Dear Readers ~

I just love bad girls.

Something about them cries out for my attention. I am drawn to them in spite of their imperfections . . . maybe even because of them. There's an old adage that says every villain is the hero of his own story. Well, I want to know what makes bad girls tick.

And there are oh, so many stories inside the walls of the Pleasure Emporium, Whitechapel's most notorious bordello. The residents of this particular "private hotel for ladies" are just yearning to tell us how they came to such reduced circumstances. And the quietest of these voices are the most impatient to be heard.

Surrounded by scarlet women, our heroines have become a bit too pink around the edges, a quality our heroes find downright irresistible. It takes a strong man to tame a bad girl, and these men are determined to teach these girls a lesson in love they are never to forget.

So light a candle and step with me over the threshold of this wicked place, where these mischievous vixens lurk in the shadows. The first of our discoveries will be April Jardine, the bordello's scullery maid with ideas above her station. The chance discovery of the Madame's erotic diary brings her the opportunity to blackmail her way to wealth, until she clashes with Riley Hawthorne, a judge with power over her freedom . . . and her heart.

Welcome to the Pleasure Emporium.

~ Michelle

When a Lady Misbehaves

MICHELLE MARCOS

St. Martin's Paperbacks

NOTE: If you purchased this book without a cover you should be aware that this book is stolen property. It was reported as "unsold and destroyed" to the publisher, and neither the author nor the publisher has received any payment for this "stripped book."

Dedication
For Jesus

This is a work of fiction. All of the characters, organizations, and events portrayed in this novel are either products of the author's imagination or are used fictitiously.

WHEN A LADY MISBEHAVES

Copyright © 2007 by Michelle Marcos.
Excerpt from *Gentlemen Behaving Badly* copyright © 2007 by Michelle Marcos.

All rights reserved. No part of this book may be used or reproduced in any manner whatsoever without written permission except in the case of brief quotations embodied in critical articles or reviews. For information address St. Martin's Press, 175 Fifth Avenue, New York, NY 10010.

ISBN: 0-312-94849-2
EAN: 978-0-312-94849-8

Printed in the United States of America

St. Martin's Paperbacks edition / November 2007

St. Martin's Paperbacks are published by St. Martin's Press, 175 Fifth Avenue, New York, NY 10010.

10 9 8 7 6 5 4 3 2 1

When a Lady Misbehaves

One

I HATE THIS PLACE.

It was the first thought of every day, but this day in particular.

Squirreled away in the still womb of the pantry, April had finally managed to steal five minutes away from the windowless scullery to read the Society pages. Clutching a pilfered candle and her newspaper, she could follow the chronicles and scandals of the titled elite, and pretend that she was among their number. And just when she began to disappear into the realm of the *haut ton,* she heard that irritating rhyme that seemed to have caught on at the brothel.

"April Jardine, come clean!"

Pluck a duck! Her hands were still stinging from the steaming dishwater, and raw from the carbolic soap that loosened the grease on the mutton pans. Now there was more cleaning to do. She shook her head, ignoring the summons from one of the working girls. But as the seconds ticked by, the remembered warning from the Madame grew louder in her head until she could no longer focus on her fantasies. She shoved the *Morning Post* into the pocket of her apron, grabbed the mop and bucket, and trudged up the stairs.

Vomit. It was all over the carpet in Glenda's bedchamber. Her customer had had too much to drink and had heaved his mysterious-looking supper onto the floor.

April stood in the doorway, her lip curled in disgust. "What in bleedin' hell..."

Glenda walked gingerly around the chunky puddle, lifting her night rail to her knees. "Hurry up, love. He's passed out cold, but he'll be awake in a minute. With a little luck, I can convince him he's already had his go and make him pay again."

April's gaze sank from the groaning mass lying facedown on the bed, to the disgusting mess on the floor. "He's your customer. You clean up after him!"

"You're the scullery maid! It's your job! And don't you give me any more of your lip or I'll tell the Madame."

April mumbled a retort as she dropped to her knees in front of the bucket.

Glenda adjusted her gelatinous breasts over her corset. "You're a silly girl, you are, April. I don't know why you do it. Slogging in the kitchens day after day, when you really don't have to. If I were you, I'd take the Madame up on her offer. We need someone to replace poor Deirdre. Why don't you come work with us girls? In the right light, you could pass for pretty. Besides, you're woman enough for a man in his cups. You could make a damn sight more money than scrubbing pots and floors all day."

April lifted a defiant gaze to Glenda's overpainted face above her. "I'd rather bend my back than lie on it, thank you very much."

Glenda put her hands on her wide hips and wriggled in derision. "Oh, look who thinks she's so bloody noble... the Dustbin Duchess!"

"Stop calling me that!" April cried, her green eyes shooting daggers at Glenda.

Glenda laughed heartily, her hennaed curls quivering

over her freckled shoulders. "I've seen you aping them nobs when you think no one's looking, talking all genteel and putting on airs. D'ye honestly think you're going to become one of them toffs in Hyde Park, all la-di-da and how-do-you-do?"

"Sod off!" April snapped.

"You mark my words, April Jardine," she said, her breasts spilling over her corset as she bent forward to face April, "this is as good as it gets for the likes of us. The minute you start filling your head with ideas above your station, somebody's going to whack it off."

A long, low groan came from the bed as the man stirred into consciousness.

"Bugger! Hurry up, girl, he's almost come to!"

April crawled over to the vinegary splatter of vomit, her face twisted into a grimace of revulsion, and poised the damp cloth over it.

"*There* you are!" exclaimed a voice from the doorway behind her.

Jenny Hare, April's best friend, grimaced at the mess on the floor. She was already in costume for the evening, a transparent chemise cinched under her breasts, and a pair of white stockings rising up to red garters. "Madame's been looking for you."

"She'll just have to wait," Glenda interjected. "April's got to clean up this mess first."

Jenny arched her shapely black eyebrows. "Then you go up there and tell her that yourself. I'm not letting April get into hot water with the Madame for you. April, you'd best go on up and see what she wants. Let Glenda clean up her own mess."

April climbed to her feet and offered Jenny a grateful smile. Jenny gave her a conspiratorial wink and handed April's cloth and bucket to Glenda, who now stood helplessly agape as Jenny shut the door behind them.

It was a typically noisy Wednesday night at the Pleasure Emporium. The tinny music from the pianoforte filled the dim salon. Waves of boisterous singing, punctuated by raucous laughter, swelled throughout the house. A girl shrieked as she was groped by a customer, and he roared in triumph when he finally hoisted her over his shoulder like a sack of meal and pounded up the stairs toward an empty bedchamber. April flattened herself against the wall to allow them to pass her, and then made straight for the Madame's study and knocked on the door.

"Come."

April lingered by the open door. "You sent for me, Madame?"

The older woman looked up from her ledger and scowled. "A half hour ago. Where have you been?"

"Sorry, Madame. I didn't hear you."

"No doubt you were engrossed in another one of your silly fantasies."

"No, Madame. I was just . . ."

"Never mind. Mrs. Critchley has been taken ill. You'll have to clean the upstairs rooms tomorrow afternoon, before the customers arrive."

"Yes, Madame." Old Mrs. Critchley was rarely too sick to work, because she could ill afford to lose a day's wages. Nevertheless, April blessed her own luck. Cleaning all the bedrooms was a load of work, but at least it would take her out of the suffocating scullery for the day.

"When you're done with the bedrooms, you can tidy up my study. I'm going to sell some of these books, so I'd like you to box them up and take them downstairs."

Stacks of books were piled high in each corner, carved from the shelves that lined each wall of the Madame's study. April puzzled over why the Madame would be selling her precious books, but dared not ask. No doubt it had something to do with the way she was frowning over her ledger.

The Madame leaned back in her chair with an exasperated sigh. "Sit down for a moment, April."

April perched herself on the edge of the chair the Madame had indicated, and waited as the woman lit a cigarette. Despite her exacting manner and brusque demeanor, Madame Vivienne Devereux was a singularly handsome woman, with the high cheekbones and wide mouth characteristic of French women. Her pale skin, though creased around the eyes and mouth, was still lovely. Her once-blond hair was now dulled with gray, but the flash of her icy-blue eyes belied her age. The Madame wore an arrogance that April always admired, a mask of quiet confidence that came from years spent in the company of nobles and royalty. A courtesan of some repute in her youth, the Madame never looked or behaved any less a lady, even now. April always wondered why she lived here, in this hovel of a bordello, instead of exchanging racy witticisms in a Paris salon, where she seemed to belong. But the Madame never spoke of the turn of events that brought her from consorting with European princes to eking out an anonymous existence in a smelly Whitechapel brothel.

"Avril . . . dis-moi. Qu'est-ce que tu as décidé?" Although April was born in England, her father was French, and she was the only other person at the brothel who could speak with Madame Devereux in her native tongue.

April blushed. "I'm sorry, Madame. I'm grateful for your offer of promotion, but I don't really want to join the girls."

The Madame's full lips tensed. "Why not?"

"I'm just too . . . bashful."

"The shyness will pass. It is the first casualty of our profession."

"I'm not as pretty as the other girls. No one will ask for me."

The Madame delicately expelled the smoke through a sideways smile. "And modesty is the second."

April shifted uncomfortably. She was running out of excuses. "I don't mean to insult you, Madame, but that isn't the way I wish to earn my living."

The Madame's eyes grew wide with incredulity. "No doubt you prefer the stench of the scullery?"

"No, Madame." She couldn't say so to the Madame, but it was a damn sight better than spreading her legs for any man with a few coins to spare.

"I would have thought a year on your hands and knees would have changed your mind in favor of less taxing work."

April didn't know how to answer. Nothing could be worse than working in the scullery. Except that.

The older woman leaned back in her chair. "You are an unusual girl. Very different from the sort of woman who comes to work for me. But you must understand, April. You are young and pretty, and your place is in the front of the house, where the men are. I let you work in the scullery for a time, hoping it would soften your maidenly resolve. But I cannot afford to keep being patient. I can get any old woman to work there. I must put you to work where you can be of greatest service."

April squeezed her hands. "But I can serve in other ways. I can read and write—"

The Madame shook her head. "Those skills are of no use to me here. In fact, the only thing of any value to me you will not part with yet. You are still a virgin, yes?"

April tried to hide the rising color in her cheeks by hanging her head. It was a humiliation to be a virgin in a place like this. "Yes, Madame."

The Madame leaned forward over the desk, her clear blue eyes glistening brightly. "Do you have any idea of the high price that you would fetch? There's a king's ransom to be had for your maidenhead. Most men have forgotten what it is like to have a virgin in their bed, and they would pay handsomely for a second chance at having a fresh girl.

It is a great advantage. In one night, you would earn more money than any of the others could make in a month. What do you say to that?"

She could not respond outright. The thought of giving herself to one of these ale-swilling, unwashed barbarians filled her with dread. In a single night, to be branded a low-class whore for the rest of her life—a perpetual consort to this pack of fishmongers, sailors, and pickpockets. It was unthinkable. She wanted better than that. To sell the only thing that truly belonged to her, her dignity . . . it was too great a price for too little a reward.

"Madame, I can't . . ."

The Madame pursed her lips in frustration. "April, I think you had better reconsider. I have never forced a girl into the profession, and I don't intend to start now. My customers come to my house because my ladies are willing and eager to please. It is a pity that you would prefer to ruin your young beauty with manual labor, but if you wish to remain in my employ, I must make use of you as best suits this establishment. My greatest need for you is in the front. It is not easy work by any means, but it is considerably more profitable than working in the kitchens. I will give you until Friday to decide. If you trust me, I will find you a generous man who will be gentle with you. If not, then I'm afraid you'll have to find employment elsewhere."

The blood drained from April's face. "Oh, Madame, please don't do that to me. Can't I just stay on in the kitchens?"

She cocked her head imperiously. "You seem to be wearing out your welcome there. Cook has been complaining that you're not putting in a full day's work."

"It's a lie! I work plenty!"

"She says that you're forever droning on about the aristocrats you read about in the papers, and that if you put as much effort into keeping the pantry as organized as you do your royal gossip, you would make an extraordinary servant."

"Cook's got it in for me, that's all."

"Is it true that you sneak away to bury your nose in the scandal pages?"

"Of course not. I can't imagine where she should get such a ridiculous notion."

The Madame walked around her desk and stood beside April. She leaned over, pulled the folded *Morning Post* out of April's pinafore, and held it aloft.

"Oh." April's earthy complexion reddened more. "I . . . it's just to pass the time."

"Pass the time? If you have the energy to follow the idle exploits of the *haut ton*, then clearly you must not be busy enough. You're lucky you're not living in France now, April. To be such a Royalist would earn you a stroll to the guillotine." She shook her head. "You and your fancies. It is a waste of your time to revere these ridiculous people," she said, waving the newspaper, "who do nothing all day but play at being gods and goddesses. And not just because they will never accept you, but because one of these days you will learn that these nobles you worship so much are anything but that."

Her words were pregnant with meaning, but April was only desperate to hear that she could keep her present job. "I won't do it anymore, Madame. You'll never hear another complaint about me, I swear. Can I stay on with Cook then?"

The moments lengthened as April waited for a declaration of amnesty.

"Unfortunately, April, circumstances dictate our choices. If it were not necessary, I could let you stay on in the kitchens. But with Deirdre in her grave these past three months, it has become impossible to make the payments on this house. We are already in arrears, and with the slow winter months coming, I cannot see us surviving into the next year. I need a new girl, and I need her now. And a virgin auction is just what this house needs to stay in business." At April's horrified expression, the Madame placed a papery hand on April's trembling one. "There is no difference between the men of St. James Place and the men of Battersea Park. When it comes to sex, *ma petite,* one man is as insignificant as the next."

"But I don't want any man," April said defensively.

The Madame's voice deadened. "That may be true. But without a husband or at least a lover, it will be impossible for you to survive."

April lowered her face, unwilling to betray her failing hope. Despite her ambitions to improve her station in life, it was foolish to believe she could ever be more than a common scullery maid. But less?

Her mind reeled at the prospect of herself in a virgin auction. She had seen it done before, and she shuddered at the thought of presenting herself before a gathering of the Madame's eight or ten most solvent patrons, dressed in nothing but a transparent shift. She would have to let their glazed eyes drink their fill of her nearly naked form, and watch as they frantically outbid each other, until only one was left. She would then take the arm of the man who won her body for the evening, and lead him to an upstairs room. She would allow his dirty hands to wander all over her body as he pressed his whiskered face onto hers, and inhale the putrid odor of alcohol in his mouth. She would feel his tongue lave at her neck while he pressed his freely perspiring body onto hers. She would open herself up to him as he tore through the wall that kept her free and pure, forever imprinted by him as her first. She would have to hear him grunt while she dutifully cooed and purred in his ears . . .

"I can't," she said, shaking her head slowly.

The older woman clasped her hands on the desk. "I offer you the promise of a better life, April, one which will benefit both you and me. The alternative will make neither of us happy. The choice is yours. Think about it. In two days, I will have your answer."

"But, Madame—"

The Madame's voice took on the resolute quality that was the hallmark of her final word on a subject. "That will be all. Return to your duties. I will call you tomorrow when you may clear away the books." She extinguished her cigarette in a saucer and picked up her quill.

April got up from her chair and silently closed the door behind her.

THAT NIGHT, IN HER ATTIC ROOM, APRIL sat up awake.

Trapped. That's what she was. Like a moth in a jar.

No matter how she turned it over in her head, she couldn't see a way out of this. A virgin auction . . . the very words turned her heart to water. But out on the streets, she'd fare much worse. It was bad enough having to look for another position and a place to live. But how was she supposed to eat with no money? At least at the Madame's, she had a roof over her head and three meals a day. If only she had someone else to turn to. Her mother had died when she was a child, and her father raised her as best as a drunkard could until his own death last year. With no other living relation, and only the squalor of the London streets to look forward to, being discharged from the Madame's employ would be tantamount to a death sentence.

And her fate didn't matter to anyone, because she was no one of consequence.

April gazed at her reflection in a shard of mirror she had collected from a dustbin. *Young beauty,* the Madame had said of her. There was nothing beautiful about the face that stared back at her. Her long reddish-brown hair curled chaotically. Her skin, bronzed by her labors in the kitchen courtyard, marked her as a working-class commoner. Her stature, lacking the height that comes from proper nutrition, contributed to the condemnation. Tears gathered at her lashes, magnifying the dark outline of her emerald eyes. Her reflection blurred in the mirror, distorting her already disheveled appearance, and her pink lips pouted in self-pity, despair, and angry impotence.

Her heart tightened painfully as her thoughts turned to the ladies she saw strolling languidly through Hyde Park on Sundays, looking willowy and radiant in their elegant Grecian frocks and long white gloves. They had no such problems over their heads. They filled their indolent days with morning rides, afternoon teas, and evening routs. They were free, like butterflies in a garden. How she longed to be one of them!

No one of consequence.

She sighed to relieve the heavy ache. Why was it that some people were favored, and others not? She was a peasant, a commoner, a nobody, and she raged against the accident of birth that made her one who didn't matter. If this was all she was meant for, why had she even been born?

DESPITE HER REPRIEVE FROM THE SCULLERY, the next day seemed interminable. Troubled by the Madame's ultimatum, she found that even her daydreams eluded her. There was no minuet when she swept the floors, no flower arranging when she replaced the spent candles, no tea service when she emptied the chamber pots. It was all cold reality.

Tomorrow. That's when the Madame would demand her answer.

It was nearly eight o'clock by the time April was able to tidy the Madame's study. There were dozens of books scattered about the floor, and she groaned at the thought of crating them all. She was tired and hungry, and she desperately wanted to get out of her filthy clothes. She placed a stack of books on the divan, and began to arrange them in the empty trunk she had brought down. Another time, she might have indulged in skimming the titles. But today, she was in no mood for stories.

When she finally brought the lid down on the packed trunk, her back felt as if there were a sword lodged in it. The divan looked so inviting, so comfortable, that April hazarded a moment to sit. But her bottom landed on something square and hard, and she sprang up from the couch.

It was a book. Camouflaged by the divan, the red leather volume had escaped her notice. There was also no title printed on it. She picked it up, and something slid to the floor. Holding it to the light of the candelabrum, she saw that it was a patch of fine, cream-colored silk. Cradling it in her dusty hand, April gingerly unfolded the pristine material. What she saw startled her.

It was a handprint. A baby's handprint. In faded blue ink. Impulsively, she brought the swatch to her nose and sniffed. She could still detect the barest trace of violet water through the musty notes acquired from the book's pages. She turned her attention to the open book. There, on the inside cover, in the same blue India ink, were the words *"Journal de Vivienne Boniface Devereux."*

And right underneath in a big bold hand, *"Privé."*

April hesitated, glancing at the closed door. Through it, the music from the pianoforte downstairs could be heard clearly, along with the loud laughter and singing from the men and the working girls. Flushing, she debated whether to turn the page, or set the book down and resume her duties, lest the Madame return and catch her. Blood thrumming in her ears, she turned the page.

The hand was bold and exquisitely rendered, the penmanship of a well-tutored woman.

17 août 1790

Pour fêter mon anniversaire aujourd'hui, le Duc de Somerset m'a donné ce journal et une plume dorée. Il est très généreux avec moi, et donc ce soir je lui donnerai quelque chose de tout aussi extraordinaire.

April's eyes widened. It was clear that the Duke of Somerset, who had given the young Vivienne this journal and a golden quill on her birthday, would be richly rewarded that evening!

A stab of guilt jarred her. It was wrong to look through a person's personal diary, especially one as intimate as this one appeared to be. The Madame had been a very famous courtesan in her day, and she had known many celebrated men. But the Duke of Somerset . . . April had read much about him. She knew him to be a highly respectable man and close friend of the Archbishop of Canterbury, and it shocked her to learn that he would have purchased the services of a courtesan. April was infected with a viral curiosity to know who else was mentioned in the book. Ignoring the reprimanding voice in her head, she hid the book in the pocket of her apron.

LATER THAT NIGHT, DURING THE BUSIEST hour for the girls in the house, April nestled into her bed. Her tiny attic room was above the third floor, so the music and the noise were faint enough not to bother her. She lit a precious tallow candle, pulled out the diary, and began to read.

THE DYING CANDLE SPUTTERED BRAVELY AS the pool of wax threatened to extinguish it. April leaned back against her pillow and rubbed her tired eyes.

This was no ordinary diary. It was a customer dossier.

The Madame had documented every tryst, every liaison, every meeting with the men who paid for her favors. She detailed everything about their assignations: what they ate, where they went, who they met, what they did. Pages upon pages of graphic details described how he liked his sex, what she did to arouse him, how much he paid. Some liked to be whipped, others to do the whipping. One man wanted her to pretend to be a dog in heat, another liked her to dress as a man. April spent the night in a state of continuous blush, her eyebrows frozen in a raised position.

And it read like a *Debrett's Peerage* of smut. Peers, playwrights, politicians—all numbered among those who had shared the Madame's bed. Many were men whose names she recognized from the newspapers, men whose accomplishments made headlines on the front pages. Gentlemen of every rank from baron to duke, members of the ruling class, appeared in the Madame's little book, their erotic predilections dishonoring their proud names.

She heaved a profound sigh. The Madame had been right. These, the so-called nobles, were just as lecherous as the working-class blokes who frequented the brothel— perhaps more so. They didn't deserve their dignified standing. She had half a mind to send the diary to the *Morning Post,* just to see how long it would take for a man to go from High Society to bottom-dweller. She chuckled. What wouldn't a man give to bury his own sordid past? Which of those men wouldn't give her as much as ten pounds just to burn this diary? Which of them wouldn't give her anything she asked? Why, she'd be able to name her price . . .

April bolted upright. She stared at the diary in her hands. No, it would never work! It was too wild, too dangerous.

Someone like her couldn't pull it off. She was a nobody, a common scullery maid. Someone like her wouldn't dare. And yet . . .

She got dressed.

"'AVE YOU TAKEN LEAVE OF YOUR SENSES?"

It was dawn by the time April dragged Jenny out of bed and into a cab, making sure both of them were dressed in black. April ordered the driver to take them to Parliament, paid him with every last penny she had, and then confessed her plans to Jenny. Jenny was unable to stop yawning and rubbing the sleep from her eyes. Until now.

"Just think of it," April answered, a gleam in her eye. "What is the one thing that toffs are most afraid of? A scandal! They can't bear public ridicule."

Jenny shook her head incredulously. "You're mad!"

"No I'm not. This little book is loaded with enough ammunition to shoot down any of the nobs named in it. We could make a fortune!"

"You mean to tell me you're going to blackmail these men?"

"No. Not blackmail. Better than that."

Jenny's large brown eyes fixed on her friend as if seeing her for the very first time.

April opened the diary and handed Jenny the swatch with the handprint. "Did you know that twenty years ago, just when the Madame was at the height of her popularity and wealth, she had a baby?"

Jenny's black eyebrows drew together in puzzlement as she fondled the cloth. "Really? Who with?"

April began to flip through the pages. "She doesn't say, but around that time, the Madame had about ten regular clients, all of them very wealthy. Here, listen to this:

"I can withstand no more of the grief. The pain of losing my child is too much for me to bear. All I possess now is the impression I made of the infant's hand, and the sad memory of a babe no longer mine.

"That's what gave me the idea. I'm close to the age that babe would have been. If I visit each of those men, posing as the child that could've been theirs, they'll do anything to keep me quiet about it. No one wants their past coming back to haunt them. If they so much as sniff the possibility that their names would show up in the papers in connection with the Madame, and that the evidence of their affairs is very much alive, their pockets will be wide open for us. It's a golden opportunity for us to make some real money."

"It's a golden opportunity for us to swing at Newgate! You've gone daft, you 'ave. No one's going to care that they cock-a-doodle-doo'd with the Madame twenty years ago."

"Oh, yes they would! As well connected as some of these men are? They'd rather fork over a few quid than have any breath of scandal light upon them."

"April, this is a serious offense! We could be put in jail for something like this!"

April's face glowed with wild enthusiasm. "That's what's so brilliant! We won't be doing anything illegal! 'Sides, no one's ever going to tell. If we get arrested, we'll have to tell the courts everything. The diary will have to be submitted as evidence. If something comes out, everything comes out, and these toffs know it. And none of them wants that to happen. Believe me, you and I will never see the inside of a courtroom."

Jenny threw herself against the back of the leather seat. "Well, I want no part in it. Driver, stop the cab."

The carriage lurched as the driver reined in the horse.

"Driver, carry on," April shouted, and blazed at her

friend. "Listen to me, Jenny. Girls of our station are never going to get ahead, don't you understand? Where do you think girls like us end up? Do you want to be like Old Margaret, toothless and dying of cirrhosis? That's how aging prostitutes end up. You have no future."

"If I get caught, I'll 'ave no future for sure! If I don't get executed, I'll be shipped straight to Australia with all the rest of the prostitutes. We'll never see each other again."

April sighed. "Jenny, if we don't at least try, we'll never see each other again anyway. Madame says if I don't join you lot up front, I'll be sacked. And I've got nowhere else to go. Even if I can find a job, what've I got to hope for, eh? A life in service? Where, maybe, if I work very hard and follow orders, in ten or twelve years I'll be able to work my way up to the lofty position of laundry maid? That's not good enough for me."

Jenny's large brown eyes narrowed on April. "I can see Glenda's right about you. No good ever comes of getting ideas above your station!"

April jerked indignantly. "How can I not? Answering to everyone, everyone my superior? You don't know what it's like to spend sixteen hours a day in that bloody scullery with your hands soaked in hot water and soda crystals! Just once I'd like to see the day when I could scrub less than three hundred pieces of cutlery and crockery. Know what? That day will never come. Never! It's up to me to make it happen. And this is what I'm going to do. Circumstances dictate our choices, the Madame said, and she was right. And if you had half a brain, you'd see that it's the only way out of having to hike up your skirts for any man that fancies you."

Despite Jenny's discontentment with her profession, April's attitude made her defensive. "What's wrong with what I do? At least I'm making a decent wage."

"At an indecent living."

"At least I'm not stealing my money."

April rubbed her forehead. "Look, all I'm saying is that either way, we're never going to get any respect in this world. But with a little money, at least we'll be able to buy some. You want that, don't you? Oh, Jenny, I know it's a risk, but it's a calculated one. I promise I won't let any harm come to you. Please help me?"

Jenny looked into April's face. She was so hopeful, so desperate. Jenny wouldn't say it out loud, but April had a valid point. Anything was better than sleeping with a stranger, pretending to love him so he'd leave more money. It ate her up inside to cater to the appetites of men who didn't have the least regard for her as a human being. At least April had her dignity. And if April's plan could help Jenny achieve some measure of independence, then by God, that was an ambition she wanted to follow.

"What do I 'ave to do?" she sighed.

As the cab clattered to a halt, April and Jenny adjusted the veils over their faces. Taking her cue from April, Jenny alighted with all the somber grace of a lady in mourning. They walked up the path to the Palace of Westminster, and approached the imposing doorway with downcast eyes. A gentleman who happened to be exiting held the door open for them and mumbled, "My condolences."

"Thank you, sir. I wonder if you could direct me to the office of the Clerk of the Parliaments?" April asked, affecting a convincing posh accent that impressed Jenny.

"Certainly, miss. It's just down that hall. Would you like me to escort you there?"

"No, thank you. Good day."

"Good day, ladies."

When they were clear of earshot, Jenny whispered, "Did you 'ear that? He called us ladies!"

April stiffly replied, "Yes, now try to act the part and shut the bloody hell up!"

They walked the rest of the way in silence. When they arrived at the Clerk's door, April knocked softly. A junior clerk answered, and she asked to speak to Sir Cedric Markham.

"Whom may I say is calling upon him?" he asked deferentially.

"I am Miss April Devereux. This is my maid, Jenny."

The man politely ushered them in and bade them sit down while he announced them.

"Cor, look at this office!" Jenny whispered after he left. "Who is this bloke anyway?"

April's lips thinned. "This 'bloke' is the most senior officer of the House of Lords. Now shush!"

A few moments later, they were allowed in to see Sir Cedric Markham, the Clerk of the Parliaments. He sat stiffly behind his desk, his rigid torso rising perpendicular to the wide mahogany plane of the desk. If he hadn't cocked his head in their direction and smiled, April would have thought that he was made out of wood as well.

He rose to greet them, straightening his tall, skeletal frame. "Miss Devereux? This is a pleasure, though I believe you have the advantage of me." He peered out at April, his eyes like small raisins balanced above his rectangular spectacles.

April raised her veil. "Yes, sir. We have not been formally introduced. But I was compelled to come see you. I did not wish to disturb you at work, but I'm certain that once I've spoken, you'll appreciate my prudence for not visiting you at home. It is a matter of some discretion."

"A matter of some discretion?" he repeated, looking puzzled.

"You see, I believe that we have a mutual acquaintance. And I regret that I am compelled to be the bearer of bad tidings about this person."

"Oh, dear. Has someone passed away?"

"Yes. My mother, Vivienne Boniface Devereux."

The vertical crease on his forehead deepened. "Er, I'm sorry for your loss, Miss Devereux, but I don't believe I know anyone by that name."

April looked stricken. "You don't remember her?"

His puzzlement turned to embarrassment. "I'm very sorry, but I can't recall the name."

"It was a long time ago. Twenty years, in fact. Do try to remember."

The man blinked repeatedly. "I believe I was in India twenty years ago."

April feigned some tears. "Oh, Jenny, he doesn't even remember her."

Jenny took her cue, and reached out for April's hand. "There, there, miss. For shame, sir. You've wounded 'er feelings."

"I'm terribly sorry," Sir Cedric stammered. "I don't know what to say."

April stiffened as she pulled out a handkerchief from inside her sleeve. "Well, allow me to refresh your memory. Vivienne Devereux was Madame Davies' most celebrated courtesan."

His head tilted back as recognition illuminated his face. Flustered, Sir Cedric took a moment to compose himself. "Er, yes, I have heard of her, though I have never had the pleasure . . . that is, I have never met her personally. You have my condolences, of course, but why are you telling *me*?"

"Sir, you torment me. How could you say you have never met her when I know full well that you were one of her best and most regular clients?"

His face blanched. "Young woman, I don't know what scandalmonger has told you these lies, but I assure you that I have never indulged in sordid dalliances with ladies of the evening."

"Sir Cedric, I am not here to judge you. Circumstances drove my poor mother into her disagreeable profession, and to judge you would require that I judge her just as harshly. There is no need to hide your past from me. She told me all about you."

"Lies," he insisted, beads of perspiration forming on his wrinkled forehead.

April quickly recalled the details from the diary. "Well, if you don't wish to believe me, perhaps we should ask Viscount Ormsbey, to whose ball you escorted my mother so many years ago. Or perhaps you need confirmation from the Italian couturier, Signor Angelico, from whom you ordered some furs for her. I believe we have the bill of sale somewhere, signed by you. She herself told me of the insulting names you used to refer to your wife while you and my mother were together."

"Good God, she didn't tell you that, did she?"

April straightened. "Does the term 'Bovine Betty' spark your memory?"

He buried his head in his bony hands. "Damn that Madame Davies! She gave me every assurance of complete discretion. I should have known better than to trust a whore."

April and Jenny sneaked a look at each other, pleased with their victory.

"Very well, then. So she's dead. Why are you telling me this? I haven't clapped eyes on her for two decades. Why would you think I'd want to know?"

"Well, you see, she also explained to me who my real father is. You."

His eyes widened. "God's nightshirt! That can't be true! Any one of a hundred men—a thousand—could be your father!"

"She told me there was no one else for her at the time. Apparently, she developed . . . *feelings* for you."

"Stuff and nonsense."

"And so, sir, here I am."

His lips thinned. "Oh, I can see where this is headed. You're trying to extort money from me, is that it? Well, it won't work!"

"No, sir, I don't want your money."

His voice boomed across the room. "Well, what do you want?"

Feigning her most innocent expression, she said, "I want to come live with you."

If the chair had suddenly come to life and joined the conversation, Sir Cedric Markham could not have appeared more surprised. "Are you mad? I can't just pick you up like a lost dog. I have a wife, a family! It's out of the question!"

It was time for histrionics. "But I have nowhere else to go! My mother was the only family I had and now she's gone! What am I to do? Oh, please, please save me!" April bawled so loudly that the junior clerk came in to see what the matter was.

"Is everything all right, sir?" asked the worried clerk.

"Yes, yes it is, Dyson," stammered Sir Cedric. "This young woman's had a death in her family, that's all. Bring her a glass of brandy, won't you?"

When the clerk left, Sir Cedric shouted under his breath. "Miss Devereux, please! I must ask you to control yourself. The Prime Minister is in the next room!"

April clawed at his sleeves. "Oh, please, sir. I have nowhere else to go. You're my last living relation. If you don't want me, I'll be compelled to enter into the same profession as my mother. I'm a good girl, a decent girl, just arrived from a finishing school. I promise I won't be any trouble. We won't take up much space, my maid and I. Just give us a place to stay!"

He tried to wrench his sleeves from April's clutches. "B-but it's unthinkable!"

Now Jenny wanted to participate. "Leave it alone, miss. Anyone can see he's got no feelin' 'eart. Imagine, seeing a nice girl turned out onto the street by 'er own father. You leave it to me, miss. We'll go see your stepmother, Lady Markham. Maybe she'll 'ave more compassion than this lout."

Sir Cedric's eyes bugged out. "No! For goodness' sake, no. Look, er, I'm sure you'll appreciate the fact that I can't take you in, but—"

April wailed loudly.

"B-but I've no wish to see you come to ruin. Here, I've got some money," he said, racing to a safe in the wall. "Let me give you something to keep you respectable, until you can figure some way out of your predicament. Shall we say, a hundred pounds?"

"A hundred p—?" The words died in April's throat.

He shook his head. "No, you're right. Let's call it two hundred. That will give you a head start in life, won't it?"

Careful not to betray her excitement, April answered delicately, "I th-think it would help us to pay our creditors, yes, and keep food on the table for me and my maid for a short while."

Sir Cedric began to count out the pound notes on his desk. "Now, I do have a condition. You must not seek me out again, do you understand? I cannot recognize paternity to the world and I cannot continue to support you once this money runs out. Will you agree to that?"

April cleared her throat. "Yes, sir. I've no wish to place you in a compromising position. I know that you cannot give me the protection of your name, but your generosity will at least allow us to keep body and soul together for a time. I assure you, you will not hear from us again."

When April had deposited the money in her reticule, the clerk knocked and entered the office carrying a snifter of brandy. April and Jenny quietly exited through the open door.

Sir Cedric seized the glass and gulped the contents down. "Dyson, bring me the bottle."

APRIL AND JENNY COULDN'T WALK FAST ENOUGH out of the building. Like two coiled springs, they strained to keep their composure until they were safely away with their money. They jumped into the next cab that happened by, and when they were finally on their way, they exploded in girlish screams.

Jenny fondled the stack of bills. "Look at all this money. It's amazing! He just gave it to us!"

"Well, what did you expect?" April declared in mock arrogance. "It was an exceptional plan, executed by two very exceptional performers."

"I've got to 'and it to you, April, you're a right clever one, you are. And that accent! Dead posh, you were! Cor, whatever are we going to do with all this money? It's a fortune!"

The gleam intensified in April's eye, her mind racing with familiar dreams of wealth and prosperity. "No, Jenny. It's a beginning! There are at least nine more blokes in this blessed little book we could touch, some with much more money to offer than our Cedric Markham. Just think of it. We'll have enough money to set us up in style for the rest of our lives!"

The smile ran away from Jenny's face. "Ooh, no, April. Two hundred pounds is a lot of money. Let's quit while we're ahead. You could retire from service and lead the life of a queen with that kind of money."

"Bullocks. Two hundred pounds won't keep us for very long and you know it. Don't be such a wet goose! You saw how easy it was. These toffs are easy targets when it comes to their precious reputations. 'Sides, you'll thank me when you and me are blowing the bubbles off our champagne at Almack's and drinking the waters at Bath."

"It'd be more fun to drink our champagne at Almack's and blow bubbles in Bath," Jenny countered, sending both girls into peals of giggles.

Returning long before noon, when the working girls normally awoke, April and Jenny packed their things, and without a word to anyone, left the Pleasure Emporium behind them.

Two

WHILE FEASTING ON A DELICIOUSLY PLENtiful breakfast in a room above the Cavern Tavern in a small village in Kent, April and Jenny planned their next movements.

Jenny leaned back in her chair. "Do we have to go just yet? This place is so quiet and peaceful. Let's stay a while."

But April was already engrossed in the diary's description of their next target, and did not answer.

Jenny brushed the bread crumbs off her sleeve. It was such a pleasure to be fully dressed indoors, especially during a cooler day like today. Back at the brothel, regardless of the temperature, she was obliged to dress as scantily or transparently as possible, so the customers would be enticed to select her. The dress that she had purchased with some of their takings was plain, but blissfully opaque. "We really should keep out of sight for a while, don't you agree?"

April mumbled a response, not bothering to look up from the diary.

"Come on, April. Let's rest up a bit. We've been on the move for a week now. The five blokes we did in London were scattered all over the place. I'm tired of riding round in a rickety stagecoach. I think it's time we had a proper holiday." At April's silence, she rose and went to the window. "I've never been outside of London before. Cor, whoever knew that the countryside was so pretty? No wonder the nobs only come to London for the Season. Who'd want to live there all bloody year?" Jenny returned to the table. "Say, April, 'ow much money we got?"

April's brows furrowed, her nose buried in the book.

"'Ow much?" Jenny insisted.

April grumbled. "A little over two thousand."

A dreamy look descended on Jenny's face. "Two thousand pounds. Blimey! If my mum coulda lived to see me a millionairess . . . Why don't we retire, April? We've got plenty of money. Let's buy a small cottage round 'ere and set up house on our own. We could hire a woman to do our cookin' and cleanin', and just live like gentlewomen on the—"

April's head shot up from the book. "Not yet! It ain't enough! We need more."

A dark frown creased Jenny's creamy brow. "What's wrong with you? Two thousand pounds is more money than you ever dreamed of in your whole life!"

"It ain't enough, Jenny," she repeated. "Nowadays, a woman ain't even a worthy prize unless she can bring ten thousand to a marriage."

Jenny cocked a fine black eyebrow. "Oh, so we're thinkin' of marriage, are we?" she asked, sarcasm dripping from her voice. "Who's the lucky fella?"

She shook her head. "That's not what I mean. I'm just sayin' for comparison. Ten thousand pounds, administered wisely, and we won't need to give any more thought to money for the rest of our lives."

Jenny crossed her arms. "That's what you said before we reached five 'undred, and before we reached a thousand. 'Ow much is enough?"

April mirrored her reprimanding look. "I'm not being consumed by greed, if that's what you're thinking, Jenny Hare. Ten thousand, and we'll stop."

"We've been to five men and all we've come up with is two thousand. There ain't enough rotters in that whole bloody book for ten thousand."

The gleam returned to April's eyes. "Yes there are. Look," she countered, placing the diary in front of Jenny as she read aloud, forgetting that the older girl couldn't read at all, much less in French. "'Today, I received a new caller, a man named Hawthorne, Duke of Westbrook. I am told by Madame Davies that he is one of the wealthiest men in all England, possessing land throughout Britain, the Continent, and even the American colonies. She informed me that she was extremely surprised to see him patronizing her establishment, given that the duke is renowned for his unfailing principles and unblemished reputation.' See? A man like that'll pay any amount to keep his name out of the papers, and he's got the ready money to pay a great deal. That's prime pickin's, that is."

Jenny glanced warily at April. "I s'pose. What else does she say about 'im?"

"She said he was really handsome. Funny thing, though. He didn't seem to want to bed her."

Jenny snorted. "Well, he can't very well have been your father, then."

"No, no, he came back." April thumbed through the next few pages until she found the one she was looking for. "It says here that he called again the following week. He brought her a strange-looking flower, a kind the Madame had never seen before. He called it *Passiflora incarnata,* and told her that it grew only in the Americas. But he had bred his own variety, and if she but kissed him, he would name it after her . . . the Vivienne Passionflower. Isn't that romantic?"

"Charmin'. Get to the part when they do it."

"Blimey, but you're crass."

Jenny's face hardened. "You'll pardon me if I don't melt at sweet words. I know men too well. All they fancy is a good toss."

April bristled. "Shows how much you know. He didn't bed her that night, either. But—"

"You seem to be barkin' up the wrong tree. Maybe he leans a little to the other side, if you take my meanin'."

"Can't you understand anything? He was wooing her."

"Ha! Pitching woo is nothin' but pitching poo."

"As I was saying," she resumed stiffly, "he didn't bed her that night, but he came back again and again. Each time, she says, he brought her a different flower from another exotic place. Finally, one night, they made love. She says he was the gentlest and sweetest lover she had ever had."

"That's what I've been waiting to 'ear. 'Ave we got anything else on 'im?"

"Very little, I'm afraid. He sort of disappears from the diary after they bed each other. After that, she goes on and on about some other bloke she calls *Ours*."

An incredulous look formed on Jenny's face. "The Madame went out with a man called 'Arse'?"

April chuckled. "No, you ninny. *Ours* is French for 'bear.'"

"Oh." She laughed nervously. "I thought it was because he was a strictly 'backdoor' kind of fellow."

"Crass, Jenny. Very crass."

Jenny rose from the table and flung herself down on the bed. "All right, then, let's go hit this man up for all he's got so we can get out of this bloody business."

"Fine by me."

Jenny watched as April went to the wardrobe and began to pack their clothes in a well-worn valise.

"April? I'm beginning to get a little nervous. We've

done pretty well so far, but don't you think we're pushin' our luck? I mean, if we get caught—"

"Would you get out of it? We're not going to get caught."

"Don't be so arrogant. One mistake, and it's the gallows for us."

April sat on the bed next to her friend and gave her a protective hug. "Don't worry, Jenny. I'll never let that happen. You and I have been through too much together. I just don't ever want to see you working 'tween the sheets again. We've got a good thing going here. Our only mistake would be if we passed up this wonderful opportunity Providence has placed in our lap. Have I ever steered you wrong?"

"It's not you I'm worried about. It's this," Jenny said, holding up the red leather diary. "I've got an awful bad feelin' about this. We've gotten away with it so far, but we can't go on forever. Our luck is bound to change, and I don't want us to be around when it does. Five blokes have given us their money without blinkin' an eye, but what if the next one is different, eh? What if the next one decides he's just not going to be taken in by a couple of gutter rats from Whitechapel?"

April gave Jenny a condescending smile. "When will you learn to trust me? By this time next month, you'll be swimming in money, filling your belly with chocolates, and wearing the very best that Paris has to offer. How does that sound?"

Jenny sighed. If there was any such thing as fool's luck, April had it. Her innocence lent her courage, which in turn gave her the audacity she needed to reach for her seemingly impossible ambitions. Shrugging off her fears and worries, Jenny smiled in response. "Only on one condition."

"What's that?"

"I get to be the daughter this time."

April cast her a sidewise glance. "You? You're too old."

"Too old? Ooh, you're for it now!"

And each girl grabbed a pillow and began to pummel each other with it until tiny fluffs of goosedown filled the room.

IF JENNY HAD HAD ANY MISGIVINGS ABOUT the wealth of their next target, they vanished when she and April drove their carriage up the gravel path to Blackheath Manor.

It was the first home they had been to outside of London, and the grandeur of the estate made all the others pale in comparison. It rose up from the surrounding forest like a mountain peak amid clouds. The mansion itself was enormous, nestled in the smiling countryside of Kent, and the picturesque tranquility of the nearby village bespoke a benevolent landlord. Although they approached the house from the front, they could glimpse sprawling gardens in the rear of the house. Clearly it had been misnamed, for it was more like a palace than a manor house, with ducal flags flying from the flagstaff. But a halo of clouds drifted over the house as they approached it, and April couldn't help feeling a little uneasy.

Not wanting to contaminate Jenny with her apprehension, April adopted a lighthearted tone. "D'ye think we can get eight thousand out of this place?"

Jenny smiled nervously. "At least!"

The clattering of hooves announced their arrival to Blackheath Manor. When they drew near the door, a footman appeared and assisted them down from the carriage. A groom emerged from the side of the house and led their horse and carriage away. At the door, they were greeted by the butler. April gave their pseudonyms, and the butler informed them that His Grace was indisposed, but that if they cared to wait in the afternoon room, he would inform His Lordship of their arrival.

As she studied the view of the gardens from the open

windows, a young man of about twenty walked in. He had a face mothers boast about: smiling blue eyes fringed with thick, dark lashes; milky skin that invited caresses; sensuous lips that commanded notice. His hair was as black as soot, glossy and straight, and his face had just begun to take on that leanness that comes with developing manhood.

"Good afternoon," he said, smiling at them. "I'm very sorry to have kept you waiting. Do try the settee," he said, waving at the sofa. "I can't say I recall being introduced to you, for I'm sure I would remember the pleasure. Have we met?"

"No, my lord. My name is April Devereux; this is my maid, Jenny. I've come to see His Grace, the Duke of Westbrook, on a matter of some discretion."

"Do you know my father personally?"

"I'm afraid not."

"Then perhaps you don't know that he is in very delicate health. His affairs are managed by my brother, Riley, the Marquess of Blackheath."

"I see. Well, I'm afraid this is a strictly confidential matter. I can speak only with His Grace. I bring him bad tidings that concern someone he knows."

"Yes, I noticed your mourning garments. Someone very close?"

"My mother."

"I *am* sorry," he said, his eyes conveying the deepest sympathy. "But therein lies the problem, you see. It would be inadvisable to trouble him with announcements of this kind. It might advance his own infirmity. If it is an urgent matter, I can send for my brother. He's away at present, but not far. I assure you he will be able to dispose of any problem you have that concerns my father, especially one of a confidential nature."

Her brows furrowed as she deliberated over what to do next. She certainly did not want to wait around for what's-his-name to come home. Her business was with the old man. She did not want to tell the younger son about his father's infidelities. The more people who knew, the less effectual the scheme; the less effectual the scheme, the likelier they were to get caught. She looked to Jenny for silent advice. Jenny's face was urging her to speak to the young man, but April believed this was not a wise course of action. Before she could take her leave, however, Jenny impetuously blurted it all out.

"My lord, beggin' yer pardon for speakin' out of turn. My mistress needs to speak to His Grace because she has good news, too. She's come to inform him that he has another child."

"Jenny . . ." April cautioned.

"You see, my lord," she continued, "Miss Devereux is his daughter."

The young man sat there looking at each one in turn, unable to speak.

April gritted her teeth. Jenny had desperately wanted this to be their last job, but she was now making mistakes—chief among them was not letting April do the thinking for them. "You see, my lord, your father and my mother were very intimate at one time. I realize that this may shock you, but my mother, Vivienne Devereux, was a courtesan with whom he committed . . . certain indiscretions twenty years ago. I have come to throw myself on the mercy of His Grace, and beg that he accept me into his family."

Nothing could have prepared her for what happened next. His eyes widened, his smile reappeared, he threw his arms around April, and began to cry.

THE NEXT FEW MINUTES EXPLODED WITH confusion.

A thousand questions poured from him so quickly that

he barely gave her time to respond. Not that she would have been able to, imprisoned in his tight embrace.

"My lord, please calm yourself! Are you all right?"

"Of course I am! This is too good to be true!"

"Perhaps you didn't quite hear me, my lord—"

"There's no need for formalities now! I'm your brother, Jeremy! I must send for Father right away. He's in Bath taking restoratives. We simply must get him back!"

April smiled weakly. "My lor— Jeremy, why don't I come back another time, say, on His Grace's scheduled return—"

"He can be here in the morning!"

"Well, we'll come back then—"

"I won't hear of it. Forrester will put you in rooms. Please make yourselves comfortable while I send word to Father and Riley. They'll be so excited!"

Before they could voice any more objections, the butler ushered them out of the room and up the stairs.

April held her tongue in check until Forrester had closed the bedroom door behind them. When she heard the door click shut, she whirled on Jenny.

"Have you gone completely insane?" she shouted under her breath. "Didn't I tell you to leave the talking to me? Why did you go and tell him the story, eh? He's no bloody good to us!"

"I don't want to 'ear it from you, April Rose Jardine. I told you to leave well enough alone, didn't I? I knew we should've never come 'ere."

"Don't you start in on that! This would've never gone wrong if you hadn't opened your big cakehole."

"It weren't *my* fault! That boy is right barmy, he is! Good Lord, he practically adopted us!"

April blinked at Jenny's remark. For the first time, she looked about the room. It was beautifully appointed, painted a cheerful yellow, with a blue brocade canopy cascading from the wall to a luxuriantly oversized bed. The narrow windows flew to the high ceiling and looked out onto the fountain and immense driveway in front of the house. The gleam returned to her eyes.

"Hmm. That doesn't sound so bad . . ."

"What doesn't?" Jenny asked suspiciously.

"Being adopted," April said, smiling broadly. "Haven't you ever wanted to live in a place like this?"

"What the devil are you playing at?"

"Listen! There's more to be had here than I first thought. If these people think me their real daughter and aren't frightened by the scandal . . . why, they'll give me anything I ask! Look where they put us and I haven't even asked for a penny yet. I told you this was prime pickin's!"

Jenny looked incredulously at her. "You've gone right over the edge with your greed, you 'ave. Haven't you stopped to think this might be a trap?"

"Why? We haven't done anything wrong. 'Sides, this ain't a prison. We can walk out anytime we like."

"Let's do it, then. I don't want to stay 'ere a moment longer."

She threw her hands in the air. "After spending the last week at every rat-ridden inn in London, haven't you wished you could stay in a room like this?"

"No!" Jenny responded petulantly. "I want to get out of 'ere. This place makes me nervous as a cat. Nothing's gone right since we came here. We're not going to get a penny from these people. Let's just go while we still can."

"Wait a minute. Let's give this place a chance. I never thought about what it would be like if someone actually took us in. Blimey, what a grand scheme that would be! Reflect a moment. If we leave now, it'll take us forever to get our ten thousand pounds. Two hundred here, four hundred there . . . we risk everything with each bloke we see. But this place is a godsend. If they decide to keep me around, I know I can get all the money we need right here. Then we'll be out of it for good."

Jenny sulked. "I don't like this. It's not working."

"Nonsense! It's working better than ever! Just look at the room he gave me! It's fit for a princess!" She bounced about the room, passing her eager hands over the marquetry side tables, escritoire, dressing table, cushioned footstool, and her very own fireplace. She could definitely become accustomed to this. April took a look through the adjoining door that Forrester had pointed out. "And this, my dear abigail, is to be *your* bedchamber."

April flung open the door and let Jenny absorb the richness of the smaller, yet equally luxurious room. "Can you possibly be persuaded to stay a day or two in this primitive dwelling?"

"I don't know, April," she answered, shaking her head. "Something bad is going to 'appen, I can feel it down to me bones."

April sighed. "All right, Jenny. If you really want to leave, we will. We'll set out before dawn, after the barmy boy has gone to sleep. But in the meantime, let's just stop for a few hours, please? I'll wager you never slept in a bed like this . . ."

April smirked as the bedroom's fine furnishings and elegant décor seduced Jenny.

"All right. Maybe just one night. I still don't like it, mind, but it's beginning to look like rain. We don't want to start driving out in these conditions."

April made no effort to hide her satisfaction.

DINNER THAT NIGHT WITH JEREMY WAS A tedious commitment. He had a thousand questions, for which she had to make up answers. Though he eagerly swallowed every answer she gave him, it was exhausting work, and as soon as dinner was finished, she begged him to let her retire early.

That night, when she was gratefully out of her mourning dress and in her chemise, she leaned back appreciatively in the soft, yielding mattress. She remembered each time she had fancied owning such a bed, and patiently counted every pleasurable sensation it afforded her right now. Absently, she gave in to her familiar thoughts of owning a house like this, with servants to feed her and look after her, and as the treacle-heavy syrup of sleep engulfed her, she found herself wishing she could stay here forever.

SNUGGLED DEEP UNDERNEATH A THICK, warm comforter, April dreamed she was duchess of her own fiefdom, walking down the halls of her artfully decorated manse. She walked past rooms where servants gleefully dusted the furniture and arranged flowers, and she sighed contentedly at the knowledge that she was safe behind the walls of her riches and titles. Suddenly, she heard a rumbling footfall behind her. She turned but saw no one. Frightened by the thundering noise, she began to run. It seemed there were hundreds of men running after her, pounding closer and closer, until she felt them reach out for her...

April woke with a start. Dazed, she heard the rumble still. It came from beneath her window, in the courtyard below—the thunder of hooves on the flagstones. Ignoring her state of dishabille, she ran to the window and threw back the curtains. The late morning sun exploded in her face. Too late to make good their planned escape.

The voices below distracted her. A number of servants had assembled in the courtyard, huddling in a semicircle around the carriage, bowing and curtsying to the open door. Two men emerged, and disappeared into the house.

Jenny stormed in, startling April. "You overslept!"

"So did you!" April retorted.

"What are we supposed to do now?" Jenny's question hung in the air.

There was a knock at the door, and an elfin chambermaid entered. "Morning, miss. Brought your breakfast tray."

"Yes, come in," April told her, ignoring Jenny's nervous pacing. "What shall I call you?"

"Susan, miss. Susan Deacons." The slender maid set the tray down on the table, and efficiently began to tidy the bed linens.

"Susan, what was all that commotion downstairs?"

"The master of the house, miss. He and his father have just come home. Sorely missed, he is. Master Riley has been too long a time away at court."

"Court? Was he attending the monarch?"

Susan giggled as she fluffed the pillow. "Oh, no, miss. Not that court. The Assizes. Master Riley serves as the Circuit Judge."

"What?" shouted April and Jenny simultaneously, making the poor maid jump.

"I mean," assuaged April, more composed, "did you say that Master Riley is a judge?"

"Why, yes, miss. We're very lucky to have our Master Riley on the bench. And it's not just 'cause he's a noble. He studied law at university. That makes him more qualified than anyone in the county to be judge. You'll not find a more moral, upright man in all England. Straight as an arrow is our Master Riley. He's as fair and true as they come. Friend to the honest man, I like to say, and worst nightmare to the ne'er-do-well. Don't you worry, miss, you're as safe as mother's milk in this house," she said proudly, and closed the door behind her.

April and Jenny looked at each other, neither able to speak.

Jenny was the first to find her tongue. "I told you to leave well enough alone, didn't I? I told you that two thousand pounds were enough, didn't I? I told you we should've stopped, didn't I?"

"Shut up! I have to think."

"We're in for it, now!" Jenny continued, her voice trembling. "We'll be arrested. He's going to throw us in jail for sure. D'ye have any idea what it's like in a women's jail? Oh, I wish I'd never left London!" Jenny began to cry.

"Don't say that!" April threw her arms around her friend. "Look, we're not in for it. He hasn't even met us yet. All we have to do is keep up the act. As long as we can convince them we're April Devereux and her maid, nothing can go wrong. You just leave it to me. Just help get me dressed, and I'll have him eating out of me palm before you can say 'flibbertigibbet.'"

WITH A CALM SHE DID NOT FEEL, APRIL descended the grand staircase toward the morning room behind Forrester. She didn't like the idea of being introduced to the men alone; single ladies never entertained men unaccompanied. But shaken by the news that they were trapped in the house of the highest judiciary officer in the county, Jenny was in no fit state to meet the judge and his father.

Forrester stopped before the ornate double doors, and April took a deep breath.

Inside, three men came to their feet. She smiled at Jeremy. He smiled right back.

"April," he began, drawing toward her with the older man, "may I present our father, Jonah Hawthorne, Duke of Westbrook. Father, this is April, whom I told you arrived yesterday. She's Vivienne's daughter."

Jonah was a large man, but clearly the ghost of a man

much taller and more robust. His hair was thinning and streaked with gray, and he leaned heavily on his cane.

The older man took her gloved hand gently. She smiled at him. "Your Grace, I'm so pleased to finally meet you." She curtsied, her hand still held by his.

His eyes never left hers. He peered at her face, assessing, remembering.

"I . . . have a daughter?"

She smiled sheepishly. "Mother told me about you, but I regret that she never told you about me. I'm very sorry for springing upon you unannounced, but I knew no other way to contact you with discretion."

Her hand still clasped tightly in his, April began to grow slightly uncomfortable under his scrutiny. She could sense him swaying from past to present, then to now, comparing her likeness to a memory. Surprise, guilt, tenderness, regret: his face was a kaleidoscope of emotions.

Jeremy spoke up again. "And this is our brother, Riley, Lord Blackheath."

A curious excitement, laced with fear, rushed through her. Her eyes swept the room, and what they saw surprised her.

She had expected to see a scholarly man, bespectacled and stooped from poring over legal tomes. She had expected to see a man whose frame was as brittle as the pages in ancient books of law. She had expected to see a man whose expression was frozen into a perpetual air of disdain.

Instead, she saw Riley. And he was magnificent.

Easily among the tallest men she had ever seen, he was as imposing as if he had been the only person in the room. He was standing beside the tea table, pouring some of the steaming liquid into a china cup, and the sight of so large a man handling so delicate a teapot was oddly fascinating.

His head was forested with hair as dense and black as a murder of crows, and it spiked over a snowy cravat. His face was harder and leaner than his brother's, but there was the trace of a little boy in the impossibly thick fringe of black lashes that seemed to be a family trait. He was considerably younger than she imagined, thirty-five, perhaps, but his bearing was as incontrovertibly authoritative as it was vibrantly confident.

He looked up, and their eyes met. They were beautiful . . . an unusual shade warring between blue and green. From beneath the thick eyebrows that feathered back toward his temples, those eyes regarded her with a keen perspicacity that unsettled her. The person standing before her was the picture of a gentleman, but something lurked behind the regal façade. It was something so instinctively male, so seductively primitive, that she was forced to look away. Her gaze lowered, mesmerized by the way his shoulders filled the beautiful swallowtail coat, its fabric taut with the width of him. Lower her eyes went, trailing down the long lines of him that narrowed at his waist and widened at the sinews that stretched his dove-gray breeches.

A flush suffused her face, she was sure, and she fervently hoped he hadn't noticed the trail her gaze had taken. Her attention flew back to his dazzling blue-green eyes, which were now narrowing suspiciously upon her.

"I'm very pleased to meet you," she said, extending her hand.

Riley stared into her face, probing beneath the pleasant smile she offered him. "Yes, I can see you are," he answered, bringing the cup to his lips.

Mortified, April retracted her hand as fast as if he had slapped it away. His face became smug as he peered at her over the brim of his cup. She had never looked at a man the way she looked at him, and to be caught doing so was more than her pride could bear.

Jeremy, uncomfortable with their tense exchange, cleared his throat politely. "Mrs. Perkins brought in the tea. May I pour you some, April?"

She blazed at Riley. "Thank you, no, Jeremy. I just came down to meet our father."

Jonah, who had not taken his eyes off April, grew weak at the knees and had to sit down. "Do forgive me, but I'm afraid this is all just a little too much to absorb."

April sat in a nearby chair. "It is I who should apologize, Your Grace. I suspected that the news would shock you. But it was imperative that I come to meet you. After all these years, I had to know my father."

Jeremy brought over a glass of brandy, and Jonah's hand trembled as he raised it to his lips. "I don't understand. Why did Vivienne keep you from me all this time?"

It was an odd question. "She spoke of you often, Your Grace, and always with fondness. But she never told me why she kept me a secret. Judging from your station in life, I can only imagine it was out of respect for your reputation. She simply didn't want to defile your family name."

He looked aggrieved. "Oh, my poor Vivienne."

While April puzzled at his response, Riley snorted derisively. "Father, don't tell me you believe this girl's fish tale."

Jeremy responded. "Oh, it's true, Riley. It's as I told you in my letter. She knew all about Vivienne: where she came from, where she lived . . . everything."

"That's hardly privileged information, Jeremy," Riley answered, never for a moment shifting his eyes from April.

"There are things she knows. Tell them, April. Tell them about Vivienne and Father."

She didn't hear the question at first. That man Riley kept staring at her. He didn't even seem to blink. If it weren't for the steady rise and fall of his chest, she would have thought him a statue.

With great force of will, she tore her eyes from Riley's. Focusing on Jonah's expectant face, she recited some of the details she had gleaned from the diary. Under the guise of reminiscences, she fabricated a vignette of a life with the Madame, made up of half-truths and carefully embellished stories from the Madame's diary. April wove in moments where the Madame had shared confidences about her love affair with Jonah. She was secretly pleased at how convincingly she incorporated herself into the Madame's life.

It would have been her finest performance yet, except that she kept glancing over at Riley, and every time she did so, her mind went blank. He was no statue, as she originally mused. He was far too alive, too alert, to be made of stone. Everything she uttered was eagerly absorbed by Jeremy and Jonah, as if her words were drops of water falling on parched soil. But that man Riley was not so receptive. He listened attentively, probingly, collecting every stutter and hesitation as if he were searching for a chink in her armor.

When April reached the part about the Madame's death, she had to stop. Jonah was almost in tears.

"She was such a good woman," he said, removing a handkerchief from a pocket. "I was wrong to let her go. I'll never forgive myself."

Jeremy threw an arm around him. "It's all right, Father. Don't mourn what you could never have."

Their reaction bewildered her, but she was careful not to betray it.

Jonah looked up at her. "I'm sorry that your mother is gone, child. She meant the world to me. She was the most wonderful woman I have ever known."

Riley bristled, and she felt an immense relief that his

attention was finally drawn elsewhere. "That is because you have very low standards, Father."

"I beg your pardon?" he said, turning toward his son.

Riley met his stare. "Firstly, I will not be drawn into a discussion wherein the praises of Vivienne Devereux are sung. And secondly, I have never heard such a heap of rubbish in my whole life. Damn it, Father, it's not like you to be so credulous. Can't you see how artfully this girl is playing upon your romantic sentiments?"

Jonah glowered at Riley. "You'll have to forgive my son, Miss Devereux. Riley is a good lad, but he's a man of the law, and therefore highly skeptical. I'll concede that I too was dubious when I received word of this. But I'm not anymore. Which makes me surprised at Riley. He is usually a very good judge of character."

Riley moved to an armchair directly opposite April, his nearness sparking an alarm within her. April got that unsettling sensation again, the distracting impression that she was sitting too close to a viper that was about to strike, just as soon as it found the right vein.

"Tell me, Miss Devereux, what evidence do you have that you are who you claim?"

Jonah frowned at him. "You heard the girl. She knows things that no one but Vivienne and I were privy to. Conversations we've had, places we'd gone. The exotic flowers I brought her. Things that took place twenty years ago. How else could she know? She must be Vivienne's daughter."

"Yes, but is she *your* daughter?"

There was a long pause. She watched as his frown dissipated into a proud smile. "Even if she isn't mine, she's Vivienne's, and that's good enough for me."

His words pulled her out from under the weight of Riley's stare. April had been surprised by his grief at Vivienne's supposed death, but she was astonished by his blind acceptance of her for Vivienne's sake. Something warmed within her. April had that feeling again, that she was somehow out of her depth. Every instinct in her told her to run, that things here were not as they seemed. But these strangers were openly offering something that April didn't even know she craved—a family of her own.

Riley leaned back in his chair. "Oh, come now, Father. Just have a look at her. I can't even tell what side of the cradle she favors. She doesn't look like the Vivienne I remember. There's absolutely no resemblance to either of you. Go on, girl. Pack your things and get out."

Jonah shot his son a pleading look. "No, Riley. Please. She's all I have left."

Riley swung his stormy gaze from his father's wistful face back to April, who straightened under his inspection. "Very well, Father. Prove it to me. Why should I believe she is who she claims?"

Jonah reached into his waistcoat pocket and pulled out his watch. He released the catch and offered it to him. "There. In there is a picture of Vivienne. Maybe that will refresh your memory. See how much they look alike? What can you possibly remember of her? You were just a boy."

Riley studied the inside of the watchcase. "Father, this is a silhouette."

"That's right. Can't you see? They have the same nose!"

Riley rolled his eyes heavenward and sighed impatiently. "Notwithstanding your nasal similarities, Miss Devereux, I fail to connect you in any way with our family. Furthermore, I do not know why you should choose to show up on our doorstep now, claiming to be some long-lost and best-forgotten relative. What, exactly, are your intentions toward us?"

April squirmed. "I . . . I want only to be reunited with my father."

Jonah's eyes softened. "You have been, child. You're part of our family now."

There it was again, that softening of her heart. The feeling of being accepted, of *belonging* . . . it filled her with a strange elation.

Riley's sensual mouth thinned, and his striking eyes retreated under his thick black eyebrows. "I can see I've been away at court too long. Have you both become so vulnerable to a woman's charms? All she needed was a little information and a pretty smile, and she got you two to take her in like a lost puppy. Need I remind you what a precarious situation she has placed us in? Her very presence here is enough to cast suspicion upon us. She is the daughter of a harlot, and very likely one herself. I don't know what you two intend, but I won't have our family name tarnished by any sort of connection with a girl like that."

Her teeth clenched uncontrollably. She could hardly believe his insufferable haughtiness. How dare he think his family above her kind, considering his own father bedded one of them! Much as it galled her, her indignation at his disdain gave way to a fierce obligation to protect those he maligned, many of whom were her friends, Jenny included.

Rising from her chair, she put on her best ladylike hauteur. "Although my mother was indeed a harlot, sir, neither she nor I were ever accustomed to being treated like one. I came only out of a desire to learn the identity of my father—and to comply with my mother's dying wish that I seek him out to ask him to look after me. I have done both. Now I shall trouble you no longer. Your Grace, Jeremy, thank you for your hospitality. Be assured I will leave as soon as my maid packs our things." Her skirts whirled as she made for the door.

Amid their protestations, she heard only one remark. "Make certain she packs *only* your things."

She cringed. She'd be damned before she left this house trounced by Lord High and Bloody Mighty. She turned upon him.

"As far as I'm concerned, your lordship, you can take the entire bloody manor and shove it right up your bottom!" With that, she turned and stormed out of the room.

FIFTEEN MINUTES LATER, APRIL GROANED into the pillow. "Oh, Jenny, I'm a fool. A right bloody brainless fool!"

Jenny sat beside her on the bed. "Stop kicking yourself. You did the right thing. Imagine the cheek!"

April jerked the pillow away from her face. "We really have to leave now, you know. There's no way they'd let us stay."

Jenny smiled sympathetically. "You know I'm not disappointed about that. I'm glad to be quit of this place. Let's just take our loss and get out."

April rolled her eyes upward. "But this house . . . and you should have seen the morning room! It was so beautiful, overlooking the gardens and all. Oh, I can't stand it!"

Jenny pried the pillow from April's face. "What good does it do to 'ave all these rooms if it makes you mean and selfish? Is that what you want, to be like that Riley fellow? All uppity and 'olier-than-thou? I don't think I'd like you very much if you became like that."

"I just wish I hadn't let my temper get the best of me, that's all. He was testing me—I could feel it. And I rose to the bait. Some 'lady' I turned out to be."

"You *are* a lady," Jenny insisted.

"Yes, but ladies don't go about telling gentlemen to stuff themselves, do they?"

Jenny giggled. "Not usually, no. But you stood up for

what you believed in, and that makes you lady enough in my book."

A knock sounded on the door, and they froze. April leapt off the bed and told Jenny to start throwing their things in their valise. April then opened the door.

She blinked in disbelief. It was Riley.

"Lord Blackheath," she breathed. "I did not expect to see you."

He looked down, a lock of black hair falling onto his forehead. "I did not expect to come. May I speak with you a moment?"

She swallowed hard. "Of course."

Now that he stood so near, she was able to appreciate his size. He was unusually tall for an Englishman, and incredibly broad about the shoulders. As he brushed past her, his masculine scent, mingled with a whisper of sandalwood, made her senses kindle in response.

The immense bedroom she so loved seemed cramped now that he stood in the center of it. He glanced at Jenny, and April realized he wanted her to dismiss her servant.

"Jenny, please excuse us."

"Yes, miss," she said haltingly, and practically ran out into the other room.

When they were finally alone, Riley spoke. "I cannot seem to dispel the memory of your parting remarks. It was rather less cordial than I am accustomed to."

Despite the stern reprimand, she would not give him the satisfaction of appearing contrite. "If you've come seeking an apology, Lord Blackheath, I fear you may have wasted your time."

"Actually, I came to make one." Riley raked his fingers through his hair in the impatient gesture of a man who was forced into a course of action that countermanded his better instincts. "My father would have you stay on a bit longer, if you've a mind to. As you may have surmised, he was quite fond of Vivienne, and you are his link to her memory. He also has no wish to turn you out. Therefore, I invite you to be our guest here at the manor, and if you would be so kind, acquaint my father with the years of Vivienne's life since he saw her last."

Wearing her triumph like a crown, she strode to the window. "I am not certain I can accept your invitation. Given what passes for a welcome here, I expect I shall be much more comfortable at the finishing school."

She could not see him, but she heard him inhale sharply. "I shall have Forrester situate you in the Queen's Bedchamber during your stay. It's the suite Her Majesty uses when she visits, the finest in my home. I trust *it* will make you comfortable."

April's heart leapt at his sweetened offer of hospitality, but she quelled the delight. "I don't think so, Lord Blackheath. I did not make arrangements for an extended stay. My things are not here. Please convey my regrets to His Grace."

Riley made a guttural noise, and she could sense his palpable irritation at his vulnerable position. "My entire household will be at your disposal. I will have Forrester assign a contingent of servants to wait upon you, and if you wish, you can order a consignment of dresses from London so that you may remain fashionable while in the country. With my compliments, of course."

April's eyes gleamed. She was glad that she was not facing him, because she could not suppress her exhilaration at his offer. Her breathing quickened, and she could not erase the smile from her lips. What a victory!

She cleared her throat. His hospitality was not Riley's own idea. He was clearly making amends at his father's behest. "Perhaps I may be persuaded to stay on for a short time, until I find alternate arrangements," she said, hoping her words cut him.

"Of course."

Out of the corner of her eye, she saw him turn toward the door.

"Is that all?" April called out, halting him.

His eyebrows drew together. "Excuse me?"

"You said you came to make an apology, and I have not yet heard it." She faced him in a bold challenge.

Riley's eyes widened, but he swallowed his flaring temper. "Yes, well, I realize I was a bit harsh on you, and I apologize if I insulted you or Vivienne Devereux."

She boldly walked up to him. "You were exceedingly harsh, sir, both to me and to the memory of my mother. I knew there would be questions, but I did not expect an interrogation."

Riley's jaw clenched. "I do beg your pardon once more."

"I must say I expected more of someone of your privileged upbringing. And indeed, of someone who is in fact my own blood relation."

He moved so quickly, April jumped. In a second, his large hands slammed against the wardrobe on either side of her, pinning her between his massive arms.

"Don't even try it! You may have charmed my father, Miss Devereux, but don't think for one moment that you have fooled me. You haven't uttered a single honest word since you entered my house, and I do not suffer liars gladly. I strongly suggest you abandon all pretenses, or you may find out what happens to those who try to deceive me. Do we understand one another?"

The heat emanating from his fiery eyes made her gasp for air. Even if she could, she dared not answer him.

He tore himself away and stormed out of her room, leaving in his wake only the sound of the vibrating wardrobe doors.

Her heart hammered against her chest. She chided herself for a fool. It had been an imprudent move to challenge him.

There was no turning back now. The war with Riley was under way.

Three

IT TOOK THE REST OF THE MORNING FOR April to convince Jenny to stay at Blackheath Manor. Jenny was horrified at the prospect of having to stay even one more night with the Circuit Judge in residence, despite April's assurances that she would eventually win Riley over. In truth, April didn't understand how Jeremy and Jonah could be so accepting of her. This was one mystery that nagged at her constantly. Nevertheless, she reasoned that being accepted as a daughter afforded her a lot more privileges than being paid off to not be one, so she decided to bide her time.

Riley's generous hospitality was just what April had been looking for, but she was hard-pressed to find ways in which it benefited her friend. Now that April was ostensibly a member of the family, she no longer needed to have an abigail. Jenny was relegated to the servants' quarters while April occupied the grandest room in the house. Ultimately, April appealed to Jenny's loyalty as a friend, and Jenny acquiesced on the condition that they be on their way, money or no, before month's end.

The Queen's Bedchamber was indeed worthy of its

namesake, occupying an enormous spread of the second floor. It comprised most of the windows overlooking the water terrace and driveway. In addition to the bedroom, it boasted a bathing area with a built-in marble tub in the floor, dressing room, and private sitting room. The grandeur of the rooms exceeded even April's dreams, and she wished that the girls at the Pleasure Emporium could see their former scullery maid brushing her hair with the Queen's own bejeweled hairbrush. She spent a long while touching, smelling, exploring every inch of the bedchamber. She marveled at how perfect it felt for her to be there after a lifetime spent wishing it were so. She congratulated herself on making her wishes come true, plan put into action, fantasy made reality. She had broken all the class barriers in one fell swoop. After all her hard work on her hands and knees, this belonged to her, it was her reward, and she deserved it. She would never leave all this splendor, and she made a mental note to work on changing Jenny's mind permanently.

True to his word, Riley had summoned a couturier from London, a Mr. Cartwright. Mr. Cartwright had brought with him a few model frocks he was in the process of completing, and April found she could just about fit them. Reluctantly, she requested that each have some black trimming or bows, in order to maintain the appearance that she was in mourning.

While his assistants worked slavishly making alterations, Mr. Cartwright showed April some of his fashion plates. April ordered a number of morning and afternoon frocks, a riding costume, and several evening dresses. She required all the accessories—hair ribbons, undergarments, bonnets—which Mr. Cartwright only too happily commissioned for her. Most definitely, the lowly sum of two thousand pounds that she and Jenny had accumulated would not have been nearly enough to be dressed to fashion. All in all, he left very pleased with the order, and she was thrilled that she was about to become the lady she had always dreamed she would be.

That evening, as Jenny fixed April's hair, she listened patiently to her friend complain about her new living quarters. Though Jenny's room was furnished and clean, she said, the bed was lumpy and the carpets needed mending. Jenny whined that she was better off at the Madame's. April ignored her for the time being, focusing her thoughts instead on dinner that night. April's mission now was to convince Riley that she was his sister, and she needed all her wits about her to strategize.

DRESSED IN ONE OF HER NEW FROCKS, April descended the grand staircase. She cursed the blasted Mr. Cartwright for leaving so much décolletage. She felt brazen and conspicuous, rather like the strumpets at Madame Devereux's. Damned if she knew how Society girls enjoyed walking about with half their bubbies out in the open. Surreptitiously tugging at her neckline, she joined the gentlemen who were already in the anteroom partaking of a brandy.

"My dear," Jonah cried, a smile spreading across his face. "You look like an angel."

She looked around the room at Riley, who was standing by the fireplace swirling the amber liquid in a glass. His thick black hair seemed to be sculpted from onyx. His long legs columned upward toward a fine jacket of black velvet. Unlike so many tall men who hunch over to minimize their height, he inhabited his body fully, extending it to its full height and width, not at all afraid to show his size, but not showing it off. He exhibited a remarkable economy of movement, barely even creasing his clothes when he did move.

He cast her a sidewise glance. Though only briefly, his eyes lingered appreciatively over her face and figure. She decided to use this to her advantage.

"If I appear angelic, it is thanks to Lord Blackheath's generosity, Your Grace. It was his idea to supplement my meager wardrobe."

"As pretty as the frock is, it doesn't do you justice. What do you think, Riley?"

This time, he focused his full attention on her, and she felt her heart beat faster. The candlelight carved out his high cheekbones, which hovered above the hollows on either side of his face. Beneath the surface of his skin, the shadowy hint of a beard accented his strong jawline.

"A cunning creation. Devilishly beautiful. I'd say it suits you perfectly."

She bristled. The sauce! She knew exactly how to get even with him. "Your Grace," she began, turning to Jonah, "may I say how grateful I am for your invitation to stop a while at Blackheath Manor. Lord Blackheath conveyed your wishes to me, and I am happy to announce that I would be very pleased to accept. I will stay at Blackheath Manor for as *long* as you would care to have me."

Riley tensed visibly, a warning emanating from his eyes.

Jonah smiled excitedly. "The pleasure is all mine. But let's not stand on ceremony. Let us call each other by our given names, shall we? We're all family now."

"Father . . ." Riley admonished.

The duke ignored him and held out his arm. "Shall we go into dinner?" She put her white-gloved hand onto his.

April was escorted to a table unlike any she had ever seen. Her place setting was filled with a glittering array of long-stemmed glasses with gold edging, and there were so many plates and serving bowls laid out that it made her light-headed at the thought of washing them all. She offered a silent prayer of sympathy for the scullery maid who had to work in this palace. God help her if she broke anything . . . the saucers alone looked like a month's wages.

She gulped as she stared down at the multiple forks, spoons, and knives arranged geometrically around her plate. There weren't half so many at dinner with Jeremy the night before. Now she regretted her earlier lie about having studied at a finishing school. She would be expected to know how to use all these pieces. Why on earth did these nobs need so many utensils?

The first test came with the soup course. When her bowl was filled, she reached for the dainty spoon above her plate, until she noticed Jeremy taking the larger one to the right of his knives. April did her best to mirror his table manners, so as not to give away her unrefined upbringing.

She wouldn't be half so nervous if it wasn't for Riley. Sitting directly across from her, he studied her every move with an intensity she found alarming. All throughout the soup course, he kept quiet, participating enough to be civil but not enough to be sociable. But he was most attentive when she spoke, watching her moves in patient watchfulness, like a relentless panther waiting for a gazelle to tire before pouncing. As clever as she believed herself to be, his vibrant intelligence was highly discerning, and it made her throat tighten with apprehension. Though he sat as immutable as a statue, danger rolled off him in waves.

"Vivienne was French, was she not?" he remarked halfway through the fish course.

April's fork froze in midair. "Yes. Yes, she was."

"What part of France did she hail from?" His eyes were alive with interest, but April had the suspicion that he had the answer to that question already.

Fortunately, she and the Madame had talked about this. "Orléans. Her father was a count. My grandfather," she added for effect.

"I'm curious. Why did she not make arrangements to

send you home to France? I'm certain there are those who might wish to know of your compromised situation." His presence filled the room, making Jeremy and Jonah seem merely shadows.

"No doubt, Lord Blackheath. If His Grace bids me pack, then I will be off to France to fall on the mercy of whatever relations are left to me."

"Nonsense," interjected Jonah. "I won't hear of it."

Riley ignored him. "Certainly that is an option. That is, if you haven't forgotten your French. But what am I saying? You would have studied French at finishing school, wouldn't you?"

The tension between them pulsed like a living thing. "Of course."

"Quel est le nom de votre école?"

A tidy little trap, she thought. "You certainly ask a lot of questions, Lord Blackheath."

"I have an inquisitive nature. Especially when I find things questionable."

Let's see how he likes this. In perfect French, she responded, "Mother sent me to Mrs. Waverly's School for Girls when I was old enough to become interesting to gentlemen. It was imperative to her that the same fate that befell her would not be visited upon me. And as her own family disowned her, it would have been imprudent for her to send me to live with them, would it not?"

Riley pursed his lips, and April gloried in the feeling of having thwarted him. His attention left April for the moment, and he began to push his food absently around his plate. His full, pensive lips were sober, weighted by the gravity of his thoughts. She could sense him struggling with the truth, trying to distinguish fact from fiction. Why couldn't he be as gullible as his father and brother? Why couldn't he just *accept* her, as they had done? A springy lock of black hair fell away from its place, and she was momentarily distracted. Her fingers twitched with the unmet desire to feather it back into place. Cor, but he was arrestingly attractive.

Arresting. The word shook her out of her foolish reverie, and reminded her of the danger of dropping her guard around him. By degrees, her mind returned to the conversation.

". . . surprise for you, April," Jeremy was saying. "By happy coincidence, we're expecting the arrival of Emily, my fiancée."

"Your fiancée?"

"Lady Emily Mountjoy. She's making a trip into London to do some shopping for our wedding, and she'll be stopping by on the way. You'll like her, I think. She'll keep you from being lonely in this big old house."

Pluck a duck! She was having enough trouble trying to win over Riley; now she must contend with someone new.

"It's an excellent match," Jonah affirmed. "Emily is a distant cousin of Her Majesty's. He did rather well for himself. I can't take any credit, I'm afraid. He discovered Emily all on his own."

"I didn't 'discover' Emily, Father; I fell in love with her. I'm only too happy she agreed to be my wife."

April shook her head. "But you're so very young, Jeremy. Why hurry into marriage?"

Jeremy beamed. "Because when you find the one who makes you into the person you were meant to be, you don't want to waste any time."

April had to meet the woman who could put this kind of smile on a man's face.

Jonah smiled. "As for Riley, however, I may need to lend him a hand."

Riley glowered at him.

"He could have his pick of any of a dozen beautiful girls from fine, noble families. I can't for the life of me understand why he can't just pick one and settle down."

"Father," Riley growled. "Please don't concern yourself with my personal affairs."

Jonah turned to him. "I will when they involve me. You're the eldest, and it is your responsibility to continue the line when I am gone. The Hawthorne lineage has stood unbroken for four hundred years, and its continuation depends solely upon you. I'm glad your brother is marrying, but I'll be made much happier when I see you wed and I am bouncing my grandson on my knee."

"Well," Jeremy chimed in, "if it's any consolation to you, Riley, Emily is being accompanied by her sister, Lady Agatha."

Riley's face was inscrutable, but he didn't appear to be made ecstatic by the news.

"Excellent!" Jonah answered. He leaned toward April. "Agatha Ravenwood is a stunning woman. Her husband passed away about six months ago, leaving her a considerable estate in Cornwall, far too much for so young a widow to administer. And she's absolutely crackers about Riley. What could be more perfect than two brothers marrying two of the most eligible sisters of the *ton*?"

Riley gritted his teeth. "Let's not get carried away with romantic fancies, especially when they involve me. Do either of you think it wise to bring outsiders into the house when we still have April to sort out?"

April bristled. "Sort out? Whatever do you mean?"

His smoldering wrath now ignited the distance between them. "What I mean, Miss Devereux, is that you cannot be allowed to wear your identity in public. Outside of this room, you cannot be passed off as our . . . *sister*," he said, hissing the last word. "As you can appreciate, that fact would cast such a pall of scandal upon this family that our four hundred years of proud nobility would end here and now. We would become objects of ridicule. Emily's father will call an end to Jeremy's marriage. I shall lose my post as Circuit Judge and my seat at Parliament. Father can forget about dandling his grandson on his knee, for no woman of noble birth would accept a father-in-law who flouted every social convention by parading his illegitimate child as a member of the family. So you see, Miss Devereux, this is why, no matter what the cost, you must never become a branch on the Hawthorne family tree."

The last word echoed in the vast dining room. He said it with such cruel conviction that April was bereft of words.

"Well, what are we to do?" Jonah asked. "We can't hide her every time we have a guest."

"Why not?" he replied coldly. "She must stay out of the public eye. God knows we have enough to contend with, avoiding servants' gossip. We don't want to call attention to the situation."

Indignant, April asked, "Am I to be made a prisoner in my own room?"

"Not what you bargained for, is it?" he countered, his flashing eyes daring her to make additional protestations.

Jeremy spared her the trouble. "Surely that will make matters worse. The servants will wonder why she is not allowed to see people."

"We'll cross that bridge when we come to it. For the time being, she is forbidden to meet anyone on the outside. I hope that is perfectly clear to you, Miss Devereux."

"As a bell, Lord Blackheath. Tell me, in your infinite wisdom, what do you think the servants ought to be told about me?"

Riley ground his teeth at her acerbic comment. "If they show any interest in you at all, Miss Devereux, you may tell them that you are my ward. Daughter of a friend who's fallen on hard times. And that is *all* you may say on the subject."

April had half a mind to bend the silver serving dish over his arrogant head.

"Do you think that will work?" Jeremy asked.

It would, she thought, but it'd be a waste of a good serving dish. "My lords, I have no wish to bring any dishonor upon you. You have been exceedingly compassionate with me, and I will never forget the kindness. I will put myself in your hands, and agree to propagate any explanation that you feel will keep these terrible things from happening."

Riley cocked an eyebrow. "That's very noble of you."

April returned his gaze. "I'll thank you to remember that as you are pruning my branch from the family tree."

His lips thinned. "Good. Then we're agreed. Please remember to confine all talk of Vivienne to private quarters, out of earshot of the servants. There will be no displays of affection when others are around. Do you trust your maid to keep silent?"

"Implicitly," she replied.

"Excellent. Then with any luck, this whole charade won't make outcasts of us all."

The conversation had made her suddenly weary. "I think, then, gentlemen, I shall leave you to your cigars," she said, rising from the table.

The three men rose, too, surprising April. No man had ever risen for her before. It made her feel like a real lady. The fact that Riley rose too made her feel all the more special.

"My dear," Jonah protested. "We can't leave you to entertain yourself. Let's retire to the game room for some whist."

Visibly alarmed, she declined. She had never played the game in her life, but she knew it was something all ladies would know.

Suspicious, Riley spoke up. "Surely you wouldn't deprive us of your company so early."

The proper answer came to her lightning fast. "My apologies, but I must inform my maid immediately of the arrangements we have made here tonight. She has spent a great deal of time with your servants today, and I wish to contain any potential breach of confidentiality."

A crease marred Riley's forehead. "Very well, then. Until tomorrow."

The house was mute as she made her way back to the Queen's Bedchamber. Her new slippers whispered over the gleaming marble floors, and the fragrant smell of flowers drifted up to her from the arrangements placed on massive chests along the walls. Each passageway led her down a more beautiful cluster of rooms, as if the manor itself were seducing her.

Two passing servants nodded in deference to her. Her back straightened, and she adopted an expression of casual entitlement, casting her eyes away as she had seen so many ladies do in Hyde Park when tradesmen tipped their caps to them.

She passed a set of tall windows, and took note of her reflection. The girl she knew to be April was gone. Reflected in the glass was a woman dressed and styled to the height of fashion, her expression glowing with the bestowed authority and affluence of a duke's daughter. In the glass, framed by the prospect of miles of land and estates, was the image of a lady. She took a deep, contented breath, and a possessive grin etched itself onto her face.

At last, she thought.

APRIL STIRRED AS THE ORNATE CLOCK ON the mantel softly chimed eight o'clock. She smiled at the distant and vague memory of a life that had had her up at the crack of dawn to scrub the floors after the men left the Pleasure Emporium. She felt far more like a lady now that she was nestled in the smooth sheets with an aromatic fire crackling nearby, sleeping as late as she pleased. She curled under the coverlet contentedly.

A few minutes later, Jenny entered the room with a tray and set it down. She jostled April's sleeping form, eliciting an irritated grumble.

Jenny smirked. "Oh, I beg yer pardon, Yer Majesty, I didn't mean to wake ye, exceptin' that I brought yer royal cocoa."

"Really? Let's have it, then."

"Save me some. They won't let us belowstairs have any." Jenny sat beside April on the sprawling bed.

April sipped the velvety chocolate. "Cor, this is good!"

"They sent me up to tell you that breakfast will be served at ten."

"Oh, cheers. I'm famished."

"I wouldn't 'ave thought so, considering the spread you 'ad last night. There was enough food to feed a regiment. You 'ad more than enough to stuff your piehole."

April giggled. "I'll say. They know how to eat, they do. Lobster, pheasant, plovers' eggs, asparagus. Never saw such things. Did you get to try the syllabub and chocolate mousse? Almost disgraced meself with them."

Jenny looked incredulously at her. "They don't give us none of that! It's only for you lot. Cook makes a steak and kidney pie for us."

April felt a stab of guilt. "Oh."

Jenny looked about the room. "Blimey, this is grand. And warm! My room is freezin'."

April handed her the steaming cup. "I'm sorry things turned out like this, Jenny. If I had my way, I'd let you sleep here in the bed next to me."

"Well, why not? Now that you're in, you can do as you please." She gulped the chocolate.

"A servant in the Queen's Bedchamber? That would be sacrilege."

Jenny almost choked. "And just who do you think you are?"

April became flustered. "What I meant was that we need to keep up appearances. To them, I'm not a servant, but you are. It wouldn't be proper to have you sleep in here with me." Eager to change the subject, she said, "Speaking of keeping up appearances, the family decided I was to be passed off as Lord Blackheath's ward, in case anyone asks. I'm to be the daughter of a friend who's fallen on hard times. Have the other servants wondered who I am?"

"Yes, but I 'aven't said anything. Anyway, they don't 'ave too much time to lark about, so I 'aven't gotten too friendly. Well, except for one bloke, who got quite chatty with me."

"Really? Go on, then."

Jenny's face lit up. "He's a real nice man, real good manners. Talks real genteel. If it weren't for his footman's uniform, anyone would think he was one of these nobs."

"Footman? You mean the tall one with the red hair?"

"It ain't red! It's auburn."

"It's red. Clearly, there's no accounting for taste."

"Sod off! It's not like that. He's a perfect gentleman."

April stood agape. "A what?"

"A gentleman," Jenny said, a smile spreading across her face. "We had our tea together yesterday, and he recited to me one of the poems he had written. It was real good!"

"A poet? How charming," she said dryly.

Jenny smiled. "He said the sweetest things to me. He said he finds my accent endearing. He said there was a musical quality to my voice. Ain't that nice?"

"Nice," April said flatly, but her heart was in turmoil. She sensed the danger of losing her best friend.

"He's so bashful. You should 'ave seen him screwin' up the courage to ask me if he could accompany me to church on Sunday! And he's ever so smart. He knows loads about drama and music and all that. He carries a book about in his jacket pocket. He's real cultured."

April laughed. "Cultured? You haven't the faintest idea

what that is. To you, anyone who doesn't first ask 'How much?' is 'cultured.' "

Jenny reacted as if she'd been slapped in the face. "Leave it to you to bring that up. At least William doesn't think of me that way." She marched toward the door.

April halted her. "I'm really sorry, Jenny, I didn't mean it like that. It's just that I find it hard to believe that a servant could be that . . . sophisticated."

Angrily, she thrust a stray lock of mahogany hair in her cap. "Maybe you're right. It's not likely a filthy scullery maid could ever pass for a lady, is it?"

April bristled. "I'm different."

"How?"

"I had noble ambitions. I made myself what I am. I worked my way out of it," she said, punching each word.

"By lying, cheating, and swindling. You deceive people into thinking you're someone that you're not. What's so noble about that? You're not better than a scullery maid. She earns her wages honestly. You're lower. You're a common thief."

April's heart went cold. "Better a thief than a whore."

Jenny's musical voice cracked. "Better a whore than a false friend."

The door slammed shut behind her.

Four

PUSHING HER QUARREL WITH JENNY OUT of her mind, April sat down to a pleasant breakfast in the Rose Parlor, a room with three sets of soaring French doors that opened out over the rose garden warming in the sun. She was joined by Jonah, who never missed an opportunity to steal a few moments with April to talk about Vivienne.

April had been in the Madame's employ for about a year, and during that time, had learned much about her. The Madame often waxed nostalgic, and April loved to listen to her glamorous escapades. The Madame recounted a youth spent accompanying Europe's crème de la crème to opera houses, masques, and even royal palaces. Not even women within Society's circle were allowed to do and see all that the Madame was permitted. Somewhere between Polite Society and the demimonde, the adventuress held sway.

April had always wondered why the Madame had abandoned this lifestyle when she was still at her peak. The Pleasure Emporium was a far cry from the palace at Versailles, but the Madame never discussed her reversal of fortune. Still, what April did know of the Madame's life was enough to satisfy Jonah's ears. He was brimming with questions, and April was touched by his tenderness toward the Madame. It was peculiar that of all the men she had tried to blackmail, he was the only one who did not regret his liaison with her.

After breakfast, they took a stroll, arm in arm. Outside, a thick stone balustrade escorted them down onto the green sea of lawn that undulated toward the enormous burbling fountain anchored in the center of the garden. The garden was Jeremy's singular passion, the older man explained, so Jeremy oversaw its maintenance personally.

"One day, Jeremy crawled away from his nursemaid and made straight for the lavender beds," he said, using his cane to point out the place. "And he's never come out. How that boy loved to root around in the earth! There was more dirt on his knees than on the ground. You could have planted potatoes under his fingernails! And now, look at him. Only twenty and he's just published his first book on botany. It's why he's always been a particular favorite of Queen Charlotte's. The monarch frequently comes to visit, because she and Jeremy share the same passion for horticulture."

April looked out across the field. Floral carpets lined the manicured lawns, a parade of colors glowing in the sun. Bushes shaped into clever formations festooned the walkways. In the distance, the trees burned orange, gold, and magenta. Never had she seen such a wondrous sight.

"A lovesome garden is the purest of human delights," he said, evidently proud of his son's achievements. "Such is our Jeremy. A pure and wholesome soul. You remind me of him."

She halted, numbed with amazement. "Why?"

He shrugged. "I expect it's probably because you and he were raised by parents who were very much alike in spirit."

They came to a bench placed strategically within sight of the entire garden. April helped him into the seat, and then took her place beside him.

"I fell in love with your mother the first moment I laid eyes on her. She was a bonny thing, the very soul of grace. I met her in the park; she was walking with another gentleman, a man whom I knew well. I bid them a good morning and struck up a conversation. She was delightful. So witty and charming. It was with much reluctance that I parted company with them.

"Well, I also knew this man's wife. So, when I saw him at Boodle's a few nights later, I asked him about the extraordinary creature he had had on his arm in the park. He informed me that she was a . . . well . . . a *fille de joie*. And he told me where I could call upon her.

"I'm ashamed to say so, because I too was married. But I thought about her constantly. I had to see her again. As smitten as a schoolboy, that was I. I don't know where I found the courage to do so, but one day I visited her at her apartments in London. You must believe me when I tell you that I never purchased her services—ever. I only wanted to speak with her. To my surprise and joy, she recognized me at once.

"Well, it didn't take us long. We began to love each other with the kind of love that comes along only once in a lifetime. I detested her vile profession, but I was convinced that even that would never separate us. She began to avoid her clients, seeing only me, and it was I who paid her lost wages."

April mentally scoured the pages of the Madame's diary. She remembered the entries concerning the man whom the Madame had been in love with. He was nameless in the diary. Could this be he?

Jonah continued. "She had a darling pet name for me. I never told a soul. It makes me laugh every time I think on it," he said, shaking his head and smiling.

The anonymous pages that followed! "Yes, I remember. She called you her *petit ours*."

"By God, she told you! The minx! I hope she didn't tell you why she called me that."

There was nothing in the diary. But April noticed that his hand, resting on the knob of the cane, was covered with dense salt-and-pepper hair. "Because you are furry?"

He laughed then, and she fell in love with the sound of it. "I believe your mother may have been far too free with the details of our past, my child." Jonah inclined his head, appearing to study the handle of his cane. "But after Jeremy was born, everything changed."

"Was this when your wife found out about you and the Mad— I mean, Mother?"

"It would seem so, yes. Somehow, rumors were bandied about that Vivienne had become diseased. It wasn't true, of course, but malicious gossip is impossible to smother. We never found out how it got started . . . maybe a client irate at her long absence from her duties. Who knows? But she quickly became a pariah in Society. She wasn't welcomed anywhere. Things were intolerable not only for her, but also for anyone who had been seen with her."

His face took on that faraway look again, as long-dead memories came to life. "I became afraid . . . I had an established position in Society, you understand, and . . . well, the rumors that hounded her began to plague me as well. It was becoming painfully clear that being connected with her . . . it would be the end of me, of my reputation. So, I . . . I had to break it off with her." He turned to April, searching her face for some measure of understanding. "I did it for my family, April. I was honor bound."

Even as he said these words, his confidence failed him. "I did it for myself, too, I suppose. I was so selfish. So proud. And it cost me the only woman I ever loved."

If regret were flesh, she was surely beholding it now. He

hung his head, his forehead lined with contrition. Tears began to pool in his eyes.

"I was a fool." He buried his face in one hand and sobbed. April patted his back, offering him solace. She realized that she had not been the only one imprisoned by her class. The Madame and the duke had suffered, too, their love unable to transcend their difference in rank. She looked at him now, a sad, broken man, and was moved to tears.

He sniffed, and mopped at his eyes. "I had no idea what it would do to me. To her. To you."

She shook her head, dodging his undeserved sympathy. "Don't fret so, Your Grace. That was many years ago. Things are different now." She wiped his cheek with her hand, which he grasped firmly in his.

"I hope you will permit me to be a father to you now. Vivienne was the light of my youth, but you . . . you shall be the light of my old age. You're right: let's have no more talk of the past. Now, we shall focus on the future. I promise I will make myself worthy of you."

His words shamed her. Never in her life had she felt so morally reprehensible. An unbidden voice screamed at her that it was she who was unworthy of him. She was overcome by a powerful desire to confess her schemes, disavow any relation, and walk away from this family. But his eyes were so earnest, so eager to make amends. He craved a chance to right the wrongs in his past, to atone for the sins of his pride. It was the least she could do to give him that chance, and let him mend his broken life.

"Yes, Your Grace. Today we bleed, but tomorrow we will heal."

RILEY DESCENDED THE GRAND STAIRCASE in a foul temper. He had spent a sleepless night with a bottle of brandy, dissecting the issue of Miss April Devereux.

The chit had turned his whole world on its ear. He had always prided himself on being an excellent judge of character; it was a trait that made him a fair and discerning judge. But this girl was a complete enigma. All the evidence supported her story, yet every fiber in his being pointed to the fact that she was not what she represented. Her very presence imperiled his family's dignified name in Society.

Damn the day that Vivienne sashayed into his father's life! Out of respect for his father's feelings, Riley did not speak of his exhilaration to learn that Vivienne was finally in her grave. With Vivienne's death, the secrets that had made his family vulnerable would finally be buried forever. But the introduction of Miss Devereux threatened once again to bring old secrets to light. Even from the grave, it seemed, Vivienne was able to exert her influence on the Hawthorne men.

Despite his father's infatuation with the idea that Vivienne had left him a daughter, Riley was convinced that April had ulterior motives. But what were they? He had lain awake till dawn contemplating what her objectives could be. As yet, she had made no overtures of blackmail, theft, coercion, or any other crime. But he'd stake his fortune on the fact that every word she uttered had been a lie. But to what end?

In spite of his irritation and growing belief that April was merely some mischief-making firebrand, he sensed that she was completely unaware of the incredible power she had to cripple his family. In more ways than he'd care to admit. He wished that he hadn't been so attracted to the saucy manner she had of standing up to him. No well-bred lady of his acquaintance would ever dare reproach a marquess—and in so vulgar a manner.

She was a good actress, he'd give her that. She had manufactured a thin veneer of cultivated propriety to mask her lack of breeding, which amused him a great deal. She had everyone fooled. But he had known far too many low-class

London lawbreakers to be deceived by this green girl. He had half a mind to put her over his knee to set her on the right path. And he would, if he wasn't so afraid of what he might do to her afterward. She was so pretty, so disarming. What if his instincts were wrong, and he really was her half brother? The thought made him frown. He had to get to the bottom of this, no matter what the cost.

As he straightened the white cuff beneath his navy blue coat, he noticed the butler withdrawing from the dining room.

"Forrester, be a good chap and send for my solicitor."

"Mr. Northam is already here, my lord," the butler replied solemnly. "His Grace sent for him this morning. They're presently in His Grace's private study."

"Ah. Thank you." Riley thought it odd that Jonah would need their solicitor, but blessed the convenience that Peter Northam was already there.

Riley threw open the doors to his father's study. "I knew there was a foul odor around this place."

"Maybe you should have a bath then," Northam countered good-naturedly, as he rose to shake hands with his old friend. Of an age with Riley, Peter Northam, with his blond hair, hazel eyes, and genial smile, inspired confidence in almost everyone he met. It was a decidedly advantageous trait for a solicitor to have.

"What are you doing here? Aren't you supposed to be working on the Capofaro murder case?"

"It's not until next week. I just brought over some papers for your father to sign."

Riley turned to his father, who was peering through his spectacles at a sheaf of parchment, the only thing on his desk. His father's study, as neat as a manicured garden, stood in sharp contrast to his own, which was littered with well-worn law books, court transcripts, and newspaper clippings. Though it appeared disorderly to everyone else, Riley could navigate through the towering piles of books and hills of paper as well as he could negotiate the terrain of his property. It was the only room he prohibited the servants from entering. "Ah. Good morning, Father."

"Good *afternoon*, Riley. By God, the slumber of the young is sound indeed."

Riley rubbed the back of his neck. "Hardly. I've been wrestling with a problem. I must have conjured you, Northam, because I was only just thinking about sending for you. You might be in a position to help me."

"Only too glad, Riley. Once His Grace has concluded his business, I'll stop by your study."

"Fine. I just got some Havanas in and a respectable burgundy. Let me know when you're done."

Just as Riley reached the doors, he overheard his father ask, "So, Northam, do you foresee any problems expediting this through the probate process?"

"Not at all," the solicitor replied. "As long as the will is executed by Your Grace and properly witnessed in the prescribed time, I should be able to sidestep some of the formalities involved in revising the will so hastily."

Riley turned. "Father? Are you amending your will?"

"That's right. I've decided to leave Clondoogan Hall to April."

Not sure whether to register fury or reason, Riley opted for the latter. "Clondoogan Hall is Jeremy's estate. It's his birthright."

Jonah peered through his spectacles at the parchment, and poised his quill over the designated spot. "Jeremy hates Scotland. And April is going to need a dowry for us to make a good marriage for her."

"Bloody hell!" Riley exploded, startling his father so badly he jarred his quill and ruined his signature.

"Damn it, Riley! See what you've made me do! Is this still acceptable, Northam?"

"I'm afraid not, Your Grace," he stammered, unsure what made Riley so angry. "But I can have fresh papers drawn up by tomorrow."

"Father, forget the damn papers! You've known her for all of two days and you're writing her into your will?"

Jonah threw the quill down testily. "Well, I certainly can't leave it up to you to look after her when I'm gone, can I?"

Riley leaned both hands on the back of a chair, gripping it so hard his knuckles turned white. "Of course," he muttered, shaking his head. "She's after the inheritance. That's her game! Once she's in the will, she's a heart attack away from a fortune!"

The older man removed his spectacles. "Why do you persist in being so suspicious of her? It wasn't her idea to be in my will; it was mine. I meant to surprise her with the news tonight over dinner."

"Can't you see that she's manipulated you into this? She's put blinders on you and Jeremy, and neither of you can see what a cunning little confidence artist you've let into this house!"

"Jeremy and I see perfectly clearly. It is you who are blinded by jealousy. Northam, draw up the papers. I'll sign them tomorrow. As for you, young man," he said, squaring up on Riley though he was far shorter, "you always were a cynic as concerned the women in my life. I'm fed up with submitting to the Hawthorne rules of propriety. It's brought me nothing but misery, I can see that now, and it will do the same to you. I suggest you step down from that pedestal of yours—before you fall off it. And from where you stand, it's a long way down." The door slammed resolutely behind him.

Riley gritted his teeth. The conniving chit could not

only ruin his reputation and his fortune, she was also driving a wedge between him and the rest of his family!

"Is everything all right, old boy?" Northam asked, unsure what to say.

Riley looked at him with steely determination. "No, it most certainly is not. I need a favor, Northam, and I must have your word as a gentleman that you'll keep this just between us." They had known each other since their days at Eton, and Northam had always proven himself a discreet confidant.

"You have it. What's the problem?"

Riley threw himself in a green leather chair. He carefully outlined the trouble that had begun when April waltzed in and bewitched his brother and father. Taking care to avoid giving away too much detail, he told Northam that April had characterized herself as the daughter of Jonah and a courtesan of his acquaintance from long ago. His father, who had been in fragile health, was vulnerable to her charm and had been duped into giving away Jeremy's inheritance.

Northam shook his head. "He told me she was a distant relation. The impertinence of the girl! Why don't you just send for the constables and have her thrown in jail?"

"I intend to. But I can't do that while Father is in love with the idea of being a father all over again."

"I understand, old boy. What can I do?"

"Before I send her down, I have to prove to him that she has deceived them. I need evidence. I'd like you to look into her past, find out who she really is. Spare no expense. Her story is full of holes, and I intend to make her fall into one of them. But I've no wish for a scandal. So please try to go about it without stirring up any dust."

"It might take some time, but I think it can be done. What do you know about her?" Northam pulled a notebook from his pocket.

"Not much beyond what she's told us. She said that her mother sent her to a finishing school, a Miss Waverly's School for Girls, but I presume that is a lie. The girl has some measure of refinement, but she hasn't yet shed the taint of the streets. She's arrived with an abigail, a Jenny Hare, though I suspect their relationship is more akin to close friends or sisters than a mistress and servant." Riley sketched out a few more observations, deductions based on April's actions rather than her words.

"I'll need a description. Do you think I could meet her?"

"Come for lunch tomorrow. You can meet her then. In the meantime, I'll try to gather more information about our protégée. It's time to replace speculation with fact."

"I'll get right on it. Don't worry about a thing."

"Thanks, old friend. But there's something else I'd like to ask." Riley stared at his clasped hands. "I respect your professional relationship with my father, so I won't ask you to disregard his commission to you to revise his will. All I ask is that you delay the process a bit. You're a master at dodging the established channels to save time; perhaps you can observe them just this once."

Northam smiled. "Of course. You can count on it."

LEFT WITH MORE QUESTIONS THAN ANSWERS following her conversation with Jonah, April drifted about the house absently. This family was a puzzle of a thousand pieces, and she couldn't even begin to glimpse at the complete picture yet.

In the midst of her wandering, April found herself in the Long Gallery. Paintings of the family ancestors throughout its history lined the hall. Men in armor, in ruffs, in military dress. April smiled as she identified the strong physical commonalities that manifested themselves in every generation.

The resemblance among the Hawthorne men was unmistakable. They were a handsome lot, proud and regal to a man.

She took a second look around, and a frown creased her brow. There were no women in any of the paintings. Where were all the paintings of the women in the family? Had this always been a household of chauvinistic men, or had the paintings of the Hawthorne women been removed? April was left pondering that last point when Riley walked up behind her.

"Claiming your place on the wall so soon?"

April let out a gasp. She turned to face him, and was met with a startling image: Riley, standing below his own portrait as a younger man. Both scowled at her from above, and she couldn't tell which was more intimidating. April's confidence failed her in the face of their unshakable aristocratic bearing.

She cleared her throat. "Hardly, my lord. There doesn't seem to be room for anyone of my sex on the wall."

"Quite right. This gallery is reserved for honoring the ancestors of the ducal line who merit veneration for their noble actions throughout the ages. The men you see here have sacrificed a great deal for the glory of England. The first Duke of Westbrook," he said, pointing to one man on horseback, "was accorded the title by Henry the Fifth for his valor on the field of battle in preserving English interests in France." He walked toward the painting of a man with a sword. "Cecil Hawthorne served as an officer in Queen Elizabeth's navy, maintaining Britain's balance of power during the defeat of the Spanish Armada. And William Hawthorne over there," he said, pointing at a more recent painting on the far wall, "was Prime Minister. At the risk of sounding immodest, I am proud of this family and its accomplishments."

"I see," she responded. "And you feel that your female

ancestors have not contributed to the family's great accomplishments?"

"I did not say that. The duchesses Westbrook have historically been a dignified collection, veritable queens in their own right. Most of them loved their husbands to distraction . . ." His voice trailed off.

"And yet?" She observed that he still exhibited his customary scowl, but now it seemed tinged with sadness. She was beginning to understand. "Where is the painting of your mother displayed, my lord?"

He turned away from her. "I believe it is somewhere in the attic. Do you care to see it?"

"What did she do to make you so angry?"

He swung his gaze back around. "This is not fit conversation, Miss Devereux. I wish to discuss another matter with you."

Ignoring him, April continued. "I can understand why you should hate Vivienne. I can hardly blame you. She stole your father away from you. But why your mother?"

"Miss Devereux, I'm warning you. You have no right to pry into my affairs."

April cocked her head. "What a curious choice of words, my lord, are uppermost in your mind. Did your mother have an affair? Is that what drove your father away?"

Riley advanced upon her with deadly menace. "I would advise you, Miss Devereux, to avoid speaking of my mother in my presence again."

April raised her chin defiantly. "For a man who places so much importance on truth, it is surprising that you should run from the sound of it where it concerns you."

His blue-green eyes narrowed upon her. His lips formed a response, but no words came forth. "She . . . was a faithless woman. There had been men in her life before she married my father, but it was he who presented the most advantageous match. He was so besotted with her that he did not care to see that she continued her liaisons well into their marriage. When my father finally found out, it was too late to do anything. He would not bring scandal upon the family name by being the first Hawthorne to divorce his wife. So he resigned himself to her adultery. Cuckolded in his very own house. Yes, you're right. She did drive my father away. To the waiting arms of a prostitute."

April's growing pity at his tale turned cold at the way he spat out the last word.

"Indeed. There were two adulterers in the marriage. Yet your father wasn't banished to the attic, for there his painting hangs."

Riley leveled his steely gaze on her. "Have a care, Miss Devereux—"

She withstood his stare with righteous indignation. "That is the difference between us, Lord Blackheath—I do have a care. I am able to overlook the faults and weaknesses of people. Humans are flawed creatures, but they are still worthy of love. Your father fell in love with a courtesan, hardly a venerable act, yet he remains here among your ancestors, this legion of pirates, assassins, and despots that lines the walls. Your mother gives her heart to another man, and she gets booted into exile, carved out of history together with the entire female half of your family. Is that the measure of your justice?"

His brilliant eyes gleamed intensely, belying the undercurrent of anger that pulsed through him. "Your opinion concerning my judgment is uninformed and unsolicited. I'll thank you to remember your place."

"Place," she repeated sarcastically. "I suppose in your world a lowly prostitute cannot presume to love a duke. It should be a sad world indeed if we begin to question from whom comes the love we receive. If you expect to be loved only by people who are your equal, I fear you may be sadly disappointed, my lord. Ordinary humans cannot ascend Mount Olympus."

With that she ran from the Long Gallery.

Five

THE NEXT DAY HAD DAWNED BEAUTIFUL, but a massive cover of angry clouds soon began to creep over the sky.

April sat down on the stone steps dejectedly. Mr. Cartwright had not yet delivered her new wardrobe, and she was forced to wear one of her plain black dresses. She cursed the fact that there would be visitors at a time like this. The tension between her and Riley was too great. Thrice they had met, and thrice they had fought, and each time they drew blood. And even though he tolerated her presence for Jonah's sake, she was careful not to miscalculate the balance of power at Blackheath Manor. In this chess game of hers, April might no longer be a pawn, but she was far from being a queen.

If only she knew how to checkmate him. As an adversary, he was far more skilled than she originally credited him with being. Her lies ricocheted off him like dull arrows on a suit of armor. What's more, he had an uncanny ability for hearing what she *didn't* say, as clearly as he heard her spoken words. Around him, she couldn't help but feel naked.

Involuntarily, her body warmed to the idea.

She shook her head. She couldn't think straight when she was around him. Those penetrating eyes both troubled and mesmerized her. If she looked straight into them, her body stopped responding to her wishes. She didn't know how other criminals felt, but bearing up under the weight of his guiltless stare was next to impossible.

Guiltless. It seemed he was the only one here who had nothing to be ashamed of. Her flaws stood out in stark contrast to his perfection. He was handsome, principled, powerful . . . and seductive as hell. In other words, Lord Perfect.

Normally, it wouldn't be so awful knowing that she was Miss Imperfect. Sometimes, she even took pride in it. But for each of his good qualities, she possessed its perfect opposite. That she could never even hope to have someone like him be interested in her . . . the thought depressed her to no end.

There it was again. Damn her weakness! How could she hope to win over him when all she thought about was how to win him over?

A sound drew her attention to the horizon. She spied a procession of carriages turning onto the fount-lined drive toward Blackheath Manor. Instinctively, April backed against the dripping ivy, flattening herself behind a potted yew tree. As the caravan drew to a stop, a footman rushed to the lead carriage, which bore a royal emblem on the door.

The door opened, and a pink-gloved hand emerged. The young woman who alighted was about eighteen, and she was dressed in the prettiest traveling costume April had ever seen. A velvet dress of the palest pink flowed becomingly from her waist, which was lined with a darker pink satin ribbon. Though the dress was cut daringly low, her bosom was modestly covered with white organdy pleats all the way to her throat. Her matching velvet bonnet adorned ringlets of shiny blond hair, framing her heart-shaped face. Her pale blue eyes, rosy lips, and creamy complexion made her the absolute picture of maidenly beauty. Lady Emily Mountjoy was exactly as Jeremy had described her.

The footman held out his hand for a second lady, who handed him a wrapped parcel. Stepping onto the footstool, the lady descended from the carriage. April was dazzled. Taller and more slender than her sister, she had the high arched brows and regal bearing of a seductress, with full lips and high cheekbones. Her eyes were as blue, but her hair was black as night. She too had a flawless complexion, made glowing by the contrast to her claret-colored traveling costume. But where Lady Emily was engagingly pretty, this woman had an unapproachably cruel beauty, at once compelling and frightening. This lady, who could only be Lady Agatha Ravenwood, was far from the image of the widow April had pictured.

Another lady descended and the breath caught in April's throat. The Queen!

Embarrassment quickly gave way to exhilaration at being so near Queen Charlotte. "Your Majesty!" April cried out, running to the carriage and curtsying humbly. "It is so great an honor to meet you. Please allow me to help you with your wrap—"

Lady Agatha slapped her hand away. "How dare you address the monarch without first being spoken to! Take your filthy hands off Her Majesty's person before I have you dismissed. If you need something to do, take these into the house," Lady Agatha commanded, flinging her bonnet and gloves at April.

April narrowed her eyes on Lady Agatha's retreating figure as she and the Queen strode into the hall. Her humiliation quickly turned to indignation at Lady Agatha's dismissive manner. She could have easily forgiven the mistaken identity. But not the rudeness.

"I'll take those, miss," said Susan meekly.

April handed the bonnet and gloves to the maid. "Thank you, Susan. Please see them safely to the dustbin."

Just as April reached the hall, Riley raced to a halt in front of the entourage.

"Majesty!" he called out, executing a hasty bow. "This is a happy surprise. Please forgive me for not meeting your carriage."

The Queen smiled placidly at Riley. "Do not trouble yourself, Blackheaz. I am not come on ze state visit. I know I was not expected."

"You are always welcome here, Your Majesty. Blackheath Manor is at your disposal. I shall have your rooms freshened at once—"

"No, I shan't be staying. My cousins informed me zat zey were stopping here before proceeding to London, and I offered to chaperone zem to Blackheaz Manor."

"You do me too much honor. Lady Agatha, Miss Emily," he said, bowing over each lady's hand, "how gratifying to see you both in good health."

"Where, pray, is your brother?" asked the Queen.

"Here I am, Your Majesty," Jeremy pronounced, coming to a stop.

"*Liebling!*" The Queen embraced him. "How very nice to see you again. You are too long away from Frogmore House."

"I have missed the pleasure of Your Majesty's company also. But I am yours to command." He smiled down at her.

"If it were so, you would to Richmond Gardens be coming viz me today. I have grown weary of Hampton Court and prefer ze less ostentatious gardens of Richmond. Next week, I am receiving a shipment of bulbs from Holland.

By spring, I shall have Buckingham House covered in tulips. You will be excited to learn zat I believe I may have found a solution for your problem viz ze breeding of your roses . . . but I shan't discuss it in Blackheaz's company, for he has no love of horticulture."

Riley shook his head. "My apologies, Your Majesty. Honesty must confess ignorance. But I am delighted to see Your Majesty pursuing her greatest passion, and taking pains to share the wealth of her expertise with my brother."

Lady Agatha held out the wrapped parcel to Riley. "And just so you don't feel left out of the wealth-sharing, Riley, I brought you a little trifle of my own."

He took the package, a curious expression on his face. "Is it my birthday and no one's told me?"

Her come-to-bed eyes smoldered. "No reason, darling. Just because."

"Well, thank you, Agatha." Riley opened the box and gingerly pulled out a pocketwatch dangling from a chain.

"It's a fob watch," she said. "It's been in the family for ages."

He held it up by the chain. "Agatha, I can't accept this. If it's a precious heirloom, it should remain within your family."

Agatha wrapped her hand around the crook of his arm and shrugged conspiratorially. "Riley, darling, I'm hoping it does."

Partly because of the disgustingly transparent marriage proposal, and partly because of the look on Riley's face, April succumbed to a fit of the giggles. All eyes turned to the corner where she had been watching quietly.

Lady Agatha leveled a contemptuous look at April. "Of all the impertinent . . . Riley, I demand that you dismiss this insolent servant immediately."

Riley tensed visibly. Damn the girl for disobeying his explicit instructions to stay out of sight! He had half a mind to thrash her now, in plain view of everyone. "Agatha . . ." he began, scrambling for an explanation.

"Do you know that she had the unmitigated gall to assault the Queen's person?"

"Tut, Agatha," admonished Queen Charlotte, "do not exaggerate so. Come here, child."

April walked toward the Queen and curtsied ceremoniously.

Riley stepped between them. "Your Majesty, may I present Miss April Rose Devereux . . . *my ward*." The words barely made it out of his clenched teeth.

"Quite lovely. And such a charming name, too."

"Thank you, Your Majesty," April responded, not sure if the giddiness she felt was from the compliment or her proximity to the Queen of England.

"Since when did you take a ward, Blackheaz?"

Riley's face was a mask of controlled fury. "It is a long story, Your Majesty. Why don't we take our rest in the Tapestry Room, and I'll ring for some refreshments?" He held out his arm to the monarch, and the ladies followed.

April took a seat at the circular table, her eyes round with excitement. She, a common girl from Whitechapel, was sitting in a luxurious salon in one of England's stateliest homes opposite none other than the Queen of England herself! Even April's fanciful dreams never dared reach these heights.

Jonah came in soon after, accompanied by another man. Jonah made his apologies and reacquainted himself with the monarch. It was clear that Jonah and the Queen were old friends, having met long ago when he paid his respects at her coronation. Riley brought the younger man to her.

"Peter Northam," Riley began, "may I introduce April Devereux, my ward."

As she gave him her hand, April inspected him. Mr. Northam was a singularly handsome man, with close-cropped sandy hair and intelligent hazel eyes. His smile revealed a row of perfectly aligned teeth. Though his buff-colored jacket and navy vest were tailored and flattering, the garments revealed their heavy use. April was relieved that she was not the only one dressed plainly. At least there was one other person sitting at this table who was not sopping in money. He slid into the seat beside her.

The conversation became animated. The Queen was a genial woman who seemed to have no pretenses. She was humble and self-deprecating, unafraid to make fun of her own occasional flubs in speech. April liked her immensely.

What she found even more incredible was that the Queen warmed to April as well. She laughed at her own folly at mistaking April for a servant, observing that it was the stuff of comedies and operas. True to her reputation for parsimony, she even went so far as to compliment April on her frugality in dress. "In zis day and age, ze price of a young lady's dress could feed a thrifty family for a year! It is extraordinary what my cousins pay for zeir clothes. Jeremy, I am warning you: be very strict viz Emily, or you may find yourself in debtor's prison before your first wedding anniversary."

Emily blushed becomingly, and Jeremy beamed at his fiancée. "Marm, if the cost of such beauty be that I spend the rest of my life in jail, then lock me away."

Everyone cooed at his words, except for Lady Agatha, whose stare remained fixed on April.

The noon meal was called. Jonah escorted the Queen into the dining room. Riley held out his arm to April, but Lady Agatha glided past her and snatched it first.

April could hardly quell the rage that heated her face. The bitch! Her fingers curled with the desire to tear out Agatha's hair and stuff it into her pillow.

She turned away, letting Jeremy accompany Emily out of the drawing room. At the end of the procession, Northam watched her as she tried to leash her anger.

"We have something in common, you and I. It appears we both fall short of being noble."

April crossed her arms. "I beg your pardon?"

Smiling, he held his hands up defensively. "I only meant that I couldn't help but notice that we two are the only ones here who don't have titles. We are therefore unfairly relegated to the end of the line into luncheon."

Her lips thinned. "I am beginning to learn that true nobility has very little to do with titles, Mr. Northam. Based on the conduct of some of the guests today, it occurs to me that integrity of character is entirely exclusive of hereditary privileges. Pity we cannot accord titles only to those who truly deserve them."

"I am entirely inclined to agree with you. There are those in my circle of acquaintance who have gotten much further in life as a result of their titles than through any personal merit. However, if, as I believe, you are referring to Lady Agatha, you really must be more charitable. Her husband died recently, and this tragedy may affect her behavior somewhat."

April glanced into the dining room, where Agatha slid her slim body seductively into the chair that Riley held out for her, making sure he could get an unimpeded view down her scandalously low neckline. "You are too kind in your estimation, Mr. Northam. Lady Agatha doesn't appear to be too heartbroken."

He looked in the direction of April's gaze, and his amiable countenance changed. Almost imperceptibly, his eyes went sharp. A muscle tightened in his jaw.

"Appearances can be deceiving. As you probably already know." The sharp hazel eyes were now aimed at her.

"Indeed that has been my experience, Mr. Northam. In fact, it surprises me that, as a man, you remark upon it. I have found that men most of all are either unable or unwilling to look past the veil of appearances. Men seem to see only what suits them." *Except Riley, more's the pity.*

He laughed, and his whole face lit up. "You know, Miss Devereux, I find that you have an intrepid quality about you, and I must confess that I find myself drawn to it. My guess is that you have a very interesting story to tell." He placed a brief kiss on her gloved hand. "I believe I shall call upon you tomorrow afternoon. I know I shan't rest until I have the opportunity to become more intimately acquainted with you, and get, as you say, past the veil." His smiling face leaned closely in on hers, his unblinking eyes glistening in bold challenge.

She was momentarily dazzled by the unmistakable presence of sex in his gaze. Wholly unlike the kind at Madame Devereux's, this was personal, and it was directed at her. He was a beautiful man, and it flattered her female vanity to be desired in that way. The heat from his naked hand spread through her gloves. Although her body responded immediately, her mind rebelled at the way he couched his sexual invitation.

"Hadn't you at least ask permission first?"

"I don't believe Riley would mind."

"*He* is not the one you need to ask," she replied archly.

He cast his eyes down, giving the illusion of being thoroughly chastened. "My humble apologies. I assure you I do not take you for granted."

"I should hope not. Although we are indeed both commoners, you are mistaken if you believe that makes me common."

His charming smile spread. "I could never think such a thing about you."

"Good. Then please escort me into the dining room. The Queen awaits."

Though only midday, the heavy rain outside cast a pall of darkness over the house, and they had to dine by candlelight.

As the food was served, Lady Agatha spoke. "Miss Devereux, Riley never mentioned he took in a ward, and I'm curious to know how you came to the house of Hawthorne."

It seemed to April that she asked this more out of suspicion than curiosity.

Riley, who was seated next to April, interceded. "April's just come to us from her father, an old friend of mine. He asked that I look after her while he resolved some business concerns overseas."

"Business?" she exclaimed with thinly veiled disgust. "What sort of *business* is your father in, Miss Devereux?"

Irritated by Agatha's typically aristocratic disdain for people in industry, April decided to have some fun with her.

"Slaves."

Shock marred her beautiful face. "I beg your pardon?"

"My father. He's a slavetrader. He's in Jamaica right now overseeing a shipment of live cargo bound for the American colonies."

Jeremy snickered. Riley was not amused.

Her voice lightened. "Father normally despises humid climates, but commerce with the colonies has been so very lucrative these days, it's all he can do to keep up with the demand."

What a natural little liar she was, Riley thought. He marveled at how easily deception came to her.

"How very peculiar," Lady Agatha exclaimed.

"Why is that, Lady Agatha?"

"Well, slavery is frowned upon. I didn't think Englishmen would invest in such things."

"On the contrary," April replied. "England deals in slaves every day. Hundreds of your own countrymen are exported each month to endure a lifetime of hard labor, working in inhospitable or dangerous conditions. Only they're not sent to America. They're sent to Australia."

Riley leaned toward her. "I believe the people you are referring to are criminals, April. Australia is Britain's penal colony. Those men are sent there to serve out their sentences."

"But not all of them are men, are they, Lord Blackheath? A goodly number are women, whose only crime is that of prostitution."

Jonah dropped his fork. Riley leaned over and rested his hand on April's, surreptitiously giving it a vicious squeeze. "April, that is not a word used at the dinner table. You'll have to excuse her, Your Majesty," he apologized somberly. "My young charge has spent entirely too much time in the city, where she was accustomed to more candid and unrestrained conversation."

"Yes," April agreed, rubbing her sore hand under the table. "In my former home, women were allowed to speak their minds without fear of reprisal."

"Well, what difference does it make whether they're male or female?" Agatha interrupted. "They are breaking the law after all."

"Perhaps," April responded, "but the law demonstrates a decided partiality. It seems that as regards prost—er, this particular crime, men are just as guilty as women, yet only the women seem to be punished. As a judge, Lord Blackheath, do you not find it odd that only the women are condemned as villains in this scenario, and the men who pay for their services are never even prosecuted?"

Riley's blue-green eyes leveled on her darkly. There was no way to answer her without casting aspersions on himself, his father, or his profession. She was clearly baiting him because of their earlier conversation, but he was furious that she would do it in front of such esteemed company. "I realize, Miss Devereux, that you have had a rather unorthodox upbringing. The fault is not yours, and so, easily forgiven. But it remains my hope that, as my ward, you will acquire the ways of polite society and learn to confine yourself to less contentious topics of conversation."

The public reprimand incensed her. "You must pardon me, my lord, if I speak too frankly. I'll warrant that I may be unsophisticated, but I am not unenlightened."

The Queen laughed then, rescuing April from the withering response she saw forming on Riley's lips. "Blackheaz, your young charge reminds me much of myself in my youth. I was far too comfortable speaking my mind. It was a fault zat ze King was often calling me to task on. Do not on her be too hard."

"Honesty is not a fault, Your Majesty," replied Riley, "and certainly not something I can accuse April of. But she is too intelligent for her own good, and I am determined to encourage her to commit her gifts to more laudable pursuits."

Mutely aghast, April was unsure whether to be offended or flattered.

The Queen regarded this exchange with lively interest. "It is typical of Blackheaz to be conservative in his praise, Miss Devereux, but it was praise nonezeless. And quite a compliment coming from such a learned man as he. Blackheaz chooses his actions carefully, but his words more so. Clearly, you must have impressed him to deserve such a rare token of esteem."

April glanced over at him. His gaze was downcast and his face was inscrutable, but the rapid rise and fall of his chest revealed that the Queen had hit a nerve.

"I would not have thought so, Your Majesty. I am afraid that my first impressions upon him have been . . . less than favorable."

"Well, my dear, even ze most trying plants yield flowers zat make ze wait worthwhile. Isn't zat right, *Liebling*?"

Jeremy put his fork down. "Yes, Your Majesty. In China, there is a grass called a bamboo plant. A gardener will plant the seed in the ground, and water and fertilize it. But very little will happen. The plant will not grow much the first year, nor the second, nor even the third. But sometime during the fifth year, the bamboo plant shoots up, and during a span of just six weeks, the plant will reach over ninety feet tall. The stalks quickly become very strong and highly resilient. In fact, if the gardener is patient and forgiving enough of the plant as it grows, he can even use the stalks to build himself a house."

"How very interesting!" the Queen exclaimed. "Ninety feet in six weeks! Imagine building a home from what is essentially common grass. Patience and forgiveness certainly have zeir reward, don't zey, Blackheaz?"

Riley shifted in his seat. "I wouldn't know, Marm. My skills at gardening are woefully inadequate."

"Neverzeless," the Queen said, smirking, "it is clear zat you appreciate ze beauty of ze blooms in your own garden."

The color rose in Riley's face, but he disguised it by dabbing his mouth with his napkin.

"Cousin," admonished Agatha pleasantly, though her smile was artificial. "Don't be so meddlesome. Anyone would think you were playing Cupid."

The creases in the monarch's eyes deepened as she grinned mischievously at April. "Nonsense. Cupid provokes love where it does not exist. Zere is very little for him to do here."

Now it was April's turn to blush.

Queen Charlotte's smile spread. "Still, you are right, cousin. I shall not intrude where I have not been invited."

Emily deflected the topic of conversation. "Speaking of invitations, Jeremy tells me all the invitations have already gone out for the Minister's Ball. All of London has confirmed."

"Will Your Majesty be honoring us with her presence?" Northam asked.

"I zink not, Mr. Norzam. As I explained to Blackheaz in my letter, ze King is in poor health, and I must look after him."

Jonah shook his head. "Yes, we were very sorry to hear that. A toast, ladies and gentlemen." He stood and raised his glass. "To the King and Queen. May good health return to His Majesty, and bless them both forever." The other guests stood and echoed the toast.

"Emily," suggested Jeremy as he resumed his seat, "why don't you and Lady Agatha stay until the ball? It seems a waste for you to leave for London only to return so soon."

Emily shook her head, her blond ringlets bouncing against her cheeks. "Darling, our wedding is little more than a month away. Do you know how much shopping I have to do? I'm a wreck as it is. I'm only too glad that Aggie has agreed to help me."

"Well, why don't you take April with you?" Jeremy offered. "She might be able to lend a hand."

Emily's face lit up. "That's a splendid idea! I could use the help. That is, if April won't mind the awful bore of it all?"

April was spared an answer by Riley. "I'm afraid that's impossible. April will be overseeing preparations for the Minister's Ball. She's needed here." He was not about to allow April to roam free about London.

Piqued by his high-handed manner, she said, "Actually, I wouldn't mind accompanying you on your excursion, Lady Emily. I know London very well. I can take you to all the toff—I mean, the best shops."

"But, April," Riley countered through clenched teeth, "with just us three bachelors here, we'll need a lady's touch in arranging the ball. Please stay." It was spoken as a request, but it was intended as an order. His face was a polite mask of carefully tethered anger, and April thought it wisest to stop provoking him.

"Curious," began Lady Agatha. "I've never seen you at the ball before. I wonder if you yourself won't need help in arranging it."

"Agatha . . ." Riley admonished.

Her eyebrows arched. "Riley, darling, I only meant that if you need help coordinating the ball, you might be able to persuade *me* to do it. I mean, if she has never attended it, how would she know how to organize it? Besides, no offense, Miss Devereux, but if you are just now being tutored in the ways of civilized society, you'll have enough to do just knowing how to behave at the ball."

April stifled the urge to drag Lady Agatha out by the hair. Back at the Pleasure Emporium, that is exactly how she would have settled this underhanded snub. But now she was not a maid in a brothel, the lowest of the low. She was a lady in a duke's family, the highest position to which a woman could aspire. In circles like these, she had to match wit for wit.

"Lady Agatha, I may not be as civilized as you, but I am familiar enough with protocol to know that, given your state of mourning, it would be bad *ton* for you to attend the ball at all, much less coordinate it. I'm certain Lord Blackheath would have preferred to ask you, but he has far too much respect for your husband's death. Though I must say I am surprised he even remembered. New widows do not typically wear red."

Agatha's face flushed to the color of her dress, but for the benefit of the guests, she answered only with a hollow smile.

April pressed her advantage on Agatha's embarrassed retreat. "Lord Blackheath, I will be delighted to stay and help you arrange the ball. It is the least I can do for my benefactor."

A slow smile spread across Riley's face, and her heart thrilled in response. It was the first time he had smiled at her, and she was unprepared for how giddy it made her feel. Whether it was the handsomeness of his face or his furtive camaraderie, she didn't know, but the fact that she had won some measure of his respect . . . it quite took her breath away. The conversation continued apace, but April's thoughts were far from it. The soft sheen of his lips, the light in his eyes . . . if she knew he would have given her such a grateful smile for so small a token of support, she would have given it sooner.

Her attention gradually returned to the discussion about the Minister's Ball. It was an unmet dream of hers, to attend a fancy ball, and she was very excited about the prospect. Contrary to her initial supposition, the Minister's Ball was not a religious event. It was a dance celebrated in honor of the Prime Minister. As a member of the House of Lords and a descendant of a former prime minister, Riley had offered to host it each year. Lady Emily, who never missed it, animatedly went on about how it was the high point of the Season and how no one in the *ton* ever declined an invitation. In fact, you didn't count unless you managed to secure an invitation. That comment made April smile. Just by showing up at the ball, April would finally become One Who Counted.

The group chatted amiably about the people who had been invited and who hadn't. Royals, nobles, gentry—everyone she ever wanted to meet. She was getting more excited by the second, until one name crashed through her enthusiasm with all the numbing shock of a bucketful of icy water poured over her head.

"I—I'm sorry," she stammered. "Wh-whom did you say would be giving the toast?"

"Sir Cedric Markham," Jonah answered. "The Clerk of the Parliaments. He's a grating bore, but it was the Prime Minister's idea."

April could feel the color drain from her face. Markham was bound to recognize her from the deception she pulled on him back in London! She couldn't possibly go to the ball now. If April showed her face, it would be the gallows for her for sure!

The rest of the lunch seemed to crawl by. It seemed an eternity before the Queen finally ushered the ladies from the table to take sherry in the drawing room, leaving the men to their port and cigars.

A SHORT WHILE LATER, RILEY GROUND OUT his half-smoked cigar in the ashtray and impatiently rose from the table. There was something amiss in April's demeanor toward the end of the meal. He wasn't certain when it happened, but April became more reticent as lunch wore on. He didn't know what had happened to turn her mood, but he would stake his fortune it had something to do with this damned charade of hers. But when the gentlemen rejoined the ladies in the drawing room, April was not there.

"She begged off with a headache, darling," Lady Agatha explained. "She really is dreadfully gauche, Riley. Whatever possessed you to take her in?"

"Aggie!" admonished Emily. "Don't be so rude!"

"Well, isn't that the general consensus? I put it to you, Mr. Northam: what are your thoughts on Riley's charge? Wouldn't you say that he has taken on a dreadful burden?"

Northam swirled the cognac in his snifter. "I cannot disagree with you, Lady Agatha. Riley does indeed have his hands full with the girl." Riley and Northam exchanged a knowing look.

"The first thing you must do, Riley, is to teach the girl about fashion. It's bad enough she dresses like a servant, but to wear gloves at the table in broad daylight is beyond deplorable."

Straining the limits of his patience, Riley attended his guests a little while longer. When he could stand no more idle chatter, he excused himself. "I think I'll go and find out if April is feeling better."

Jonah grinned expansively. "Well, that's very thoughtful of you, m'boy. I hope you can persuade her to come down. Tell her that I have a surprise waiting for her."

Riley's scowl blackened as he remembered Jonah's surprise—that he had named April in his will. He cast Northam a look, but Northam simply shrugged helplessly.

Once free from the oppressive confinement of his forced hospitality, Riley relaxed. Now it was time to move in for the kill. Slowly, his long legs carried him across the polished marble hall, the heels of his boots pounding the floor at long intervals. His eyes prowled the rooms in search of his prey. He swore that before the afternoon was over, he would have the truth out of her.

The library was open and he crept up to the door. She was there, her back turned toward him. As he approached, he saw her curled up in a leather chair, her legs tucked up beneath her. Her face was focused intently on her lap, where she cradled a book.

He regarded the downturned profile outlined in the candlelight. Her delicate brow waved into an upturned nose, divided by the thick shadow of her eyelashes. Her lips pursed in thoughtful study, flanked by a long wayward tendril of hair. It was the face of a little girl absorbed in quiet play.

He felt a strange sensation, one completely alien to him. Though he couldn't name it, it had a profound effect on his senses. At once, he was taken with the urge to enfold the girl in his arms, caress her hair, and place a gentle kiss on her forehead. Yet there was something else, something more primitive, that overtook it. A savage instinct, one that brought forth visions of desire, of heated embraces and bodies ignited. Of legs stroking in the dance of passion . . .

A shadow fell across April's book. She looked up. A startled gasp escaped her lips.

"What are you doing here?"

"I live here," he said sardonically, removing the tinderbox from his waistcoat pocket. "Or have you chosen to forget that?" He turned and lit the wax candles nestled in the candelabrum. The candle glow encompassed them in an intimate circle of light, and the rest of the world vanished in darkness.

When her heart had returned to its natural rhythm, she glanced down. The Madame's diary lay open in her lap! With lightning speed, she snatched it up and tucked it in the fold between the cushion and back of the chair. There was a slight creaking noise, and she prayed he didn't hear it.

"I meant, what are you doing in the library? Why aren't you with the others?"

"I wanted to have a word with you." The candle glow bathed his face with its warm light. His hair became a midnight blue, and his dark eyes flickered in the candle's beams. He leaned his tall frame against the writing desk, only inches from her chair, and allowed one long leg to dangle carelessly over the edge. The nearness of him sent her body heat spiraling.

"Allow me to preface my comments by expressing my gratitude to you."

April frowned in puzzlement. "Gratitude? For what?"

"For my father. He's looking very well, and I know you had a great deal to do with that."

The softness in his voice relaxed her coiled response.

He stared down at his clasped hands. "I haven't seen him so cheerful in a long time. Whatever the reason for your coming to Blackheath Manor, I will always be grateful to you for his . . . awakening."

Her gaze followed his. She was very attracted to hands on a man, and the size of his provoked something carnal within her.

"Therefore, I would like to make you a proposition. For your miraculous influence upon my father, I would like to offer you a token of my appreciation in the amount of ten thousand pounds."

April's eyes widened.

"In exchange for which you will leave Blackheath Manor and never speak of your visit here again."

April took a breath, unaware she had been holding it. Ten thousand pounds! It was exactly what she had been hoping for since she started on this campaign of hers. Ten thousand was more than she could earn in ten lifetimes. She and Jenny could live modest but comfortable lives, and never have to work again. He was offering her what she had set out to achieve: a life of independence.

"I flatter myself you will not consider my proposal entirely disagreeable," he said, elegantly folding his arms.

But Riley's proposal didn't bring her the enthusiasm she expected. Perhaps if he had made this proposal when she first arrived . . . But things were different now.

"It is an exceedingly generous offer, my lord, especially considering that you were on the point of having me arrested not three days ago. May I ask what prompted this proposal?"

He had expected a wholehearted and resounding "yes." It was only a test after all; he was sure she was only after his money, and he wanted to give her the perfect opportunity to expose her true intentions. But now that she was known to the Queen, and therefore all of Society by proxy, he could not have her arrested—could not even throw her out—without igniting a scandal. Paying her off was his only tenable course of action. But for now, all he wanted was to understand her motives, know her mind. He simply had to get inside her.

If only that thought didn't bring such a rush of pleasure to his loins.

"My father has named you as a beneficiary in his will. I am giving you the opportunity to make away with your fortune now, rather than waiting until my father passes away, which may not be for some time. And I promise you that before long, I will convince him of his folly and he will withdraw your name from his will anyway. If you take my offer, you are sure to make good on your scheme."

April heard nothing after his first sentence. Jonah had named her to his will! He had included her in his heart among his own flesh-and-blood children. Her own father once threw her out of the house when she refused to marry a man he had lost a wager to. But now, a perfect stranger had adopted her and counted her as family. How much must Jonah truly love her to do this thing? Touched in places she had never known, the sentiment brought tears to her eyes, and she silently embraced Jonah in her heart. Here was the real treasure—a family—and it was beyond price.

She stood and faced him squarely. "Lord Blackheath, I regret to tell you that I would not leave for ten times that amount. I cannot tell you how happy it makes me to be Jonah's daughter, even if I can only be so in secret. I don't want his money. Or yours, for that matter. Unlike you, I have never known the joy of having a father. Now that I have it, you ask that I give it away. How unbearably selfish you are! And never mind my own feelings in the matter. Your father cares for me, and yet you would have me disappear, without even so much as a word to him? Have you considered how it would crush him?"

"He would recover," Riley said impassively.

"You have no feeling in you. I was told you were a fair, compassionate man. I was told you were legendary for your devotion to your family. But now, having met you, I can see that legends diminish in grandeur when you get up close."

He rose to his full height, and April backed away instinctively. "Govern your tongue, Miss Devereux, unless it is to admit you made all of this up." He stalked her around the room, her alarm intensifying with every inch he drew near. "I can see the deception in your eyes, and I will not rest until I have a confession from your lips. Tell me who you are!"

"I have told you!" The apprehension tightened in her throat.

"I demand the truth!"

"I'm telling you the truth!"

"One bastard in the family is enough!"

"What?"

"I will not have you for my sister!"

"You have no choice!"

"You are *not* my sister!"

"How can you be so sure?"

He seized her arms in an unyielding grip, lifting her effortlessly off her feet. With a quiet snarl, his head swooped to conquer her lips. Stunned, she opened her mouth to protest, but her mouth was imprisoned underneath his. Her hands splayed across his chest, pushing with all her strength, but she was powerless to free herself. On and on, his lips drove, hungrily, savagely, driving her head back.

But the shock wore off, and she refused to retreat anymore. Adamantly, she turned the kiss against him, her lips mirroring the boldness in his. Now, it was his turn to be shocked. His hands loosened their hold, and he lifted his mouth from hers.

Defiance blazed in her face, her chest rising and falling rapidly with unvoiced emotions. The air between them still throbbed with their heated exchange. Slowly, the expression on his face softened. His gaze wandered over her face, as if he were regarding her for the very first time.

The intimacy of his look relaxed her coiled response. Her palms were still flattened against his chest, only now they began to absorb the sensation of his heart hammering against the warm wall of muscle. His breathing quickened, the searing gusts of air fanning her already kindled senses. He bent toward her once more, slowly, his eyelids lowering as his lips softly touched hers.

The gentle contact of his lips ignited a blaze of emotions that April could not name, let alone understand. But it melted her resistance—to him and to her unexpressed feelings. The flavor of his mouth, the heat of his chest, the warm scent of his skin—all made her drunk with longing. Voices in her head screamed at her to stop the madness, but she wanted more. When his thick arms entwined around her, she placed her hands on his velvet sleeves in a vain attempt to push them away . . . but the feel of the muscles beneath dizzied her. His mouth trailed down her jawline to a spot under her earlobe, weakening her resolve even more. His tongue darted out, and the hot contact sent liquid pleasure coursing through her body. As she softened against his form, the arousing contact of her breasts pressed against his chest melted the last vestige of outraged dignity. Every part of her that touched him yearned to become fused with him, as though each nerve was a vine that reached out to embrace him.

His lips reclaimed hers, and her mouth was receptive when his warm tongue danced upon hers, coaxing, wooing, winning. She finally indulged the desire of her fingers to thread themselves through his silky black locks, and, dear God, the pleasure it gave her! She heard a groan deep within his throat, and it resonated within her, as though their pleasure had reached the same harmonious pitch. His large hands spanned her back, stroking it, branding it, and she arched against him. He had her from all sides; she was completely surrounded by a fortress of muscle. She hung in his embrace, shrugging off the realization that the wanton force keeping her pressed against him was not his, but her own. Somewhere in the distance, she heard a soft, pleading moan, and recognized that she herself was making the sound. Her desire mounted until she felt an urge to enfold him, to climb him, and absently, one leg lifted in a desire to do just that. It was as if her body had taken leave of her, so intent was it on experiencing this pleasure. Her rational mind railed against her surrender, but its protests were drowned in a flood of new sensations.

In response to her body's desire, her mind begged for more, more . . . until abruptly, he tore his lips from hers.

"That's how," he responded, releasing her and walking out the door.

Six

IN THE PERIOD FOLLOWING THEIR QUARrel, Jenny missed April's company very much. April had said some cruel things to her, and even though Jenny could never hate April, she would never forget the betrayal.

It weighed heavily upon her, because she would have liked to have confided in her best friend now. Jenny was eager to share her growing attraction to William Bainbridge, head footman at Blackheath Manor. He was awakening feelings in her that were unfamiliar, feelings she never thought she could ever get with a man again. Illusions of romance, which had long ago faded, came to life again. The time she spent with William showed her that her heart had not died, but had only been sleeping.

She had never known anyone like him before. He was the first man to ever wonder what she actually *thought* about. It was difficult for her to communicate this way. He didn't ogle or grab her—that she could deal with. He wasn't crude or vulgar—that she understood. No, here was a man who was proper, decent, and humble; a different breed of man from what she was used to. He wanted to like her for her *self,* and she wasn't sure she wanted to show him who that was.

They spent a great deal of time together now that arrangements were under way for the Minister's Ball. The servants were fevered by their many assignments in preparing the entire manor, bedrooms and all, for the festivities. The housekeeper was quick to realize that Jenny had fallen out of favor with her mistress, so she put Jenny to work. Jenny didn't mind at all, because she was frequently put to work alongside William.

It was nearing seven o'clock, and Jenny and William hurried to set the table for the family's supper. The footman brought out the unwieldy tablecloth spindle, and Jenny helped him to unroll the pristine white cloth onto the tabletop.

She watched his expression as he meticulously checked the length of the cloth on each side of the table. His look of concentration endeared him to her. He always took his responsibilities so seriously, making sure that he shined at everything he was assigned to do. He cut a fine figure in his navy blue evening livery, which emphasized his auburn hair.

Furtively, she stole glances at him while he smoothed the wrinkles out of the table linen. The white cloth illuminated his warm brown eyes, which danced around the table seeking out defects and creases. Jenny drew a stack of clean dishes from the sideboard, but he jumped in front of her.

"Allow me. Those are too heavy for a lady."

Flattered by his gallantry, she blushed. She followed him around the table, laying out the silver after he arranged the plates.

"Do you like being in service, William?"

He shrugged. "It's not such a bad life when you get right down to it. I'm only twenty-eight, but in a few years' time I could ascend to the position of butler. Mr. Forrester is getting on in years, and Lord Blackheath has been pleased with my work. I imagine that by the time Mr. Forrester is ready to retire, I'll be asked to take over. I was the youngest head footman ever at Blackheath, so maybe I'll become the youngest butler and all."

"So you intend to make a career out of it?"

He smiled at her. "There are worse ways to earn a living."

Jenny's heart sank, as she once again pondered what he would think if she ever told him how she had spent the past nine years.

"What about you? Don't you like being a lady's maid?"

"There are worse ways to earn a living," she repeated sheepishly.

He regarded her with amusement. "I think you would make an excellent couturière."

"Me?"

"Yes, you."

"You're daft."

"Just look at you," he said, pointing to the tiny white wildflowers she had woven into her hair. "You're wearing the same servant's dress as all the other girls in the house, yet you still find a way to make even that drab costume seem like a ball gown. Even if you didn't add your own special touch, you'd still stand out from all the rest. You're . . . different. Unique." His face reddened. "You're like a diamond of many facets. And I find myself wanting to know them all."

She smiled in spite of herself.

"I don't want to frighten you, Jenny, but I just can't keep my feelings hidden any longer."

This is what she had been waiting for. Since the moment they met, she had entertained visions of stealing away with him to the stables. Wrapping her arms and her legs around him. Taking his head to her breast. Showing him with her body how she felt in her heart. If he asked her, she'd say yes.

"Yes, William?"

"You're the kindest, most wonderful girl I've ever met. And ... well ... I was wondering if you and I ..."

"Yes, William?"

He closed his eyes and began again. "I was wondering if you would give me permission to court you."

Jenny blinked in disbelief. "You want to *court* me?"

He straightened. "I have only the most honorable intentions," he said earnestly. "I like you very, very much, Jenny, and I would never do anything to hurt or compromise you in any way. Please say you'll allow me the privilege of taking you out tomorrow night. I would be the proudest of men if you would let me escort you."

His esteem for her made her heart sing. She was bursting with the yeses that were welling up inside her. Coyness was alien to her, and she wanted to show him how he made her feel. Closing the distance between them, she pressed her lips upon his with the overwhelming affection she had for him, and found herself smiling through the kiss.

"Yes, William. Yes."

THEIR AFTERNOON OFF WAS NOTHING SHORT of heaven. Arm in arm, Jenny and William walked into town. William beamed as he greeted people, taking great pride in introducing Jenny to everyone he knew. Once, he stopped at a dry-goods shop to purchase an expensive brick of chocolate so that "his lady might also have hot chocolate in the morning."

Jenny had never felt so safe and so cared for in her life. The paradox made her smile: he was trying so hard to woo her, and she had already made up her mind to be completely his.

They stopped to have their tea in a small but cozy pub called the Copper Kettle. The pubkeeper greeted William warmly.

"Tea and biscuits for us, please, John." They sat down at a table by a curtained window. "Are you warm enough?"

Jenny nodded. She felt warm all over when she was with him.

The pubkeeper brought over their tray. "Careful with these biscuits. The wife just made 'em. They're still hot. So how're things up at the manor?"

"Just fine, John. It's a bit busy, though. Getting ready for the Minister's Ball."

"Think they'll be borrowing servants from Altimore Castle again?"

"Most likely. They're putting everybody to work. Even the ladies' maids," he said, waving across the table. "This is Jenny Hare. She's just arrived."

John's eyebrows shot upward. "Lady's maid, eh? You must be working for that girl that's visiting Blackheath Manor."

"Yes," she answered, surprised that the publican would know this.

"I forget her name. It's a month, ain't it? June or May?"

"It's April. Devereux," she answered.

"That's it. Them Frenchies always did have the hot blood in 'em. Dirty business, that."

Jenny's brows knit together. "What do you mean?"

John held up both hands defensively. "No disrespect, mind you. I've got nothing against your mistress, m'self. It's the wife. It's all she can talk about these days. She's been living here all her life, so naturally she's always been loyal to them at the manor. I've never known her to say a bad word about the duke. I'm sure your mistress is just a poor innocent in this sordid mess, but folks in town are a bit cross that she would bring the duke's past out in the open, him being such an important man."

"What are you on about?"

Embarrassed, John grabbed his tray. "Look, it's no business o' mine. You folks pay me no mind. Enjoy your tea."

Jenny called out to him, but he kept walking. "What in blazes was he talkin' about?"

William had the decency to become flushed. "I'm sorry, Jenny. But you should know that it's not a secret anymore. Mr. Forrester did tell us that Miss April was Master Riley's ward, but we found out that that wasn't true. Everyone knows that it was just a lie to cover for the real truth. That Miss April is the duke's *bastard*." He whispered the last word.

Jenny blanched. "My God."

"It's true, isn't it?"

Jenny lowered her hand from her mouth. "No, William. It's not. 'Ow did the servants get wind of that story?"

"I don't know. It was something I heard in passing over the kitchen table. Apparently, we aren't the only ones talking about it if the townspeople know as well."

Jenny was silent for a long time, contemplating the imminent catastrophe if the whole world knew of this. Their past crimes were sure to come to light now, and Jenny could almost feel the noose tightening around their necks.

"Jenny, the last thing I want is for you to be hurt by a scandal like this. I've been talking it over with Mr. Forrester, and he told me that if you resigned from your employment with Miss April, he'd put you on the staff. It'd be a demotion—you wouldn't be an upper servant anymore—but at least you'd have nothing to do with Miss April, and we would be together always."

A tear pooled in Jenny's eye. "I can't do that. She's my friend."

"Friends build you up, they don't bring you down. This secret was all over the servants' quarters, but I didn't know it had reached outside the manor. Now that she's been found out, she won't be able to show her face in the village. And I don't want you to be anywhere near her when she becomes an outcast. Please say yes."

His expression was so concerned, so supplicating. At that moment, Jenny was sure that he loved her. More frightening than that, she was sure she loved him back. She could commit her body to him, and now she knew she was certain she could entrust her heart as well. There was nothing he could ask of her that she would not say yes to. Except this. Jenny could not betray her best friend. And she would not stand by and watch April go down.

She shook her head. "When you fall, friends are the ones who stoop to pick you up. I'm sorry, William, I have to go." With that, she slid off her seat and ran out the door.

"Jenny, wait!" he shouted, but she did not stop.

APRIL SLUMPED ON THE BED, A FORLORN expression on her face, atop her newly arrived dresses. All her accessories—the matching hair ribbons, undergarments, reticules, slippers—were neatly wrapped and waiting for the maid to put away. Had April been in her usual frame of mind, she would have reveled in their exquisite beauty, which surpassed the vision and detail of Mr. Cartwright's fashion plates. But April was not in her usual frame of mind; she hadn't been since she and Jenny fought. April sighed. Although she had finally realized the dream of owning such beautiful clothes, she had no one to share her joy with, rendering her dream a hollow success.

But there was a darker factor that contributed to her depression, and it concerned her last encounter with Riley. To April's immense relief, he had left Blackheath for London the morning after the Queen's visit. But he had left her with a definite and indisputable message: she had failed to convince him. She shuddered to accept the last stroke of defeat, but she could no longer ignore the rapier sticking out of her chest. She had fought her best, but she had lost.

The memory of that kiss still haunted her. Her self-control, which she believed as unbreakable as an oak, had crumbled like a dry leaf in his embrace. That her body responded to him of its own volition, heedless of her wishes, disturbed her to no end. If she couldn't trust her own body, how could she hope to deceive him? She could not allow herself to lose her wits again. It was only a matter of time before Riley exposed her and Jenny. Every stratagem she considered, every move and countermove, pointed to one incontrovertible course of action.

Abandon Blackheath Manor.

Suddenly, April heard running footfalls in the hall. Her door burst open. Jenny.

They looked at each other, both silently speaking volumes in that moment. The next moment, they joined in a fierce embrace.

"I'm sorry," they chorused.

"Let's never fight again," April said.

"No. Never. I missed you," Jenny answered.

"Me too. Forgive me?"

"'Course!"

"Friends then?"

"Always." Jenny's smile quickly faded. "But I have something to tell you."

"Me too."

"We have to run away," they said in unison.

"What?" they said in unison.

"You first," they said in unison.

"Oh, shut up and listen to me," April said. "We have to leave before the Minister's Ball. Do you know who our guest of honor is? Sir Cedric Markham, that first bloke we swindled in London. I can't let him see me. He'll recognize me right away."

Jenny shook her head. "It's worse than that. I was just in the village. The word is out. Everyone is talking about you. As the duke's bastard."

"What? How did they hear that?"

"I don't know. But even the servants here found out that the yarn Riley came up with about you being his ward wasn't true."

"How? Only a handful of people know about me. The family, you. Who else knows?"

Jenny shook her head. "It's falling apart, April. It's getting too hot for us here. If the village knows, all of Society is bound to know by now. It'll be a right scandal. They'll pull you to pieces."

"Oh, no." April crumpled onto her expansive bed, though it offered her no comfort now. "What about the family? What'll happen to them?"

Jenny had no answer.

"We can't get away clean now," April contended.

"What choice do we have?"

"The family has been very good to me, Jenny. Do you know that Jonah wrote me into his will? He left me one of his estates in Scotland. Can you believe it? My own father never gave a brass farthing about me, and this kind old man whom I've done nothing but lie to gives me my very own manor house. I don't want to leave him with a corpse to bury."

"It won't be as bad as that. People will forget in time."

"No, Jenny. I read the Society papers. You don't know these toffs like I do. Rumors like this never die. Especially not when they're about a duke. God, Riley is in the bloody House of Lords. He'll be ruined!"

"Oh, April. We'll need to warn him."

"We can't do that! We'll be forced to admit that we made all this up!"

"Aren't we a little beyond that now? It's the least we can do. They'll be scorned from now until kingdom come, and the rumor ain't even true."

April latched on to that small glimmer of hope. "You're right. Maybe since it isn't true, the rumor *will* die down. It's possible, isn't it?"

"I hope so." Jenny groaned. "When we first got here, I couldn't wait to leave. But now that we have to go, I want to stay."

"It's that footman, isn't it?"

Jenny's dreamy smile answered for her.

It had been a long time since she had seen Jenny so enthused about something. Now that she had found love, she had to leave it behind. It was yet another hindrance to their escape. There was nothing they could do now but cut themselves clean away.

"Tonight, Jenny. We'll leave under cover of darkness."

THE HORSES WERE STEAMING IN THE SHEETing rain when Riley reined them in on the flagstones that night outside the manor. Before the phaeton even halted, he leapt from the conveyance. A footman barely had a chance to open the front door before Riley pushed past him.

Forrester was still putting on his coat when he reached the hall. "Sir, I do beg your pardon, but you were not expected for another week." *And certainly not at two in the morning,* he thought.

Riley pulled at the clasp of his full-length cape, which was pouring rainwater onto the marble floor.

The butler helped him out of it. "I'll order a fire started in your bedroom immediately."

"Never mind that. I want you to go and bring April to me

at once. Yank her out of bed if you have to. Dressed, undressed, it doesn't matter. I will see her in the library *now*."

Without a fire, the library was cold and drafty. Riley poured a glass of port down his throat to warm himself up. He was soaked to the skin, but he refused to take even a moment to change. As he poured himself another glass, the butler returned.

"My lord, Miss April is not in her room," he said, flustered. "The bed has not even been slept in. I took the liberty of alerting her maid, Jenny, but she too is missing."

Riley's expression stormed over. "Find them."

The servants were roused and ordered to rout out the entire house. Jonah and Jeremy were awakened by the commotion.

"What the devil is going on here?" Jonah demanded when he reached the library. "Riley! What has happened?"

"I'll tell you what has happened. My worst nightmare."

"Steady on," Jeremy soothed. "Tell us what's wrong."

Riley wiped the rainwater from his face as he paced inside the library. His wet hair spiked out from his head like tiny black daggers.

"I went to my club tonight. Apparently, my young 'ward' has become quite the *on-dit* of London. I should have suspected something was wrong when I walked into the club. It suddenly leveled to a pronounced quiet. I greeted some of my acquaintances, only to be met with silence. Friends came up to offer their assistance should I need it. Then I overheard a cluster of men whispering and laughing. Do you know what they were saying? 'There goes the Lord of Bastard Manor.'"

"Oh, my God," Jeremy exclaimed.

"Surely you were mistaken," Jonah contended.

"Really? What would you call it if that drunken fool Lord Beecham stumbled toward you to declare that your family was now the only one in England with a barrister and a bar sinister?"

"How on earth did they find out about April?" Jonah muttered to himself.

"I say, you don't think that remark was meant about me, do you?" Jeremy asked nervously.

Riley's large hand tightened around the glass. "No. For now, I think your bloodline is not under scrutiny. I don't believe anyone suspects that you're Vivienne's son. Damn that girl for stirring up the past!"

"It's not her fault, Riley," Jeremy said. "She has just as much right to be with her true father as I."

Riley set his glass down so hard Jeremy thought it would shatter. "Can't you get it through your heads, either of you? This girl is not related to you. She's a prankster, an impostor, a confidence trickster. I'm not saying that she came to deliberately destroy us, but the chit just happened to stumble upon the very con game that was guaranteed to bring us to ruin. If anyone finds out that Jeremy is really Vivienne's son, there's no telling how much damage it could cause. Not only would it ruin our family name, but since Jeremy is marrying the Queen's cousin, it would be a humiliation for the crown as well." For the hundredth time that night, Riley cursed Northam for not turning up any information on April Devereux.

"Let's not lose our heads," Jonah said. "Surely we can find a way to recover from this scandal. We'll try to quash the rumor before it lands upon Jeremy. For April's sake."

"For her sake?"

"Yes, Riley. I just can't believe that she's been deceiving us."

"Oh, no? Her absence isn't proof enough?"

A knock was heard at the door. The butler entered.

"My lords, the Misses April and Jenny are nowhere to be found."

Riley's jaw tightened. "Saddle a fresh horse and bring him round to the front. I'm going after them."

"My lord, it's heavy with rain. Allow me to prepare a carriage—"

"No. It'll only slow me down. Tell the groom he has two minutes to ready my mount."

"Yes, sir," answered the butler, and ran to the stables as fast as his old legs would carry him.

Riley turned to his father. "If it's proof you want, it's proof you'll get. And as you won't believe me, you're going to hear the truth directly from someone you will believe." Riley downed the contents of his glass in one gulp and bolted for the door.

PACING THE DUSTY FLOOR OF THE ROOM above the tavern, April punched her open hand. She foolishly had left the Madame's diary back at Blackheath Manor.

"We're not going back for it," Jenny declared. "So you can put that idea out of your head right now, April."

April rubbed her forehead. How could she have been so careless? "It's early yet. No one will notice we're missing till morning. We could sneak back into the house, take the diary, and be back before dawn. Don't shake your head at me. We need that diary."

"How can you say that? That bloody book has brought us nothing but trouble. We are one step away from being caught, I can feel it. I won't have any more part in your schemes."

"Oh? And just what do you plan to do? Go back to living your life on your back?"

"My old life was simpler. I'm just not cut out for life on the run."

"You mean to tell me that you'd prefer a life of sexual slavery to a life of independence? Why make a few shillings in a brothel when you can make a few *hundred pounds* for just a few minutes of playacting?"

"I'm not doing this anymore."

"Well, pray, enlighten me. What are we going to do now?"

Jenny crossed her arms. "If we go back to Blackheath, we go back to stay."

April threw her head back. "Oh, I see! It's your ruddy footman, isn't it?"

"Don't say it like that. William is very special to me. It's tearing my heart out to leave him like this, without so much as an explanation, even a dishonest one. I won't go through that again. I don't expect you to understand. You're too busy playing 'her ladyship' to give us servants a second thought."

April bristled, but bit back a venomous reply. "All right. Let's not get carried away. We both made a lot of mistakes on this job. We got too emotionally involved. We can learn from this. We'll be better next time. For now, let's concentrate on getting that damn book back!"

It sounded like a thunderclap. The door flew backward on its hinges. A great, black shadow stood in the doorframe, blocking out the light from the hall. Water poured from a full-length cape.

He advanced slowly, his leather boots creaking, each footfall making the rotten wooden floor shake.

She knew who it was before she could see his face. Few men equaled Riley's size. But when he neared the candles burning on the table beside her, she wished she *couldn't* see his face. It held a look of such controlled rage that it made her legs unsteady.

"Lord Blackheath." It was all she could manage.

He cornered her, forming a wall of indomitable strength between her and escape. The sharp planes of his face, glistening with rainwater, were cast in shadow. But not his eyes. His unblinking eyes burned with a green fire that incinerated the air between them.

"I shall make this very simple for you. I will ask you a question, and I expect from you a single word—yes or no. If I do not get an honest answer, you will finally learn what it means to cross me."

It was impossible to ignore the steely purpose in his eyes. Her chest rose and fell rapidly as she weighed the risk.

"Ever since he set eyes on you, you have been trying to convince my father that you are his daughter. Were you speaking the truth?"

April blinked, her mouth agape. The honest answer could get her thrown in prison. Even so, the other answer was not coming easily. She vainly searched his face for a hint of some emotion she could at least appeal to, if not manipulate. As it was, the only thing she saw was determination—a cold, fierce, dispassionate determination, which conveyed to her that all he wanted at that moment was to get the truth out of her, and nothing was going to stop him from accomplishing his aim.

She swallowed dryly. "My lord, let me explain—"

"Yes or no. I advise you, April, come clean."

In a flash of recollection, she saw herself back at the brothel, mop in hand, those same loathsome words echoing through the house: *April Jardine, come clean!* The memory of that other life filled her with dread. That wasn't her, not anymore. And even though she knew he was past believing, fierce pride made her cling to her claim of innocence.

She tilted her chin upward defiantly. "It's the truth."

A large hand shot out from beneath his cape and clamped on her arm. He dragged her to the edge of the bed, and sitting down, jerked her across his flat and very firm lap.

April lost all control over her actions. One moment her nose was turned up against the mask of fury, the next it was inches from the dusty floorboards.

"What are you doing?" she cried, panic registering in her voice. The front of her dress soaked up freezing rainwater from his breeches.

"You will find, April," he said, flipping his cloak back over his broad shoulder, "that where it concerns the protection of what's mine, I will spare nothing, including the rod."

She gasped, appalled by the reality of her humiliating position.

"You wouldn't dare!" The panic in her voice belied her brave challenge, as her legs scissored helplessly in the air. She struggled to free herself before he had the opportunity to—

Whap! He brought the flat of his hand down on her upturned posterior. Hard.

It was the last thing in the world she expected. She cried out, more from surprise than pain. Until the force of the next swat drove the pain home.

"Now, as I seem to have your undivided attention, perhaps you will be wise enough to tell me the truth about why you've come to Blackheath Manor."

She tried in vain to stand up, but his left hand on her back made her feel as if she were trapped under heavy furniture. A fierce indignation spiraled within her, and she reached for the only weapon she had—her razor-sharp tongue. Calling on every shred of anger she could muster, she shouted a stream of epithets at Riley that made his eyebrows lift in surprise.

His lips thinning with determination, he began to swat her upturned behind with precision and force. Now she rued the size of his hands, which were making her entire bottom glow hotly. She tried to shield her smarting backside with her free hand, but he pinned it to her side, leaving her defenseless. And desperate. Her protests quickly turned to pleas, but they fell on deaf ears. She called to Jenny to help her.

Riley stayed his hand momentarily to stab his finger in

Jenny's direction. "If I don't get the truth from April, you're next."

Jenny's eyes grew round as saucers. "April, tell him!"

"There is nothing to tell!" she growled at Jenny, but received a few whacks for her interference. Suddenly, a plan formed in her mind.

"All right! I'll tell you what you want to know. Let me up!"

He pulled her effortlessly to a standing position, but her wrist was still imprisoned in his hand as securely as if it had been a metal cuff. Taking advantage of her free hand, she tightened it into a fist and swung it at his cheek.

It was a solid punch that spun his head. She bolted for the door, but found that although she had caught him by surprise, he never loosened his grip.

"Not so fast!" He yanked her back across his lap, and delivered another volley of whacks on her burning posterior with the force of an arrow shot from a bow, acquainting her with new levels of pain. All her squirming and bucking and kicking could not rescue her; in fact, it only winded her more quickly.

"My lord, stop, I beg you!" It was Jenny. "She's too stubborn to confess. She's trying to protect us both. I'll tell you all you want to know."

"Jenny, no!"

"I shall have the truth from April's own lips!"

The futility of her position finally sank in. He was serious about teaching her a lesson, and he wasn't going to let up until she learned it well.

"Very well," cried April. "I'll tell you the truth! Please, no more!"

Riley hauled April to her feet.

As much as her bottom stung, her pride was far more wounded. Tears burned at her miserable state. She had failed utterly, and she could do nothing about it. She had lost the tenuous hold on the only true family she had ever known, the diary was no longer in her possession, and now, she was in the clutches of her accuser. No pretense could rescue her now. Even if there was one, it eluded her. The only things that came to her mind were the pain of her smarting backside, and the image of a mop and bucket behind prison walls. Only then did April begin to cry.

Spinning her around to face him, Riley took her face gently in his hands. There was no anger in his face anymore. In fact, there was only tenderness and compassion in his eyes. "You needn't be afraid of me, April," he said softly, as he wiped the tears away with his thumbs. "Tell me the truth. I promise you that whatever it is, I will protect you."

He said it with such earnest tenderness, and she so desperately wanted to believe him.

"Swear?"

"I give you my word."

She couldn't look him in the face anymore. Her despairing heart reached out for the only lifeline it was offered, and she seized it in a fierce grip.

It surprised her when that lifeline wrapped his arms around her too.

RILEY HIRED A LANDAU AT THE TAVERN, AND the three of them rode back to Blackheath Manor. The chilly silence in the coach echoed the early freeze that had descended upon the moor in the aftermath of the rain. As the horses slowed on the driveway, the full weight of April's actions descended upon her, and she found it hard to breathe. Her attempt at flight had failed, and now she was forced to face the consequences of her deceptions.

She stepped out into the remaining drizzle. Though nearly frozen, she was grateful that the rain obscured the fresh tears that spilled down her cheeks. Riley ordered Jenny to go directly to April's bedroom.

April glanced at the footmen who stood at the front doors with raised candelabra. Their customary cheerful expressions were gone; instead, their stony faces looked upon her with irritation. The floor clock in the hall chimed four as she followed Riley into the house. The servants, some still in dressing gowns, stared at her in silent judgment, upset at their loss of sleep on her account. She had the vague impression that the servants would eat her alive if Riley left her alone. Dutifully, she followed closely behind him into the library.

In the far corner, Jeremy and Jonah came to their feet.

"My dear," Jonah said, taking her hand. "Are you all right? You must be frozen to death. Come sit by the fire."

She allowed herself to be ushered toward the fireplace. Jonah threw a coverlet over her and sat in the chair opposite her. Jeremy handed Riley a snifter of brandy, and poised himself on the arm of Jonah's chair.

Riley disappeared into the shadows of the room.

"Why did you run away?" Jonah asked, his brow creased with fatherly concern.

April couldn't look at either of them. What she was about to say would prove that she had been a wolf in the midst of sheep. It wasn't so much her own shame she was trying to prevent; it was the humiliation they would feel at their own gullibility. She had tried to spare them that by running away. Now it could not be avoided.

"My name is not April Devereux. It's April Jardine."

They stared at her in puzzlement.

She tried to swallow, but a lump formed in her throat. "I am not your daughter, sir. It was a lie."

Jonah straightened. "Why did you say you were?"

The weight of her guilt was becoming more than she could bear. "You were so welcoming, so hospitable. And this was such a lovely place. My own father, you see, never loved me, and I never had brothers, and I wanted it to be so. I always dreamed of having a family, and I so wanted to be a part of yours. I can't begin to express how sorry I am for lying to you as I did. You gave me everything I ever needed, and I was in love with the idea of belonging here."

He looked so disappointed, so crestfallen, she could hardly stand to look at him. He didn't speak for several moments. Then he took a deep breath and slapped his thigh.

"So what if you're not mine? I can't say that I didn't enjoy your company these past weeks. And I don't want you to go away. I don't know who your father is, but he is a fool if he didn't love you. I will be happy to give you a home. You may not be my child, but you're Vivienne's child, and that's enough for me."

April's heart sank again. How could he be so considerate? Her brimming eyes scanned the shadows, looking for Riley. She hoped he would allow just this one lie to stand, so she wouldn't have to admit this, her greatest deception. But no reprieve was forthcoming.

She hated herself.

"No, sir. You see, Vivienne . . ."—her chin began to tremble—"is not my mother. I am not related to either one of you."

"What?" he whispered.

Her tears fell in long hot trails. "I am only . . ." *No one of consequence.* The confession caught in her throat. "I was Madame Devereux's scullery maid. I found her diary. There was mention of a child. A child who would have been my age about now. I thought I could masquerade as that grown-up child. I thought if I could convince you I'm your daughter, you would fear a scandal, and would pay me to keep silent about it." Her lies tasted like spoilt milk in her mouth. "But you didn't pay me off. You took me in, and gave me everything I never had. It felt so wonderful to finally have a proper bed and enough to eat. But more than that, I was treated like a lady here. And you can't imagine what that meant to me. I intended to enjoy your hospitality for a short while, and then leave without taking a penny. Really I was. But then you gave me something I hadn't counted on—the love of a family. And I couldn't tear myself away from that. It had become more valuable to me than anything on earth."

She reached for Jonah's hand. He pulled it away as swiftly as if she had scalded him. The look of pain on his face had chilled to disdain. He stood up, his downturned mouth stiffened against her. Without a word, he walked away until all she heard was the door shut with a hiss.

She waited until her heart started beating again, and then she looked up at Jeremy.

"You got more than you bargained for, April. You've broken his heart. To say nothing of mine." Then he too left.

April sat in the wing chair, her life in tatters around her. Even the fire in the fireplace retreated away from her, leaving her to sit in the growing dark. She watched the shrinking flames through tears.

In the shadows, two eyes studied her. "That was very difficult for you."

"I hate you for making me do that."

"It needed to be done."

"You have no idea what that confession cost me."

"What was never yours to begin with."

She hung her head. "I never meant to hurt anyone. Least of all them. They didn't deserve my betrayal."

"No, they did not."

"How was it that you knew all along?"

"Is that important?"

No, it wasn't. Not anymore. She had branded herself a thief and a liar. She was now a known criminal. She had lost it all—but there was one more price to pay.

"I realize you will need to send for the law. But let Jenny go. This whole thing was my idea. She had nothing to do with it."

"She is an accomplice to a crime."

April shook her head, releasing a fresh set of tears. "I dragged her into it. She came along only to protect me. I'm the one you want. Let her go. Please."

The shadows were silent for a long time.

"I will take your punishments under consideration. For now, you're both confined to your room. We'll talk again tomorrow."

Seven

SLEEP DID NOT COME EASILY THAT NIGHT. April lay awake, looking about at the ornate bedchamber that had now become her prison. Too late she realized that these, the trappings of a lady, had been just that—a trap. The canopy bed, the marble bathtub, the Queen's bejeweled hairbrush—all of it lost its allure. Her newfound family, her freedom, and possibly her very life hung in the balance. This room held nothing of importance anymore.

Except for Jenny. April looked at Jenny's tear-streaked, sleeping face. If anything happened to Jenny... she would never forgive herself.

Bleary-eyed and exhausted, April finally drifted off to a restless slumber just after dawn. When the knock at the door awakened her several hours later, it felt as if she had been asleep for only five minutes.

It was Susan, the chambermaid. "The master summons you to his private study."

The master summons you. How naked she felt without her position. Her fiction had given her sway. Because of that counterfeit identity, Jonah had championed her and kept Riley at bay. Without it, she was reduced to her true form: a wayward scullery maid summoned before the master of the house.

A short while later, April knocked softly on the study door.

He appeared so enormous and forbidding behind his desk. She saw him for what he really was: Circuit Judge of the Assizes and Marquess of Blackheath, heir apparent to the dukedom of Westbrook, Member of the House of Lords, nineteenth in line to the crown of England. Her jailer.

She stood before his mahogany desk. "You sent for me?"

Riley leaned back in his chair, his hands clasped in his lap. He was dressed immaculately in a blue velvet coat and dark gray waistcoat. A light gray silk cravat nested at his throat. "We need to discuss your immediate future. Sit down."

There it was. Not even so much as a "please" anymore. The civility with which he had treated her before was now gone. Now that she was nothing but a maid, no respect needed to be accorded her. But she swallowed her pride, because now she had to accomplish her one and only objective.

"My lord, I will accept whatever sentence you deem fair, but I must insist that you release Jenny at once."

One black eyebrow flew upward. "You are not in a position to insist upon anything. In fact, if I were in your position, I would curb my tongue."

April's throat tightened in impotence. Once again, she stood behind the bars of the class barrier, condemned to being polite to those intent on keeping her in her place. Angry tears threatened to betray her composure.

Riley studied her, his eyes glinting with curiosity. "Many cases come before me each month. While most of the prisoners are men, I do try a few women, mostly for domestic offenses. I can't help but feel intrigued by you, April. Blackmail, theft, fraud . . . these are not crimes committed by women. In fact, they are rather extraordinary crimes for anyone."

"Perhaps my lord will agree that I am not an ordinary person."

He regarded her thoughtfully. "That I'll grant you. But why would a young girl like you embrace a career of such irregular crimes? To use your considerable intelligence to profit by corrupt means . . . it's inconceivable to me."

"To what other purpose can I use it? For a scullery maid, intelligence is irrelevant; in fact, it's detrimental. I am only as good as my hands, and useless otherwise."

"That is an exceedingly poor defense. I expect that being a scullery maid doesn't seem so terrible now that you're faced with imprisonment."

"Of course it is."

He blinked in disbelief. "I beg your pardon?"

Her brows drew together. "It *is* terrible. I don't yearn for my past any more than I look forward to my future."

He leaned his tall frame forward over the desk. "Do you mean to tell me that you don't regret your crimes?"

Her lashes fanned against her cheeks. "The only thing I regret is the pain I caused the people I care for. But it cost me too much to escape that other life. I don't want it back."

"You would rather hang at Newgate for fraud than return to your life in service?"

She sighed. "Either way, it is the same, my lord. On the one hand, I must give up my life; on the other, I must cease to live."

"That is a trifle dramatic, don't you think? The backbone of England's work force is comprised of those in service. Thousands of people in London alone. What is so intolerable about that?"

"Allow me to pose a question to you, my lord. Why did you pursue a career in the law?"

He cocked his head, surprised by the question. "I've harbored a passion for the law all my life."

"Why?"

He reflected a moment. "Because I despise injustice. Even as a little boy, I could see that there was one law for the titled and privileged, and another for the lower classes. I've known men who would rather continue suffering at the hands of a criminal than bear the sting of injustice at the hands of the court. It's an appalling state of affairs in this country, and I've always felt a desire to reverse it."

"What obstacles did you face in the pursuit of your goal?"

He cracked a smile. "Well, Father for one. He was never pleased that I wanted to study the law. He's always thought the post of judge was one best suited to men of lesser nobility. But I wanted more than just to be a landowner, like all the Hawthornes before me. I wanted my life to have meaning."

April leaned forward. "So it is with me. Like you, I had ambitions beyond the role that was determined for me at birth. I wanted to become something greater than what I was predestined to be. But unlike you, there is little I can do if I desire advancement in life. A person of my sex and station is not permitted to achieve any level of independence, financial or social. I would never be permitted to pursue a great passion as you have done."

Lines appeared on his forehead. He knew better than to dispute the veracity of her words. It was a tragic thing when someone in April's position had ambitions. "Have you no other dreams or aspirations to sustain you?"

"I have realized my dreams, my lord. As fleeting as it was, I have done what I set out to do."

He rubbed his chin. "But why this? Most young women dream of marriage, children, that sort of thing."

"Perhaps for most women, it is enough. I wanted more."

"And you had to resort to crime to get what you wanted?"

April sighed. "Maybe if I was a man, it would have been easier for me to transcend my class without breaking the law. Maybe then I wouldn't find myself on this side of the desk. But as the gamblers say, where the risks are big, so are the rewards."

"And the dangers. Was it worth the risk, this dream of yours?"

She squeezed her hands. "I don't know."

"I do. If you must break the law to achieve an ambition, then it is time to reevaluate that ambition. And as the *religious* men say, the love of money is the root of all evil."

Her eyebrows lifted in resignation. "So is the lack of it, my lord."

Riley chuckled in spite of himself. He leaned back in his chair, absently running his fingertips down the length of a quill pen. "And yet you turned me down when I offered you ten thousand pounds. Why?"

"I found something more valuable."

"A life of luxury?"

April shook her head meaningfully. "A loving family."

He looked at her evenly, scanning for a hint of insincerity. There wasn't any.

"You may regret using that word, for now I must decide what is to become of you."

Apprehension gripped her by the throat. His handsome face was inscrutable, his expression darkened by the responsibility to execute his duty. She licked her lips. At least it had been Riley who had captured her. She knew she deserved to be punished for her crimes, and Riley was renowned for his sense of fairness. She sensed that whatever punishment he decreed would not only be fitting, but fair. Despite everything, at least she could trust him for that.

But it wasn't herself she was worried about. It didn't matter what happened to her. She had roped Jenny into this mess, and for Jenny's sake, she needed to seek his charity. If for no other reason, she hoped that the scales of justice in Riley's head would tip in her favor.

He heaved a weighty sigh. "I told you back at the inn that I would protect you. And I am a man of my word. I shan't summon the constabulary. Not yet anyway."

April blinked expectantly at him.

"While I do not condone your actions, I am moved by your demonstration of remorse. I will grant you an opportunity to redeem yourselves, and put right what you made wrong. I will not prefer charges against you or Jenny, provided you meet the following conditions. First, you must produce Vivienne's diary, and hand it over to me. If my father is somehow compromised by this book, then I want it destroyed. Second, you must carry on as before, maintaining your little charade for the world at large. You will remain at Blackheath as my ward, until I tell you otherwise. If any of these conditions is not met, then you will have to be remanded to the authorities immediately. Is that understood?"

April nodded, as she weighed his conditions. "How long do you intend for me to stay?"

"As long as it takes to find a suitable excuse for your departure."

She gulped. "Will we be able to leave before the Minister's Ball?"

Riley's brows drew together. "Why?"

She dared not tell him that there were other victims of her crimes. It would only complicate matters. "I just thought that you might want me out of the way before such a public event."

"On the contrary. I have every intention of presenting you openly and publicly to the entire world."

"No!" April blanched. "I mean, wouldn't that make my eventual departure more difficult to explain?"

"Perhaps. But as news of your so-called parentage has now reached London, you must help me to establish the appearance that you are *only* my ward. Regrettably, we are now in a position where we must transform fiction into reality."

Her heart beat a staccato at the base of her throat. "And after the ball? What's to become of us then?"

There was that look again, that look of a concerned ... lover? The pleasant thought warred with the certain futility of that possibility.

"We'll see."

APRIL RETURNED TO HER ROOM, PUZZLED. Jenny was sitting on the edge of the bed, her nightdress clutched in her hands.

"The oddest thing just happened. I never thought the day would come when—" April was interrupted by Jenny's sob. She flew to her side. "What happened?"

Jenny swiped at her eyes with the nightdress. "He left me."

"Who?"

"William," she cried impatiently. "He was just here. He came to ask why we had run away last night. He said he was worried sick over me, out at night with all the highwaymen about." She chuckled pitiably. "He was worried about my honor."

April took the damp dress from Jenny's hands and dabbed at her friend's face. "And then what happened?"

"He kissed me. Tender and sweetlike. Almost like the kind of kiss you'd give a child. I never felt so safe with anyone in my life. It was as if my heart started beating for the first time." She dissolved into fresh sobs as a torrent of tears fell down her face.

April's heart sank. "But why are you crying?"

"I don't know what came over me. I wanted to be totally honest with him. I wanted him to love me for who I really was. So I told him . . . I told him about my past at Madame Devereux's, what I'd been doing all these years. He just got this strange expression on his face. 'You're a harlot?' was all he kept saying. I tried to tell him that I didn't do that no more, that I started a new life, and that I wanted him to be a part of it. But he just kept pushing me away. 'How could you?' was all he said. And then he left." Jenny broke down and sobbed on April's shoulder.

April patted her gently on the back, annoyed by the irony. Now that Riley wanted them to stay, it became a torture for Jenny to do so. She tried valiantly to console her overwrought friend, but it was hard to do while she was trying to quell her own anger at any man who would spurn such a tenderhearted girl.

"Jenny, if he can't see beyond your past, then he isn't worthy of you. Is he so perfect he has never done anything shameful? Just like a man to give up on love so easily. Let's give William a chance to think about it for a while. If he still cannot see in you all the beautiful and wondrous things I do, then sod him. Dry those tears, now. All will turn out for the best. I promise."

If only April could believe that herself.

Eight

AS HAPPENED EVERY YEAR SINCE RILEY WAS confirmed into the House of Lords, Blackheath Manor began to swell with people who came from as far as Scotland and Ireland to attend the Minister's Ball. The most coveted invitation of the social calendar, the ball drew the crème de la crème of society and politics, about four hundred people, for the grandest and most entertaining celebration since the close of the Season.

Riley had planned a program of festivities to amuse the group of forty or so who would be lodging at the manor until the ball. There would be a fox hunt and card games on Friday, archery and a picnic on Saturday, and finally, the ball on Sunday. Today, Thursday, the overnight guests began descending en masse on Blackheath Manor. With more than eighty bedchambers, in addition to the vast servants' quarters, the manor was equipped to accommodate all the overnight guests and their valets or maids comfortably.

April and Jenny spent the better part of the day squirreled away in their room. Ensconced on the window seat overlooking the driveway, April could hear the carriages arrive one by one. At one time, on her afternoons off, she would sit in Hyde Park and gaze in admiration at these same carriages bearing the members of the ruling class. Now, each conveyance that stopped under her window brought a sense of dread that it might contain Sir Cedric Markham. She wished that he would meet with some minor tragedy—that he would break a leg or become bedridden with influenza—anything that would keep him away from Blackheath Manor this weekend.

The afternoon sun had begun to descend on the rise of hills outside her window, and a chill wind was beginning to blow. April shut the window and returned to the dressing table. Thoughts of the future weighed heavily upon her, and she sighed for the hundredth time as she considered the upcoming weekend spent in the company of the two people who least wanted to see her: Jeremy and Jonah. Not to mention that bitch, Lady Agatha.

The clock on the mantel chimed five, and April decided to take advantage of the stillness to go and look for the diary. The last time she remembered having it was in the library. She and Jenny tiptoed down the servants' staircase, and waited for a lull in the traffic to slip into the library undetected.

The library had two floors, each with its own entrance from the rest of the house. Thousands of books lined the massive shelves. Two ornate rolling staircases, one on each floor, allowed access to the highest shelves. Through a set of double glass doors, which led out onto a gardened loggia, streamed in the fading rays from the afternoon sun.

Though no one was there, the room was full of memories. It was here, amid the smells of wood and leather, that she confessed her guilt in duping the people who had opened their home and hearts to her. But there was another, more insistent memory that troubled her. It was also where she had discovered her weakness. And it took the shape of Riley Hawthorne.

There was no doubt about it. It was this weakness that had caused her downfall. She could trace the reversal of her luck back to that one momentary lapse of reason in which she kissed him.

Mentally, she replayed the moments she found herself enfolded in his powerful arms, her body responding to his soft yet dominating kiss. She could almost feel the gentle pressure on her mouth again, and her lips grew warm at the thought. The remembered sensation of his solid body enveloping every inch of her set her ablaze once more.

She shook her head in self-reproach. If she had responded the way she should have, she and Jenny would not be in their current position now. Why she did not slap him for his impertinence, or even rebuke him for the offense, was beyond her comprehension. No, she just hung in his embrace, wrapped in his arms, the granite reserve she had taken such pains to cultivate crumbling under the weight of a single kiss. Once again, she saw herself as he must have seen her, her eyes dreamily closed with a satisfied smile—a smile!—offered up to him.

April stomped over to the leather chairs and flung each of the cushions off, sending a spray of dust motes into the air. She cringed at the memory of her vulnerability. She almost deserved his arrogant reply. How could she have succumbed so easily to his masculine charm? And why was she so attracted to this man in particular? She had seen hundreds of men come through Madame Devereux's brothel . . . why did this one unsettle her so?

April turned the question over in her mind. Perhaps it was the way he saw beyond her pretenses, through her lies. He saw her as she truly was, the person she was trying so hard to hide. She had to give him credit for his keen intuition and powerful perception. He was as impervious to lies as a roof to rain. He had a kind of patrician reserve, a patient watchfulness that made it difficult for her to be persuasive. It was like trying to convince a man that the sky is green. Still, it was a great relief not to have to lie about her identity anymore. And yet, there was that niggling regret that it was just a matter of time before she was ousted from Blackheath Manor altogether, and there would be no more kisses like that one.

From far away, she heard a voice. It was Jenny.

"What?"

"I said it's not 'ere. What's the matter, you got cloth in your ears or something?"

"No, I . . . what do you mean it's not here? It's got to be . . . I left it here, in this chair."

"We've searched them all. Maybe one of them parlormaids put it away. I swear, these girls are the most efficient servants in all of England. We could do with some of them down at Madame Devereux's with the lot we've got."

Jenny's playful jibe did not register with April. Her mind was reeling with the possibility that the diary could have fallen into the wrong hands. It was too catastrophic to contemplate.

"We have to find it, Jenny. It must be found. Help me search the shelves for it."

"But I can't read."

April sighed impatiently. "You know what it looks like! About this big, bound in red leather, smells a bit musty with a hint of jasmine perfume."

April perched herself atop one of the ladders scanning the upper shelves while Jenny searched the lower ones. They were so concentrated on finding the book that they didn't hear Lady Agatha come in from the loggia.

"Ahem!"

April spun around to see Lady Agatha, dressed as always like a fashion plate from a ladies' magazine. Her pale blue dinner dress was a confection of artistry. The bodice stretched over her full breasts, and it was festooned by bands of blue satin at her trim waist and sleeves. Beaded appliqués of roses lined the hem of the gown. A gauze wrap draped becomingly from the crook of her arms, completing the soignée ensemble.

April's face grew red as she descended the ladder. She had taken great pains to dress as plainly as possible, too ashamed to dress in elegant clothes following her disgrace from Jonah's favor. Her light brown morning dress was simple and unembellished.

"Good evening," April said, smoothing out the skirt, as if that would somehow improve its appearance. "We were just looking for some light reading for tonight." She took pleasure in noticing that Lady Agatha had donned black gloves and placed black feathers in her hair, proof that her comment about Agatha's breach of mourning protocol had found its mark.

"Indeed?" remarked Lady Agatha. "Won't you be joining us for dinner?"

"I don't think so," April replied. "I've come down with a bit of a headache."

"Again?" she responded, one elegant eyebrow raised in malicious curiosity. "You really ought to see a physician about that, dear. It might be an early indication of a more serious and embarrassing condition."

The veiled insult riled April. "Thank you for your concern, Lady Agatha, but that won't be necessary. My headache is brought on by the company I seem to be keeping."

Lady Agatha's nostrils flared, but she retained her malevolent smile. "No doubt living among slave traders has ruined your taste for refined company. Speaking of servants, why is yours sniffing the bookcase?"

April's biting response died when she whirled around to see Jenny searching for the Madame's perfumed diary, her nose scanning the shelves. Humiliated, April hunted for a plausible excuse.

"She is not *sniffing*. She is merely nearsighted, and must . . . peer closely at the titles."

Lady Agatha chuckled. "Yes, I've seen her at work with one of the footmen in Riley's employ. She seemed quite 'nearsighted' with him as well. Scandalous the way they ogled each other. Considering her behavior, you might do well to get an abigail for your abigail."

April bristled at the insult to her friend. "She follows your example of propriety, Lady Agatha." April turned around and asked Jenny to leave the room. When the door closed behind her, April gave Agatha a withering look.

"Now that we're alone, let me pay you the courtesy of speaking plainly. I don't like you. I find you a revolting hypocrite with the face of a convent novice and the manner of a terrier in heat. I've seen penny-harlots that were less obvious than you. The title of 'lady' is laughably inappropriate on you, rather like putting a crinoline on a milk cow. The widow act is an interesting choice of costume, though I'd have hated to be the poor sod who had to give up the ghost in order to give it to you. It must buy you sympathy, but I'm sure that's not the kind of comforting you're looking for. And as for my servant, at least she seeks out gentlemen of her own station. Unlike you, she has no intention of marrying up the ladder of English aristocracy one rung at a time. And so, *Lady* Agatha, I'll leave you in possession of the library." She strode toward the door, but Lady Agatha's parting remark stopped her.

"You've forgotten your reading material, my dear."

"I beg your pardon?" It was not the response that April would have expected.

"I believe you came for a book. Riley does keep some very unique books. I myself have found an interesting volume or two here."

April's blood froze.

Observing April's ashen face, Lady Agatha continued. "By all means, don't let me keep you from your search. If you like, I can suggest something I've found to be enormously entertaining."

The mountain peak April had been standing on just a moment before crumbled beneath her. Her worst nightmare had come true—the diary *had* fallen into the wrong hands. Riley would kill her when he found out.

"Lady Agatha, please . . ." It was a supplication that cost her every shred of pride she had.

"Try this one first," she said in mock helpfulness. She picked up a large but slender folio and handed it to April. "It's a genealogy of the House of Hawthorne. Since you both enjoy 'peering at titles,' you'd do well to learn it. You have a lot of catching up to do."

April felt as if her stomach had turned to water. There was no telling what havoc someone like Lady Agatha would wreak. She could bring down the family with one careless word.

April's earlier arrogance lay in pieces around her like discarded clothes. She had put this family through so much. She simply had to get the diary back at any price. "What do you want?" she muttered in defeat.

Lady Agatha's smile vanished. "Well, as you've already chosen the weapons, allow me to reciprocate. I don't like you, either. You are impertinent, ill-mannered, and uncouth. You're nothing but a cheeky little bounder trying to pass herself off as a member of Society, but you cannot shake off the stink of the working class. You accuse me of being a social climber, and yet here you are seeking a passable countenance to cover your bastardy . . . and you can still call *me* a hypocrite?" She laughed at April's stricken expression. "Oh, yes. Did you honestly think that anyone believed that drivel about your being Riley's ward? Even the servants know you are nothing but an unwanted misbegotten who's taken this opportunity to sponge off Riley's family. You may have blackmailed him into a corner, but I'm not afraid of you, pet. I hope you got what you came for, because it will be the last thing you ever take from him. I'll see to that. You're right about one thing. I do intend to become the future Marchioness of Blackheath, and my first duty as Riley's fiancée will be to see you married off and out of his hair. Or you can run away again, I don't particularly care which. Either way, I'm certain that both he and his father will thank me for getting rid of you. Now," she said, resuming her forced smile, "I advise you to make gainful use of this weekend to find a suitable man to marry you, because failing that, come Monday morning you will be engaged to someone of my own choosing, like it or not. Do you understand, my dear?"

April leveled her stormy gaze at Lady Agatha. Her first and most powerful impulse was to drag the woman across the library carpet by her flawless coiffure. April restrained herself only by convincing herself that, in this situation at least, Lady Agatha held the upper hand. Lady Agatha didn't love Riley; of that April was sure. It was his title and wealth she coveted. April was too honest not to recognize elements of herself in Lady Agatha, and her own superficial ambitions rose up like bile in her throat. Agatha might not use the diary to expose the family to disgrace, as she clearly wanted to marry into it. But April didn't know Lady Agatha well enough. If April antagonized her, she might do just that out of pure malicious spite, and then find some other rich lord to marry. It made April all the more determined to defend the family against harm. At all costs, she must get the diary back . . . and destroy it.

Lady Agatha's smile became more genuine as she savored April's defeat.

"Yes, Lady Agatha, I understand you perfectly. But let us have an understanding. I will leave Blackheath at the first opportunity. But I want the diary back. It is of no earthly good to you, but it is my only price for leaving Blackheath . . . and forsaking my claim to my share of the inheritance. Do we have a deal?"

Lady Agatha turned to face the fireplace as she seemed to consider this carefully. After what seemed like an eternity, she finally spoke.

"Agreed."

"Now, Lady Agatha. I must have the diary now."

"You are in no position to threaten me, my dear. You'll get it when your engagement is announced, and not a moment before."

April fumed at her overbearing manner, but held back flinging herself at the older woman's turned back. "Fine. But you'd do well to remember just who has more to lose in this transaction." Unable to stand being in the same room a moment longer with the awful woman, April slammed the library doors behind her.

TAKING ADVANTAGE OF THE TEMPORARY lull, Riley retreated to his study for a moment of solitude. He had already tired of the tediousness of greeting his arriving houseguests.

Thoughts of another houseguest had distracted him all day. That girl, April.

He felt vindicated now that he knew she had been lying. His chief worry—that she knew about Jeremy's parentage and was out to ruin them—was finally laid to rest. She was naught but an upstart, a presumptuous malapert with aspirations of being a lady. She never even knew the Madame as well as she claimed. He chuckled. He couldn't believe the impudence of this common housemaid to flout every established convention, daring to pass herself off as a duke's daughter. What cheek!

But that wasn't what gave him the greatest pleasure. It was the idea that he had her where he wanted her, and that she was going to stay there for as long as he desired.

Desire. That was his problem. Because where he wanted her was in his bed. He wanted her naked and breathless for him, her passion mounting until she begged him to take her. He wanted her to be filled with the length of him, writhing under his weight, her legs embracing his. He wanted her to be as desperate for him as he seemed to be getting for her.

His blood raced at the mere thought of her. He wondered if she was as audacious in bed as she was in mixed company. She had the complexion of a saint, but the mind of a devil. He loved the challenge of her, all full of snap and bite. Among all the women he'd met, he'd never seen her equal.

He walked to the window of his study, which overlooked the broad serpentine river that wound behind the gardens, through the pasture and beyond to the woods. There, as if he had conjured her, was April, walking through the winter garden. She was dressed plainly, but she was a vision of loveliness to him. Her beauty was so earthy and uncomplicated, and he shook his head at her misguided aspirations to attain a more refined and artificial beauty.

It made him wonder why she seemed to take great pains to hide herself from view of the guests who were strolling in the fading daylight. She began to pick a handful of winter irises. He found it odd that she kept glancing to the right, in the direction of the lakefront.

When she had filled the crook of her arm with the lavender blooms, she made her way to the lakefront. His eyes preceded her path and landed on the bench under the shade of an old maple facing the lake. It was his father's favorite spot, and Riley saw him there now, wholly unaware that April approached him from behind.

She neared slowly, cautiously. She must have called out

his name, because he turned. He watched his father look at her momentarily, then turn and face the lake once more. Slowly, she walked out in front of him and spoke to him, but he acted oblivious to her. She crouched down in front of him, and placed her carefully picked bouquet in his lap. He made no gesture of recognition. She spoke to him, more earnestly this time, her palms face up in supplication. His father stretched out his cane and stood up, letting all the flowers fall to the ground, and walked over them back to the house.

Riley heaved a sigh. Poor April. There was no way she could make amends with his father over this. She had wounded him in a place that had never fully healed, and most likely never would be.

But she tried. And that spoke volumes to Riley. It confirmed that what she told him earlier had been true: she may have had avaricious intentions at one point, but they had since changed. Now she craved the love of a family. But it was too late.

He watched her begin to weep, and took pity on her.

Nine

THE DAY DAWNED SLOWLY. A COLD MIST HAD descended on the land in the night, and lay over the grounds like a white gossamer blanket. Belowstairs, the household began to stir, as dozens of the guests rose to take part in the planned fox hunt.

Susan brought in the morning tea and offered to help April dress. April was about to decline, but she had no desire to explain to Susan why she wasn't going on the hunt. She let Susan lay out her riding habit, a dress of hunter green velvet with a wide skirt and demi-train. She asked to speak to Master Riley, and Susan informed her that he was at the stables overseeing the preparation of the horses.

Donning her warmest gloves, April made her way to the stables. She wanted to catch him before the hunt began. She had to try to convince Riley to let her and Jenny stay in their room this weekend. Riley had no idea of the danger he was in by letting her be presented openly in public with Sir Cedric Markham around. As easy a target as Markham had been, April doubted he'd forget the two girls who'd had two hundred pounds off him. Riley didn't know that she had blackmailed others, and she had no wish to confess it to him. As far as Riley was concerned, Jonah had been their only target. It was a potentially explosive situation, so she and Jenny must stay out of sight at all costs. Even being out in the open air now made April nervous, but there would be little opportunity to speak to Riley for the rest of the day.

Whereas Jeremy's passion was horticulture, Riley's was horseflesh. Their respective hobbies helped to make Blackheath Manor the grandest and most magnificent seat in the entire county. The Blackheath stable was legendary, as was his skill for breeding the finest and fastest horses in England. She turned the corner toward the stables, and found him standing in the middle of the courtyard.

He was speaking to a groom while stroking the neck of a large mare, but April noticed nothing but him. The red velvet coat and white breeches he wore hugged his magnificent frame, and she marveled at the line of him. The early morning light fell on his black hair and spilled onto his wide shoulders, bathing him in a rosy hue, and her breath caught in her throat. His hair, still wet at the temples where he had washed, ruffled in the light breeze, and her fingers yearned to thread themselves in that mane again. She watched him issue instructions to the groom. He had such an authoritative manner, it was little wonder he was so well liked and respected. The servant rushed away to carry out his orders, and Riley was finally alone.

Slowly, she approached him, her boots making no sound on the flagstones. Unaware of her, he continued to pat the horse, all the while cooing affectionately in its ear. April remembered something the Madame had told the girls a long time ago—that they could tell a lot about a man by the way he treated his horse. What was it she said? *He who will not be merciful to his beast is a beast himself.* Smiling at the way his gloved hand caressed the animal, April felt her body grow warm.

The horse became aware of her presence before Riley did. The mare's giant head craned in her direction, and Riley finally turned to face her.

"April," he breathed, and smiled.

She was taken aback.

He had never smiled at her that way before, and she was astonished at how it made her feel. A strange lightness filled her, rendering her speechless. His expressive eyes registered something she was unfamiliar with. Could it have been . . . affection?

"You look very . . . I was just choosing a mount for you," he said. "Her name is Symphony. She's a suitable horse for a lady."

A curious elation welled up when he mentioned that word. Strange he should continue to call her a lady when he knew she was nothing but a servant. "Thank you, my lord, but that won't be necessary."

"Would you prefer rider's prerogative and choose your own mount?" he asked gallantly.

"No, you see, I shan't be participating in the hunt. I merely wanted to ask—"

"You're not coming? Why not?"

She hadn't counted on his look of disappointment. It threw off her concentration. "Well," she began tentatively, looking at the horse, "my seat isn't what it used to be."

He smirked, and a dimple appeared in the hollow of his cheek. "It's your own fault. You deserved that thrashing. I hope you'll think twice before lying to me again."

The memory of the spanking made her blush darkly. "I didn't—"

"Good. Because the next time you wind up facedown over my knee, I shan't be so lenient."

Her jaw dropped at the mere possibility that the pain on her bottom could be worse than it had been. But the amused twinkle in his eye told her he was enjoying himself immensely at her expense.

Her lips thinned. "Yes, I suspected when I met you that you would be a pain in the arse."

He threw back his head and laughed, and it gave her much pleasure when he did so. The sound resonated in the still courtyard, and tore down her defenses.

"What I meant, my lord, is that I've never ridden a horse in my life. The only thing I know about horses is how to dodge them on the streets of London."

The thick fringe of his lashes widened with boyish enthusiasm. "Then you haven't truly discovered their splendor. Come, let me show you." Impetuously, he took her hand in his and led her toward the paddock.

Behind the stables was a square area fenced by white clapboard. There were two beautiful horses inside the paddock, as lovely a pair of animals as she'd ever seen. The larger of the two had a coat the color of worn leather, with rich brown tones melting into black stockings. He pranced around the fence line encircling the smaller one, who was doing a fine job of ignoring him. She was an elegant-looking horse, a flaxen chestnut with feet the color of milk.

"Adonis there has had a very auspicious career. Fourteen victories from twenty-five starts, and last year's champion at Newmarket. He stands a shade over seventeen hands. Isn't he beautiful? No other Thoroughbred in my stables has such a splendid build, or such staying powers. He does have a bit of a temper—the wild animal in him is strong—but his pedigree is unparalleled. Among horses, he's practically royalty."

"Will you be riding him?" she asked.

"Not today," he answered her, leaning against the white fencepost. "Adonis is otherwise engaged."

"What with?"

"Today he will breed."

She turned to the blond horse in the center of the paddock. "She doesn't seem to be too interested."

He looked down at April. "She will be."

She matched his stare. "How can you be so sure?"

"The horse in there is a maiden mare. We put Adonis there to tease her. He will entice her to mate."

Her eyes remained fixed on his, even though she felt the color rise in her cheeks. "What if the mare has no wish to mate with your Adonis?"

"That won't happen."

"Why not?"

"Because she can't help herself. It's in her nature to desire him."

"Aren't you presuming a great deal? Perhaps she has chosen another mate already."

"Impossible. He's perfect for her. They are ideally matched."

"So say you."

He nodded arrogantly, confidence dripping from him like warm honey.

She looked out onto the paddock. Adonis approached the mare from behind, his large head extended in front of him to sniff her tail, and she bolted. "Well, you appear to be mistaken. She is clearly not as fond of him as you have decreed she should be."

He leaned in close. His eyes had little gold specks in them. She had never noticed that before. "She'll come around. Adonis is patient. As am I."

She could smell the soap on his freshly shaved skin. "If she is a maiden mare, she may be fearful."

His fingers moved a lock of her uncoiffed hair off her shoulder. "Nature has a way of breaking down the defenses of even the most obstinate of females. She may appear to take no notice of him, but his presence alone has already sparked a desire in her. The nearer he comes to her, the more she will accept it of him. When she decides to give in to her yearning, it is she herself who will invite him in."

Her eyes danced around his masculine face as he drew closer. His nose brushed hers, and his hot breath fell on her cheek. Her lips parted in anticipation, her own breathing quickening as she warred with her impulses. Riley's mouth hovered maddeningly above hers, like a delectably ripe fruit. All she had to do was reach up and taste it.

She cursed her weakness, and gave herself to the kiss.

The softness of his mouth filled her senses to the brim. His lips smoothed over hers again and again, as if her mouth were a slice of orange and he wanted every last drop. All thought, all reason, evaporated. Only one sensation remained—*pleasure*.

Dear God, why did she crave him so? When he was around, she lost all hold on who she was. Around him, she became someone else. Someone she liked all too much. And when his arms came up and wrapped around her body, she knew why. *Safe*. In the warm cocoon of his embrace, her troubles and fears became distant, and the stronghold of her loneliness crumbled.

He pulled away, his eyes still closed as he savored the last of her kiss. Slowly, his eyes opened and refocused on her. "God, but you're sweet."

It amazed her that he could make her feel so alive . . . so feminine. She blushed, ashamed of her defenselessness around him. In the awkward silence, she glanced at the horses once more.

"Perhaps you're right. She may come to welcome his attentions after all. He's a handsome stallion, and she's a beauty, too."

His eyes never wavered from her face. "Yes, she is."

There was that fluttering again. Breathless and alive at

the same time. Title or no, he made her feel like a real lady. No . . . like a real woman.

"Would you like to pet her?" he asked. Without waiting for an answer, he puckered his lips and gave a shrill whistle. The mare's ears swiveled in his direction, and recognizing him, ambled lazily toward the fence and his outstretched hand.

He grabbed the strap of her bridle and pulled her golden head over the fence. "Don't be afraid. She likes to be touched."

April raised a timid hand and touched her blond forelock.

"Touch her here," he said, rubbing her muzzle. "It's her softest part. Feel how silky it is."

April did so.

"No, no. Take your gloves off."

An alarm went off inside her. "No. That's quite all right. I can see it is soft."

"Come along. She won't bite, I promise."

"I know she won't. But we really should go now."

The dimple returned to his cheek. "I never pegged you for a coward. Are you afraid?"

"Certainly not!" she retorted. "I'm not afraid of anything."

"All right, then. Give us your hand." He gripped her hand, and began to pull off her glove.

"No!" she cried, and tried to push him away. But he had already pried it off, and the cold air made contact with her naked hand.

Mortified, she tried to reclaim her hand, but he held it fast in his own. There, stamped on the cracked, callused skin, tiny scars, and uneven nails, was a painful reminder of who she was.

And still remained.

She yanked the glove out of his hand and spun around to

put it back on, even though she knew it was too late. The lovely cloud she had been floating on dissipated, sending her crashing back down to earth. So much for being thought a lady. Now that her ugly laborer's hands had been served up to his eyes, she was back to being common as dirt.

She felt his hands encircle her arms, and gently he turned her around to face him. Her downcast head retreated between her shoulders. She couldn't bear to look at him.

He pried apart her hands and pulled away her gloves.

His hands were strong and warm as they rubbed her own.

"I didn't want you to see that."

His voice was tender. "Why?"

"They're man's hands."

"They're your hands."

"I know," she said miserably, and started to replace her gloves.

He pulled them off impatiently, and flung them away. "When will you learn to stop hiding from me?"

She folded her arms, a hopeless tear stinging at the corner of her eye. "I won't ever be like her, will I?"

"Who?"

"Lady Agatha."

He snickered. "Why would you want to be like her?"

"I don't really . . . it's just . . . she's so bloody beautiful and so bloody rich, and she's a lady, and I'm . . ." Her voice cracked. She hadn't intended to show her weakness. "I'm no one."

He laughed, drawing her attention to his face.

"What's so bloody funny?"

"You've turned my whole world upside down, and you can stand there and say you're no one?"

"No one of consequence, I mean."

His hand caressed her face, his amusement softening to a tender regard. "You're someone to me."

As if to drive home his point, the mare nickered softly

and began to chomp on a curly tress. Riley chuckled. "Apparently, Bervilia finds you as delectable as I do."

She pulled her hair free of the horse's mouth. "Eww. You lied to me. She does bite."

He laughed at April's discomfiture, pulling her by one hand. "Only on Fridays. Come on, let's give her a little respite from Adonis. Absence makes the heart grow fonder."

"Where are you taking me?" she called to his back as he opened the gate to the paddock.

"The three of us are going for a ride."

She pulled away from him. "I told you, I can't."

"Yesterday, you couldn't. But today, you will." He placed a hand on the crest of Bervilia's neck, and jumped up on her bare back. "There is no greater pleasure in life than being on the back of a horse at full gallop. Come, let me show you." He stretched out his hand.

A dozen excuses leapt to April's mind, but they vanished when her eyes locked with his. They were playful, inviting . . . and asking for her trust. With a will of its own, her hand found its way into his.

He lifted her effortlessly onto the horse in front of him. Uneasy, she shifted on the animal, her feet finding no purchase. "My lord, are ladies supposed to ride astride like this?"

"They can hardly ride sidesaddle when there is no saddle." Reins in hand, Riley nestled closely behind her. "We haven't much time before the hunt, so you'll have to be a quick study."

"I don't mind waiting until the next hunt, truly," she said nervously. The animal began to move, and panic seized her. "I'm going to fall!"

"You won't," he reassured her, using the same gentle tone he used on the horse. "Hold on to me."

He wrapped a strong arm around her middle, holding her fast against him. She could feel his rock-solid chest and abdomen press against her back, and his legs bracing hers. The sensation of being completely enfolded by his body brought her an immediate sense of security. She clasped her hands against the powerful arm encircling her, and the fear ebbed.

"Now let me show you what it feels like to truly live."

His long legs dug into the sides of the horse, and the horse bolted, carrying them into the thick December mist.

Wide-eyed and rigid, April's gaze never wavered from the ground. Sensing her fear, Riley lowered his head and whispered into her ear. "Breathe."

She took a deep breath, unaware she had been holding it. The clean air that filled her lungs uncoiled her body's panicked response.

"Don't be afraid. You won't fall as long as I'm here. Just relax against me, and let the horse rock beneath you . . . that's it . . . keep your head high, but give in to her stride. I'll hold on to you."

Guided by Riley's controlled rocking, April let her body relax. That's when she noticed that the crisp air that stung her cheeks was perfumed with the smell of damp earth and crushed leaves. She lifted her gaze, and was amazed. The sun emerged from between two far-off hills, and they were galloping straight for it. April had never felt so free, so wild, as she did in this chase against the sunrise. Riley gave the horse her head, and they flew across the dewy ground, leaving eddies of mist spiraling behind them.

April gloried in the cool, fresh moisture that clung to her face and left a cobweb of dew on her velvet riding habit. The chill wind whipped through her russety hair, which entwined itself in his black locks. Up and down the hills they flew, crashing through tiny rainbows in the mist. Larger and larger the sun grew, until it filled the sky with an array of beams in reds and purples. It was an awesome sight, and for the first time, April Rose Jardine felt what it was like to be truly alive.

Gradually, the growing sunlight drove away the silvery mist, and Riley slowed the horse to a walk. He guided it across a stone bridge that sprawled over a thread of the river that rushed through the estate, and over to a copse of trees at the foot of a gathering of hills. Maple leaves were scattered on the ground like the pieces of a forgotten jigsaw puzzle. The horse continued a slow gait, forcing them to rock slowly against one another. April could feel every part of him against her, and her body responded immediately to the sensation. He must have felt the same pleasure, because although there was no more danger of falling, Riley's grip on her waist tightened.

As the horse swayed gently beneath them, her mind entertained unbidden thoughts of having a different sort of beast between her legs. His mouth brushed against her ear, and instinctively she inclined her head to receive the sensation. The morning was so still and quiet, it seemed like they were the only two people in the whole world.

The horse stopped at a clearing and began to graze at a small shrub. Riley kissed a tender spot behind April's ear. A warm hand on her chin turned her face until her mouth was underneath his. The kiss was gentle and passionate, with an almost pained tenderness. His lips covered hers completely, and April felt she would swoon from the sheer pleasure of it.

His hands traveled slowly from her waist to her bodice. Somewhere inside her, modesty protested, but his large warm hands on her breasts silenced any objection. His lips trailed down her neck, blazing a tingling trail down to her shoulder. April finally satisfied her desire to run her fingers in his hair. The silky wisps waved through her fingers, and she heard him groan.

His tongue darted out, igniting a spot on her throat, and traced a path back to her ear. When he took her earlobe into his mouth, it was her turn to moan. All her senses responded at once to the searing softness of his heavenly tongue.

Deftly, his fingers unclasped the buttons at her bodice, and her body yielded to his touch. As his palms stroked her rising nipples through her chemise, her body quivered. She felt surrounded by him, like a lone turret under assault from all sides. Except that she wanted to fall.

He reached down and began to pull up her skirt. The cold air on her legs brought her up out of her daze, and she halted his hand on her thigh.

He anticipated her protests. "Don't be afraid," he breathed, his voice deep and persuasive, and she closed her eyes against his gentle firmness. "Let me."

April gasped at the sensation, but let him explore her. Tendrils of pleasure snaked through her body. Wedged between his powerful legs, all she could do was arch her back against him as his hand deftly found its way to her core. He took her lips in a consuming kiss, savoring the taste of her. Her body thrummed at the sensation.

His fingers soon discovered the rhythm that incited her passion. She was overcome by the heat that spread swiftly through her body. She began to rock against him as he coaxed her toward ecstasy. She hugged the muscular arm in front of her, opening for him, to him, and was rewarded by a pleasure unlike any other she had ever dreamed of.

She sagged against him, bathed in contentment, and he resumed his sensual kisses of her neck. What a sensation! She had never felt anything like that before. When her head cleared, she turned toward him. Her eyes were dreamy, and he kissed her lips gently.

"My God," he said, smiling. "I've wanted to see that look on your face since the moment I met you."

She chuckled softly, holding one hand to his freshly shaved cheek. He was damnably handsome when he smiled thus, and April found herself yearning for him again. He kissed her mouth intensely, hungrily, and April's feelings for him deepened into something she dared not name. All she wanted now was to let him have his pleasure, too, to let him join her in this world of bliss.

"Riley," she said, and he smiled at the sound of his name on her lips.

"Yes, my sweet?" he said, resting his cheek on her forehead.

"It's your turn."

His hand stopped stroking her hair, and he lowered his head to her level. "Are you sure?"

She nodded her head. "I want you to finish my riding lesson."

Riley flushed. He jumped off the horse, and stood beside it with his arms stretched toward her. April waited a moment, reveling in the look of aching impatience on his face. It pleased her immeasurably to see the high-and-mighty marquess so hungry for her.

"It's all right," he implored. "I'll catch you."

Smiling mischievously, she replied, "I think I've changed my mind."

His eyes widened. "What?"

Turning her nose up at him, she replied crisply, "I think I'll claim rider's prerogative and choose another mount."

Giggling, she nudged her heels into the mare's flanks, prodding the horse forward. Riley lunged at her, catching her by the waist, and jerked her off the horse. She shrieked, but landed safely in his arms.

She laughed gaily at the murderous look on his face, which was softening by his growing smile.

"I knew you were going to be a troublesome mare to mate."

She tilted her head back to look him in the eye. "That's because I want only the finest in the stable. But you'll do."

He seized her by her windblown tresses and covered her mouth in a possessive kiss. He picked her up in his arms and laid her on a carpet of rusty leaves at the foot of a large tree. She looked up at him, so determined to claim her, and she reveled in the heady feeling of power she had over his body. He was so handsome, so regal, so civilized . . . and she brought out the animal in him.

He knelt over her, and peeled away his jacket and cravat. She bit her lip as he pulled his shirt over his head. His midriff was grooved with rows of muscle, looking so hard and yet so warm. His chest was forested with black hair, which narrowed to a line that disappeared into his trousers, and she ached to find out how far down it went.

He lay down on top of her, and the heaviness of his muscular body pressing on her ignited another flame of arousal inside her.

But just as he reached down to unbutton his breeches, a horn sounded from far away. His thick eyelashes pressed against his cheeks in agonized frustration.

"What is it?" she asked breathlessly.

"The hunt. It's about to start." His jaw clenched in angry frustration. "We have to go back."

His silky hair tumbled from his crown and whispered over her forehead. She gazed into his eyes, desperate with unmet need, and caressed his face with both hands. "Not yet," she begged. "There's time."

He kissed her pouty lips. "No. I'm going to take my time with you." He stole one last helpless moment pressed against her through his clothes, and with a grumbled curse, he rose to his feet.

He helped her to stand, and dusted the leaves off her dress before putting on his shirt. He looked so disappointed, and she had so wanted to give him his pleasure. "I'm sorry."

He chuckled. "No more than I," he said, buttoning her dress up in the front. He regarded her long, windblown tresses and the pink blossom in her cheeks, kissed by the frosty wind and suffused with the warmth of passion. "You know, I was wrong," he said, wrapping his arms around her. "There is a greater pleasure than being on a horse at full gallop."

"What?"

"Taking that ride with you."

She smiled, her eyes closed. They clung to each other, and she grew dizzy with the feeling of love and acceptance that his embrace gave her. She would do anything for him at that moment, anything at all, if he promised never to let her go.

A few moments later, they emerged from the copse, she on Bervilia and he walking beside them. From a ways off, they could see a large crowd gathering on the stable cobblestones. Several of the guests had already mounted their horses, and were exercising them around the courtyard.

April suddenly remembered why she had come out to see Riley in the first place. "Er, it seems the entire county is here for the hunt. Are all the guests riding out?"

"Just about, it seems. Damn it all. I was looking forward to the foxhunt a little while ago. Now, all I want to do is finish what we began."

April warmed at the thought, but dispelled the romantic musings from her head. "Which one is the toastmaster?"

"Markham? Oh, he's not due here until Sunday. Parliamentary matters are keeping him in London this weekend." He did not seem to notice April's sigh of relief.

They soon reached the courtyard. Riley, slipping into his role of the consummate host, began to issue last-minute instructions to the grooms. Promising to return to help her dismount, Riley went to fetch Symphony's saddle.

April stared after him, lost in admiration. An ecstatic smile spread across her face, and she bit her lip just to keep herself grounded. What a man! So handsome, so noble, so brilliant, so powerful, so . . . *perfect*. And he wanted *her*. Lord Perfect desired her, and that made her feel feminine, charismatic, beautiful. Although she was no one of consequence, she mattered to him.

And she didn't have to pretend to be someone else anymore. He wanted her in spite of who she was. Maybe even *because* of it.

It emboldened her to dare him to love her.

Maybe one day, she would become Lady Perfect. The thought made her so giddy, she began to hum a tune to hide her excitement.

"My dear," called Lady Agatha, bringing her horse alongside Bervilia. She was the very picture of the feminine equestrian, and April gritted her teeth in irritation. Her riding costume was electric blue, with white swansdown lining every hem. The woman's fashion sense was unimpeachable, and she never failed to make April feel at a marked disadvantage.

"I do hate to sound like a matron aunt," Lady Agatha admonished, "but it is passing unseemly for a woman to ride astride, and even more scandalous that there is nothing between you and the beast. Whatever are you thinking?"

"Lady Agatha, you do not want to know what I am thinking."

"No doubt, my dear. But I daresay Riley has an old saddle you can use. There's no need to ride like an island native. If you don't adopt a more modest appearance, you will not be successful in landing a marriage proposal. Riley!"

April bit back her retort as Lady Agatha trotted toward Riley, who emerged from the stables with a groom carrying an ornately tooled leather sidesaddle.

"Agatha. Good morning," Riley said, bowing his head politely. "How are you today?"

"Very well, thank you," she replied. "It's a marvelous day for a hunt, isn't it?"

"The day has certainly started out well," he said, smiling at April. "Allow me to help you dismount, April."

"Riley, darling," Lady Agatha complained, "I hope you're not planning to start the hunt just yet. I must intercede on April's behalf. Let me take her into the house to comb her hair. She looks as if she's been out farming."

April was spared a response by Riley. "I disagree, Lady Agatha. I think she looks bewitching. In fact, April, I forbid you to change your appearance in the slightest. I never laid eyes on a prettier, healthier-looking English girl. As the poets say, 'Loveliness needs not the foreign aid of ornament, but is when unadorned adorned the most.'"

"Thank you, my lord," she responded, her eyes brightening.

"Et moi?" Lady Agatha asked coquettishly.

Ever the gentleman, Riley offered up a compliment for her as well. *"Vous êtes ravissante.* I am a lucky man to have two such beautiful ladies at my hunt." He took her proffered hand and placed a kiss upon it.

April's blood boiled. There were so many reasons she was angry, it was hard to focus on just one. She didn't know whether to register disgust at Lady Agatha's plea for flattery, or pique at Riley for submitting to that obvious ploy for attention. Or that his compliment of Lady Agatha was so true. Regardless, April now resented Lady Agatha's presupposed claim on the position of Riley's wife. She also regretted their agreement in the library. In hindsight, April had been far too cavalier about her ties to the family. After this morning's astonishing encounter in the forest, she was determined that nothing would separate her from Riley.

Riley helped April onto Symphony. The sidesaddle was terribly uncomfortable, and it made her feel completely insecure. Riley seated his horse, and the huntmaster sounded the horn. The hounds were released, and the company of riders took off behind them.

It did not take long for April to tire of the fox hunt. Aside from the fact that she longed to explore the affection that Riley had for her, she was afraid for the life of the she-fox that had become their target. The pack of dogs chased her relentlessly, and April eagerly hoped she would escape through some inaccessible thicket. Despite April's worry, the fox proved far too swift and clever for the hounds, and she even stopped in mid-chase to hunt down a field mouse before resuming her flight from the yowling dogs. Finally, after nearly an hour's chase, they appeared to lose her scent.

The hunters gathered in a clearing to strategize. The huntmaster decided to split the team into four groups, and scatter them to the four points to pick up the chase once more. April was selected for the West Team along with Riley, and was immensely grateful when Agatha was chosen for the South Team. Lady Agatha pouted prettily and asked the huntmaster to place her on the West Team, because they'd be riding in the direction of the stream and she wanted her horse to water there. April smiled when Agatha's plan backfired; the huntmaster informed her that the river lay to the south.

As their team galloped forth, Riley and April hung back from the rest of the party. Her heart raced for him, and she wondered if he felt the same about her. After their intimacy in the forest, she longed to unmask completely to him. The desire to confess to him about Markham and the others swelled within her. Now she understood why Jenny had revealed her past to William. Honesty seemed to be the first desire of love. His words reverberated through her thoughts: *When will you learn to stop hiding from me?* If he truly loved her, then he would forgive her.

"Why didn't you have me arrested?"

He looked quizzically at her.

"The other night, when I confessed having lied to all of you. You didn't send for the constabulary. Why?"

He drew a long, ponderous sigh. His face became a mask of bronze; only the tightening of his jaw betrayed his humanity.

"I should have, you know. For attempting to defraud my father, I would have been obliged to summon the police. In fact, I myself could get into a lot of trouble for harboring a suspected criminal. By keeping you from the law, I'm jeopardizing my reputation, my judicial seat, my very freedom. I've a thousand reasons to turn you over to the authorities."

It was not the answer she hoped for. "Why don't you?"

His eyes scanned the horizon. "I've given much thought over the last few days to how I would consider your case if it appeared before me in my court. You see, I've always believed that true Justice can never be blind. What does it profit Her if a poor man who stole a loaf of bread is sentenced to death for it? She must be able to see into a man's heart, as well as to weigh a man's deeds. I can sympathize with the circumstances that drove you to your crime. And although I do not condone your actions, in many ways you are like that hungry man with the loaf of bread. When I put myself in your place, I cannot help but wonder if I would not do the same. I don't know that my decision is an act of justice so much as an act of conscience. Perhaps the only thing that has kept me from turning you in was your demonstration of remorse. I believe you. I do hope my trust is not misplaced."

His trust had suddenly become very important to her. "No, Riley. I shudder now to think how I repaid the kindness that Jeremy and Jonah once showed me. I regret betraying their friendship."

"I won't refute the fact that turning you in would not be in our best interest as well. The subsequent trial would implicate this family, and the last thing I want is to launch a scandal. Had this been a graver crime, I would feel absolutely no compunction about doing so. Fortunately for you, your actions have merely been ancillary to a legal transgression, but not the transgression itself. Other than misrepresenting yourself, which caused mental anguish and hardship to my family, an action which would make you civilly liable, you failed to actually extort money from us, which would constitute criminal misconduct. So, having weighed the legal issues in my mind, and knowing what I do of the reasons that contributed to these transgressions, I cannot in good conscience believe Justice would be served if you were remanded to the authorities."

April breathed a sigh of relief.

"Besides," he continued, "I made you a promise to protect you, and I will honor that promise."

She swallowed hard. "I don't know what to say. It would appear I owe you a great deal."

"No. But in the spirit of Justice, just see to it that I never regret the risks I have taken."

April's eyes fell. How could she confess her guilty secret now? Would he be so forgiving if she admitted there were others she had *successfully* defrauded? It would make her a criminal *in fact,* something he didn't know. She believed him when he said he would turn her in, in spite of the damage it would do to the family. He would not be so magnanimous if she told him there had been others. How would his precious Justice regard her if he learned that she had been withholding the entire truth all this time?

And if she confessed that one of her victims was a guest of honor at the ball on Sunday? Good God, Riley would never pardon her then! Promise or no, he'd have her bound and gagged, and send for the law immediately!

And it wasn't the constables she feared anymore, but strangely enough, the thought that she would lose the fragile affection that had begun to blossom between them. She never thought she would feel this way about any man, least of all her archenemy, Riley. So many things had changed.

She wrestled with the decision over whether to trust him completely. No matter how she turned it over in her head, it would not do if he knew about Markham and the others. There was much to be gained by her silence, and too much to lose from her confession.

Better that she just stay away from the ball on Sunday. All else would fall into place.

Wouldn't it?

Ten

AS THE SHADOWS LENGTHENED ON FRIDAY afternoon, Riley stood up from the porcelain bath basin, allowing the water to drip from his body. His valet handed him a towel, and he rubbed it on his head and chest, where his black hair was thickest. He refused the proffered dressing gown, opting instead to wrap the damp towel around his waist. Knowing that the master preferred to shave himself, the valet left the bathing area and went to the wardrobe to lay out Riley's clothes for the evening.

As he lathered his face, his mind wandered for the hundredth time to his interrupted mating with April. God, what he wouldn't give now to have gone through with it, and the consequences be damned! What an extraordinary girl she was. A complete study in contrasts. His hands had told him she was a virgin. But how had she managed to retain her innocence working in a bordello? Even her lips were pure, as if she had never kissed a man with passion. He couldn't get enough of those lips, so uncertain and so seductive at the same time, and he smiled at the taste of honeyed tea that lingered on them. She exuded a kind of distant knowledge of lovemaking, like a country girl who knows how colts are made. It was such an odd mixture of innocence and awareness, and his body responded to it in a way that surprised even him. He felt his manhood threaten to rise from beneath his towel, and he shook his head at the effect the chit had on him.

He stroked the razor across his cheek. She was an original, he'd grant her that. The women of his intimate acquaintance consistently fell into two basic categories: ideals of demure chastity, who later proved to be anything but; or forward jezebels, who took the sport out of the chase. They all seemed so colorless and unexciting, paling in comparison to April. Her expression of ardor was timid but natural, not practiced and artificial like other women attempted in order to incite his passion. It was when she was most herself, thusly, that he was drawn to her the most. Not just with his body, but with his heart.

Her heart was a different story. It was tightly furled and closed off, like a rosebud afraid to blossom. She was so inscrutable, so mysterious. It would be impossible to force the petals open. He would have to seduce them open.

He rinsed the razor in the basin. It was precisely this enigmatic quality that unnerved him so. Even after he exposed her to his father and brother, he could not shake the feeling that she was still hiding something. There was more to this girl than he originally supposed . . . but what?

He frowned. She was an exceptional liar. He hated that about her. She also had nerve and intellect, all of which conspired to make her a highly daring criminal. Not to mention an amazing right-handed punch. But she also had youth and a soft heart, which he hoped would make her tractable and re-educable. Riley prided himself on being a good judge of character, and April had it. He knew it when he summoned her to his office, the morning after she ran away.

He sighed. Half the time he wanted to wrap his hands around her neck, and the other half he wanted to cover it with kisses. It was making him miserable.

He hurled the towel onto the floor. He strode to the bed, his long, muscular legs pounding the carpeted floorboards, and sat down. He thrust his legs into a pair of pristine white stockings and breeches. Next came the white shirtsleeves and gold brocade vest. As the valet began to tie the intricate knot in his cravat, he studied his appearance in the glass.

The more he began to look like the Marquess of Blackheath, the more he began to question the wisdom of pursuing April Rose Jardine. Despite all pretenses, she was not a noblewoman, and never would be by blood. She fell far below his station in the order of things. Not that he could convince his body otherwise. Lady or no, she was exactly what his body craved. But he had to question his intentions toward her. Should he plan to bed her and be done with it—use her as she had used him and his family? It would be no less than she deserved. But his heart was not set on revenge. Retribution was not the sort of satisfaction he sought. He wanted more.

Marriage? He knew the answer to that before he even asked the question. He could never marry her. She was a commoner. There had been many marriages between the gentry and the lower class, and they had seldom been happy ones. But between a peer of the realm and a servant girl? It was unheard of. Hadn't the King himself flown into a rage when his brother married a woman below his station, so much so that he established the Royal Marriages Act to prevent any of his progeny from committing the same grave mistake?

His mind flew to the Queen. Now that he had presented April to the monarch as his ward, he had crafted his own reality. He must now proceed as if April were in fact his ward, and fulfill the duties that would fall to him as her benefactor.

And the greatest of these duties would be to find her a suitable husband. It was, he decided, the wisest course of action for all concerned.

His valet helped him into his elegant black tailcoat, finalizing the attire of the Marquess of Blackheath. The image in the glass was proud, confident, refined. It was the image of a man assured in his every decision. The image reflected who he wanted to be.

But wasn't.

JENNY WAS HELPING APRIL SELECT A DRESS for dinner when they heard a knock at the door.

"Come in."

Susan came in bearing a small tray and a huge smile. "Master Riley sends you a present, miss."

A puzzled grin spread across April's face. On the tray was a jar of multicolored glass. "What is it?"

Susan beamed. "It's a vial of hand cream, miss. Master Riley sent one of the footmen away to London for it special."

April bit her lip, tickled by the considerate gesture. She uncovered the jar. The musky aroma of vanilla and amber rose up to greet her. She took a little of the cold salve in her fingertips and rubbed it between her hands. Her parched skin imbibed its moisture like a desert does rain, making her moan contentedly. Heavenly.

"It's ever s'expensive," Susan commented. "It's got sperm in it."

Jenny gasped in disgust.

April laughed. "She means 'spermaceti.' Whale oil."

Her look of revulsion softened. "Not much better, is it?"

"Here, you try." She took some and smeared it on Jenny's hands.

Jenny rubbed it into her skin. "Smells kind of nice and all."

"Susan, bring me that clean teacup over there." The maid did as April asked, and April poured half of the cream into it. "Here, take this belowstairs, and share it with all the maids."

Susan's eyes expanded. "Oh, no, miss. Master Riley bought this for you."

April squared off on her. "Do as I say. I want every single maid to use this, especially the scullery maids. Is that understood?"

"Yes, miss," she answered automatically, though an enthusiastic smile spread across her face. "Thank you, miss." The diminutive maid left holding the teacup as if it were a priceless Oriental vase.

Jenny recapped the jar and put it on April's dressing table. "Well, 'Master Riley' has certainly taken a shine to you now. How'd you accomplish that?"

April caressed her softened hands against her lips. "Honestly, Jenny, I don't know. I mean, why me? I'm not a ravishing beauty like Agatha. I'm not demure and sweet like Emily. I'm not highborn or wealthy. I haven't even been especially kind to him. Why would someone like him be attracted to someone like me?"

Jenny shrugged. "Remember that painting of Cupid in the hallway back at Madame Devereux's?"

"Yes."

"Did you ever notice that he's got a blindfold on?"

"So?"

"Cor, you can be thick sometimes. What that means is that love is blind. Cupid can't see where he's shootin' his arrows. So love can strike even a strange pair like you two."

April faced the mirror on the vanity.

Love?

◆ ◆ ◆

PETER NORTHAM FITTED THE ARROW IN his bow, and drew back the bowstring. The arrow sliced through the air, and thudded onto the wooden target, landing somewhere inside an outer ring.

Lady Agatha clapped. "Good shot, Mr. Northam."

"Thank you, Lady Agatha." His hazel eyes glowed gratefully.

"I am reluctant to contradict you, Lady Agatha," said Riley, "but I think it was an appallingly bad shot. In case you didn't know, Northam, the idea is to get the arrow to land inside the bull's-eye."

Northam looked askance at Riley. "All right, old boy. You can't brag without proving you can do better. Go on, it's your turn."

"Very well." Riley aligned his black Hessian boots on the toeline. He squared his shoulders, lifted his bow, and pulled taut the bowstring. He glanced at the leaves of a nearby tree, gauging the direction and strength of the wind. Closing one eye, he retargeted his arrow, and released.

The arrow whipped through the air and landed a hairsbreadth inside the bull's-eye.

"Perfect! Well done, Riley!"

Riley beamed, and bowed curtly to Agatha. "There, you see, Northam? That's how it ought to be done."

"Hardly."

"What do you mean?"

"Well, old boy, any simple bowhunter can hit a target at this distance. But a skilled archer gets as far as he can from the target. The distance with which an archer can vanquish his enemy is the measure of his ability."

Riley shook his head. "My friend, the attorney. You always did enjoy the adversarial process more than getting at the truth."

"Which is?"

"That I'm better than you."

Northam laughed jovially. "Then truth is relative, old boy."

From beneath her parasol, Agatha continued to watch them taunt one another. Northam was a handsome man, with an intellectual face and a faultless manner. His sandy hair gleamed in the midday sun like fine gold thread, setting off the caramel-colored coat. He had a casual, friendly air about him, and an easy smile that he offered all too frequently. He would make a fine husband someday.

But not for her.

She looked over at the man who clapped Northam on the back. Her eyes raked down Riley's form. What a beautiful specimen of manhood. He fairly radiated money, the kind that lasts for generations, like a waterfall that never goes dry. The vines of his social connections entwined around every family of significance in Britain. A man with great influence, and with the power to exert it.

Power. Precisely what sparked her desire for him. She was drawn to strength in a man like a compass needle points true north. And with Riley, that allure was much more potent. His body, his mind, his position—all of them screamed *power.* She purred to think what a man like that could do for her if she possessed his heart.

If only she had been wise enough to keep it when she had it.

She cast her mind back to the days when he was nothing but a callow youth, all intellect and no experience. To him, she was beautiful, brazen, seductive, and worldly, all the things he found irresistible. He was romantic, idealistic, and young, and deeply in love with her. She had laughed when he tried to court her, like so many besotted lovers in poems. Those pleasantries were far beneath the jaded circles in which she moved. Back then, as she initiated him into the pleasures of physical love, she was the one with the power—power over him. If only she could have envisioned the man he would become. She had him then where she wanted him now.

And where she would have him once more.

They ordered a footman to move the target twenty yards farther afield. The landscape stretched green as far as the eye could see, all of it Riley's property. She smiled as her eyes scanned the horizon, drinking in the acres in every direction. An erotic tendril of possessive pleasure snaked up from her loins. Until her eyes fell on a figure walking toward them from the house.

April made her way down the walking path. Eight targets had been laid out on the field, and the lawn was filled with small clusters of guests taking part in the archery games. Two large canopies, one on each side of the river, allowed the guests to enjoy refreshments and shade.

Northam was the first to greet her. "Miss Devereux! I hope you are well this day."

"Very well, thank you, Mr. Northam. I apologize for my tardiness. I hope I haven't held up the game."

"Not at all. In fact, Riley and I were just about to make a small wager on who can hit closest to the bull's-eye at fifty yards."

Riley heaved a sigh. "If you say so. Five pounds, then?"

The corner of Northam's mouth lifted. "Not very confident of yourself, are you?"

Riley cocked a black eyebrow. "Ten pounds?"

"I'm averse to taking your money so easily. Not to mention humiliating you in front of the ladies."

April chuckled at their playful exchange. "Aren't you playing, Lady Agatha?"

Agatha tilted her parasol slightly. "No, my dear. Archery

is a man's game. A woman has no practical use for such a sport."

April looked around. There were not many females participating in the games. "Perhaps not. But it looks like fun. Can I take part in the wager, too?"

Lady Agatha shook her head. "Honestly, Miss Devereux, you are an embarrassment to our host. Proper ladies do not wager money on sport."

April raised a defiant chin. "Well, I can't just sit about under an umbrella like an old woman, can I?"

Biting her lips into a narrow red line, Lady Agatha countered politely, "Some ladies choose to avoid becoming as freckled and brown as a dustman. But fear not. A swarthy complexion suits you well, my dear."

Riley tried to contain his laughter long enough to interrupt their quarrel. "Yes, April, you may place a wager on this round. I shall countenance the bet for you."

April flounced over to the quiver and picked up an arrow. "Thank you, Riley, but that won't be necessary. I'm looking forward to collecting ten quid from you."

Agatha bristled. *Riley* and *April,* were they? They weren't on such familiar terms the last time she visited. Perhaps there was more to their relationship than she had originally been led to believe. Watching them now together—the way their eyes met knowingly, how they shared a laugh, how their glances lingered—it was becoming apparent that these two were *not* related. But more importantly, it was clear that there was something deeper brewing between Riley and the impertinent commoner. This would not do.

"Riley, darling, would you accompany me to get a cool drink? The day seems to have turned unseasonably warm."

"Of course, Agatha." He held out his hand to help her stand, and with feline grace, she nestled her arm in his.

Linked, they walked to the canopy. Agatha relished the feeling of him beside her. The muscles beneath his morning coat swelled through the fabric, making her skin tingle. "I must say how refreshing it is to be back at Blackheath Manor."

"My home has always been open to you, Agatha."

"Yes. But now that our siblings are marrying one another, we shall truly become family."

His face stiffened. "If memory serves, I offered you a permanent place in my family long ago."

"Darling, you were too young then. We both were."

Riley closed his eyes. "And yet you married him instead of me."

"You were still at university. You were intent on your studies. And Quincy was more, more—"

"Wealthy?"

"—settled," she finished.

He chuckled cynically. "Those years at university were the hardest. All I could do was think about you. I couldn't wait for summer holidays, when I could come back to you. When I think of all those soppy, sentimental letters I wrote . . . how it must have amused you."

"Darling, you know I'm not maudlin about such things as letters."

He took two glasses of lemonade from the table under the canopy, and handed one to her. "I'll never forget the last correspondence you sent me. An invitation to your wedding."

She gave a small shrug, her nose crinkling. "Oh, darling, you must forget all of that unpleasantness. You know very well the duties of our station. We marry out of necessity and never out of love. You must know that I never loved Quincy. Even as I said my vows, I thought only of you. You were such a strong, passionate lover, and Quincy was . . . well, he wasn't a young man. I certainly didn't expect him to last as long as he did. You can't imagine how difficult these last fifteen years have been for me."

He took a swallow of the tangy drink, and the strong lemon flavor curdled his expression. "As difficult as knowing the woman you loved was in the arms of another man?"

Perhaps it wasn't the drink that curdled his expression after all. Agatha's crystal-blue eyes looked up at him through a curtain of lash. "Riley, don't be so dramatic. You're not still a romantic, are you?"

He heaved a profound sigh. "Not anymore, Agatha. It was your most practical lesson in my education. Love is a misspent commodity of one's time and energy. It's illogical, unreasonable, and fraught with difficulty. It's thanks to you I excelled so much at my studies. I found the law more dispassionate, far less complicated, and infinitely less painful."

"Exactly my point, darling. We are not given to affairs of the heart, you and I. Our brand of love is a fluid thing. It's what's made our relationship so special. And so enduring. Surely you can see how perfect we are for one another. Now that Fortune has given us another chance at a happy life together, please don't throw it away."

She put her hand on his arm, and watched as her words carved their effect on him. His expressions shifted, as conflicting emotions quicksilvered on his face. Finally, he looked at her, resignation reflected in those beautiful absinthe-colored eyes.

"Yes, Agatha, we are ideally matched."

As they made their way back to the group, Agatha hung on his arm possessively, success settling on her face.

Of course, she realized that he still had reservations. She was too shrewd to underestimate his lingering friendship with April. Agatha's victory wouldn't be complete until she obliterated her rival. But for now, she was happy to have snatched the trophy.

Fortune was definitely smiling on her today. As they neared their group, she noticed Northam embracing April. Though his back was turned to them, he had her completely enfolded in his arms.

Riley's pensive eyes were fixed on the ground, and he did not see.

"They make a splendid couple, don't they, darling?"

He looked up from the ground at her, and then followed her gaze in the direction of Northam and April.

He stopped in mid-stride, and Agatha felt his bicep tighten, as if the strength from his entire body were gathering there in his right arm. His jaw clenched, and a look of murderous jealousy stormed over his handsome features.

Just then, Northam stepped to one side, and they saw April with a raised bow. Agatha sensed him relax—a little—as he realized that Northam had just been teaching her how to hold the weapon. Riley recommenced their slow walk, with only a barely detectable quickening of his breath to betray his unraveling anger.

Clearly, thought Agatha, this was more than just a passing infatuation. Much more. "Have you given any thought to April's future?"

"Some," he answered stoically.

"I know scores of eligible bachelors. Would you like me to help you make a match for her?"

"Perhaps later, Agatha."

Even after they rejoined the group, Riley's mood did not lift. Agatha always knew he was irascible and mercurial—and, in that state of mind, very, very dangerous. It was the perfect catalyst for her to make him sever his ties to that girl.

"How about that ten-pound shot now?" Northam pounded him on the back.

"Fine. You first."

Northam stood at the toeline, aimed his arrow with a

look of intense concentration, and fired. The arrow arched gracefully over the field, but it lodged in the ring just outside the bull's-eye.

He groaned, and April giggled. "You've missed the mark again, Mr. Northam. I will not have you tutor me in the skills of archery if you keep this up."

"The fault was not mine, Miss Devereux. The wind tossed it."

"In life, we must allow for such storms. Riley, it's your turn."

His nostrils flared at their chumminess. This was working out better than Agatha had hoped.

Riley plucked an arrow from the quiver and walked to the line. With built-up force, he drew back the bowstring easily, and adjusted his aim. Behind him, Northam whispered something, and April laughed. The arrow loosed.

It flew from the bow in a high arc, but Riley had used too much force. The arrow shot well over the target, missing it completely.

Northam cheered. "It appears you owe me a tenner, old boy."

April stopped him with a raised hand. "Not so fast, Mr. Northam. You're forgetting that I too am in this contest."

"Miss Devereux, are you certain? You are only just learning, and the target is too far for a woman."

April gave him a sidewise smile. "You'd be surprised how well a woman can handle a shaft."

Northam laughed heartily, but Riley was not amused by her vulgar joke. Agatha couldn't contain her delight at seeing how easily April was tangling herself in Riley's displeasure.

She selected an arrow with pretty blue fletching, and stood at the toeline. She fumbled a little with the positioning of the arrow, but finally grasped it as Northam had taught her. Her eye leveled on the target. She drew back the bowstring as hard as she could, and aimed high to allow for a proper trajectory. She released, and the arrow flew true, landing with a *fwump* well within the red circle.

She hooted in excitement, drawing the attention of nearby archers.

"I believe I will collect my twenty pounds now, gentlemen." She beamed, immensely pleased with herself.

Northam reached for his billfold. "I'll never understand the vagaries of beginner's luck."

"Nor I," added Riley.

"May I demonstrate my good sportsmanship by getting the winner a cool drink?" Northam asked, offering his arm to her.

"You may indeed."

THE PAPER MONEY IN HER HAND FELT AS cool as the lemonade that poured down her throat, each delicious in its own way.

Northam drained his glass. "You and Riley have certainly gotten on. Do I detect a budding romance? I'm not trying to pry, mind you, but Riley and I are old friends, and I care a great deal about him."

April looked down. "We are friends, nothing more."

"The color in your cheeks tells me otherwise."

The heat rose in her face. "Let us just say that I care about him, too."

He raised a blond eyebrow. "How delightfully surprising. Does he feel the same about you?"

April had been hoping someone could answer that question for her. "I believe so. Tell me, Mr. Northam, as Riley's friend, do you think that I am . . . the sort of woman that he would fancy?"

His handsome face smiled down at her. "If you're not, then he's a bigger fool than I already believe him to be."

She grinned humbly at the compliment.

"If Riley *has* developed feelings for you, he hasn't yet confided in me. But I think I can set your heart at ease by telling you this: I've known Riley since we were boys, and there are only two ways that he could possibly miss that shot. The first would be if a hurricane suddenly passed over Blackheath Manor and blew the arrow away. And the second, I've just learned, is if he is distracted by you."

Something inside her fluttered. "Thank you, Mr. Northam, for your shared confidence. And for teaching me to shoot. Your tutelage has certainly proven profitable," she crowed, holding up her winnings.

He smiled genuinely. "The student has surpassed the instructor. Next time, I shall be much more judicious in the lessons I teach you."

They walked out from under the canopy, nodding to a couple of guests who had come in for some shade. As they started back toward their spot, she noticed with pique that Agatha was sitting closely beside Riley on the bench. Too close.

"I wonder, Miss Devereux, if you would allow me the honor of a dance tomorrow?"

"Mr. Northam!" she exclaimed in reproof.

His genial smile gleamed in the sun. "I know what you're thinking. You're thinking what a shameless, amoral reprobate I am, and you're absolutely right. I am a lawyer, and therefore admit to having no scruples to speak of. But Riley and I have always been fierce competitors, and I would never forgive myself if I did not at least attempt to win your affections from him."

April rolled her eyes, disguising the fact that she was secretly pleased by his interest. Even though she was not going to the ball, the fact that he wanted a place on her dance card flattered her. "You are indeed amoral, sir. I am not some prize to be won."

Northam stopped walking, turning to face her. "Oh, but you are. Quite a lovely prize. You just don't know it yet."

She blushed. "Mr. Northam, please—"

The smile ran away from his face. "I know in the eyes of the world, Riley is a much worthier marriage prize than I could ever be. But in *our* humble circles, love counts for a great deal more than it does in his. I would like a chance to see if that is indeed true of you and me."

She shifted in embarrassment. "Mr. Northam, in light of what I just told you, you know it would be inappropriate."

"Yes, I do. But equally I know that living by the rules is no way to get ahead in life. Surely *you* can understand that."

She nodded. "I understand. Nevertheless, we can't be untrue to our principles."

"Principles, like rules, can be flexible. One dance."

She found that smile irresistibly charming. But she would never allow anyone to come between her and Riley. "If circumstances had been different, I would have loved to. But—"

"Please don't say no. Surely, if someone like Lady Agatha can accord me one dance, then you can."

That tore it. Her buttery flattered mood chilled. "I think it would be inadvisable, Mr. Northam. I am, how does one say, out of your league."

His smile dissolved, draining his face of any human expression. "You cut me deeply, Miss Devereux."

She was unmoved. "You're right about one thing. Agatha seems much more the sort who would welcome a gentleman's attentions, and by the look of her, any gentleman will do."

His hazel eyes grew flinty at April's veiled insult, and his face deadened to a cold mask. "The *lady* you speak of is an exceptional woman and a diamond of the first water. Her beauty and goodness are unsurpassed in the realm of the female. I have had the privilege of calling myself her ardent devotee for some time now, and I know her well enough to know that she truly is 'out of my league.'"

April looked down the path to the bench where they were seated. Agatha laughed prettily, and unseen by the other guests, her hand slid onto Riley's thigh. His *upper* thigh, to be exact.

"Where women are concerned, Mr. Northam, your powers of discrimination require a great deal of refinement."

She stomped over to a nearby grouping of archers and seized a bow and arrow. She took aim and let the arrow fly.

It whooshed through the air and embedded itself in the bench—right between Agatha's legs. She screamed, the shaft quivering between her thighs like an erect phallus. Riley looked in the direction the arrow had come from, and his gaze locked on April. He returned his attention to Agatha, hysterically trying to remove the arrow without touching it. With a firm yank, he dislodged it from the bench.

"Oh! I've never been so humiliated in all my life! Just look at my beautiful dress!"

He crooked his finger in April's direction, beckoning her. "Did you shoot this?" he said, holding up the arrow.

She stood before him, her arms crossed in front of her. "It slipped."

Agatha turned her full fury on April, grinding out every word. "Of all the evil, wicked, criminal— Riley, I demand that you arrest this, this . . . murderer!"

Riley shook his head. "Agatha, please calm yourself."

"How can you tell me to calm myself when that malefactor tried to kill me?"

He turned his most scolding look upon April. "I want you to apologize to Lady Agatha this instant."

"Apologize?" Agatha cried incredulously. "She nearly skewered me!"

April chuckled, but reined in her merriment. "I was just trying to ventilate your dress. It seemed to me that things were getting a bit hot down there."

Riley tried valiantly to keep from laughing, but the corners of his mouth lifted against his will.

Northam flew to Agatha's side. "This is outrageous! Riley, I demand that you take matters in hand!"

Riley cleared his throat and regained his angry composure. "April, apologize immediately."

She looked away. "I'm sorry I missed."

"April!" he scolded. "If I have to tell you again, I'll break this shaft across your backside!"

Her lips thinned. "Fine. I apologize for shooting your dress."

Agatha's eyes narrowed to vengeful slits. "You're not sorry, but you will be, pet. You haven't heard the last from me. No one treats me like that, least of all a conniving little bitch like you. Count your days, Miss Devereux, for you won't enjoy them long."

She stormed off, with Northam close behind.

Riley shook his head wearily. "Was that really necessary?"

"No," she answered, "but it really felt good."

His laughter rolled across the lawn. "Hellcat! You'd better learn to control that temper of yours around Lady Agatha. She can be very vindictive when she wants to be."

"Well, she gets up my nose." April lifted a defiant chin. "And up your leg, I noticed, but it didn't seem to bother you half as much."

"Jealous?"

She folded her arms. "No," she said, but the statement lacked the conviction she hoped for.

He laughed again. "Look, I need you on your best behavior for the rest of this weekend. We have four hundred people driving in for the ball tomorrow, and you, my sweet, are the main attraction. Now promise me there will be pax between you and Agatha."

Her lighthearted mood was quickly overcast by the ominous danger the ball represented. She needed to find a way out.

Eleven

WHERE ONCE THERE WAS ANTICIPATION, April now looked forward to the Minister's Ball with a sense of foreboding and dread. With each passing hour, as the miles shortened between Sir Cedric Markham's carriage and Blackheath Manor, April felt the weight of impending doom grow heavier. Though her fevered mind explored every option, she could not imagine a way to remain in the same house with the man who could reveal the full measure of her crimes. Even if she wanted to hide, there was no place to go; the entire manor was overflowing with people. She simply had no choice: she must leave Blackheath Manor until the danger passed.

As she removed her valise from the wardrobe and filled it with a few days' worth of clothes, her mind turned to the memory of her flowering relationship with Riley. What was happening to her? He was having an effect on her that she found unsettling . . . but deliciously delightful. Their lovemaking in the woods was a complete revelation, and she marveled at his tenderness.

And skill. She sighed. Her body had been like a musical instrument, resonating harmoniously at the touch of his masterful fingers. The experience left her with a craving that she found unbearable. Now, being in his company was nothing but a sweet torture. Even in the most innocuous situations, her mind quickly leapt at fantasies of them in all sorts of passionate embraces. High tea this afternoon was a torment for her, as she played out in her head a different sort of ending to their riding session. It was all she could do to keep her weakened fingers from dropping her cup.

She scribbled a note for Riley and left it on the mantel. She hoped he would forgive her this one last act. Since the fox hunt, all she could think about was the way he made her feel: beautiful, desirable, safe. The image of his face in her hands leapt to her mind, and she felt a tug on her heart. *One day, I'll explain everything,* she communicated to the note on the mantel, as if the apology would somehow become imprinted on it. She went downstairs to fetch Jenny.

RILEY WAS IN THE KITCHENS INSPECTING the progress on the evening's dinner. The servants were all bustling, but surprisingly not in each other's way, moving about with a practiced precision that never failed to impress him. He took great pride in the diligence with which they exercised their functions, and he decided that he would give bonuses to all of them when this weekend was over.

Closing the arched wooden door on the kitchen, he made his way down the basement corridor that served as a cold room. Having shut out the din of the kitchen, the only sounds he now heard were his own footsteps on the stone floor. But his ears picked up a second set of footfalls, and he looked up to see someone coming down the stairs at the far end.

"April," he remarked out loud, not unmindful of the lightness of mood that he experienced. Dressed in a light green frock with her long brown curls gathered loosely at her crown, she looked like a long-stemmed wildflower.

She seemed surprised to see him. "Riley! I didn't expect to see you here," she breathed, flushing noticeably.

"Nor I you. I thought you'd be upstairs getting ready for the ball. What are you doing down here?" He couldn't wait to see what she looked like in her gown.

He drew up in front of her, with only the stone balustrade between them. She had stopped a few steps from the bottom, so her eyes were at a level with his.

"Um, I was looking for Jenny. I know that she's been helping out a great deal readying tonight's meal."

"I'll have her sent to your room. Is everything all right?"

"Of course," she responded nervously. "Why wouldn't it be?"

"No particular reason. I just wanted you to feel at ease tonight. I presume this is your first ball?"

She nodded.

"There's nothing to it, really. Just a bit of dancing, a bit of drinking, and a lot of useless persiflage. Usually, in that order." He smiled, revealing a row of white teeth that glowed even in this darkened corridor. "If you're nervous, don't be. Your part is very simple. I'll introduce you about, present you to all the right people, and all you have to do is make a bit of small talk. They'll be curious, naturally, and they'll ask indirect questions about your relationship to me. If you keep your answers brief, and try not to embellish too much, we should be able to convince everyone that you're only my ward and not my half sister. If you do your job properly, the evening won't end in catastrophe and you won't ever have to endure any more of these uncomfortable situations again."

She nodded stiffly.

"We have much to accomplish tonight, but I have every faith in you. You'll do a fine job." Her hand was gripping the top of the stone balustrade, and he covered it reassuringly with his own.

She looked down at his hand. Impulsively, he retracted it. A little too obviously.

"Riley," she began uncertainly, "if you and I hadn't met the way we did . . . if we had met, say, on the street, do you think we would have . . . you know?"

He looked down at his polished boots. "I don't know. Perhaps not. We move in different circles, you and I. It's unlikely that we would have met at all, actually. It's just not the sort of association that Society encourages."

She pursed her mouth. "I see."

"You know, April," he said, "I've been giving a lot of thought to our encounter the other day, before the fox hunt."

She mirrored his knowing look. "So have I."

"And I want to you to know that I behaved rather foolishly."

The smile ran away from her face.

"It was wrong of me to take advantage of you like that, and I hope that I didn't frighten you in any way."

Her neck became rigid. "No," she responded stiffly. "Did I frighten you?"

A half smile touched his lips. "No. But now that we have represented ourselves to Society as ward and protector, we should probably adhere to those roles. And as your protector, I would be very distraught if I felt that I had jeopardized your trust in my protection."

She did not respond. Riley sighed heavily. "Please don't for a second mistake my meaning. You're a beautiful girl, and I find you completely intoxicating. But it would not be fair to you. There will be many fine gentlemen in search of a wife at the ball. And you stand a greater chance of winning a husband if you are . . . unsullied."

April blinked. "Winning a—what?"

He gulped. "As your protector, it is my duty to see you married off to an eligible—"

"Married *off*? So I'm to be . . . what? Hawked to your

guests as a potential bride? Auctioned off to the highest bidder?" The memories of the Madame's ultimatum came rushing back to her, her maidenhead for sale. "Is that why you want me to attend the ball?"

"Of course not."

"Are you trying to get rid of me?" Her lip trembled.

Concern marred his face. "Damn it, April, you know you can't stay here."

A tear sprang to her eye. "Too bloody right!" She took off back up the stairs.

He caught up with her on the first landing. "April, wait! You misunderstand me. What I mean is, you and I... *shouldn't* love each other. We're too different. We... would not suit."

She turned on him. "You'll have to pardon me, my lord, but I'm only a poor, dumb servant girl. Is that a marquess's way of saying he's too good for the likes of me?"

Her sarcasm made it obvious that she was more perspicacious than he had supposed. On her lips, the truth made him feel small.

Agatha's words echoed in his head. "We marry out of necessity, and never out of love. I have responsibilities to my family name. It is a point of honor, nothing more. You cannot understand the difficulties placed on those of my station."

Her eyes narrowed on him. "Ooh, you *are* an insufferable snob! Don't you dare lecture me on the difficulties of station! You've never had to root through other people's garbage looking for something to eat. Or spend an entire winter sleeping on the kitchen floor because it was the warmest place in the house. Or sleep with one eye open because your father's friends are over for a boozer and he's too drunk to care about protecting you. You sit here in this... this palace, with your belly full and your mind at ease, unconcerned with the constant worry of how to survive, let alone advance in life, and you're going to lecture me on *difficulties*? You'll forgive me, my lord, if I don't care this much about your sad lot in life. And as for your notions of marriage, I advise you to take a good, hard look at your own father. You're both cut from the same cloth, you are. Too proud to look down your nose, even if it's to gaze at a woman who cares for you. Well, the devil can have you both!"

She swung something at his head. Fortunately, he saw it and ducked. The valise struck the stone wall behind him and broke open, spilling its contents onto the steps.

He seized her from behind, lifting her off the ground, gripping her wrist tightly until the empty valise fell from her weakened fingers.

"Let me go," she shouted, but he held her fast. She fought him valiantly, righteous indignation fueling her spirit. "Let me go, I said!"

"As soon as you stop trying to split my skull open."

"You need it, you arrogant brute. Maybe it'll let some of the hot air out of that overinflated head of yours!" She bucked her legs in the air, and landed him a solid kick at his shins.

"Ow! I'm warning you, stop kicking me, or you'll be very sorry."

"I'm already sorry. Sorry I ever met you." Weakened by self-pity, the fight slowly left her. Angry tears burned at her eyes, but she refused to betray the emotion.

"That's better," he said, and set her down roughly. She lost her balance and her behind landed solidly on the third step up from the landing.

He bent down and picked up the open valise. "What's this? Going somewhere?"

"Yes. As far away from you as I can get!"

Her cutting remark stung him. "You'll get your wish soon enough. But not tonight."

Her chest rose and fell in deep breaths. "I regret to

inform you, Lord Blackheath, that I shan't be attending the gathering tonight."

"What?"

"I ain't going to your bloody ball!"

"You damn well will," he said, squaring up on her. "I'll thank you to remember—"

"My place?" she shot up at him, one eyebrow cocked.

"—our arrangement," he finished impatiently. "My memory tells me that in exchange for my protection, you agreed to two conditions only: attend the ball, and give me Vivienne's diary. So far, you have done neither."

"Well, I don't want your protection anymore. I want nothing to do with you."

"Well, that is a shame, my sweet, as you have assured your place in this house when you became such good friends with the Queen."

"I don't care."

"I do. People are whispering all over England that my father is housing a bastard daughter. Now I intend to silence all the scandalmongers once and for all. And like it or not," he said as he hauled her to a standing position, "you are going to do exactly as you promised and give credence to our little fiction."

"You don't need me. Rumors die down. People forget."

"*I* don't forget, especially not promises. Mine or yours. This is not a request, April. It is a command."

"Command? You don't own me!"

The air nearly steamed from the heat of his irritation. "While you are my responsibility, I own the very air you breathe."

Her chin jutted up defiantly. "And if I don't comply?"

"You have no choice in the matter."

"Oh, don't I?" she said, showing him the full extent of her bravado. "Yours is not the only fiction that can be given credence to."

His scowl blackened. "If you're threatening to sabotage me, I advise you to school yourself. I assure you that you will regret it to the end of your days. And I, unlike you, do not make idle promises." He manacled her wrist in a fist of steel and dragged her toward the kitchens.

"Where are you taking me?" she called out to him, but her cries fell on deaf ears. He opened the heavy wooden door effortlessly, and quickly spotted his footman William. He ordered him to fetch Jenny, who was trimming candles, and follow him up to Miss April's bedchamber.

William hurried off to do the master's bidding and Riley pulled April behind him as he made his way up the three flights of stairs to her floor.

When they finally reached her door, Jenny and William were almost there.

Riley pointed at Jenny. "I want you to help this creature get ready for tonight. Make her understand that in whatever state of dress she's in, she will be downstairs to receive our guests in exactly one hour's time."

He turned his attention to William. "I want you to stand guard outside this door. If she so much as sets one foot outside this room before the appointed time, you are to notify me immediately. Do you understand?"

"Yes, my lord," they said in unison.

"And as for you," he said, narrowing his eyes on her. "Don't even think of crossing me tonight. My existence in your life may be abhorrent to you now, but it will be nothing compared to what will happen if you disobey me. If you're a good girl and behave yourself, maybe you'll catch the eye of some nice young man and you'll be free from the torment of my protection. But while you fall under that protection, you will do exactly as I say. Is that clear?"

If she could shoot daggers from her eyes, he'd be skewered from head to toe.

"I said, is that clear?"

She ground her teeth. "Perfectly."

He turned and walked away, pulling at his shirt cuffs. She stuck her tongue out at his retreating back.

"Next time you do that, I'll wash your mouth out," he said without even looking.

Surprised and mortified, she opened her bedchamber door and slammed it shut behind her.

APRIL PACED ABOUT THE WIDE ROOM LIKE a caged tiger.

"Of all the insufferable, arrogant, conceited blackguards in the world, why on earth did I have to wind up at the mercy of the most self-righteous and lordly one of them all? If I'm under his protection, who in blazes is going to protect me from him? Lord Blackheath . . . they should have called him Lord Blackhearted! Do you know what he had the nerve to tell me?"

"I don't care," Jenny replied, dipping her hand in the now cold bathwater. "We need to get you in the tub. Hurry up!"

"Don't tell me he's got you jumping around? You're not scared of Lord What's-his-name, are you?"

"Come on, give us your frock."

"No! I'm not doing what he says." April threw herself on the bed and crossed her arms.

"April!"

"No! When he sees I'm not dressed, he'll let me stay in my room."

Jenny crossed her arms in front of her. "Not bloody likely. Didn't you see the state he was in? He was fit to kill, that one."

"Ha! Nothing but the bluster of a big, oafish bully."

"April, you're flirtin' with danger, you are. I don't need to remind you what that 'bully' is capable of. If I were you, I'd do as he says."

She jumped off the bed, and stomped over to the window. "He thinks he's so bloody superior." She raised the pitch of her voice, mocking him. *"We move in different circles! We would not suit! My station is so bloody difficult!* Pluck a duck!"

Jenny stood with her mouth agape. "April Rose Jardine, are you in love with Master Riley?"

April spun around. "Certainly not! What a disagreeable thought!"

Jenny started laughing. "You are!"

"I am not!"

Jenny fell upon the bed in hysterics. "I never thought I'd live to see the day. The Dustbin Duchess and the Marquess of Blackheath! You outrank him at that!"

April rolled her eyes in disgust.

Wiping her face, Jenny sat up. "I mean, what are you thinking? Imagine, a girl like you with a man like him!"

"Not you as well? What's so bloody incredible about that?"

Jenny stabbed the air with her finger. "Ha! Got you! You do love him!"

"Oh, sod off!"

There was a knock at the door. Jenny went to open it.

William stuck his head in. "Sorry. I heard a lot of yelling in here. Is everything all right?"

"Depends on who you're asking about," Jenny replied.

"Eh?"

"April is fine—now. But she won't be for long if she goes through with this death wish of hers."

"Sorry, I don't follow."

"She won't get dressed."

"Oh, I see. Well, if you don't mind my saying so, miss, you're behaving very selfishly."

April whirled upon him. "I beg your pardon?"

"Master Riley has seen fit to take you under his wing,

and present you at a fancy party like this, and you won't even have the courtesy to get ready for it. That's selfish in my book."

April rolled her eyes heavenward. "Men!"

"If you don't mind my saying so, miss, you ought to be ashamed of yourself. Master Riley's a fine, upstanding man, and those of us who work for him are right proud to serve him. I've never met a more noble gentleman or a wiser soul. I'd do anything he asked me to do, because I know that he always has everyone's best interests at heart. I know that like all men, he has his failings and imperfections," he said, turning to face Jenny, "and like many men, he's proud to a fault. I'm sure that if he wronged you, he's very sorry about it, and he wishes he could fix it so that he never hurt you. Because it really doesn't matter who you are, or what you've done in the past. All that matters is what you do now and tomorrow. None of us has the power to change who we've been, only who we're going to be. And if you let me, Jenny, I'll be the man for you, the one who'll make sure you never get hurt by anyone again. If you let me, I'll love you always." He took her hand and placed an earnest kiss on it.

Jenny took his hand and kissed it. "Yes, Will, yes."

THE TRAFFIC AT THE RECEPTION LINE had slowed to a trickle, and the hall was swollen with guests. Riley lifted his watch from his pocket and glanced at it. The chit was ten minutes late for their appointed time.

Jonah leaned in. "Where in blazes is that firebrand?"

Riley shook his head in frustration at his father's favorite epithet for her. " 'April,' Father. She has a name."

His nostrils flared. "Not to me, she doesn't. I apologize, my boy. You were right about her all along."

"I'm still right about her. She's worthy of your forgiveness."

"Forgiveness?" he asked incredulously. "She's a thief, a liar . . . the biggest felon unhung."

"She's also a human being."

His father muttered something under his breath, which Riley was only too happy to ignore. He wished that there would be peace between his father and April, but he knew that it would take time. Vaguely, he remembered his decision to marry her off, and his irritation intensified to the point of alarm. He excused himself from the receiving line, and went to fetch her.

It took some time to jostle his way through the packed hall. When he finally reached the foot of the grand stairs, he looked up at the topmost step.

It couldn't be her.

But it was.

His breath caught in his throat as she began her slow descent. Her dress was a brilliant white, and it cascaded down the length of her body. The gold thread woven through the fabric sparkled in the candlelight. Her breasts curved over the low neckline, which was trimmed in a delicate gold braid, as was the long white train that followed her down. The short scalloped sleeves puffed out at her shoulders, floating above long white gloves. Her hair was a riot of brown curls arranged ornately atop her head. And her face . . .

She rested her silk-slippered feet on the step just above his, a look of expectant hesitation stamped on her features.

"Do I meet with your approval?"

He answered out of pure reflex. "You dazzle me."

A smile broke free of her apprehensive expression. "Thank you."

His eyes drank in the vision of her loveliness. She was like a painting that was far too valuable to be priced. The thought of her as another man's wife punched him painfully again, and it was becoming increasingly hard to recover from those blows.

"Wait. Something isn't quite right."

"What is it?" She looked puzzled.

"You look too . . . too perfect."

She blushed, clearly pleased by the compliment. He reached up and pulled a ringlet from its place, and let it cascade down the side of her face.

"That's better. I prefer you thus."

"Imperfect?" she offered.

"Just so."

She smiled at him, and he found himself hungering for the touch of those soft pink lips on his own. He stepped to one side, and put out his arm. They descended together, and all eyes turned to follow them.

The room grew progressively quieter as Riley escorted April to meet the guest of honor.

"Prime Minister," Riley began, "may I present Miss April Rose Devereux, my ward. April, this is the Right Honorable Spencer Perceval."

"A pleasure," he said, bowing ceremoniously over her hand.

The Prime Minister of England was bowing before *her*, April Rose Jardine, the Right Honorable Nobody of Whitechapel, London. "The honor is mine, sir."

"Blackheath tells me that you helped him arrange the ball this year. My compliments . . . and my gratitude."

"He is too kind, Prime Minister. I am incapable of imagining the grandeur and spectacle of this kind of social event. He is the one who deserves our gratitude, not I. The only part I play is in joining him to pay tribute to you here tonight."

"I am in your debt. May I present the Dowager Baroness Marsby."

The older lady was dressed in the modern Grecian style,

but in a fabric more befitting an earlier day. In style and manner, she exuded an ostentatious wealth. "How very nice to finally meet you. I have heard so much about you."

"Oh? I did not think I was important enough to be remarked about."

"Nonsense. You're quite the *on-dit* of Almack's."

"Really? In what way, Lady Marsby?"

"Well, I've heard only the most flattering things," the older woman said. "I'd been told that Riley had a new, er, addition to his household."

April looked at Riley, whose face was expressionless. But his eyes spoke volumes as he waited to hear how April would respond. She discovered that she relished seeing his silent anguish. Against her will, she had initially allowed herself to be pleased by his flattery. But she remembered his intended mission for the night—to see her married off— and the compliment lost its flavor. Clearly to him, she was finally beautiful enough for someone else. She returned her gaze to Lady Marsby.

"Do you know, Lady Marsby, I shudder to think where I should be if it were not for Lord Blackheath. Since my own father went overseas and left me in the care of Lord Blackheath, he has proven himself a most noble and worthy benefactor. If it were not for Lord Blackheath, you might very well find me scrubbing and polishing floors."

"Now, April," Riley said through a forced chuckle, "don't exaggerate so." Only April heard the warning in his voice.

And she took great pleasure in ignoring it. "Oh, but it's true, my lord. As your ward, I am not too proud to admit that I am deeply beholden to you for your protection. If it were not for the embrace of that protection, I might find my maidenly honor compromised at the hands of any reprehensible rogue." She threw him a knowing look that revisited their intimate morning on the horse.

"Yes, I am a force to be reckoned with," he said through clenched teeth, the flash of green fire in his eyes sending back a warning.

"Good lad," remarked the Prime Minister. "One can't be too careful with such a pretty, young thing as Miss Devereux."

"And my own dear father will reward you amply when he returns from his trip abroad."

"Do I know your father, Miss Devereux?" asked Lady Marsby.

"I dare not think you do. We are not an aristocratic family, you understand. My father is a businessman, and his commerce takes him all over the world. Presently, his return has been delayed in His Majesty's island colonies."

"I do hope his detainment is not for reasons of health," said the Prime Minister, offering a glass of champagne to April from a passing salver.

April took a sip. "No, thank goodness. He is enjoying excellent health at the moment. His delay is due to an unexpectedly sluggish harvest of . . . of sugar. He writes that he will be returning to England very soon, and then we'll no doubt be leaving for the Orient."

"The Orient? Why so far?" asked Lady Marsby.

"Papa has always indulged a fondness for the exotic, and India has always held a certain mystique for him. Under your leadership, Prime Minister, Britain seems to have a presence in a great many nations the world over. Perhaps my father's ambition is to know them all." The Prime Minister and Lady Marsby laughed politely. "Still, I pray that he returns to England swiftly, for I fear that I may have overstayed my welcome under Lord Blackheath's wing."

Riley smiled stiffly. "I think what Miss Devereux means is that she has tired of my unwavering supervision. She has begun to chafe at the restrictions I must place upon her.

No doubt her eagerness to leave for the Orient stems from a desire to live under less dictatorial circumstances."

His lordly attitude rankled her. "Indeed, I would rather live under an Oriental despot than an English tyrant."

The men shared a laugh at her expense, and it irritated her to no end.

Lady Marsby interceded. "I can certainly sympathize with your circumstances, Miss Devereux, a plight that must be compounded by living in a house with no less than three men. But tell me, do you not sense any impropriety at this arrangement? I do not mind admitting that at Almack's, we have often wondered at the unseemliness of an unmarried woman living with three single gentlemen."

April grew defensive. "I do hope the ladies at Almack's do not mean to impugn my honor, or indeed that of the duke?"

"Not at all. But it has been observed that if you and the duke were related, Society might consider that your living arrangements met with the standards of decency..."

Lady Marsby was good, April noted. The baroness was clearly baiting her. But she would not get by April today.

"People may govern a society, Lady Marsby, but Society must never govern people. A woman of your intelligence should know better than to subscribe to the waves of prevailing opinion."

Lady Marsby grew flustered, unable to respond to such a double-edged compliment.

"Indeed," April continued, "I seem to recall reading a scurrilous piece of gossip about you in the *Morning Post* involving a liaison with a decidedly younger man, but I dared not believe it. I have always held fast the unyielding belief that gossip and truth are not natural bedfellows."

Aghast, the corners of the Lady Marsby's mouth were drawn low, as if lead weights were attached to them. Riley stepped in.

"Lady Marsby, while you clearly have Miss Devereux's best interests in mind, please accept my personal assurance that she is perfectly safe in our keeping. We are not unaware of the principles of gentlemanly comportment, nor unmindful of the integrity of her reputation. She is accompanied by an abigail at all times; however, at a formal function such as this one, you are correct in observing that she lacks impartial supervision. I therefore entreat you to do us the honor of serving in the role of her chaperone during the ball. It would do much to put my mind at ease, and April's honor would be vouchsafed, countenanced by your presence."

April's expression was livid, but he ignored it. They took their leave, and Riley escorted her to meet some more of his guests.

As they walked together, she took the opportunity to hiss at him, "What are you on about, leaving me to be guarded by that ogre?"

"That 'ogre' is one of the lady patronesses of Almack's," he muttered. "What she believes is what Society knows. And I want her to know we're unafraid of scrutiny."

"I don't want to spend the rest of the evening with 'er breathing down my back."

"You had it coming. I told you not to embellish so much. Now behave yourself!" They were quickly beset by a group of four dandies, who came to pay their respects.

And so it went. With single-minded determination, Riley continued to parade her in front of the other guests. April spent the better part of the evening repeating the same story to everyone they met. At first, she found it exciting to be acquainted with the crème de la crème of Society, people whom she had only read about in *Debrett's Peerage* or in the scandal pages of the *Morning Post*. And it was doubly exhilarating that everyone who met her still didn't *know* her. She could be anyone she wanted to be, say practically anything she wanted to, and they wouldn't know one way or the other.

But after a while, she grew tired of trying to convince people of the veracity of her tale, especially the less gullible. And as if that weren't exhausting enough, she continued to scan the faces in the crush of people, looking for Markham, because when she found him, she must at all costs avoid him. Fortunately, he didn't seem to have arrived. April fervently hoped he had met with some benign tragedy.

For the hundredth time, April turned her attention to the dance floor. The music was gay and sweet, and the floor was filled with couples whirling about in synchronized movement to the music. Restive, April yearned to join them. What was more surprising, she longed to dance with Riley. He had such an elegant, athletic body, and she couldn't help wondering what it would be like to twirl around the floor with him. But she quickly put the thought out of her head, adamantly resolute that after tonight, she would never speak to him again.

She heard Riley laugh as he parted from Northam, who had come to congratulate him on such a well-stocked spirits table.

"I'll inform Forrester to keep you away from it for the rest of the evening," Riley jibed.

"You haven't got enough servants, old boy," he returned, clapping him on the shoulder.

Riley smirked as he continued toward the next cluster of people, but April's fingers slipped from the crook of his elbow. He turned around, and saw April, stiff as a post, her face white as alabaster. If it weren't for the rich brown of her hair, anyone would have mistaken her for a Greek statue.

"What is it?" he asked, but her gaze was fixed on a point beyond him. He turned, but could see nothing that would startle her so.

"April, what's wrong?"

She took a labored breath. Viscount Earnshaw! Here she was afraid of running into Markham, and she hadn't even contemplated the fact that the other men she blackmailed might also be attending the ball!

"I—I'm not feeling well, Riley. Perhaps a breath of fresh air will help?"

Riley looked concerned. "Certainly. Come with me." He escorted her toward one of the ceiling-high doors that led to the balcony.

As soon as they neared it, April skidded to a stop. Dear God, it was the Marquess of Clarendon! She had taken five hundred pounds from him! Four hundred people in this bloody place, and she had almost run into not one but *two* of the men she swindled.

She turned around just as Clarendon called out to Riley. Without waiting for Riley, she briskly walked to the far end of the ballroom, her head growing dizzier with each step.

She flung open the doors to the West Balcony, grateful that no one was there, and leaned over the railing to steady herself. She fought for breath. Though the breeze was chilly, it did nothing to cool the burning in her face.

Trapped. She looked over the balustrade; if she jumped onto the hedges below, she might break her neck. But better that than have to go back into the ballroom.

However many people were at this ball, there was no way she could avoid running into *two* of the men she blackmailed. Earnshaw and Clarendon would recognize her. She shuddered to think what would happen if they both recognized her at the same time. There was nothing for it. She simply had to get away. But how?

Riley stole up behind her. "Are you all right?"

"I've suddenly come over very strange. Would it be all right if I went up to my room for a bit?"

Riley gave her a sidewise glance. "April, if this is one of your tricks . . ."

"No, Riley. Just a quick lie-down. Five minutes, I promise. Really." That's how long it would take her to change her clothes and sneak away through the stables.

He eyed her suspiciously. "You know, I've been watching you for so long, I can tell when you're lying. And you're doing it right now."

April heaved an exasperated sigh. "I'm not! I just need some time alone."

Riley looked at her through knitted brows. "Not until you tell me what's going on!"

April stomped down the length of the darkened balcony. She turned around to face him. He stood at the opposite end from her, bathed in the light from the ballroom, an impatient look of worry etched on his face. As she stood in darkness, she debated whether to trust him. There were two men in there who could have her thrown in prison; she couldn't afford to make another enemy in the person of the man in front of her. She would need his help if she was to get through that throng safely. She had to tell him something, even if it meant that he would never trust her again. He was planning to get rid of her anyway, she decided, unable to ignore the ache in her heart, so essentially, she had nothing to lose.

"Riley," she began tremulously, her thumbnail pressing against her teeth, "I have a confession to make."

"Blackheath, there you are!" He turned to face the voice that called from the open door. A voice that sounded lamentably familiar to April.

"Markham! I was afraid something had happened to you."

"Dreadfully sorry, my lord, I was buried in a pile of paperwork, and it was all I could do to dig my way out in time."

"Remind me to petition the House to purchase you a larger shovel."

"Indeed, thank you." The older man laughed.

"Sir Cedric Markham, may I present my ward, Miss April . . ."

Riley's voice trailed off when he noticed April feverishly trying to turn the locked doorknobs to the other two sets of doors leading back to the ballroom.

Massive potted holly bushes, freckled with red berries, lined the wide balcony. April darted behind one of them and waved at him. "How do you do?"

Puzzled, Riley continued. "April, this is Sir Cedric Markham, Clerk of the Parliaments."

Ever the gentleman, Sir Cedric walked down the length of the balcony, his bony hand outstretched. "I'm very pleased to meet you, Miss—"

He stopped suddenly. He adjusted the spectacles on his nose, and peered more closely at her. "Have we met before?"

"No, sir, I don't believe we have."

"I was sure . . . forgive me, my vision is not what it used to be. And the darkness does not help. Perhaps we could step into the hall?"

"Perhaps later. Lord Blackheath and I were just about to discuss a matter of some discretion."

"A matter of some—" Illumination slowly dawned on him. "You!"

April's heart froze as she saw his expression transform from polite curiosity to angry recognition. April saw his nostrils flare and his lips tighten into a thin line.

"It must be my mistake. I beg your pardon. Blackheath, I regret I am unable to stay after all. I find your choice in guests entirely distasteful. If you'll excuse me."

He turned around and pushed his way past Riley. Surprised at his reaction, Riley advanced upon her.

"What was all that about?"

"That's what I've been trying to tell you. Sir Cedric and I . . . have already had dealings."

"Dealings? What dealings could you possibly have with Markham?"

April couldn't respond. Oddly enough, she no longer feared Markham's recognition as much as Riley's displeasure.

He seized her by the arms, his face inches from hers. "Damn it, April, answer me!"

"His name was in the diary, too."

Riley couldn't make the association. "I don't . . . wait, you tried to blackmail him, too?"

April swallowed hard. "I had two hundred pounds off him."

Riley's blue-green eyes blinked at her as if he were seeing her for the first time. "Do you have any idea what you've done? That's a hanging offense."

She couldn't tell which elicited greater pain in her: the gravity of the words coming from the mouth of a jurist, or the crushing disappointment in Riley Hawthorne's face.

"I know. That's why you have to let me leave here. Now."

"You've implicated this whole family in a capital crime!"

She never felt so much shame in her life. "I'm so sorry."

"Sorry," he repeated, shaking his head. He collapsed on a nearby bench. The darkness cast ominous shadows along the planes of his face. He was quiet for several moments, and she couldn't imagine what he was thinking.

"Is there more I should know?"

April nodded weakly. "There were others."

He closed his eyes, his lashes pressing against his cheek. "How many?"

"Five. Not counting your father, five."

He hung his head over his lap and swore. "Who?"

April walked slowly to the adjacent bench and sat down gingerly, as if any sudden movement would cause him to explode.

"The Marquess of Clarendon. Viscount Earnshaw. Sir Eustace Glendale. Lord Charles Poole. And Markham."

He harrumphed. "The five most honorable men of the nobility."

April cocked her head. "Well, not so honorable they didn't have skeletons in their closets."

His head shot up suddenly, making her gasp. "Do you find this funny? Is this a laughing matter to you?"

"N-no, sir," she managed, as she sidled away from his menacing advance. She had never seen him so angry.

His lips thinned to a grim line and the whites of his eyes glowed brightly as he valiantly tried to control his temper. "I want to talk to you in my study *now*."

"Alone?" She gulped. She'd rather be thrown in a lion's den.

"Get up." He walked on ahead of her.

"But Riley—"

He froze in the light of the open balcony doors. He turned on her slowly, and his steely look withered her. "My name on your lips is a profanity. Never again presume to address me informally. From now on, I am Lord Blackheath. Do I make myself understood?"

His gaze chilled the air between them. "Yes . . . Lord Blackheath." It wounded her deeply to be dressed down in this fashion, but she had no intention of quarreling with him in his present state. "However, Clarendon and Earnshaw are in there, and I don't think it wise that they should see me."

"I did not invite them."

"Nevertheless, they are here."

He looked askance. "We've got to get you out of sight so we can sort this out. Wait here." He went inside and asked a lady for her fan. "Here, use this to cover your face. And stay close behind me."

April fumbled a little with the fan. She got it to open and then noticed that he was staring down at her. His face softened, revealing the tenderness that she knew he bore for her. If he offered to help her out of this mess, she swore she would never tell another lie as long as she lived.

But like ripples in a pond, the expression was quickly covered, first by disappointment and then resentment.

"So help me, April, you're going to pay for this."

Twelve

RILEY LED THE WAY THROUGH THE MASS of people in the ballroom, with April following behind, fanning herself closely. As it turned out, they didn't really need to push their way through the crowd. People made way for them.

Even though he was furious, he couldn't ignore the fact that the clusters of people he walked past seemed to change the subject of their conversation . . . or stop talking altogether.

Peter Northam walked up to him, his expression grave. "Riley, I need to have a word with you."

"Not now, Northam. I have another matter I must attend to."

"Not more important than this, old boy," he insisted, tugging on the taller man's arm.

Riley pursed his lips. He turned to April and led her to a wall lined with chairs where a number of children were sitting. "Stay here. Don't move."

Though anxious to leave, April had no desire to contradict him in his current temper. She sat in the chair closest to a small potted tree.

Northam conducted Riley to an adjacent salon that had been designated as the men's smoking room. As they approached the door, Northam halted and Riley barreled into him.

"What the—" Riley exclaimed.

"Shh!" he whispered. "We're not going inside. Listen from out here." Northam guided him to a secluded corner.

Riley protested. "You want me to eavesdrop?"

Northam silenced him. "Would you set aside your moral imperatives for one moment? You need to hear this, old boy."

"I'm not comfortable with this, Northam."

"Sometimes there's a need to be diabolical. Now be quiet."

Riley shook his head, but complied with his friend's request. By degrees, he began to pick up the thread of the conversation inside.

". . . nothing but a halfling."

"A what?"

"You know, a half-breed . . . what's the Latin term for it? A *nothus*."

"*Notha*," a third man corrected.

"Right you are. *Notha*."

"Nonsense."

"I have it on the highest authority. Lady Marsby herself told me that the chit is nothing more than the duke's bastard. No one believes that 'ward' story. Blackheath is merely trying to explain away her presence. Sort of hiding her in plain sight, as it were. He thinks that by flouting her in front of our noses, we won't suspect. How gullible does he think we are?"

"I can't believe that. I know Blackheath. He's not the sort of man who would fabricate a story like that. He's too damned honorable. More's the pity."

"Don't be absurd. The only reason he's thought so

proper is because he does such a thorough job of hiding all the family's peccadilloes."

"What do you mean?"

"Come now. You must remember Jonah's wife. We all do down at the club. Everyone knew what a little doxy she was. Didn't you ever think it odd how much time she spent in Austria? It was by no means a happy marriage."

"I hadn't heard that."

"Of course. Jonah's sporting more horns than a herd of Scottish cattle."

"Hmm. Then perhaps little Miss April Devereux isn't the only bastard in the family."

"Of course not! With all the time Jonah's wife spent with that foul German count and that Spaniard chum of hers, it'd be no surprise to me if all three of them had different fathers." All the men began to laugh in assent.

It had finally happened. The whispers of scandal had turned into full voices, and they were screaming attention upon Jeremy.

Riley muttered every expletive he could think of. "This has gone far enough! There's only one way that this rumor is ever going to die. Follow me."

APRIL SAT PATIENTLY IN HER CHAIR FANning herself, hiding her face as best she could. She didn't recall the ballroom being so bright before; in fact, the two chandeliers in the hall, like twin suns, seemed to magnify their brilliance upon her. To her relief, no one approached her, except for a servant who offered her a glass of champagne.

"No, thank you. I'm not thirsty."

"It's for the toast, miss. The Master is about to address the audience."

"Oh?" She took the proffered glass. She couldn't believe that Riley would consider giving the toast more important than secreting her out of the room at a time like this. Just like him to carry out his duty above all things.

"You certainly aren't going to find a husband sitting over here, my dear."

April looked up to see Lady Agatha slithering over to her, dressed in the most daring gown April had ever seen. Her lush breasts undulated over the low neckline of the bodice, which revealed more than it covered. The topmost layer of her cream-colored dress was made of the sheerest gossamer fabric, and it whispered above a second, much tighter underdress, which was scandalously damped down so as to cling even more to each of her perfect curves as she walked.

"Good evening, Lady *Hagatha*. Did you get caught in the rain?"

She forced a laugh. "You seem a little *old* to be sitting among the children. But I suppose if your conversation is as mature as your humor, then you may have been seated correctly."

April stifled the urge to throw her champagne in Agatha's lap. She might have done it, too, if she didn't suspect that it would make Agatha's dress look even more seductive on her.

"My humor right now, Lady Agatha, is as black as your heart. For your own sake, I suggest that you seek your fun elsewhere."

"But my dear," continued Lady Agatha, "I came to bring you good news. I have found you the perfect husband. He's a baronet by rank, but penniless by circumstance. He's fond of the drink, you see. But with the dowry that Riley will no doubt put up, the baron will at least make an honest woman of you. He's quite a bit older than you—he's buried two wives—but you could do much worse."

"Lady Agatha," April replied impatiently, "I hate to ruin your evening, but I have absolutely no intention of marrying your sodding baron, or anyone else, for that matter."

"Yes, I thought you might feel that way, my dear. That is why I have already arranged it with Riley's father on your behalf."

"What?"

"I talked to the duke yesterday about my idea. He thinks it a splendid match. Not only that, he's willing to put up any amount of money as your dowry to the first eligible man who'll have you. Apparently, he can't wait to see the last of you."

"That's not true . . ." April protested, but it lacked conviction.

"Oh, but it is. In fact, he told me that as soon as Riley and I become engaged, that I am to assume full control over assuring your matrimonial future."

April was bereft. Jonah's rejection wounded her deeply. April may have wronged him, but that was before she grew to care for him.

The only thing that hurt more than Jonah's betrayal was the thought of Agatha as Riley's wife. Now she understood why he wanted to marry her off. He wanted to make way for Agatha.

She swallowed the tears that burned her eyes, and turned her pain to indignation. In that, at least, Riley and his father were identical: they were pitiless and unforgiving. They would rather take a vindictive Agatha to their bosom than a repentant April. If they wanted Agatha, they could have her. They deserved her.

As if on cue, she looked up to see Jonah and Riley stand on the musicians' dais on the other end of the dance floor, just as the musicians finished the piece they had been playing. Then Jonah tapped a crystal goblet with the handle of his walking stick.

"Ladies and gentlemen, pray silence. Sir Cedric Markham, Clerk of the Parliaments, was supposed to address you tonight, but he was called away urgently. In his place, my son would like to speak a few words. Riley?"

Riley took the dais, and waited for the applause to fade. He cast a nervous glance over the gathering.

"Thank you, Father. With apologies to Sir Cedric, I shall attempt to represent him as best I can tonight. As most of you know, my great-grandfather, the eighth Duke of Westbrook, served His Majesty gratefully in the post of Prime Minister. Since that time, Blackheath Manor has been home to a celebration honoring the gentlemen who so love this country that they have dedicated their lives to serving in the honorable Houses of Parliament."

His statements were met with resounding applause.

"It is now my happy privilege to pay tribute to our guests here tonight. When asked to honor the work of Britain's government, our thoughts immediately turn to its political leader. He is a man who must shoulder the burdens and trials of a country at war, but who stands for peace, humanity, and justice. We continue to benefit from his great heart, experience, and unflagging loyalty to His Majesty. Let us raise a glass to the Right Honorable Spencer Perceval, and to the royal servants of the House of Commons and the House of Lords. May your services be forever remembered."

The guests drank in unison.

"And now, ladies and gentlemen, if you'll endure me one moment longer, I'd like to make a very special announcement. Having reached my advanced years without ever having married, it was not difficult to arrive at the conclusion that I was born without a heart. Or so I thought. Recently, I learned that a feeling heart does beat inside me after all. The irony is that, having discovered it, I immediately gave it away . . . to a very special lady, one who has very graciously accepted my offer of matrimony."

The blood rushed from April's face. "No!" The whispered scream escaped her lips. Despite her angry declarations, she didn't want Riley to end up with Agatha. Despite her guilty shame, she didn't want Riley to end up with anyone else but her.

"Darling!" Agatha gushed, and excitedly began to straighten her dress as she walked toward the stage.

Riley took a deep breath. "Having received her father's consent by post only this morning, I have the very great pleasure of announcing my upcoming wedding to Miss April Rose Devereux."

No one made a sound.

No one even breathed.

The stunned silence dragged on, broken at last by Northam, who raised his glass. "To the happy couple!"

"To the happy couple," echoed the crowd uncertainly.

Jonah turned on his son, his face florid with rage. Below his breath, he growled at Riley. "What in blazes do you think you are doing?"

"Not now, Father," he responded, shaking hands with the men closest to the dais.

"What is the meaning of this?" demanded Jeremy when he finally reached his brother. "Have you taken leave of your senses?"

"Let's discuss this in my study."

The audience slowly resumed its festivities, relief replacing shock. Society's finest seemed to have heaved a collective sigh, as the question mark that had hung in the air all night finally vanished. No one dared believe that an incestuous marriage had just been proclaimed; it was far more sensible to believe that the rumor of Riley's filial relationship to April had been false. As Riley made his way past the clusters of people who gathered to chat, he was awash with relief to pick up snippets of conversation like

"Who on earth came up with that nonsense?" and "I never believed it for a minute."

The music began again, and couples returned to the dance floor.

Riley was glad-handed and congratulated as he made his way toward April. But when he reached the seat where he had left her, he was not surprised to see that she was gone. He expected little else of such a wayward girl.

The three of them tramped into Riley's study, bursting with unvoiced objections. To their surprise, April was already there, and stole their thunder.

"What in bleedin' hell d'ye think you're doing?" she shouted, not caring who listened.

Riley, his lips thinning with rage, shut the door for privacy, muffling the sounds of the music and conversation outside.

"Riley, I demand an explanation this instant," echoed Jonah, his cheeks reddening.

"Listen to me, all of you. We tried and we failed. The rumor about April's illegitimacy proved too salacious and insidious to defeat. Our best efforts to convince the public otherwise were laughably inadequate to the task. There was only one way to declare that there was no relation between us, and that is for there to be a marriage."

April crossed her arms. "Without even consulting me? Don't you think I have a say in this?"

Riley advanced upon her stealthily, his eyes wide with incredulity. "You ceased to have a say the moment you set foot in this house with your scheme to defraud my father."

Jonah leaned his weight on his cane. "You can't marry her! You are the future Duke of Westbrook! She is nothing but a servant girl."

Her hands perched on her hips. "A servant girl, perhaps,

but one with high standards. I wouldn't marry your son if he were the last man on earth."

Riley folded his arms, one eyebrow cocked. "You have no choice in the matter, my sweet. If I were you, I'd be grateful that I'm holding to my promise to protect you."

"You're not trying to protect me. You're only trying to protect yourself."

"Really? Well, I advise you to reevaluate your position. Right now, I'm the only thing standing between you and six counts of extortion and fraud, each carrying a minimum penalty of five years' hard labor. And as no woman has ever survived more than three years of hard labor, I'd say that effectively, I'm saving your life. And Jenny's."

Jenny. April schooled herself. No harm must come to her friend. "We cannot marry. *We would not suit,*" she said, throwing his own words back at him.

"For once, Miss Jardine, I'm inclined to agree with you. Unfortunately, you have done everything in your power to make this marriage essential, unwanted or not. Once you marry me, however, I can promise you that it will seem far worse than a prison sentence. Don't fool yourself with notions of happy domesticity. This wedding is not a celebration. It's an execution. The death of your freedom. And as your jailer, I can promise you that you will regret your crimes. Day by agonizing day, you will pay your debt to society. For now, I've got to worry about paying the debt you owe to the other victims."

"Other victims?" asked Jeremy. "What other victims?"

Riley poured himself a brandy. "It seems that we are not the only gullible fools in England. Miss Jardine here has pretended to be the daughter of no less than five other upstanding gentlemen."

Jeremy and Jonah turned to her, casting the full weight of their shocked disbelief upon her. She wished the ground would swallow her up.

"And with characteristically pathological calculation, she has wrested from their purses . . . er, how much would you say?"

Her voice was barely audible. "Two th-thousand."

"Hmm, impressive. Yes, two thousand pounds from the likes of Glendale, Poole, Clarendon, Earnshaw . . . and Sir Cedric Markham."

April had never seen Jonah's face so purple. "Do you mean that Markham recognized her? Is that why he left so abruptly?"

Riley leaned his back upon the drinks cabinet, and brought the glass to his lips. "Yes."

"This is inexcusable! Is there no end to your infamy, girl? Do you know who these men are? Riley, we can't be associated with April any longer. Let her pack her things and get out, before any of the rest of them see her."

"It's too late now, Father. It has been since the moment I introduced her to the Queen. Besides, they've probably already seen her. They're all here."

"What? Why in blazes did you invite them?"

"I didn't. I thought you did."

They turned to Jeremy. "Not I," he answered their questioning look.

The three of them turned to April.

"Well, it certainly wasn't me," she said emphatically.

A puzzled look came over Riley. "Well, if none of us invited them, what are they doing here? Who else knows about your extortion scheme?"

"Only Jenny."

"You don't suppose she's told anyone?"

April's stomach plunged. Jenny had wanted to be completely honest with William, but she couldn't be so foolish as to have told him *that*. "No, my lord, it could not have been Jenny. All those men were named in the diary. Clearly, whoever has the diary invited them here tonight."

Riley straightened. "What do you mean, 'whoever has the diary'? Haven't you got it?"

She cursed herself for letting that slip out before she had a chance to recover the book. "Well, not exactly."

Suddenly, Jonah started coughing and wheezing. April gasped when it seemed he was going to swoon, and Riley flew to his side to bear him up. Jeremy fetched a glass of brandy, and they sat him down on a chair and loosened his neckcloth.

Riley shook his head and buried his face in his hands. "This affair has been deplorably handled. I should have taken matters in hand much sooner."

April cringed. "I'm so very sorry. I'll fix everything, honest."

A thundercloud of anger darkened his expression. "Honest? You haven't the least idea what that word means. Since you came here, I've spent half the time berating my father and my brother for believing you, and now that I've proven myself right, I fall for your devious tricks myself. I even managed to fool myself into believing that you cared for me. But now I see that every word you've ever spoken is a lie. Congratulations, madam, you have managed to dupe *all* the Hawthorne men. I'm sorry I ever met you, doubly so now I've agreed to shackle myself to you for the rest of my life."

Thirteen

"OF ALL THE INSUFFERABLE, UNSPEAKable, appalling . . ."

Agatha punctuated each word by tearing another piece out of Riley and April's wedding invitation. "How dare he do this to me?"

"Aggie, calm down," Emily said, dropping to the floor to collect the tattered bits of card. "Their wedding has nothing to do with you."

"He was supposed to marry *me*!" she roared. "His father said so."

Emily sighed. "But it was Riley's decision."

She paced about the drawing room in her London town house, her customary feline grace replaced by the mad rush of a bull. "Fifteen years I've been waiting for that man! He said we were ideally matched. That's as good as a marriage proposal. And now that Quincy has left me in some peace, Riley gets affianced to that—that bitch!"

"Aggie!"

"I knew she was up to no good the second I laid eyes on her."

"You didn't even acknowledge her the second you laid eyes on her."

"And can you blame me? She's as common as muck. How could he choose her over me? I'll never be able to live down this humiliation."

The butler came in and discreetly whispered into her ear.

"Show him in."

"Who is it?" Emily asked, as the butler withdrew.

"Peter Northam."

"Mr. Northam? Why are you entertaining him?"

Agatha flopped down on the settee. "I could use the company. No offense, dear sister, but you are not being particularly consoling."

Emily pursed her pink lips. "Very well. I can see you're in one of your moods. I suppose you're not taking me shopping, then?"

Agatha's glower answered Emily.

"Fine. I'll get Nanny Wendy to come with me." She reached the door and turned around. "You know, Aggie, I really hope you learn to get along with April. Once Jeremy and I are married, I want to have you over often, but not if you're going to be such a bear. I'm going to be her sister-in-law, and I intend for us to be a happy family." The door closed softly behind her.

Sister-in-law! The word set Agatha's teeth on edge. And there was nothing left to tear up! Just then, the butler announced Peter Northam.

"Good afternoon, Lady Agatha."

He looked especially polished today, sporting a rust-colored morning coat and beige lawn breeches. His sandy hair was windblown, though not artificially so. He handed his riding crop and gloves to the butler as the servant withdrew.

"I hate to seem indecorous, Peter, but you picked the wrong day for a visit. I'm in no mood to be hospitable."

Northam eyed a piece of paper on the floor which bore Jonah's crest on it. He picked it up and held it out to her. "Yes, I thought you might be in a state today."

She glanced at it and slapped it away. "It's scandalous. That's what it is. First, it's all over London that Riley and April are siblings, and now it turns out that they were lovers. It's scandalous."

He smiled. "Riley certainly has made himself a subject of gossip, hasn't he?"

"It's all that girl's fault. What on earth does he see in her? Do you suppose she has some nefarious influence over him? That she's blackmailing him in some way?"

Northam seated himself in a winged chair opposite Agatha's settee. "That's certainly a possibility."

"Can't you do anything to help him? You know all about laws and things. Can't you find some way to put her in jail?"

"Would that make you happy?"

"It would be my fondest wish."

He cocked his head. "If it were in my power, Agatha, I would do anything to please you. But I suspect that getting April out of the way would only be half your wish—the other being that Riley would marry you instead."

Agatha made no reply. She flounced over to the secretary and sat at the desk, looking for some paper.

"Agatha," he said, following her. "Agatha, marry me."

She heaved an exasperated sigh. "Darling, don't start that again. You know I can't."

"I love you, Agatha."

The earnestness in his voice made her look away. "Darling, please."

"Look at me, Agatha. I love you. I always have. I always will. I've never wanted any other woman. Why isn't that enough for you?"

She shook her head. "Darling, it's a point of sheer

economics. Quincy wasn't very good at managing our finances. We spent far more than we could afford. I'm on the verge of losing the estate. Riley . . . just has more, that's all."

"It won't always be like this for me, Agatha. You know how ambitious I am. I have plans for us. Lucrative plans. I want to make you happy, and I promise I will." His voice turned husky. "Pledge of good faith." He bent over the desk and covered her mouth with his own.

"Not today, darling. I have work to do."

He took the quill out of her fingers and stroked its feather tip along the curve of her breasts. The sensation immediately awakened every nerve, and she gasped.

"I know. I have every intention of making you work." He bent low until his face was on a level with hers. Their lips touched in that certain way that always made her body sizzle. His hand caressed the side of one breast, moving slowly to her back, pulling her toward him.

Agatha tried to move away from him. Northam knew her ways, and he could play her body like a fine instrument. Before she could stop him, he reached up and pulled the combs out of her hair, and her black tresses fell heavily down her back. And that was it, the key to unlocking her passion. Once her hair was free of the confines of the lady's coif, she ceased to play the part. Damn Northam for knowing her so well, and damn Riley for not wanting to.

But there was someone in front of her *now*. And now that the animal in her was unleashed, she didn't care who it was, as long as he was male. She stood, driving her hungry mouth onto his, pushing his body backward until it collided with the wall. She tore at his cravat, feasting on his exposed neck. She laved at the salty flesh, sucking at the tender skin at the base of his throat. Her lips drew his blood to the surface, until she could almost taste its coppery flavor. He moaned, his fingers threading themselves through her black mane. He's enjoying it too much, she thought, and nipped at the dark spot with her teeth until he cried out.

With a pained curse, he pushed her away, and she smiled at the savage look on his face. He threw his muscled arms around her, lifting her off her feet, and with a loud grunt, dropped her onto the sofa. Hovering above her, he flung his coat off, and his waistcoat and shirtsleeves landed next to it on the floor. Her soft hands stroked up and down his naked chest, undulating over the ridges that formed his abdomen. He was a great golden lion of a man, his wide shoulders forming a crossbar to the narrowing triangle that was his torso. His breeches hung low from his waist, and like so many sculpted bodies she was fond of, he had angled muscles on both his hips that pointed the way to the rising chisel between them.

Her eyes studied his face with interest. As he gazed down at her through a haze of lust, her fingertips caressed his nipples, and his eyes closed to revel in the erotic delight. She grinned at his defenselessness. One simply couldn't let a man have too much pleasure. Crooking her fingers, she dragged her right hand down the center of his chest, his flayed skin curling under her fingernails.

"What are you doing?" he shouted, horrified at the four lines that were now reddening on his chest.

Ignoring him, she nonchalantly began to pick out his skin from underneath her claws with the nails of her left hand. He seized one wrist and fell on top of her, tearing the shoulders of her dress down until the fabric pinned her arms to her sides.

That's more like it, she thought. Her tutelage in the savagery of love seemed not to have been wasted. He was proving most apt.

As he feasted on her bare breasts, he began to unbutton the flap on his breeches. But he would not take her so easily today. She ran her open hand through his blond hair, relishing how the curls tickled her skin. She closed her fingers around a large handful of his hair and pulled him off her, making him wince with pain. She raised one slippered foot to his chest, and with all her might, pushed him onto the floor.

She fell upon him, straddling his prostrate body. Snarling, Northam raised himself, but she used her superior position to flatten him against the floor, and took his body in hers. His handsome face took on a feral intensity, a look she found intensely erotic. She rocked on top of him, exulting in the power she had to give him his pleasure—or pain. Her eyes became slits as she watched him struggle with his hastening pleasure. Using the stiff wall of muscle for leverage, her nails flexed into his chest with every pleasurable movement of him inside her. He tried to slow her rhythm, but her own climax was imminent, and she instead quickened her pace. Her long, black hair lashed around her face as she selfishly took her pleasure. He writhed underneath, buffeted by the warring desires to consummate his lust and delay it. Seconds before he lost control, she climaxed, her body pulsing with molten lava, pleasure flowing from every pore, her back arched in the delectable posture of feminine ecstasy.

This is what she lived for, she thought, as the fog cleared from her mind. Being inside a man's head, and having his head deep inside her.

Now it was Riley's turn.

APRIL WALKED ALONE THROUGH THE ARboretum. The encroaching winter had robbed the trees of their leaves, their branches now only skeletal silhouettes clawing at the sky.

It had been a whole week since Riley had left for London, and she had spent it in the most dreadful loneliness of her life. She would never forget the terrible things that Riley said to her, because she deserved every word. She had betrayed his trust, betrayed his protection, betrayed his affection. Worse than that, she put him in jeopardy of losing his reputation, his livelihood, even his freedom—everything he valued. She had come to Blackheath Manor to rob him, and she'd been all too successful at accomplishing her aim. If there was a way she could reverse everything she had done, she would do it in a heartbeat. Even if it meant burying herself in the Madame's scullery again for the rest of her life.

It would almost be a blessing, she thought ruefully as she wended her way through the conservatory. No one here spoke to her anymore. Riley was gone. Jenny was so besotted with her red-haired footman that it seemed a chore for her to be in April's company. Jonah made it patently clear that she was nothing but a pariah. And Jeremy had—

Just crashed into her. The potted plant he was carrying tipped over and spilled cold earth down the front of her dress.

"Oh, dear, I *am* sorry. Let me help you."

April looked up at him in amazement. "You're speaking to me."

Jeremy's face colored. But he took a handkerchief out of his sleeve and handed it to her. "You can dust yourself off with this."

"Thank you," she said, and wiped away as much soil as she could from her green pelisse. The tense silence seemed to yawn between them, and April felt compelled to break it. "Look, I don't know if you'll give me another chance to say this, so I'll say it now. I'm sorry for everything I've done. But I never meant to hurt any of you. Everything

I did wrong, I did before I grew to care about all of you. You must know that."

Jeremy shook his head. "Oh, April. You have no idea how much I've wished that things had turned out differently."

Regret twisted her face. "So do I. I've ruined everything, and I wish to goodness I knew how to make things right again. But I've made so many mistakes, I wouldn't know where to begin."

"Your greatest mistake was in not trusting my brother with the truth."

She sighed. "I wanted to. Very desperately. But I was . . . so afraid."

"Afraid of what?"

The answer to that question gushed forth from her heart on a stream of unshed tears.

"Of losing him."

"April . . ." he said, tossing a brotherly arm around her.

The compassionate gesture loosed the torrent from her eyes. "I was afraid if he knew everything about me, how bad I'd been, he would hate me. But as it turned out, he hates me anyway."

His breath fell warmly on her forehead. "He doesn't hate you. What he hates are secrets. He's spent the better part of his life hiding things best left buried, and what you've done is dug them up all over again."

"What do you mean? I never divulged anything about your father's affair with Vivienne, honest!"

Jeremy shook his head. "No, April. It isn't the affair he's been trying so hard to cover up. It's the product of it." At her perplexed expression, he sighed deeply. "Me, April. I'm the illegitimate one in the family."

"What?"

"Vivienne was my mother."

Stunned, April slid down onto a bench. Vivienne's real

child had died . . . hadn't it? "I always thought . . . that is, it was my understanding that Vivienne's child had perished."

"Is that what her diary said?"

"Well . . ." Her mind flew across the pages of the diary she had memorized, scanning the faded brown ink containing the remembrances of the child. Madame had not precisely written that her child had died, only that she grieved for its untimely separation from her bosom. "No, I suppose it didn't. But why did you and Jonah believe me when I claimed to be Vivienne's child, if you knew the identity of the child already?"

"To know that, you have to understand the nature of my father's love affair with Vivienne. Come with me."

He took her on a stroll through the immense greenhouse, a cathedral of flowers blooming amid a dearth of color. Though the array of plants frothed with buds and blooms, her eyes never left Jeremy's face. She must certainly be addlepated if she could not see the resemblance. His eyes were the same as the Madame's, his mouth . . .

"As my father tells it, no two people were ever more in love. And when Vivienne became with child, it brought them even closer together. He mirrored her love for me, and when I was born, they became inseparable. They even talked of having another babe."

They walked through the propagation room, lined with small pots birthing seedlings and saplings of varied heights. "Father's wife, the Duchess of Westbrook, had paramours of her own, so she tolerated his affair with Vivienne. She lived mostly on the Continent, so his infidelity really didn't bother her much. Eventually, though, she got wind of a parlor room rumor that Vivienne had developed syphilis. She insisted that Father stop seeing Vivienne, if for no other reason than to stem any gossip that she too might be infected. He refused at first, but the duchess would not be swayed. It was agonizing for him to break off with Vivienne, but he could not bear to be parted from me. He consented to the duchess's demands, but only on the condition that he could bring me up himself. The duchess had no love for the idea, or for me, for that matter. But she agreed to propagate the subterfuge that she had given birth to me while she was away from England."

He walked her through the hothouse, a room dripping with ferns, cycads, palms, and other green foliage from tropical regions around the world. "Of course, Father still had to persuade Vivienne to give me up. He tried to convince her of the foolishness of leaving me to be raised in a bordello. There were arguments. But my father eventually persuaded her, and she finally agreed to part with me. He has never been proud of taking me from her, but he says he would do it a thousand times over for my sake. They were together one last night, before they parted forever. It was this special night that he thought had conceived you."

She let his words sink in. "Now I understand why you two were so excited to meet me. Jonah assumed Vivienne had never told him about me because she feared he would have taken me away as well."

"Exactly. But your arrival brought back a host of unpleasant memories for Riley. Legitimizing my birth wasn't easy, and Riley perhaps suffered the most for it. He was a lad when I was an infant, and away at school. There was a great deal of gossip then, and boys can be very cruel when they find something to pick on. But no matter how much they rebuked him, he defended me and my birthright. The more they ridiculed him because of me, the more staunchly he proclaimed our family honor and dignity. And he's been doing it ever since. Riley has had to be the model of an English gentleman all his life, proper to a fault, just so no one could point the finger of scandal in our direction. And never to protect himself, but only to protect me. So you see, April, I would never have been able to be a part of this family if it hadn't been for Riley. I've always been grateful to him that he's kept our secret so well, especially after I met Emily. His Majesty would never countenance Emily's marriage to a bastard. And I do love her so. So when you came around with that story of being Vivienne's child, Riley did everything he could to avert any hint of impropriety, for fear that scandal might alight on me."

April looked away. She began to see Riley in an entirely new light. The more her respect and admiration for him grew, the more painful the realization that he now hated her so.

As if he read her mind, Jeremy stood in front of her and said, "If Riley promised to protect you, he would do so at any cost to himself."

New tears of regret stung her eyes. "Why should he? I don't deserve his protection."

He smiled benevolently at her. "All the more reason you should be grateful when he gives it." He pointed to a large plant that looked like a thorny log with great arms that pointed skyward. "Do you see this tree behind me? It's called a cactus tree. A saguaro cactus, to be exact. It grows in the desert, amid scorching temperatures and very little rain. But when it does rain, this tree can soak up water by the ton. Naturally, this makes it a powerful target for thirsty predators, but these long, sharp spines keep predators at bay. It protects not just itself, but also its seedlings, which flourish under its protection." He took her hands in his. "I know Riley can be very prickly at times, but when it comes to protecting those he loves, he is as fierce as they come."

"He doesn't love me. You heard what he said. He's sorry to have to be shackled to me for the rest of his life."

"Those were angry words. But I know deep down he's pleased about forcing you to marry him. This way, he doesn't run the risk of your turning him down."

Hope whispered in her heart, but she silenced it. "I know you must be wrong about that. I'm not good enough for him."

He shrugged. "Even twisted branches eventually grow upward. Listen, Riley is my brother, and I'd like to kill him half the time. But if there is one thing that makes him special above most people I know, it's his unique ability to look into a person's heart and recognize the good. He must like what he sees in you, April. If he can trust the good in you, why can't you?"

"THANK YOU, LORD POOLE. I TRUST THIS sum will be more than adequate compensation for any inconvenience you may have received at the hands of my fiancée. I will not speak as to the motives behind her actions, but you have my word as a gentleman that you shall never again be troubled by this unfortunate misunderstanding."

The older man took the bank draft from Riley's hands and his eyes bulged when he read the sum. He adjusted his spectacles.

"Lord Blackheath, I feel very awkward taking your money. As I told you at the outset, I do not have any knowledge of an April Devereux, nor am I the victim of any extortion attempt." His face was turned to Riley, but his eyes were closed as he spoke. Riley was irritated that he clung so tenaciously to his lie, but he could certainly understand the man's hesitation to speak frankly.

"Regardless of its veracity, my fiancée has admitted this misdeed to me. And as a responsible man, I must act on it. If, as you say, it is not true, then let us call this a gift. If it is true, then a man of your intelligence can certainly be considerate of my own delicate position in the matter. Although a confession of this sort would give me the grounds to break our marriage contract, I have no wish to cast her into disrepute. I hope you will consider yourself repaid for your trouble, and allow me to start my marriage with a clean slate. As a grateful husband, I will remain in your debt for your understanding, and assure you that you may rely upon our discretion for as long as we have yours."

"You do indeed have it, sir," he said as he folded the draft and tucked it into his coat pocket. "Do send my compliments to your charming bride."

Riley rose to take his leave. "Oh, one last question, Lord Poole. You are, of course, invited to our wedding as my honored guest. But I must admit that you were not on my list for the Minister's Ball, only because you do not regularly serve at Parliament. Did you, by any chance, come as someone else's guest?"

"Not at all. I received an invitation with your very own seal. I'm sorry if I was not meant to be there. You must have sent it in error."

Riley frowned. "Clearly that is the case. Well, thank you again, and I look forward to your presence at our upcoming nuptials."

As his carriage lurched forward toward his London town house, Riley rubbed his tired eyes. He had taken care of Poole, Glendale, Earnshaw, and Clarendon. Only Markham remained to be dealt with, and he was being exceedingly difficult. Markham wouldn't receive Riley when he came to call. He would have to call on him again tomorrow.

It was late, and the pressures of the day had given him a headache.

But that wasn't what was making him miserable. The fact was, he missed her.

He hadn't realized how dull his world had become until she landed in the middle of it. Suddenly, there was a broad splash of color in his otherwise gray life, and he found himself yearning for more of it. Every aspect of his existence seemed fresh now that she was in it, rendering his life an entirely new adventure.

A beleaguered smile played on his lips. She was so busy trying to become a person of influence that she didn't realize how influential she already was. But trying to convince her of that was a battle in and of itself. She was all full of hiss and spit, stuck in the instinctive posture of a wild kitten before it learns how comforting and delightful a touch can be. How could he make her see that she was not alone anymore? He longed to protect her from the ravaging dogs of the world, and she was too busy clawing at him to see what he was trying to do. But he was determined to tame her, with the greater force of his love and compassion.

The carriage pulled up to the curb. The butler opened the door for him.

"My lord, you have a visitor."

He pursed his lips. "Tell whoever it is I'm not at home."

"I'm very sorry, my lord, but she is already in your bedchamber."

"Oh?" He smiled at the pleasant surprise. Though he had intended to be angry at April for all that she had put him through, he could not ignore the rush of excitement he felt at seeing her again. He could only imagine she had driven down to London to apologize for keeping the truth from him. And the fact that she had gone directly to his bedchamber indicated that she intended to atone for her wrongdoing in a way that made his blood surge. "Very well. Send up a bottle of wine, please."

"Yes, sir."

Riley took the stairs to his room two at a time. Outside his door, he paused to reflect. He reminded himself that she had made fools of his entire family, and must be taught a lesson. She must not find him too eager. Instead, he would make her own desire serve as her punishment. He would make her beg to be pleasured. Depending on the eloquence of her apologies, he would then decide whether or not she deserved it. His body already began to stir in anticipation of his planned torment.

He opened the door to find the room dimmed, illuminated only by the light of the fire crackling in the fireplace. From behind the dressing screen emerged a tall, lithe figure robed in sheer white lace. The firelight behind her made her garment vanish, leaving only the silhouette of perfect bare curves.

"Riley, darling, I'm so glad you're home."

Agatha.

She slithered over to him, her transparent lace peignoir billowing behind her. "I thought you might like some company while you were in London. I did miss you so." She slipped her arms up around his neck. "Did you miss me?"

"Dreadfully," he said, prying her hands off. "Aren't you supposed to be chaperoning Emily?"

"I'm bored shopping for Emily's trousseau. I'd much rather shop for my own..." She grasped his lapels and brought his lips down upon hers.

He came up for air. "Agatha, you're not even out of mourning yet."

"Oh, don't be so stodgy," she said, helping him out of his tailcoat. "We may have to wait another six months for the wedding, but we don't have to wait one more minute for the wedding night."

Agatha threaded her fingers through his hair, a sensation that heated his body, and pressed her full lips against his. The feel of her ripe breasts flattened against his chest brought a flood of tantalizing memories back. Her hands traveled down the curve of his back and along the crest of his buttocks, and the feel of her fingernails through his lawn breeches made him go hard. With the skill he remembered, she reached in front and deftly unfastened the buttons in his pants. As her long soft fingers began to encircle his stiffening muscle, Riley gripped her wrist.

"Stop." His breath came in ragged draws. "I can't."

Her mouth curled upward. "Darling, you most certainly *can*. And you most certainly *may*." She pulled at a knot at her bosom, and the entire peignoir slipped off her shoulders. Her lissome body glowed in the firelight, every delectable curve revealed to Riley's hungry eyes. Her black silky hair trailed down to the nest between her legs, as if pointing the way.

As a younger, more inexperienced man, he would have eagerly leapt to such a tantalizing offer. He would have scooped her into his arms and flung her onto the bed, and thrust into her without so much as a kiss. But he was not so inexperienced anymore; Agatha herself had seen to that. His mind flew to the brown-haired girl who challenged him at every turn, who teased him with her mysterious eyes, who discovered her own pleasure at his hands. He yearned to cover *her* in kisses, to explore *her* mind and body, to merge every part of her with his. It was she he wanted in his bed.

"Agatha. Let's not make this more difficult than it has to be. I'm getting married to someone else."

"Oh, but Riley, you can't seriously be thinking of going through with this marriage to that, that—"

"April. And yes, I must go through with it."

"Riley, darling, she's so common, so gauche."

He turned to button the front of his breeches. "Pedigree is not a prerequisite for a marriage. Breeding doesn't pair people. Love does."

Agatha stared at him intently. "Love? Are you . . . in love with her?"

His brows drew together. He hadn't admitted it to himself, much less to April. "I don't know. Perhaps. Yes."

Agatha's jaw tightened, but she forced herself to smile. "But Riley, she doesn't love you. She told me as much herself."

"When did she?"

"At the Minister's Ball. She said that she had no intention of marrying anyone, least of all you. Why would you want to subject yourself to a frigid shrew when you can have a willing woman in your bed every night? One who loves you desperately?"

He looked down at Agatha's face, and regret stabbed at him. He had loved Agatha once. She was a sweet woman then, much like Emily. But she became entangled in a romance with money, and it ruined her beautiful heart. Now, she was an entirely different person.

His thoughts flew to April. She didn't care about his titles, his fortune, or his name. She was content to have his love and nothing more. What a fool he was to think he could give her away to someone else. She was far too precious. He could never live without her.

"Agatha, you are a ravishing creature," he said, placing a tender kiss on her cheek. "But our friendship is in the past. It was sweetest when we were young. We are both now wise enough to know that it would never work between us."

"Darling, don't say that. It shall work. Because I love you. I want you to have the very best," she said, wrapping her arms on his neck, melding the length of her body to his. "Especially the best woman."

Her lips joined his, and their rounded fullness opened and closed over his mouth, drawing out his passion, showing him with her mouth what her sex could do for his manhood. He placed his hands on her shoulders, and firmly pushed her away.

"Agatha, *she* is the best woman."

If he had slapped her in the face, she would not have looked so affronted.

"I see," she said crisply, stepping out of her discarded peignoir. She walked over to the fur-lined coat that was draped over the armchair. "You've changed a great deal, Riley. You're not the same man I once knew."

"Perhaps not. There's been a new influence in my life, and I sincerely regret that it's changed the course of our friendship. I very much enjoyed our intimacies, Agatha." He placed a kiss on her hand. "For they are among my fondest memories."

Her lip trembled slightly before she stiffened it. "Is that what we are now? A memory?"

Riley held out his arm. "Let me walk you to the door."

"WHAT THE 'ELL IS WRONG WITH YOU?" Jenny looked down at her friend, still curled in bed at noon.

"Go away," came the muffled reply from underneath the covers.

"I won't," Jenny insisted, yanking the blanket off.

"Sod off, why don't you?" April retorted, pulling the covers back on.

"Are you sick?"

"Yes. Sick of being interrogated. Get lost."

"Not until you get your arse out of this bed."

"Why? So Jonah can shoot me dirty looks? Or you can ignore me some more?"

"April Rose Jardine! I never thought to see the day when you would start to feel sorry for yourself. Goin' around looking gloomy and sullen . . . livin' among the toffs has made you go soft."

"I can't help it." She pouted and sat up in bed. "Everything's gone horribly wrong, can't you see?"

"Not from where I'm standing. You're about to marry the best matrimonial prize in all England! You've snagged the man of every woman's dreams and you're too proud to admit you're crackers about him. That's the most ridiculous thing I've seen. Just look at you: the scullery maid who thinks she's too good for the lord of the manor, who'd rather be the 'Dustbin Duchess' than a real one. You must be barking mad."

"Jenny, you just don't understand."

"Oh, yes I do. Because you and I have the same problem. We're both smitten with men who are properer than us, men who are decent and respectable. And us from the grotty side of the street, we're bloody lucky to have snagged their hearts. They may not be perfect, but they've had to overlook a great deal to fall in love with the likes of us, and we should count ourselves lucky."

Her eyes grew misty. "He doesn't love me. He can't even stand to be in the same city as me, much less in the same room."

"Oh? Then 'ow come he just drove up in his carriage?"

"What?"

"He's downstairs now greeting His Grace."

"Bugger all!" April sprang out of bed and flew to the washstand. "Why didn't you say something sooner?"

"I didn't think you cared."

"You can be a real bitch sometimes, you can."

Jenny chuckled and helped April into an afternoon dress.

Ten minutes later, April was furiously trying to brush the knots out of her hair when they heard a knock at the door.

"Come in."

The door opened and Riley stood in the doorway. He looked so elegant in his deep green tailcoat and cream-colored waistcoat, it made April's breath catch. "My lord," April said, rising. "You've returned."

"Welcome back, my lord," echoed Jenny, smiling.

"Thank you. Jenny, would you excuse us for a moment?"

As Jenny made her way to the door, April's nerves began to rattle. Although she had longed to talk to him for a week, now that he stood before her, words escaped her. She felt awkward and inadequate, as if she should have done something useful during his absence, like repair the damage she had done to his family. Instead, things were nearly as askew as when he left.

But as she regarded him, she couldn't help but notice that he looked different from when last they spoke. He was no less handsome, but there were shadows beneath his eyes and the hollows in his cheeks appeared even more sunken. "You look weary, my lord."

He smiled weakly. "As do you."

She began to smooth out the ruffled coverlet on her bed. "Would you like to sit down?"

"Not especially. The ride from London felt more confining than usual, and it's a relief to be able to stretch my legs again."

The awkwardness yawned between them. "Can I send for some refreshment?"

"No. I came to tell you . . . that is, I wanted to say that I . . ." He glanced nervously at his boots, and cleared his throat. "That I've fixed everything with the men you robbed. Clarendon, Poole, Earnshaw, Glendale . . . they all accepted my restitution. Markham is proving more than a little recalcitrant, but I'll work on him. I can't blame them for being so uncomfortable talking to me about it, but I suppose we're fortunate that they are four of the greediest men in all of England. So for now, I think that you'll be safe from anyone swearing out any charges against you."

April hung her head, even more ashamed of herself for

meeting him empty-handed. "Thank you for straightening that out."

Riley nodded, and the silence stretched between them. "The plans for the wedding are progressing apace. I've put my secretary to work on the arrangements. He's been instructed to make it the most public wedding ever. And with all the haste that propriety will allow."

Her chest caved with regret. All of his acquaintances and colleagues would soon meet her as Riley's wife, and they would no doubt feel just as disappointed as he. If she hadn't elbowed herself into his life, he would be marrying a woman more befitting his breeding and standing. More importantly, someone he truly loved. A man like him could have any woman he wanted. But in order to save his family from ruin, he was now forced into marrying her. She had robbed him of the privilege to choose his own wife, and of all the things she stole from him, this was the most despicable.

"Your chief and only duty now is to design your wedding gown. However, you may want to consider these in your design." He took a long box out from under his arm. He bade her sit down in front of the dressing table, placed the box upon it, and opened it.

The noon sun streaming in through the window ignited the diamonds in the necklace, dazzling her with their sparkling fire.

She gasped as he took the necklace out and encircled it around her neck. The jewels cast tiny rainbows on her skin. She watched him in the mirror as he fastened the catch behind her. His touch at her nape sent a current of electricity through her body.

"These pieces have been in my family for generations. My mother wore them at her wedding, and now they will be yours." His fingers stroked the place behind her ears as he affixed the earbobs. The shiver of pleasure made her light-headed.

"Oh, I couldn't," she said, as he placed the simple pearl-drop and diamond tiara on her still disheveled hair. "They're too good for the likes of me, my lord," she said in earnest self-reproach.

His face was next to hers as they looked at her reflection together.

"You look like a duchess."

Bowing her head to hide her tears, she disengaged the tiara from her hair. "I don't feel like a duchess. Yes I do. A Dustbin Duchess!"

He gave a bewildered chuckle. "A what?"

The tears made her voice squeak. "A fraud. An impostor. A counterfeit. I'm not a duchess. I'm a lowly, contemptible creature. I haven't done anything to deserve these jewels. All I've done is bring you trouble and misfortune. But I didn't mean to. If I could, I'd take it all back."

He put his hands up to quiet her, but she ignored him.

"I'm really sorry, Riley. For everything I've put you through. Oh, I'm not supposed to call you that . . . I'm sorry for that, too."

An amused smile spread across his face. "April, wait—"

But she had far too much to say, and she was in a hurry to say it. "I know you're sorry you ever met me. I don't blame you. But I never wanted to make you unhappy, honest. I know you don't believe me; why should you? I've lied to you too many times in the past. But I won't anymore. I won't ever lie to you again, I promise."

He chuckled. "April, listen to me. I—"

"I want you to marry the woman of your choice, the one you truly love. I know that you'd rather these jewels were worn by Lady Agatha. She's . . . she's . . . everything I'm not. I know I've been catty with her, but it's only because I was jealous of how beautiful and perfect she was. I can't fault you for loving her instead of me. I'll find a way to leave quietly, without any gossip, I promise. You'll never even hear from me again. I want you to be happy. Just tell me you don't hate me. Because if you hate me—"

He clamped his hand over her mouth, amusement livening his expression. "Enough! By God, woman, can't I have a say?"

She mumbled something incoherent.

He removed his hand from her mouth, and wiped her wet cheeks. "I don't hate you. Quite the opposite, in fact."

"What?" she squeaked.

"April . . ." he began, shaking his head. "Wherever did you get the idea that I was in love with Agatha?"

"Aren't you?"

He shook his head. "She's not the woman of my choice. You are."

"Why?" It was an inane question, and she wished she could retract it. "What I mean is . . . why?"

"Turn around." He put his hands on her shoulders until she faced the mirror once more. "What do you see?"

She gazed at her reflection. Her brown hair tumbled chaotically down her back, while wayward curls adhered to her damp cheeks. Her eyes were swollen and pitiable, and her mouth formed an irrepressible pout. Beneath her face, a heavy lattice of diamonds chilled the skin on her throat. It looked outrageously out of place.

Her eyes met his, which hovered over her right shoulder. "A hideous mess only slightly less attractive than a small animal run over by a wagon wheel."

He laughed. "Look deeper."

She was afraid he would say that. She didn't want to look closer, because she knew what she would find. Beneath the tousled hair and wretched face, there was a person she did not recognize, a person who had made stupid choices and hurt a lot of people. A person who had betrayed her integrity in the pursuit of lucre. A person whose sense of value was so misguided, so skewed, that she even ridiculed her best friend when she had found the only thing of any real value: the love of a good man with the promise of a happy life together.

"Now what do you see?" he asked softly.

Her eyes watered. "A worthless woman wearing priceless jewels."

He leaned in closely, and brought his lips to her ear. "Want to know what I see? I see a woman noble of heart, even if not noble of birth. I see a woman buffeted by fear . . . of poverty, of degradation, of being imprisoned into becoming less than she is capable of. I see a woman who's been despised for one reason or another; whether for her station, her circumstance, or her talents, but always for reasons that were beyond her control. I see a woman who's hardened herself to people, for fear that they'd trample on her soft, feminine heart. A woman who's loyal to those she cares about, who's willing to protect them with her life. I see a woman whose heart is as brave as a lion's in the face of danger, but as timid as a mouse's in the face of love. I see a woman who loves deeply, but is deeply afraid of being loved. I see a woman who, if given just half a chance, will show the world exactly what she is made of, and will one day dazzle us all with the complexity and brilliance of her spirit. I see . . ." he said, turning her to face him, "a priceless jewel wearing worthless diamonds."

She looked at him, awe and gratitude swimming in her eyes. And although she tried to respond, the tears strangled her words.

He cradled her face in his large hands. "A mirror won't tell you any of that. But you can look at your reflection in my face."

Just then, she saw it. His eyes said it, screamed it, whispered it. *I love you.* And with nothing else between them, she reached out and embraced him, and held him so tight that no force of nature could pry him from her arms.

And now that she held the man she loved in her arms, with the promise of a happy life together, the tangle of diamonds at her throat finally warmed to the temperature of her skin.

Fourteen

THE NEXT DAY, RILEY AND APRIL SET OUT on horseback. They rode for miles over the vast hills that comprised his property until they came to a large green rise wooded heavily on all sides. The hill ended abruptly over a rocky outcropping that poured into a thundering stream. They dismounted and gingerly stepped down the face of the crag until they came to a small, hidden cave just a few feet above the rushing water.

April had never been in such a place, and was captivated by the earthy smell of damp rock. The chill wind that whipped through the clearing outside lost its sting in the dark womb of the cave, and even the sound of the roaring water seemed to grow distant. After the trenchant light of day, the dimness was a welcome respite.

She heard, rather than saw, Riley light a lantern from the large basket he carried, casting a yellow glimmer on the cave walls. He hung it on a nail that protruded from the wall, and now she could see all around her.

The narrow opening of the cave widened into a large cavern, which was littered with forgotten objects. Dusty books, toys, and hats were scattered against the corners. There were markings on the cave walls.

"What is all this?" she asked him, overturning one of the many discarded baskets.

He kicked away a loose rock in the center of the cavern and spread out a woolen blanket he pulled from the basket. "This is my own special place. It was my sanctuary as a child, my playroom as a young boy . . . my study room on holidays from university. I used to spend hours every day here during the summers. I would bring a basket with a whole day's worth of food, and go fishing and swimming in the stream."

"All by yourself?" she asked, studying the markings on the walls in the flickering light. From the lowest stratum to the highest, the walls bore a child's drawings, then geometry problems, then legal terms. She could chart Riley's growth by the scribbles on the walls.

"No one else knows about this place. One time, after Father thrashed me for setting fire to Jeremy's toys, I ran away and hid here for three days. Father searched and searched for me, but he never found my secret cave. I came home eventually."

"Why did you do that?"

"Because I got hungry."

April smiled, and sat next to him on the blanket. "No, I mean why did you burn Jeremy's toys?"

"I was an intensely troublesome child."

"You? Lord Perfect?"

He looked askance at her. "Lord Perfect? When did I earn that moniker? Or are you being sarcastic?"

She blushed, embarrassed to admit that he possessed every quality she found ideal in a man. "No . . . it's just that . . . well, I don't think I've ever met a more upright person in my life."

He laughed. "Upright? In case you haven't noticed, I'm lying down."

She grinned through an exasperated sigh. "Don't be so literal. You know what I mean."

He faced her, resting his weight on one elbow. "No. What do you mean?"

"All right, all right. Honorable, then."

"You think me honorable?"

Her hand flew to the lapels of her pelisse in exaggerated modesty. "If I didn't, sir, I wouldn't be here alone with you unchaperoned."

He chuckled. "Well, appearances can be deceiving."

Her brows drew together. "How so?"

He made an attempt once or twice to answer, but it was a long time before he finally spoke. "Father's adoption of Jeremy was very difficult for me. I was only about fourteen years old when Father brought him to stay with us. I'd never seen Father so happy as he was then. He doted on the boy. Here was this child, the son of a prostitute, but by the look of Father, anyone would think that Jeremy was next in line to the throne. I can remember how Father seemed almost ashamed of Mother and me, even though we were the only respectable part of his life.

"But instead of hating Father, I began to hate Jeremy. A child's logic, I suppose. Yet no matter what mischief I did to Jeremy, the boy never stopped following me around, or imitating me in everything I did. He never took anything from others without first asking something for me, and he always offered me half of whatever he had. One day, I can't remember why, I hit him. Hard. He started bleeding, but that wasn't what frightened me. He just stood there, not making a sound, just staring at me with those innocent eyes, tears running down his trembling cheek alongside a rivulet of blood. That look of betrayed trust in his child's eyes—it shamed me deeply. I never hated him after that."

April instinctively reached out her hand to his. He grasped it firmly.

"Perhaps that's one of the reasons I was so unkind to you, too, when you first came to Blackheath. Father became as he was then, besotted with a child of Vivienne's. It brought back painful memories of childhood sins."

"Sins? Riley, you mustn't be so hard on yourself. Children are like to lash out at things that cause them pain. It doesn't make them bad."

He sat up. "There's more to the story. I've . . . never told anyone, but I did something of which I'm very much ashamed."

Riley hung his head, his black hair flopping over one brow.

"What is it?"

"I ruined someone's life."

April sat back on her haunches and waited for him to speak. He stared down into his hands, absently turning over one of the tiny tin soldiers that were scattered about. "You see, even though my mother herself carried a string of lovers, she was usually very discreet about her liaisons. I learned early on that a good reputation amid Society could cover all offenses—and a bad one could expose every weakness. Society itself can be an effective weapon.

"When Father began to openly fawn on Vivienne, I was afraid that news of it would bring our house down. We were on the verge of being a laughingstock. So I came up with a way to get Vivienne out of our lives."

He paused, and April's heart began to pound in her ears.

"Vivienne was a very famous and sought-after courtesan. One of the most expensive and exclusive ladies of the evening. I thought . . . if Vivienne's renown could be damaged, if I could fix it so that no one would ever ask for her services again, she would have to leave England to ply her trade somewhere else. It would solve all my problems. No more embarrassment of a father, no more threat of scandal, no more Jeremy. So, I found a well-respected doctor, and . . . and I paid him to spread rumors that Vivienne had contracted syphilis."

He paused again. "It worked, too, more effectively than I expected. All at once, her clientele fell away. She became a salon joke, as did anyone she was seen with. Everywhere she went, she was pointed out. Mother and I hounded Father to break it off with Vivienne, before it destroyed us all. He finally relented, but on the condition that we accept Jeremy into the family.

"I didn't properly conceive all that would happen as a result of my actions. I just wanted Vivienne out of our lives. I never imagined it would cause her penury—or to abandon her own child. I'm very ashamed of what I did. I used my money and my power to destroy a person's life. I don't know why I should tell you now, except . . . I believe you would understand my . . . my regrets."

Riley had always seemed so unassailable, so invincible. But now, his mantle of invincibility was gone, and underneath was a man so profoundly human that it drew her to him like a magnet.

"How honorable do you think me now? Am I still 'Lord Perfect'?"

She put her hand in his. "Absolutely."

He grinned jadedly. "You have a very distorted view of perfection."

"No I don't. Honor doesn't come from never making mistakes. It comes from what we do once we've made them. I know that once you accepted Jeremy, you went to great lengths to protect the family's reputation for his sake. If it wasn't for your sacrifices, Jeremy wouldn't be able to marry the woman he loves. I won't allow you to forget that."

Riley smiled at her then, a smile full of gratitude and relief. "You know, it just dawned on me. I set in motion all the events that led to Jeremy's arrival, and ultimately, to yours. In a way, I suppose you've become my destiny."

"And your punishment," she decreed, enjoying the way his laughter brightened his face.

APRIL RETURNED WITH RILEY TO THE cave several times over the next two weeks. It was a strange courtship, spent entirely in the solitude of Riley's secret place. There was a time when she fantasized about being pursued at soirées and operas. But she would not have traded a single moment of that fortnight for all the balls and parties in England.

One afternoon, they took refuge in the cave from a gathering snowstorm. The air in the cave was warm and perfumed with the smell of damp earth, and the heavy snowfall outside made them a curtain of privacy. April sat on one edge of the blanket, collecting a pile of forgotten toys in her lap, studying the debris of a child's idle hours. Riley lay down on his side, regarding her intently.

"What are you thinking about?"

She grinned. She was picturing him as a little boy, playing with these tin soldiers and wooden weapons, playing at being grown-up while dreaming of becoming so. "I used to have a place like this cave. Behind the scullery was a pantry, and whenever Cook wasn't looking, I'd hide in there and dream of being a real lady. Manners, money, moniker . . . the lot."

"Then your dream is about to come true. When we're married, you'll become Lady Blackheath," he said, stretching out lazily to his full length, "with all the privileges and rights thereunto. Does this please you?"

She shook her head. "Funny how dreams change. I don't seem to crave that anymore." The only thing she wanted, the only dream she had, was to make Riley happy. It was the only thing that she knew would give her life substance. "I mean, look at Lady Agatha. She's not happy, and she's got it all . . . a title, a fortune, more clothes than she can wear, all the right friends, and bloody gorgeous to boot."

He sat up. "Just a moment . . . who made Agatha the paragon of womanly perfection?"

"You did. You offered her marriage once."

"So I did. What of it?"

"You loved her."

"Once upon a time."

April bit her lip. "Do you still?"

He smirked, amusement bubbling up in his blue-green eyes. "Aren't you the curious cat?"

She gritted her teeth, irritated by the way he dodged the question. "I just think that if we are going to be married, we should make a clean breast of things, so we can start life together hand in hand instead of head-to-head."

The smile cut across his face. "Very noble objective. But who I give my heart to is none of your concern." His teasing eyes met hers in bold challenge.

She drew a tin dagger from her lap, a toy weapon but sharp nevertheless, and aimed it straight at his chest. "Your heart belongs to me . . . even if I have to carve it out of your chest."

He raised his hands in defense. "Do you know how to use that thing?"

She nodded. "Point and penetrate."

His eyes narrowed on her. "You're a bloodthirsty little thing, aren't you?"

She knelt above him. "Answer my question. Do you still find her attractive?"

"You know, a confession under duress can't be held in evidence against me—"

His words died as she shoved the tip of the dagger under his jaw, dimpling his skin. "Answer me!"

His laughter resonated on the ancient walls of the cavern. "I can see it's going to be a challenge being married to you."

"This is your last chance. Any more prevarication and I shall be forced to run you through."

In a blur of motion, he seized her wrist and pried the dagger from her outstretched arm. He yanked her toward him, pulling her off balance, and she fell beside him. Deftly, he climbed over her and pinned her wrists above her head.

His body covered hers completely. "Let's discuss your strategy of point and penetrate, and see if we can apply it to other, less adversarial situations."

She writhed under him, trying valiantly to escape from under his superior position, but she couldn't budge him. A man his size moved only when he wanted to.

"I'm going to kill you for this!"

"You can certainly try," he answered casually.

Angered by his dismissive attitude, she opted to use her flexibility. She wriggled, trying to shimmy out from under him, but managed only to lodge him firmly between her legs. "Damn it, Riley!"

"Language! Any more of that and I shall be forced to run *you* through. And I warn you, I shan't need a sword."

Her exertions left her winded. And angry. "You *are* still attracted to her!"

He smirked, his teasing eyes hidden behind a thick mesh of black lashes. "I can't help it. I'm a red-blooded male, after all."

Her chin jutted forward. "I intend to spill some of that blood. Let me go!"

His smile revealed a row of straight white teeth, as he began to play with the decorative bows on her bodice. "First show me what you meant by a clean breast."

She no longer found the game funny. He had admitted

his attraction to Lady Agatha, and a red-hot poker of jealousy stabbed her. No matter how much she cared for him, no matter how indispensable a part of her life he had become, she would never allow him to cuckold her the way his father and mother had with each other.

"Go to her, then! Go to your bit of fluff. I shan't stop you. But don't expect me to wait around for you. I'll be long gone before you ever get back."

He laughed heartily, his chest vibrating above hers. She felt foolish for feeling so wounded, but she couldn't help it. His large hand left her wrists and cupped her chin, turning her to face him.

"April . . . you're my bride. Not her. I don't want Agatha. I don't want anyone else but you. Only you. And if you ever even mention the idea of leaving me again, I'll . . ." Riley shook his head to clear the thought. "Just don't. Because I won't ever let you go."

The vitriolic jealousy that burned inside her subsided, smothered by her heart's response to the passionate determination in his face.

His hand stroked her cheek. "There's something I've been meaning to ask you. A question that I never got a proper answer to."

"What?"

The mirth disappeared from his eyes, and now, they were illuminated by the most unearthly warmth, and tinged with the tenderest vulnerability. "Will you marry me?"

And there it was. In that wonderful, magical instant, the doubts and fears that had plagued her heart evaporated on an exhaled breath. A warmth filled her soul, emanating from the glow of love she saw in his eyes. She couldn't believe her amazing fortune to have found this man. This good, beautiful, perfect man. He was her rescuer, her hero, her partner, her lover, her friend. And to think that he was pursuing *her*. She was no rare beauty. No princess. No one of consequence. But he fought for her as if she were the greatest prize on earth, admired her as if she were the most beautiful thing on earth, loved her as if she were the noblest cause on earth. And he wanted to spend the rest of his life doing those things. How could she not give him her heart?

"I love you." Nothing else felt true in her world but these three words. Nothing else mattered except the man she spoke them to.

He closed his eyes, and opened them again, and this time, the connection was forged between them. His mouth descended on hers in a kiss neither of surrender nor of passion, but a fusion of two human souls bound by shared love. They spoke a thousand words of love in that one kiss, neither of them willing to break the spell, a pouring forth of emotions long silenced by the tyranny of pride. Opening their eyes, they beheld each other as new creatures.

It was always April's belief that one is only worth what someone else is willing to sacrifice. To her father, she was worth a five-pound card wager. To the Madame, she was worth, at best, twenty pounds in a virgin auction. To Riley, she was worth his heart for a lifetime. April Rose Jardine had just become the richest woman who ever lived.

THEY SPENT THE ENTIRE AFTERNOON kissing, holding each other, laughing. They spoke of their past, and made plans for their future. They stared into each other's eyes, caressing, promising each other heavenly delights on the night of their wedding, just a few days away. And safely ensconced in each other's arms, they fell blissfully asleep.

A short while later, she awoke to the sound of scratching. She turned in the direction of the sound, and saw Riley standing in front of the wall, the lantern held aloft by a muscled arm. He was writing something on the wall with a rock, on the highest point, just above the markings from his days at university.

She rose from the floor, and wrapped the woolen blanket around herself. She walked up behind Riley and enfolded him in the blanket, glorying in the feel of his wide chest against her palms, and his hard buttocks on her tummy. Her breasts flattened against his back.

"What are you doing?"

Riley pressed his arms against her embrace. "I'm preserving the moment."

"Which moment would that be?"

"Have a look for yourself."

He raised the lantern high above his head, casting light on his engraving.

25 November 1810:
I fell in love with April Rose Jardine.

"Riley . . ." she said, so happy that she was frightened she would burst.

He turned around in her embrace, and kissed her on the temple. "I want to remember this day, the happiest of my entire life."

She cradled his face in her hands, and placed a tender kiss on his lips. "But you left something out. You must add 'and she loves me, too.'"

His eyes narrowed through a sidewise smile. "Damn it, woman, is this how you intend to start our marriage? Ordering your lord and husband around?"

One eyebrow rose in defiance. "It is, unless he wishes my name on another man's cave."

Riley reached down and lifted her into the air, causing April to shriek in surprise. He pressed her frame against the smooth cave wall, inches below her name, and looked up into her laughing face.

"Witch! You are going to be the end of me!"

She kissed him tenderly. "No, my love. We are only just beginning."

AGATHA HELD THE RED CANDLE OVER THE folded cream-colored paper, letting the wax pool on the flap. When the seal cooled, she got up from the desk in her bedroom and tugged on the bell cord by the fireplace to summon her lady's maid.

Her razor-blade smile widened as she fanned the letter in her hand. She sat upon her bed, still rumpled from her sexual skirmish. Though it had been some time, her vanity was still stinging from Riley's rejection, and she needed the sort of comforting that only another man could provide. This evening, she was more angry than hurt, and her lovemaking was particularly savage. Thank God for Peter Northam, upon whom she could always rely to endure all the wrath that she had to spew.

Fifteen

ON THE AFTERNOON BEFORE HER WEDDING, April sat at her dressing table, slowly brushing her hair. Though she was looking at her reflection in the glass, she saw only Riley. His dazzling smile, which turned her knees to water; his soft black hair, which made her fingers ache to run through it; his sensual lips, which brought a heated flush to her face. But it was his eyes, those profound, warm eyes, that spoke to her heart. Words of love, meant only for her. Never did she think she'd fall in love, let alone with such a man as this. He might not be Lord Perfect, but he certainly was Lord Perfect For Her.

The door opened, stirring her out of her reverie.

"Well, look at you," Jenny commented. "I could snuff out the candles and there'd still be light in this room from the glow on your face." She took the hairbrush and began to brush April's hair in earnest.

"Oh, Jenny. He's so . . . wonderful. I can't explain it. I know I don't deserve him. And yet he loves me. Not for anything I've done, or for who I am, but because of who *he* is."

"Doesn't make sense, does it? That's the mystery of love."

She leaned toward the mirror. "From now on," she vowed, "I'm going to make him happy. Whatever it takes."

Jenny grinned. "Ooh, you *are* gone, aren't you? I always knew it would take a man with a title in his pants to conquer you."

Even Jenny's vulgar jibes couldn't wipe the smile off April's face.

"I take it you are no longer dreading your wedding."

"It's not dread I feel. It's nerves. My hands start shaking every time I think about it." From what she'd been told, every single one of the two thousand guests invited sent their acceptances. St. Paul's Cathedral could not accommodate another soul.

Jenny stopped brushing. "Oh, dear. Well, I suppose with your sainted mother gone, maybe I should be the one to give you some practical wedding-night advice." Jenny dragged a chair over to April and sat in front of her.

"Jenny, you don't understand . . ."

"No, I don't mind. If there's one thing I was ever any good at, it's what goes on between a man and a woman behind closed doors."

"I think I know enough about what goes on. I'm not stupid."

"But there's a great deal more to it than that. You want to make him happy, right? Well, the secret to making a man happy is to think of yourself as a fireplace: whether he blows hot or cold, you must always warm up to him."

"Thanks just the same, mum, but I think Riley and I can sort things out for ourselves."

"So, it's like that, is it?" she replied archly. "Just for that, I won't tell you about William and me."

April's mouth dropped. "You didn't!"

"We did."

"You brazen tart!"

Jenny giggled, a dreamy look descending on her face.

"It was wonderful. He's the best thing that ever happened to me, April. You remember all them stories we hear as little girls . . . like Robin Hood and Maid Marian, Lancelot and Guinevere? That's what he treats me like. Like I'm a fair maiden, and he's this brave hero out to rescue and protect me."

April nodded. "I know *exactly* what you mean."

They continued to chat dreamily while Jenny fixed April's hair. Most brides look upon their wedding as a solemn ritual to execute or a social commitment to endure. She looked forward to hers as an opportunity to publicly say to Riley what she was feeling in her heart.

Thinking of him now, she regretted agreeing to his suggestion that he observe the strictures of propriety by spending the remaining days until their wedding at his London town house. He thought it only proper that they travel to the church from separate residences, and she found the thought endearing. She was overcome by an irresistible desire to see him again. Now that she was in love, she couldn't bear to be apart from him. Now that she had given her heart to him, it was agony to have it so far away.

She wondered if her handsome caveman was as eager to consummate their vows as she was. Throwing all decorum to the wind, she decided to send him a provocative note to whet his appetite. She seized notepaper from the desk, and dipping the quill into the India ink, April scratched a few words onto the paper:

Dearest Riley:

I very much enjoyed our little conversations in the cave; they were most engaging. Indeed, during the fox hunt, you proved yourself quite a master debater. But once we are married, it is my wish that you will develop into a cunning linguist. Then, I shall look forward to the opportunity to sit upon your lap, and we shall discuss the first thing that comes up.

Yours forever,
April

She smiled mischievously, trying to imagine his expression as he read her lascivious note. "Jenny, will you please deliver this to Riley in London? It's very private, and I don't want a footman to do it." And Jenny couldn't read.

"What does it say?"

"I said it's private."

"And you won't tell *me*?"

"Not this time." Lovers' secrets are better kept in the dark.

"Well, all right, but consider this your wedding present."

A SHORT WHILE LATER, MR. CARTWRIGHT delivered her wedding gown. Miles of white moiré silk gathered under her high-waisted bodice, which was cut daringly low in front to allow for the web of diamonds at her throat. The bodice was encrusted with teardrop pearls, like the ones dangling from the tiara Riley had given her. Mr. Cartwright had sewn onto it a veil of Honiton lace, which trailed over the train that draped from the bodice in the back. April had never seen its equal.

She gazed at herself in the glass. In her most fanciful daydreams, she never imagined she would be garbed in so radiant a dress or so dazzling a set of jewelry. The experience far exceeded her greatest expectations, and she was bursting with happiness. She assessed her appearance through Riley's eyes, and dearly hoped that he found her a beautiful bride, fit for a marquess. Above all, she wanted him to be pleased.

As she tried on each of the seven pairs of shoes Mr. Cartwright had brought, a footman came in bearing an envelope. Amazed that Riley could have answered so quickly, she smiled at the cream-colored envelope. She couldn't wait another minute to read his response to her brazen challenge, so she sent Mr. Cartwright and his seamstresses out of the room to have this moment all to herself.

She tore open the envelope. Her heart froze.

It was a page from the Madame's diary.

Written across the faded brown ink of the Madame's hand, in bold red letters, was the message:

Naughty girl.

Someone must pay for your crimes. Will it be you or your bridegroom?

Bring £20,000 to the Hoof & Talon at midnight tonight, the eve of your wedding, or the rest of this diary goes to the constabulary. Tell no one, or you shall discover the true meaning of the word "scandal."

April's knees buckled, and her crisp silk dress crumpled as she slumped to the floor. The page trembled in her hands as she read it over and over to make sure that this was not a poorly conceived joke.

Her anxious mind played out the image of her arrest, Riley's humiliation, Jeremy's disgrace. It was more than her heart could take. Now she understood why her schemes worked so well on all those men. This world of nobility was a prison of its own. It was made of paper walls and clay bars, but they were just as confining as if they had been mortar and iron.

Tell no one, the note said. If Riley wasn't so far away in

London, she would have been able to confide in him. But there was no time to reach him and still act before midnight. Now, she could not share her despair with a living soul. She felt as if she were adrift at sea with no one to hear her cries for help. She began to whimper.

Struggling to regain control of her ragged breathing, she scrambled up on a nearby chair and forced herself to think rationally. Who knew about her guilty past?

There were the men she took money from: Markham, Clarendon, Poole, Glendale, and Earnshaw. But they wouldn't expose themselves to scandal, even if only to spite her.

Lady Agatha! She had the diary, didn't she? And goodness knows she already hated April enough to do it, without adding the insult of being passed over by Riley. But Lady Agatha didn't know April had blackmailed anyone. Why would she threaten April, instead of say, Jonah, or any of the other men in the diary? It didn't make sense.

Even Jonah was not above suspicion. He'd despised her since her confession, and he made no secret of how much he disagreed with Riley's decision to marry her. But it was illogical to suppose he would carry out a threat that would implicate himself as much as her. Besides, he didn't need the money.

Clearly, she would find out soon enough who was behind this blackmail attempt, because she had no choice but to comply with the demands of the note. But twenty thousand pounds was a king's ransom. Where would she get that kind of money? She worried her lip absently as her eyes scanned the room, as if twenty thousand pounds were lying on a table or in a corner. Her eyes fell on the full-length mirror across the room. In the reflection, she saw her piteous, frightened expression.

And the diamonds encircling her neck.

Her hands flew to her throat. It was a fortune in jewels!

She shook her head violently. What was she thinking? These gems had been in Riley's family for generations. He'd have her head on a platter if she sold them. What explanation would she give for showing up at the wedding without them? Bugger it all, if she didn't sell them, *she* wouldn't be able to show up at the wedding either! She'd deal with Riley's wrath later; for now, she had another problem to resolve.

Minutes later, she was changed and in a carriage speeding toward the village clutching a reticule full of jewelry.

RILEY'S CARRIAGE CLATTERED TO A HALT in front of Blackheath Manor, grateful for the end of what seemed the longest carriage ride he'd ever taken.

What a lusty wench April was! She had a penchant for intellectual sex, and her dirty mouth never failed to spark the flame of arousal in him. By God, he would show her just what a "cunning linguist" he was, and he was not about to wait until the wedding night to do it.

While wicked thoughts danced in his head, he struggled to maintain control over his body's response. He took the stairs up to the entrance of Blackheath Manor three at a time. Forrester opened the doors for him.

"My lord, I thought you were staying at the St. James residence."

"I am," he said brushing past him toward the grand staircase. "Is my bride in her rooms?"

"Miss April is not here, sir."

Riley stopped on the landing and looked over the banister at the butler, a frown darkening his expression. "Where is she?"

"Miss April departed for the village. There was a final purchase that she had to make."

"Why did she not send one of the servants?"

"She insisted on going herself, sir."

"Who accompanied her?"

"No one."

"She went alone?"

"She was most adamant on that point, sir."

"Curious. Well, I'll wait for her in my study. Let me know the minute she returns."

RILEY HAD BEEN PACING IN HIS ROOM ALL night. He'd talked himself through every emotion from anger to despondency.

It all started with the surprise visit that evening from the jewelers at Pettigrew & Sons. They were dismayed because they thought the Hawthornes were no longer satisfied clientele. Pettigrew & Sons had proudly displayed the ducal crest ever since Riley's grandfather had commissioned the wedding set, and now they were distraught that the pieces were being returned by the future Lady Hawthorne.

Apparently, the jewelers were more loyal to the family than April would ever be.

Riley couldn't wrap his mind around it. He couldn't fathom a reason why April would sell the jewelry he gave her—that is, other than the fact that she had been after his money all along. It didn't make sense, and he didn't want to believe it. And yet, the evidence pointed to that very conclusion. And as April was also missing, he couldn't even give her the benefit of the doubt.

He raked his hand through his hair and looked at the clock. It was after eleven. Where was she? He feared for her safety, and for himself and the marriage on which he was basing his every future happiness.

THE JEWELER'S REACTION WAS NOT AT ALL what she expected. HE seemed more preoccupied with *why* she was selling the pieces than *how much* she wanted for them. But in the end, he gave her a bank draft for more than she needed—£25,000—with enough time to change the draft for legal tender notes at the King & County Bank. She stuffed the banknotes in a large satchel, clipped it to a belt which she strapped on under her rib cage, and let the satchel dangle behind her. Under the hooded cloak she wore, her secret cache was invisible.

By the time she reached the manor, she was physically exhausted and emotionally drained—and she still had to keep her midnight appointment with the blackmailer. She shivered in the freezing night air as she stepped off the carriage, which she stationed in the field. She wished she could have taken Riley's carriage to her rendezvous, but all his carriages bore the ducal crest. In the interest of anonymity, she would need to have a horse saddled. She had to wake a groom.

The stable hall was dark and cold, but a small fire smoldered behind a grate at one end. Farthest from the fire, and closest to the door, slept the apprentice, a young lad of fifteen named Ian. April opened the large door, letting in a draft, and he stirred uncomfortably.

April threw back her hood so he would recognize her in the dim light. She placed a gloved hand over his mouth, and he jerked awake. She motioned for him to follow her quietly outside to the stable close.

Her whispered breath blew puffs of smoke in the frosty air. "I'm sorry to wake you, Ian, but I need a favor."

"Anything, miss."

"I need you to saddle a horse for me."

She saw his forehead furrow. "You wish to ride at this hour, miss?"

"Yes, I need to go into town for something. It's important."

"Shall I get you a carriage instead?"

"No, I want a horse, and don't put that blasted sidesaddle on him, either. I want a proper one."

She followed him to the tack room, where he pulled a saddle from the rack and carried it over to a mare.

"Is anyone going with you, miss?" he asked.

"No. Just me. I'll be fine. It's not far."

April could sense his tension even in the dark. "Mr. Wilkins will have my hide for this, miss."

"He won't. I promise. Here," she said, slipping a crown into his hand. "This is for your trouble. And for your secrecy. It's very important you don't tell a soul. I'm counting on your discretion."

"Yes, miss!" he said, ecstatic over the coin in his hand. He helped her onto the mare, and held on to the bridle while she got her bearings. As the mare stepped out into the courtyard, the racket of her hooves resounded like gunplay in the night. April feared the entire household would be roused. She urged the horse in the direction of the fields, and disappeared into the thick soup of darkness.

A NOISE IN THE COURTYARD BELOW BROUGHT Riley to his window. In the moonlight, a hooded figure made off on one of his horses into the night, while a servant bolted shut the stable door.

Moments later, Riley pounded on the door of the grooms' quarters.

"Which one of you released a horse?"

The groomsmen all arose unsteadily, wiping sleep from their eyes—except one. The young apprentice who opened the door still had his jacket on.

Riley's green eyes narrowed as he looked down at the lad, who stood transfixed by the look of the angry master.

"I—I did, sir."

"Who took it out?"

"I'm not supposed to say."

Mr. Wilkins, the head groom, stomped to the doorway and smacked the boy on the back of his head. "Daft boy! Tell the master what he wants to know or you'll feel the leather girth on your backside!"

Ian rubbed his head, his breathing accelerated by fear. "She made me promise not to say."

"She?" Riley seized the boy by his lapels. "Is Miss April out there riding by herself?"

"Y-yes, sir," said the terrified boy. "She gave me a crown to keep quiet about it. Here it is; take it, sir. I was just doing what she told me. I didn't mean to be no trouble, sir."

Riley released the boy. "No. It's all right, son. You keep the money. Just tell me where she went."

"She said she had to go to town, sir. She said it was something important, and then she went down the meadow toward the main road. That's all I know, sir."

Riley's head thundered. What was so important she had to take off in the dead of night all alone on a horse she could hardly ride? He didn't know what was on her mind, but he certainly knew how her mind worked. If she told the boy she was going to town, then she was almost certainly planning to go in the opposite direction.

"Saddle my horse."

RILEY FOUND BERVILIA TETHERED TO THE Hoof & Talon Inn about a half hour's ride out of Blackheath.

Despite the quiet of the sleeping village, the Hoof & Talon was alive with the bustle of men celebrating the end of a week's work. Though warm inside, the smoke-filled air was pungent with the smell of unwashed bodies and alcohol.

Riley pushed his hat down lower over his face and sidled

behind an empty table in a dark corner. From his vantage point, he could survey the entire room: a bar at the far end behind a crush of men three deep, a table-filled salon with dozens of burly workmen, a stairwell that led up to the rooms. At a table by the adjacent wall, like a daisy in a field of crabgrass, sat April Rose Jardine.

He wasn't sure whether to feel relieved that she was all right, or furious that she would come to a place like this. He debated whether he should haul her out by the ear and then carry her back to the manor, or walk out and forget he ever laid eyes on her. Neither, he decided, would tell him what he wanted to know, and so he resolved to watch over her until he knew why she was there.

She was wearing a lavender hooded cape, which she tugged on to conceal her identity. He could only catch glimpses of her face when she turned occasionally to glance at the door.

A serving woman came to take his order. He didn't wish to reveal his identity, so he answered without looking up. At that moment, April motioned to the woman, and Riley hunched over the table as far as he could. The serving woman asked him to repeat his order, which he did as loudly as he could without lifting his face. She shrugged and walked over to April's table, and took away April's beaker.

The door flew open and in came a man. Riley was prevented from seeing his face by the men in the table in front of his, who stood up to make a drunken toast. The man walked over to April's table and sat down, his back to Riley.

From this position, he could clearly see April's face, but not the man's. On her face he saw shock and disbelief, but it quickly darkened to fury. The man spoke for a while, during which time April's expression melted from anger to worry. She looked around her to make sure no one was looking, and then began to unfasten her bodice. The man reached out a hand to stop her.

Riley jerked up from his chair when the man's hand touched hers. But he schooled himself and sat back down. His heart was hammering in his chest, and his hands clenched in controlled fury.

The man motioned for her to come with him, and she hesitated. He spoke a few words more, and finally April got up. Holding the hood close to her face, she followed him to the unlit stairs. They reappeared on the second floor, the man led her into a darkened bedroom, and then the door slammed shut.

Riley sat there, unwilling to believe his eyes. How could he, when they told him that he had just witnessed his beloved bride go into a bedroom with another man? He shook his head as if to answer the questions in his head. When he finally breathed, the air fanned flames of jealousy. He thought the anguish would kill him.

He could go up there and stop them. He could call the man out in the name of honor. He could take her home and lock her up for the rest of her life. But that wouldn't change the knowledge that April went with him.

Willingly.

That word was a dagger that pierced a hole in his chest and skewered his heart. She kept the truth from him, sold his gift, escaped from his home in the night, and went to the arms of another man on the eve of her wedding to him.

Willingly.

He tried to rebuild the wall around his heart, the one he had constructed to protect him from all the faithless women in his life, but it was too late. The damage had already been done.

He desperately considered what he should do now. Suddenly, their door opened and April flew out. She scurried down the stairs, her hood flown back, and ran out the door, her eyes brimming with tears. He fought the urge to run after her and help her, and instead leveled his gaze on the open bedroom door, waiting to see who stepped out.

A few moments later, the man emerged. His face was in shadow as he stooped to light a cigarette. And then he looked up.

Riley stopped breathing.

Sixteen

THE SMOKE SWIRLING FROM THE MAN'S lips dispersed to reveal a face Riley knew well. A face he'd seen since his youth, at university, and throughout his career. It was the face of a trusted friend and personal confidant. It was the face of Peter Northam.

Riley ran up to that face, and punched it with the angry strength of a betrayed husband.

He stood over Northam's crumpled figure. "If you ever touch her again, I'll kill you."

Northam rubbed his stinging cheekbone, which was now bleeding profusely. "You'll regret that, old boy."

"I trusted you, you son of a bitch. You were my friend."

"I trusted her not to tell anyone. Seems you can't trust anyone these days."

Riley growled and hauled Northam up by his shirtfront. "How could you do this to me? On the day before my wedding?"

"What are you upset about—that it happened today or that it happened at all?"

Riley was in no mood for flippant remarks. He cocked

his arm back and drove it into Northam's gut. The man fell to the floor in a heap, gasping for air.

"Come near her again and it'll be the last thing you do. That's not a threat. It's a prediction."

He strode out of the inn and jumped on his horse. Afraid he'd kill April if he returned to the manor, he rode his horse all the way back to his London town house.

APRIL RETURNED TO THE MANOR IN MISery. Her tears were freezing to her face, and her heart felt just as cold. She didn't seem to be able to awaken from this nightmare. In fact, it was getting worse.

Northam's blackmail, she reasoned, was not to hurt her, but to hurt Riley. Her fiancé had no idea that his oldest and dearest friend bore him the most profound hatred. Even after she went to his room to hand him the twenty-thousand-pound payoff, he still did not produce the diary. Instead, he increased his price. Now he wanted *her*.

Horrified, she refused. He whispered to her that she could either submit to him, or be passed from guard to guard at Newgate. He admitted that he wanted her body only to see Riley's face when he told him he'd been cuckolded, and to prove it, he would describe every curve and freckle of her body to him in nauseatingly accurate detail. She slapped him, adamantly refusing to ever hurt Riley in that way. Northam grabbed her, squeezing her arms painfully, warning her that if she did not give herself to him, she would be arrested and the diary would be sent to the *Post*. With his wife in prison and his whoreson brother in disgrace, Riley would become the greatest laughingstock in English history. Either way she decided, Northam would relish every last moment of it.

Faced with choosing between two such disastrous courses of action, April did the only thing she could think of doing: run. And that she did, all the way to Blackheath Manor, perhaps for the very last time.

Now more than ever, she needed to confide in Riley. She had to warn him that his supposed friend was a traitorous villain. She had doubts as to whether he'd believe her now, and he certainly wouldn't appreciate how she came by the information, but all that paled in comparison to what would happen if she didn't trust him with the truth.

THE WEDDING DAY DAWNED, A BRIGHT January morning filled with promise. The servants awoke earlier than usual, in order to prepare the wedding party. All of them were in good spirits, in anticipation of their own celebration at the manor in honor of the master's marriage. But for the present, everyone knew his role, and they all went about their duties with clockwork precision.

Had April been even half as enthusiastic as they, she might have given the impression of a nervous but optimistic bride. As it was, she wished she could remain abed for the rest of the day. Her lack of sleep made her nauseous, her face was swollen from crying, and her head ached from her unresolved anxiety. Numbly, she allowed the maids to bathe her and dress her. It wasn't until she was ushered into the chilly carriage that she even took stock of what was happening to her.

She turned the matter over and over in her mind as the town coach rumbled to London. Jeremy struck up a conversation with Admiral Wolfe of the Royal Navy, a friend of Jonah's who'd be giving her away, and April was immensely happy they didn't involve her overmuch. When the carriage turned onto Newgate Street and passed the jail, she shuddered. Newgate Prison was infamous at Madame Devereux's; any working girl unfortunate enough to get imprisoned there was never heard from again.

April could not cast off the image of herself disappearing into the bowels of the prison, even when the carriage lurched to a halt in front of St. Paul's Cathedral. In her beleaguered mind, instead of walking up the steps of the church, she was approaching the impenetrable iron gate of the jail. She was not marching down the aisle of the church alongside Admiral Wolfe, but being escorted to her cell by a large prison guard. The beaming expressions of the wedding guests refocused into the snarling faces of two thousand inmates. Jeremy's exotic blooms in her bouquet quivered uncontrollably in her hands, like the shackles that she imagined she wore.

But when she finally neared the altar and her eyes landed on Riley, everything changed.

Her nightmare dissolved, and her world became a dream again. How beautiful he was in his royal-blue tailcoat, silver waistcoat, and white breeches. How elegant his snowy cravat, how stylishly combed his black hair. He was the most beautiful man she'd ever seen, both inside and out. Her pace quickened, eager to make the dream come true before the nightmare returned to steal her happiness. He held out his arm, and his eyes met hers. They were swimming with the most profound emotions, something she tried to name. Love? Tenderness? Then just as quickly, it disappeared. The faint lines on the corners of his eyes deepened, his proud chest caved, and his smile vanished. She placed her gloved hand upon his, and was it just her imagination again, or did he give off the bitterest chill?

The archbishop spoke ponderously, but his words were lost on her. She stole occasional glances at Riley, and his expression was dour. Was he angry about the fact that her diamonds were missing? He turned to her and began to speak his vows, but on his lips they sounded sarcastic and hollow. What's more, it seemed she was the only one who detected it. As he placed the ring upon her finger, she desperately hoped that he meant his wedding vows, because she certainly meant every word of hers.

THE WEDDING BREAKFAST WAS HELD AT Riley's London home. People swarmed around them at all times, and they were never alone. Riley seemed distracted, aloof, troubled. When she tried to pull him aside to talk in private, he refused. He rushed through the pleasantries, barely touched his food, and just when the party was truly getting under way, he announced their departure.

Ensconced in their new matrimonial town coach, April finally turned on him. "What the devil is the matter with you?"

Riley leveled his stormy gaze on her. "I have done my duty for Jeremy's sake, and you have done yours. But from now on, your duty is to me. And by God, you're going to do it. I will see to that."

"What are you talking about?"

"Just as I have traded in my future happiness for propriety's sake, you will do likewise. You may expect to live your life henceforth as the very soul of wifely modesty, for I will expect nothing less."

April heaved a sigh. "I'll thank you to not speak in riddles today, Riley. I haven't slept well and I'm in a frightful temper."

He whirled on her. "I didn't sleep at all, knowing that I was to be marrying a faithless woman."

"Faithless—what has gotten into you?"

"I should have known. Women are the same the world over. There isn't a virtuous one in the lot. My mother cuckolded my father time and again, and my father accepted the humiliation of it. Well, not I, madam. If you think that I will roll over while you leapfrog from my bed into another man's, you are epically mistaken. But if you expect to find me in your bed at all, I fear you will also be disappointed. I will not accept another man's used property."

Her astonishment could not have been more palpable. "What?"

His voice boomed in the carriage. "I saw you with Northam last night! I saw you go into his room! On the eve of your wedding, madam. You betrayed me for a *hired servant*."

"Oh, Riley." Relief washed over her after his baffling attack. "You misunderstood. I was just—"

"Spare me the pitiful excuses. You always were an inventive liar. This time, I witnessed it with my own eyes."

"You're mistaken. What you saw—"

"Are you not happy unless you are pitching this family into one scandal or another? I hope your encounter with Northam was good, because it will be the last one you ever have with any man. Hereafter, you will be confined. You will never again set foot outside Blackheath Manor."

"What?"

"You heard me. As prisons go, it's hardly a tortured existence, so I will accept your gratitude for being so lenient."

April's gaze chilled. "Surely now that I am *marchioness*, I trust I may come and go as I please?"

"You are my wife. You come and go as I tell you."

"Just a moment! You're ready to try and convict me without allowing me to offer a defense? And this from a judge renowned for his fairness and justice?"

"I am in hell!" His voice split the air, making the horses jerk. "The thought of another man touching you makes me want to kill him. But the thought of you touching another man makes me want to kill myself!" His eyes misted, and he squeezed them to keep the tears from spilling out.

"Riley, my love, I—"

"Don't . . . *ever* . . . speak of love to me. I loved you once, and that has cost me everything, including my own sanity. I want nothing more to do with love. And nothing more to do with you!"

He pounded on the carriage ceiling, signaling the driver to stop, and got off.

"Riley. Don't say that. I don't exist without you." It was true. She owed everything she'd become to him. And there was no turning back.

Despair marred his face. "Right now, I wish you had never existed at all."

His words punched a hole in her heart.

"Take the lady to Blackheath Manor. See her safely to the door, then tell Forrester that she is not to leave, nor is she in to visitors. You disobey my instructions at your peril."

"Yes, sir," replied the surprised coachman.

Riley looked at her through the open door, his expression betraying his profound pain. "I would have made you a good husband. No man ever loved a woman more than I loved you. The tragedy is that I love you still. I hope, with all my heart, that putting time and distance between us will lessen the pain. Maybe someday I can look upon you without hearing my heart break. Until then, my lady marchioness, enjoy the rest of your life."

The door closed with a sharp report, and the horses broke into a gallop. She cried out to the driver to stop, but he ignored her. She turned to look out the rear window, but all she saw was his diminishing outline, retreating ever farther away.

THE TEARS WERE STILL SPILLING DOWN her cheeks when the carriage approached Blackheath Manor. It was humiliating enough to be dispatched home alone on her wedding night. But when her arrival interrupted the festivities of the servants and villagers at Blackheath Manor, held in her and Riley's honor, the look of shock and embarrassment on their faces was more than she could bear.

She flew to her bedchamber and cried herself to sleep.

WHILE THE CREAM OF SOCIETY CELEBRATED his wedding at his town house, Riley walked the streets of London alone all day. By nightfall, he'd been through two bottles of whiskey.

Why did he fall in love with her? Perhaps the insult of adultery would have been easier to bear if he did not desire all of her caresses for himself, if he did not crave all of her kisses and moans. Those eyes that looked at him with a mixture of awe and desire and affection. How could he not love her?

Perhaps he saw only what he wanted to see. He was not a man given to fancy, but April instilled in him a hunger to be loved. He hadn't known how much he needed it until she offered it to him.

She must be a better actress than he credited her. He could swear on his life that there was love in her eyes when she looked at him. He considered himself a competent judge of people, always able to spot a liar. How could it have been an act?

Then again, he also had failed to foresee Northam's treachery. Like a cancer, Northam had been silently killing off his life, bit by bit, until it was too late to reverse the damage. His tortured mind imagined all sorts of revenge against his supposed friend. Riley downed the last of the bottle and hurled it at an alley wall. Damn his eyes! He would demand satisfaction. He didn't care if the whole world found out that his wife had taken a lover the day before their wedding. He wanted to taste Northam's blood.

Riley stumbled up the stairs to his now-darkened town house. Even in the biting January wind, he was perspiring. He patted his pockets for the key, then realized he was still in his wedding clothes. He pounded on the door until a servant let him in.

He staggered to the library, poured himself a whiskey, and threw himself in a chair. April would not approve of his drinking to ease his pain. Well, damn her, too. She was the cause of it.

He used his cravat, which he had long since loosened and was now hanging limply from his neck, to wipe his face. At last, he was beginning to feel anesthetized to the torment. He surveyed the room through half-closed eyes. There, in the far corner, was a wall of luggage, packed for their honeymoon to Greece. They were supposed to be leaving in a week. Through a drunken haze, Riley peered at the initials emblazoned on the trunks: *AH*.

The contents of his glass spilled onto the floor as he buried his face in his hands.

HAMMERING.

Someone was hammering in the room.

Riley stirred from sleep and mumbled an incoherent protest, but it didn't stop. He vowed to sack the servant who dared to make such a racket in his presence—and in his present state. Forcing himself to emerge from the numbing syrup of unconsciousness to silence the noise, he sat up, and an intense throbbing battered his temples. His hands flew to his head, as if he needed to keep his brains from exploding out of his ears. Was that dreadful noise in his own head?

There it was again. Someone was banging on the front door.

The clock on the mantel read four-thirty. In the morning.

A wave of nausea passed over him as he attempted to stand. He steadied himself, and then walked gingerly to the front door.

"Who?" The taste in his mouth was redolent of horse turds.

"Open the door in the name of the law."

He unbolted the door, fighting another wave of sickness. Three brawny men shouldered their way past him.

"Lord Blackheath? We've orders to take the Marchioness of Blackheath into custody of the constabulary."

"Who?"

"Your wife, sir."

"Oh." Riley wiped his open palm down his face, and rubbed the stubble that had spread across his chin. "On what charge, Constable?"

"On the charge of extortion, sir. Will you direct my men to her location, please, sir?"

"Just a moment. On what grounds is this accusation made?"

"The magistrate has evidence of her guilt in this matter."

"Evidence? Who procured this evidence?"

"I have orders to bring her in, sir. Do I need to search the house?"

"I demand to know who brings this charge against my wife."

"Sir, if you don't cooperate—"

"Constable, do you know who I am? I am a Circuit Judge of His Majesty's—"

"He knows who you are, Riley." Northam stepped into the doorway. "We all do."

Riley took a step back. "You!"

Northam still bore an angry welt on his left cheek, an island of white in a sea of blue-black. "I hate to interrupt your wedding night, old boy, but I have a duty to Lady Justice."

Riley's eyes burned with unfulfilled bloodlust. "Lady Justice demands that you and I also have a reckoning."

"Soon. For now, there is another matter to settle. Find her, men."

"She's not here," Riley said, his eyes never leaving Northam's.

"Come now. You don't expect us to believe that she jilted you on your wedding night, too, do you?"

Riley's eyes flashed green fire, his hands throbbing with the desire to wrap his fingers around Northam's throat. "She's not here."

"You must be losing your touch, old boy. Search the place."

"Don't bother. If my wife is accused of a crime, I will answer for it. Take me instead."

The constables glanced uncertainly at Northam.

Northam pasted his expansive grin back onto his face. "How noble of you. But April is the one—"

"Under the law of coverture, the husband must answer for the wife's crimes and debts. You'd know that if you were any good at jurisprudence."

Northam flinched at the insult, but Riley could tell from his expression that he had upset Northam's plans.

Northam crossed his arms. "In the interest of our past friendship, I will give you another opportunity to send down the girl. Think of your career, your reputation. Besides, I don't need to tell you what it would be like for you to be incarcerated with the same villains and deviants that you yourself put there. Give me the girl, and let her answer to her own crimes. Accept my advice; it's the last I'll ever give you as your solicitor and as your friend."

Riley had already considered it. But the thought of April in a place like Newgate filled him with dread. Despite what she had done, and despite his attempt to drink her out of his heart, he loved her too much to subject her to such an ordeal. This decision confirmed what he knew since the moment he met her: loving Miss April Rose Jardine was the greatest happiness he had ever known—and an irreversible curse. Besides, he wouldn't give Northam the satisfaction. "Good friends make the best enemies, do they not? But only a fool takes the advice of an adversary."

Northam tilted his head. "So be it." He leaned in close to whisper in Riley's ear. "You know, I'm looking forward to seeing you in the morning, when the realization of what you've done hits you full force. I'll remind you of right now, when you were too blind stinking drunk to tell which one of you should be in prison."

Riley matched his bold stare. "You may be right. Some asses have four legs and some have two, and at the moment, I'm too drunk to tell which one you are."

Northam's victorious smile melted, and he sent his fist flying into Riley's stomach.

Riley doubled over, warring with the urge to spew.

"Take him away!"

Seventeen

WHEN APRIL AWOKE ALMOST TWELVE hours after she fell asleep, she was remarkably clearheaded. And angry as a hornet.

Who the bloody hell was he to speak to her like that? How dare he ruin her wedding day deliberately, in order to punish her for a misunderstanding! It was beyond intolerable, and she was going to march straight to London and *force* him to listen to her side of it, even if she had to tie him up to do it.

And bugger Northam and his clandestine blackmail, too. There were too many damned secrets in this family already without her having to keep another one. She would tell Riley everything that happened. She needed to. His so-called friend was a dangerous blackguard, and he must know this. To prove it, she would show him the page from the diary with the blackmail note written upon it.

She descended the grand staircase and confronted the butler. "Forrester, please have Mr. Wilkins prepare a carriage for me."

"I'm sorry, miss. The master has left precise instructions that you are not to leave the manor under any circumstances."

April bit back a venomous reply. She had only Riley to blame for that high-handed and degrading treatment. She would have words with him about that, as well.

"Going somewhere?" Jonah emerged from his study.

"Your Grace. As a matter of fact, I was on my way to see my husband."

Jonah snorted derisively. "You won't go far without a pickaxe and a shovel. He's in Newgate Prison, thanks to you."

Her eyes bulged. "What?"

"He was arrested this morning. A footman at the town house arrived with the news two hours ago."

"And you're only just telling me?" she asked, her voice frantic. "What did he do wrong?"

"He married you."

"How is that a crime?"

"It isn't. The only crimes have been committed by you. My poor son is the one who must suffer the consequences."

April gave an exasperated sigh. "You're not making any sense. Why is he in jail?"

"As if you didn't know! Does the term *feme covert* ring any bells? That's what you became as soon as you married my son. You knew that once you married into his protection, Riley would become responsible for all legal actions concerning you, including your crimes. You'd be guiltless and he would be accountable. But you planned this right from the start, didn't you?"

His words buzzed around in her head, but didn't quite settle into any sort of logic. "I—I need to see him. Tell the servants to get me a carriage."

"So you can inflict more damage? Never!"

Rage fomented within her. "Listen, old man, I'm not going to sit here while my husband rots in Newgate. You tell them to get me a carriage, or I will make you regret your hesitation!"

"How dare you threaten me!"

She squared off on him. "I haven't begun to threaten you. Do it!" She stormed back up the staircase to her room.

Jonah charged after her, his jowls jiggling with indignation. "How dare you insult me in my own home? Who do you think you are?"

"I am the Marchioness of Blackheath, and Riley's wife," she responded, tossing the words over her shoulder. "He's not going to sit in prison one more second on my account. I'm going to take his place."

"You've done quite enough as it is. You aren't going anywhere."

She stomped into her bedroom. "And remain here with you doing nothing? I think not." She grabbed the picnic basket from the wardrobe and upended it over her bed. The tiny tin soldiers and Riley's other toys she had kept as a reminder of their days in the cave fell onto the rumpled bedsheets. She then began to throw in any remaining clothing from the wardrobe, whatever hadn't been packed for their honeymoon.

Jonah burst in after her. "Now you listen here. You will address me with respect. I will tolerate your offensive attitude no longer."

"You won't have to, you vinegary old coot. I'm leaving."

His face purpled. "I knew you were nothing but trouble. I told Riley to find you another husband."

She laughed bitterly. "I'm quite certain you mentioned it to Agatha, as well."

"Yes, I did! She always suspected you were an impostor. Clearly, there's no substitute for good breeding."

She turned on him. "You weren't so fickle when you believed me to be the bastard daughter of a prostitute. Now that you know me to be decently born, I am not fit to be married to your son."

"My son deserves a wife of noble blood."

"Your son deserves a wife who loves him."

"Rubbish! Love makes fools of us all. Look at him now. His magistracy, his position, his reputation—in tatters because of some ridiculous romantic impulse. He's an object of ridicule now."

His words stung her. "There was a time when you yourself would have given everything up for love. Maybe that might have made a happier man out of you. Now, look at you. Your heart is as dry and brittle as the logs in the hearth. Is that what you want for your son?"

"Is this any better?"

April pursed her lips. "No. But I'm going to sort it all out."

Jonah laughed. "What are you going to do? Walk up and demand they release him?"

She sat on the bed and began to button up her boots. "It'll do for a start."

"Stupid girl! He's going to be tried in open court! He doesn't need you. He needs his solicitor. I've just sent for him. That's what *I've* been doing."

She harrumphed. "If it's Peter Northam you've consulted, I suggest you hire someone else. He's very likely the man who had Riley arrested."

"Northam? He's been a friend of the family since he was a boy."

April rolled her eyes. "You really are a gullible old fool! He's been duping you for years. I don't know why Northam hates Riley so much, but he was biding his time until he could make Riley suffer. But stupid me, I'm the one who finally gave him the opportunity."

She closed the lid on the basket and faced Jonah, who stood in the doorway. "Are you going to send for my carriage?"

"No. Riley doesn't want you with him, or else he wouldn't have ordered that you remain at Blackheath. You're not going anywhere." He straightened in the doorway, blocking her exit with his full height.

"That's what you think." With the waist of his breeches exposed, she tugged on the uppermost button, and the fabric fell away. She shouldered past him as the duke struggled to pull his pants back up.

APRIL BEGAN THE LONG WALK TO THE nearest inn, where she could hire a stagecoach. She walked amid the trees, avoiding the main road for fear that Jonah would send men out to recapture her. It was slowing her down, but she had to keep to this hidden path until she was sure that no one was following her.

Before long, she heard a carriage approach. She hid behind the hedgerows, waiting for it to pass. But then she heard Jenny's voice calling her.

She stepped out of hiding and walked to the main road, where Jenny and William sat ensconced in the driver's bench.

"There you are!" Jenny cried. "I was so afraid something had happened to you."

"If His Grace sent you out to collect me . . ."

Jenny shook her head. "No, he doesn't know. We told Mr. Wilkins we were going to town to do the shoppin'. We're here to help you get to London to see Riley."

"How did you know?"

"I was listenin' at the door."

April sighed gratefully. "I'm so glad you're incorrigible. Remind me to buy you something really special."

"How about a weddin' dress?" she responded, her face brightening.

LADY AGATHA STORMED THROUGH PETER Northam's front door. In her rage, she had completely lost any interest in protocol, thoroughly unmindful of the unseemliness of a woman entering a bachelor's apartments in broad daylight.

"Agatha," deadpanned Northam. "How lovely to see you. Do come in."

She tossed her wrap on the settee and unfastened her bonnet. "Don't give me that. What in blazes is Riley doing in jail?"

"Change of plans."

"You said you'd take *her* out of the picture. Riley's no good to me in prison."

Northam tethered his insulted pride. "Why should that concern you now? He's never been good to you anyway."

Agatha gritted her perfect teeth. "You promised me that you would have her thrown in prison. Why is she still free?"

"Keep your voice down." He walked over to her and placed his hands on her bottom, grinding seductively against her. "She paid the blackmail, you know. All twenty thousand pounds. Marry me, Agatha, and all your financial troubles will be over."

She pulled away from him in disgust. "My furs alone cost more than that."

He muttered an oath. "You still won't marry me? I'm giving you everything I have, including my love, and you still won't have me?"

"Darling." She smiled stiffly. "What we have is so much better. Why ruin it with all this guff about marriage? We can always carry on with our . . . understanding."

Northam's nostrils flared. "While you're married to him, is that it?"

"One of the things I've always liked about you is your antimatrimonial ideals. Please don't disappoint me now."

"Agatha, I love you. Haven't I proven that? Riley won't risk all that he has for you as I've done."

She glided over to him, and rubbed her hands up and

down his chest, a touch she knew he always found intensely erotic. "I can't be bothered with his love, darling," she purred. "I couldn't care a whit about Riley. You, on the other hand, I do care about. I've always been grateful you've been so devoted to me. I wish things were different between us, Peter, really I do. But you see, with Riley, there are . . . compensations. It's no reflection on you. But twenty thousand means nothing to a man of his resources. If I were to become Marchioness of Blackheath, there would be no end to the money you and I could enjoy."

Northam looked at her suspiciously. "I'm not a fool, Agatha. I know you want him."

"Darling, don't be so jealous. You know I find you irresistible. Riley can't hold a candle to you. But as his wife, I'll be entitled to a vast fortune that you and I can share."

But Northam knew she was manipulating him. He had always known. "And just how did you expect to become his wife? He's turned you down on a number of occasions."

Agatha closed her eyes, but her ubiquitous smile emerged. "The diary, darling. The plan was that when April is convicted, Riley can annul her. And if she hangs . . . well, so much the better. Once she's out of his hair, I could get another crack at him. And if he still won't marry me, I could threaten to turn over the diary to the scandal pages. I'm quite certain there will be no further obstacles to our union."

Northam shook his head. "Your plan failed to account for his selflessness. He took her place under the principle of coverture."

Her hands froze. "You mean he went to jail . . . for her?"

Northam nodded. "He'll be tried tomorrow."

Agatha turned away. "That fool! That stupid fool! What sort of a hold does that tart have over him? It's inconceivable."

"Perhaps to you, but the fact remains that he passed you over for that tart. But I'm sure it's no reflection on you," he said, throwing her own words back at her.

Now he had made her mad. She walked up to him and held out her hand. "Enough. Give me the diary. Riley won't get convicted. He'll find a way to get out. And when he's released, I'll need that book. Give it to me."

He squinted. "I don't think so."

"Give me the diary," she insisted. "I can't blackmail him if you have it."

"Forget it. It stays with me. I want him ruined."

Agatha was aghast. "You lied to me! You didn't just want the twenty thousand pounds. You were going to use the diary to ruin him anyway."

"I did what you asked, Agatha, and it didn't work. Now, we're going to try things my way."

"No! It can still work. Our plan goes forward."

"Circumstances are proving even more favorable than we planned, Agatha. Just sit back and watch them unfold."

A frown marred her elegant face. "I don't want him ruined. He's useless to me if you bring him down."

Northam beamed. "I know. In fact, I'm counting on it. Don't worry, Agatha. If you want his fortune, you can have it. But you'll have to go through me first."

RILEY SAT IN HIS CELL, WEIGHING THE decision whether or not he was hungry enough to eat the only meal he would be given that day. Despite his raging hangover, which made his stomach churn at the mere thought of food, the plate before him did nothing to appeal to his appetite. One piece of bread as hard and dense as a brick, a cup of watery broth that smelled like dirty laundry, and a square of questionable-looking meat. He shook his head. At least there were no insects in it.

They'd be coming for the plate soon. Until then, he had another quarter of an hour to convince himself to eat.

He stood and walked to the cell's only window to stand in its muted light, seeking some warmth from the paralyzing cold. Although he was well over six feet tall, he could not see out of it. The cell was so narrow that if he stretched out his arms, he could touch the opposite walls. For his necessities, there was a hole in one corner, but the fumes that wafted up from it drove him back. He would never again take the open air for granted.

Or indeed any of his other luxuries. Even here, he recognized, he was living as a prince among prisoners. He was being held in a cell reserved for those awaiting trial, which were cleaner and more private than those for the people who were serving out their sentences. He had passed those cells as he was brought to his own. They were dank and filthy pens housing three men each, and they reeked of human waste and bodies unwashed for years. Insects crunched under his feet as he walked, and the rats walked freely through the cells as though the inmates were the vermin.

He shook his head, urging himself to focus his mind on more constructive pursuits, like strategizing for his defense. How easily one loses hope in a place like this. His thoughts drifted again to April. It might have felt better if he were protecting a faithful woman, but it wouldn't have affected his decision. He couldn't see himself living at Blackheath while April merely subsisted behind a foot and a half of solid brick, buried in the bowels of a prison that was as inhospitable to women as it was hospitable to disease. He couldn't imagine the desolation in her eyes as the prison guards stole her dignity. He couldn't stand it if she begged to be impregnated so that she could plead a belly when it came time for her execution. No matter what she had done to him, no matter how she had made him suffer, he couldn't let anything bad happen to her.

He sighed. Of course, his defense wouldn't be any easier now that she was on the outside. How could it? She was guilty. His only hope was that the Chief Justices would show mercy. Riley knew that at the very least, the trial would cost him his seat on the bench and his position in Society. But all that paled in comparison to the only thing of any real importance now: to win back his freedom.

The metal gate down the hall opened, and he heard footsteps approach his cell. A key was inserted into his door, and with a loud metallic grind, the lock turned. The door groaned as it was pulled open. He squinted in the light, until the shadow in the door transformed into the outline of Peter Northam.

Riley leapt at Northam's throat, with the sole intention of squeezing it until he begged for mercy. But a burly guard tackled him, pinning him to the far wall, and manacled his wrists to the chains bolted to the mortar.

"Thank you, Constable. I won't be a moment," Northam said, adjusting his rumpled neckcloth. "Well, as I live and breathe. Lord Blackheath! I never thought to see you in such, shall we say, *reduced* circumstances. It's a far cry from the splendors of Blackheath Manor, isn't it?"

Perspiration sheened on Riley's face. "Why have you done this to me?"

"Poor Riley. Do you truly feel done by? Has life treated you unfairly? You have my deepest sympathies."

"I thought I had your friendship!" His voice reverberated in the small enclosure.

"Friendship?" He snickered, shaking his golden head. "Your idea of friendship is typical of the aristocracy, old boy. Only offered when something is expected. And never when really needed."

His handsome features twisted in bewilderment. "What are you talking about? I never treated you like that. You were practically a member of my family. In many ways, closer than a brother. I trusted you! How could you repay me like this?"

"Repay? You expect to be repaid? For what? For keeping me in your shadow? For being able to afford to become a bloody barrister when all I could hope for was enough business to keep my job at the firm? For enduring the humiliation of being your humble solicitor while you ascended all the way to the judicial seat in half the time it takes most other men?"

"Is that what this is about? Professional jealousy?"

"Don't flatter yourself, Riley. You're not that good. The only reason you made it so quickly was because of your title and your wealth. If you weren't so full of yourself you'd see that."

Betrayal ignited into fury. "And if you weren't always hiding your professional inadequacy behind a mask of privation, you'd see that you had just as many opportunities as I did."

"Did I? Remember who you're talking to, old boy. I've been rooming with you all throughout Eton and Oxford. I'm surprised you managed to learn anything with all the professors falling over themselves for the privilege of licking your boots. And don't tell me that your father's generous endowments to the schools had nothing to do with it."

"You're always trying to blame my family's money for your shortcomings. My father didn't buy my skills or my high marks on exams. You can't become a barrister without knowing the law, and you can't become a judge without being a bloody good barrister."

Northam poked at the untouched food on Riley's plate. "What I don't understand is why you had to pursue the law in the first place. You had your titles, an estate of your own. You're the first son, with all the privileges and honors that it buys you. Why give other men the competition? You don't even need to work. But you're so bloody selfish, you begrudge lesser men the crumbs off your table."

"I won't be blamed for your misfortunes. Like you or any other man, I have the right to pursue my own passions."

"Pursue your passions . . ." he repeated. "Like you pursued Agatha?"

Riley blinked. "What?"

"You bested me in school, you snatched the barristership, and then you took Agatha away from me. How can you stand there and call us brothers?"

"I didn't know you wanted Agatha. She and I . . . I meant nothing to her."

"Oh, but you did. Her love is just something else your money and titles bought."

"You're wrong about that. I couldn't afford her. That's why she married Ravenwood."

"You fool. She married him because you loved your career more. And now you choose the thieving little tramp April over her. Do you have any idea how that made her feel?"

"At the time, it was necessary to become engaged to April. The rumors would have destroyed our family."

"Yes, I know, old boy. I'm the one who started them."

Riley's breath caught in his chest, as surely as if Northam had punched him there. "You?"

"You have only her to blame, you know. It was a mistake for you to take her into your family. She made you vulnerable. Your Achilles' heel, as it were. It left your reputation wide open to attack. All I had to do was leave a few well-placed words, and then sit back and watch you dance."

Riley jerked at his chains, but his futile attempt made Northam chuckle.

"That girl was a godsend to me. After these many years, she gave me the perfect opportunity to finally see you suffer. She even left behind a weapon I hadn't counted on."

Anger pulsed through Riley. "The diary!"

"The diary. She's quite clever, that one. I'm surprised she was able to swindle so many high-ranking, educated men."

"You invited them to the Minister's Ball, didn't you? To trap April!"

Northam nodded. "I must admit I enjoyed watching her squirm. What I didn't understand is why you paid those men off, when you could have sided with them and cut her loose. And then I knew: you had fallen in love with her. That was a happy and unexpected turn of events. It made blackmailing her all the more effective."

"What?"

Northam's mouth gaped. "She didn't tell you?"

Riley was overcome with remorse. That's why April sold her jewels and went to see Northam that night! She went to pay him off!

Northam watched his face. "No, I can see that she didn't. How touching."

Riley cursed himself. He was a fool for doubting her love. He would not make that mistake ever again. "Is that why you were out for April's blood? Because Agatha wanted me over you?"

"It's only your money, old boy. She doesn't really want you. You're nothing but an accident of birth. Once you're out of the picture, she'll see who the better man really is."

Riley could almost spit with disgust. "A better man might have declared his intentions, might have called me out for the right to her hand. A better man would have fought for her. What kind of an honorless, impotent coward skulks about plotting the downfall of another man to win a lady's affection?"

Northam rose to his full height. "Don't lecture me on your perceptions of honor. I won't accept it from a man whose accomplishments all came as a result of his titles.

Look at you now. Your name is worthless. No one will have anything to do with you. Your precious reputation... ruined. From now on, the name Blackheath will always be a drawing room punchline. You'll be torn to shreds whenever your name is uttered. But don't worry. I've spared you the ignominy of hearing it firsthand. You won't be exposed to many drawing rooms behind the bars of Newgate or Marshalsea. I'll content myself with that for now. Once you succumb to jail fever, or die at the hands of the criminals you once convicted, your wife will become a very rich widow. And I'll make certain she doesn't stay a widow for long."

Riley strained at his chains. "Damn it, Northam, you stay away from her!"

"Don't worry, old boy. I won't keep her long. It's not her I want. Once I marry into her money and estates, Agatha won't be able to turn me away. And then we'll have no more use for your April."

Riley struggled against his chains until he was winded.

Northam chuckled. "Who's impotent now?" He lit a cigar using the only candle in the cell. "See you at the trial, old boy."

THE CAB CAME TO A STOP IN FRONT OF THE Pleasure Emporium, and April heaved a nervous sigh.

"You sure you want to go in there, miss?" asked the driver. "That's a house of ill repute. You go in there unescorted, people are like to mistake you for one o' them strumpets, if you'll pardon the word."

April reached into her reticule, and placed a few coins into his hand. "Thank you. I'm sure I'll be all right."

"I'd go in with ye, exceptin' my missus'd have my head if I ever set foot in a place like that."

April was not looking forward to it, either. Having just come from Newgate Prison, where she had to be forcibly and roughly ejected after she was refused permission to see Riley, she decided this would be the best course of action. She walked to the front door and turned the handle.

The warm smell of sex and liquor that assaulted her was at once repugnant and familiar. The pianoforte in the other room was playing a boisterous tune, and she could hear the same voices laughing and singing along. The old feelings of weakness and despair came flooding back. If she had heard the words "April Jardine, come clean," she would have begun to look for a mop.

"Can I 'elp you?"

The voice made her jump. She whirled around.

The thick makeup did nothing to hide her age. "Glenda?"

"Yes?"

"It's me. April."

A frown creased her brow, and then illumination dawned. "April Jardine?" She looked April up and down in amazement. "Cor, you done well for yourself, 'aven't you? But what you doin' back 'ere? Madame was in such a state when you left. If she sees you now, she'll have your guts for garters."

April swallowed. "I came to see her, Glenda. Is she here?"

The prostitute's eyes grew round. "You sure?"

April nodded, her mouth too dry to speak. Glenda went into the salon.

The seconds stretched into eternities, and it was this—time alone with her frenzied thoughts—that she had come to dread. Now, her thoughts turned to the memory of the walks that she and Riley took near the cave, the snow making sharp crescents on either side of the path. One time, she slipped on a patch of frost, and he caught her. Back then, she knew—just knew—he would always catch her, no matter how often she fell. Well, now it was Riley who was about to hit the floor, and she'd be damned before she'd let that happen. Once again, she wished she could turn back the hands of the clock to a more innocent time, when her heart was not a jungle of fear, tangled by the vines of regret. But then she would not have known the indescribable joy of falling in love with Riley.

Finally, the Madame came out, followed by a gaggle of girls. It was a moment she had dreamed of since she had left the brothel: when all the girls she used to clean up after would gawk at her with awe and envy. But April's mind was far from childish boasts. She was here to beg the Madame for her help in freeing her husband.

The Madame stood before her, looking like a queen who'd just been insulted by a serf. April's palms began to sweat into her French silk gloves.

"Madame," she began, her voice faltering, "a moment of your time?" Suddenly, April felt like an upstart scullery maid caught in the act of dressing up as the Marchioness of Blackheath.

The Madame's eyebrow shot up imperiously, her elegant mouth expressing her disdain. Her head turned ever so surreptitiously in the direction of the girls crowding in behind her. "Get back to work!" she barked. April jumped and almost started for the kitchens.

The Madame led the way up to her office. She sat behind her desk, and once again, April felt like a misbehaving servant about to receive the sack.

The silence yawned between them.

"Madame," April began, speaking in French. "I've come to ask for your pardon."

The Madame leaned back in her chair, her mouth a moue of impatience.

April squeezed the handle of her reticule. "I stole your personal diary and made away with it. I persuaded Jenny to come with me, and together we left you without a word. I took advantage of your trust in me, and I crippled your business. For these things, I humbly beg your forgiveness."

"Very eloquent. But why are you here?"

"Madame?"

"Why do you seek my forgiveness? I believe I can safely deduce from the quality of your clothes that you have not come to ask for your job back. Yet I am equally confident that you would never have set foot in my establishment again, if you did not require something of me. So I repeat, why are you here?"

As always, the Madame's characteristic perspicacity and directness made April completely uncomfortable. "It's my husband. He's in jail. And you have it in your power to help him get out."

The Madame smiled, the slow, lazy grin of someone who's just discovered she has the winning hand in a card game. "Ah, now we have it. Please, carry on," she said, and lit a cigarette.

April explained how she used the diary to pose as the Madame's daughter and successfully extracted money from the men who feared they had fathered her. She explained how the diary had fallen into the hands of a man more nefarious than herself, who used it to have her arrested, but took her husband in her place. April's voice choked when she came to that part.

"And what would you have me do?" the Madame asked.

"Your diary is the only evidence against us. Show up in court, and claim that it is a forgery."

"Preposterous. You ask that I commit perjury?"

"It would not be the first time you broke an English law."

"Why should I? Why should I risk my own freedom for your husband's?"

April reached into her reticule. "Here is seven thousand

pounds. It is all the money that I have in the world. It is everything I have been given by the men I deceived, plus a great deal more. If it is not enough, I can arrange to get you whatever price you name."

The Madame let a column of smoke curl up from her lips. "Your money will do me no good in prison. No."

"Then, if you will not do it for my husband, will you do it for my father-in-law?"

The Madame laughed, reaching out to flick her ashes. "One man is as inconsequential to me as the next."

"His name is Jonah Hawthorne, Duke of Westbrook."

The cigarette stopped in mid-air, causing the ash to miss the saucer and fall on the desk. "So you married into the Hawthorne family? You read my diary, so you know that he and I used to mean something to each other. But it has been a lifetime since then. Our love died long ago."

April shook her head. "You still mean a great deal to him. He talks of you with great longing. And regret."

"I don't believe that."

"It's true. He is in agony still."

"Agony?" she said, her nostrils flaring with rage. "He hasn't experienced anything close to the agony that I have known." She stood and went to the window, staring out at the London night.

"I know all about the babe that he took from you. He broke his relationship off with you, and then wrested the child from your arms to raise in luxury while you were forced to fend for yourself. I know he hurt you. And so does he."

April could not see the Madame's face. She stood in front of the window with her arms crossed.

"But Madame, if you could see that child now . . . He's grown into a fine, compassionate man. Noble, gallant. And he's about to be married. To a cousin of Queen Charlotte herself! You would be so proud. He resembles you so very much . . ."

The Madame made no sound, but April could tell her words were getting through.

"This is why it is doubly important for you to renounce this diary. If suspicion lands on the facts of Jeremy's birth, he will be disgraced. The scandal will reach all the way up to the monarchy itself. The Queen will call off the wedding, and that would destroy him. He is most desperately in love with Emily, you see."

Still, the Madame said nothing.

"Madame, I realize that I have wronged you terribly. And so has Jonah. But I implore you, if for no other reason, please help us for the sake of your son. Riley has struggled his entire life to protect his brother from the scandal of his real birth, and in just a few weeks, I have managed to bring all of his efforts to naught. I will give you anything you ask if you help me to rescue the people that I have grown to love with all my heart. I know I don't deserve your mercy, and yet . . . Will you do this?"

The Madame cleared her throat. But she did not turn away from the window. "The woman who would have said yes to you died a long time ago. Those people are nothing to me now. I'm sorry."

April's heart fell. "Madame, I beg you to reconsider . . ."

The Madame's voice took on the tone that April remembered only too well as her final word on a subject. "No. Now go before I have *you* arrested. You can join your beloved husband on the gallows for aught I care."

Mustering all the courage she had, April stood up on unsteady legs. "If this is the limit of the love a mother has for a child, then I hope to God I never conceive. I'm glad that Jeremy never knew you as his mother. It would appear that even his stepmother, who cared for him not at all, loved him more than you." Amid tears for her inability to help Riley, April flew down the stairs and out into the night.

THE MADAME WATCHED APRIL CROSS UN-
der her window and run down the street. She lost track of how long she stood there, just staring out onto the street. It was her fifth cigarette—or was it her sixth?—when one of the girls knocked on the door and told her that a gentleman was there to see her.

"Who is it?"

The girl brought over the man's calling card.

"Ah, yes. Send Mr. Northam in."

Eighteen

"PRAY, SILENCE. BE UPSTANDING IN COURT all persons who have anything to do before my lords, the King's Justices of *oyer* and *terminer* and for the jurisdiction of the Sessions House, draw near and give your attendance. God save the King."

The Old Bailey was filling to the rafters with people who had come to witness the most talked-about trial in years. The buzz around the court began to hush as the chief justices walked in, and assumed their seats with the usual formalities.

Riley stood. As barrister, he had argued countless times from the bar, but never, in his worst nightmares, had he ever imagined that he'd be addressing the judge from the dock. Here, the air was dense with the smell of old wood and frayed nerves.

A hand swiped his face absently, the three-day growth of beard pricking his skin. He still wore his wedding clothes, which were now rumpled and smudged from the two days he had spent in the cell awaiting trial. He looked around the room, anxiously scanning the court for April.

His sleepless eyes scoured the room. Hundreds of curious

faces looked back at him, but none resembled the familiar one he sought. And as everyone resumed their seat, only one person remained standing.

April.

Although she looked terrified and exhausted, her presence there gave him the strength that had failed him. Regret over the appalling things he had said to her when they last had parted still burned in his conscience, and he was overjoyed to see her. Her lips moved. *I love you,* she mouthed, and it filled him with a sense of elation . . . and panic.

The court clerk's voice boomed across the room once more, tearing his attention away from April's face. "Riley James Patrick Hawthorne, Lord Blackheath, you stand charged on the indictment that April Rose Hawthorne, Lady Blackheath, did extort money from one Cedric Markham, knight of the realm, on the twelfth of October last, in the County of London. How say you, Lord Blackheath? Are you guilty or not guilty?"

The spectators held their collective breath.

Riley's knuckles whitened on the wooden bar in front of him. "Not guilty."

The judge, a wizened but shrewd-looking man, looked up from the dossier before him to Riley. The round spectacles sitting on his nose were the same diameter as the curls on his white periwig.

"Before I instruct the jury, Lord Blackheath, I understand that you wish to stand trial on behalf of your wife, under the principle of coverture."

"If it please you, m'lord."

"It is *de rigueur* in civil proceedings, as I'm sure you are aware, but in a criminal trial, this is very irregular."

"There exists a precedent, m'lord. In the matter of *the King* versus *Whiting*, 1747, the husband appeared in place of his wife when she was accused of robbery."

He peered down at the papers in front of him. "From what I gather, Lord Blackheath, the crime your wife is accused of was perpetrated prior to your legal union, was it not?"

"We were married after the fact, m'lord, yes."

"Your wife was not a *feme covert* at the time of the crime, then?"

"No, m'lord."

"Then I'm afraid I will have to rule against your motion to stand in for your wife. Bailiff, is Lady Blackheath presently in the court?"

"She is, my lord," the bailiff replied.

"Please usher her to the dock. The prisoner is free to go."

An excited murmur rippled through the courtroom as the principal players in this trial changed. Everyone waited to see the woman whose name was splashed across all the newspapers. The stocky bailiff waddled down the aisle to where April was seated, and escorted her to the dock. All eyes watched her go.

She passed in front of Riley, a valiant smile on her lips. She whispered, "*I* deserve this, not you. Don't fear. I'll always love you."

A cold dread smothered him. She was guilty . . . there was no way she would be able to win this trial. But she would not go down alone.

"M'lord," Riley said, "may it please you, I am a barrister of record in this courtroom, and would like to serve as my wife's defense counsel."

"So be it," the judge answered. "Who stands for the prosecution?"

Northam rose. "I do, m'lord. Though I am not a great barrister as is my learned friend, I shall endeavor to represent the King's interests as ably as I can, as befitting the honor and dignity of the Crown."

He glanced down the bench to where Northam was sitting. The bastard was actually pleased with himself. No matter which of them was convicted, it suited his plans just fine. Riley looked down, the burden of freeing April weighing even more heavily upon him. Even if he could convince the jury not to hang her, she would not be able to survive a heavy term of imprisonment. Her life was now in his hands.

As April was being sworn in, Riley felt a tap on his shoulder. He turned to see Agatha sitting behind him, looking flawless in an ermine-lined burgundy pelisse.

"You're a fool, Riley. That wife of yours is going to cost you everything you hold dear."

He glanced at April. "She *is* what I hold dear."

Her pretty nostrils flared. "But you won't hold her long. If only you had been man enough to take me when you had the chance."

His brows furrowed. "Why, Agatha? You don't love me."

A red grin cut across her mouth, and her eyes looked askance at Northam. "That's right. And you're about to find out how much I don't."

The threat surprised Riley, who looked in Northam's direction. With an air of bravado, Northam nodded deferentially at him, thoroughly enjoying a victory that only they seemed to know about.

The judge removed his spectacles and turned to the jury box. "Gentlemen of the jury, the prisoner stands indicted for that she, on the twelfth day of October, did extort money from Sir Cedric Markham. To this indictment, a plea of not guilty has been registered, and it is your charge to say, having heard the evidence, whether she be guilty or not. You have taken an oath to try this case impartially and without prejudice. You must base your judgment only on the evidence presented in this court." He faced the bar. "Mr. Northam, you may proceed with the case for the prosecution."

"Thank you, m'lord." Northam stood, looking sleek and polished in a brand-new coat of rich burgundy velvet, oozing charm and self-assurance. Northam's fashionable clothes, golden hair, and winning smile was making a favorable impression upon the six men in the jury box, while Riley, unwashed, unshaven, and unkempt, most likely had the opposite effect. The trial hadn't even started yet, and already Riley was at a marked disadvantage.

"Gentlemen of the jury," Northam began, "the facts in this case are simple. The prisoner who stands before you bears every appearance of being a lady. But today you will learn that she is anything but that. Not only is she of common birth and occupation, but she has led a life that would scandalize others of her fair sex. Today, you will discover the depravity of her character, the ruthlessness of her greed, and the wantonness of her ambition. In short, you will be shown evidence as to how this innocent-looking woman stole her trusting employer's diary, this book I now hold in my hand, and used it to blackmail a high-ranking officer of His Majesty's government. He is not, I may add, her only victim. The prosecution knows of five other men who fell into her trap of deception, but for reasons I am sure you will appreciate, they were reluctant to present testimony in open court. In fact, had I not confiscated this diary six weeks ago, there might have been even more unwitting victims of this conniving woman's extortion schemes. Do not let the fact that the prisoner is the wife of a judge sway your decision away from a guilty verdict. Even my worthy opponent will agree that the law is meaningless if not applied consistently. In the words of William Shakespeare, we must not make a scarecrow of the law."

Riley watched as the men of the jury nodded their assent.

"I will now call her principal victim, Sir Cedric Markham, Clerk of the Parliaments."

The room buzzed as the call for the witness echoed down the courtroom. Markham was escorted from an outer room to the witness box.

A tornado of anger stormed inside Riley. Many times, he had tried to see Markham to make restitution and come to some agreement of peace, but he refused to even see Riley. Now he knew why. At whatever cost to himself, Markham wanted vengeance against April.

Markham was handed the Bible and a statement to read. "I swear by Almighty God that the evidence I shall give be the truth, the whole truth, and nothing but the truth."

Northam faced the witness. "Sir Cedric, would you please tell the court how you came to know the prisoner?"

"She came to my offices in Westminster on October the twelfth."

"What name did she give?"

"She called herself April Devereux."

"To what purpose did she visit you?"

"She told me that I was her father, and as her mother had just died, that I ought to support her."

"And who did she claim was her mother?"

"Vivienne Devereux."

"And who is that, sir?"

"She is a courtesan."

The room buzzed.

"Did you believe her story?"

"Certainly not! It was preposterous. She accused me of having a tawdry affair with this woman. I have always been faithful to my wife." His wooden face brooked no doubt.

"And you paid her blackmail?"

"Well, yes. It was a scandalous story, and I didn't want

my reputation tarnished. People in my position make easy targets for attack, and frequently, fighting back only prejudices us further. Sometimes, our only defense is to concede. I hoped that by paying her off, I would never have to set eyes on her again."

"Thank you, Sir Cedric. No more questions, m'lord."

The judge turned to Riley. "Lord Blackheath, your cross-examination?"

Riley stood and faced the witness. "Sir Cedric, how much did she ask for?"

"I beg your pardon?"

"How much money did the prisoner ask you for?"

"I gave her two hundred pounds."

"Ah. Is that greater or less than what she asked?"

"No, she named no price. I offered her the money, and she took it."

"You fixed the price?"

"Yes."

"I see. After you paid her, did she submit the diary to you?"

Markham hesitated. "I knew nothing of a diary."

Riley appeared puzzled. "You didn't know that there was a diary with your name in it, implicating you in an adulterous affair with a public female?"

"No, I did not."

"What evidence did she have against you? Damaging letters?"

"No."

"Witnesses?"

"No."

"What did she threaten you with?"

Markham grew flustered. "Sh-she wanted to come live with me."

There was laughter in the court.

Riley stole a glance at April. "Having lived with the

prisoner myself, I can certainly understand your alarm." The laughter rose, and the judge beat his gavel to call for quiet. April was not amused.

"I am a married man, sir," insisted Markham. "She would have informed my wife."

"You claimed it was a fiction."

"It would have been very damaging to me."

"How? If I approached your wife and told her that you had just been named the crown prince of Prussia, would she believe me?"

"Of course not."

"Then why would she believe the prisoner's fiction? Sir Cedric? Is your wife capable of distinguishing fact from fantasy?"

Markham's lips thinned. "Yes."

"Did the prisoner physically compel you to give her money?"

"No."

"So, is it your testimony that an ordinary girl walked into your offices in broad daylight, told you a story that she was your daughter which you didn't believe, offered you no proof of her claims, did not threaten you with any harm, asked you for no money . . . yet you paid her the sum of two hundred pounds?"

Markham began to stammer.

"Sir Cedric, this court is not interested in how you spend your money. You can fling out pound notes from your office window if you like. But this prisoner is on trial for her life, and for her to be found guilty of the crime of extortion, it must be made very clear as to whether or not she threatened you with harm if you did not give her money. Therefore, I must have an answer: did the prisoner, or did she not, promise you dire consequences if you did not pay her?"

Markham appeared crestfallen. "Not exactly, but—"

Riley's shoulders relaxed. "Thank you, sir. I have no more questions." He looked at April, and she smiled at him.

"Just a moment, Sir Cedric," Northam said. "Would you say that the prisoner approached you under false pretenses?"

"Yes, I would."

"And would you say that the prisoner successfully deceived you and made away with two hundred pounds of your money?"

"Yes, she did."

"Then, m'lord, I respectfully request that the charge be changed to larceny by trickery."

Riley sprang to his feet. "M'lord, I must protest! First extortion and now larceny by trickery—does the prosecution intend to charge her with the entire canon of English common law until he finds her guilty of . . . pig snatching?"

Northam held up his hands. "Not at all, m'lord. My learned friend is attempting to get the prisoner, his wife, excused on a technicality of the law. Let us charge her properly. It will become evident to the court that a crime was indeed committed. We cannot in good conscience allow the prisoner to set a precedent for this type of crime."

The judge removed his spectacles. "I must agree. The jury will acknowledge the new charge. Please proceed with your case, Mr. Northam."

Riley sat down stiffly. He had been so pleased with himself. He might have had the case dismissed after that very first witness. But the son of a bitch was right: it was only a technicality. On principle, she was as guilty as sin.

"May it please the court, I would now like to call Jonah Hawthorne, Duke of Westbrook."

Again, Riley rose. "M'lord, I must object. He was not on the list of witnesses, sir."

"He is in the courtroom now, m'lord," Northam explained, "and I believe he can shed some light on this case. However, the prosecution reserves the right to treat him as a hostile witness, given the fact that he is the prisoner's father-in-law."

"I will allow it," said the judge.

"M'lord, this does not follow procedure—" Riley insisted.

"Your objection is overruled, Lord Blackheath! Please continue, Mr. Northam."

Riley watched his father step up to the witness box and speak the oath. He knew exactly where Northam was headed with this.

"Your Grace," began Northam, "I know you were present when Sir Cedric Markham gave his testimony. Did the prisoner approach you with the same subterfuge?"

"Yes," said Jonah, the corners of his mouth turned down in indignation against Northam.

"Did you ever give her any money?"

"Never."

"Did she ask for any?"

"No, she did not."

Northam handed Jonah three parchments. "Would you please tell the court what these documents are?"

Jonah pulled out his spectacles and balanced them on his face. "They're copies of my last will and testament."

Northam paced in front of the witness stand. "Allow me to clarify. They are *versions* of your last will and testament. The earliest and longest-standing version was amended to the second version, which is dated the day after you met the prisoner. Can you please explain why you changed your will?"

Jonah gave Northam a withering look. "I added April to it as a beneficiary."

"Interesting. What did you bequeath her?"

"My Scottish estate, Clondoogan Hall."

The audience gasped.

"Your Grace, you knew the prisoner for all of two days, and you leave her an entire estate in your will? Why?"

"She claimed to be my daughter. I wanted to provide for her."

"And was she in fact your daughter?"

"No, she wasn't."

"Hence, your third will, in which you effectively disinherited her."

"Yes."

"The clearest and most profitable case of larceny by trickery this country has ever seen," Northam crowed.

Riley stood. "Objection, m'lord. Please remind my inexperienced colleague that he is drawing conclusions. I believe that falls in the jury's purview."

For once, the judge sided with Riley. Northam withdrew the statement, but he continued to beam.

"Your Grace," Northam continued, "do you know this book?" He held up the Madame's diary.

Jonah peered at it. "I've never seen that book before in my life."

"Shall I read to you what the author of this book says about you, Your Grace?"

Riley sprang from his chair. "Objection, m'lord! The prosecution is attempting to tarnish the characters of two well-known gentlemen, implying their impropriety through association with a courtesan's private memoir. Assuming this diary has anything to do with the case at hand, it behooves the prosecution to prove that first, the diary is not a forgery, and second, that the events described therein are factual."

The judge turned to Northam. "I am inclined to agree with Lord Blackheath. A diary is, by definition, highly subjective, making it a very unreliable document, doubly so if it was supposedly written by a woman of loose moral character. If you wish to use this document as evidence, Mr. Northam, you will have to prove its authenticity."

Riley sat down, relieved. Northam would never be able to bring the dead to life.

"As you wish, m'lord," Northam conceded. "That will be all for now, Your Grace. You may step down. May it please the court, the prosecution would now like to call Vivienne Boniface Devereux."

Riley's heart missed a beat. He looked at his father, who had frozen halfway down the witness box. Jeremy was transfixed by the person walking down the courtroom. April's face was buried in her hands.

She was just as Riley remembered her. Handsome, proud, regal, unflappable. She crossed paths with Jonah. They stared at each other for a long time, and a current of recognition passed between them. The bailiff spoke her name, breaking their contact, and she glided up the stairs into the witness box. She swore her oath with the same lilting French accent that Riley recalled.

Northam drank in Riley's shock, then turned his attention to the witness. "Madame Devereux, would you kindly state your occupation for the court."

"I am the proprietress of a gentlemen's club."

"A gentlemen's club?"

"Yes. An establishment where gentlemen take their leisure."

"And in this establishment, are sexual favors purchased?"

"Sometimes."

"Was the prisoner an employee at your establishment?"

"Yes."

"Did she exchange sexual favors for money?"

The spectators leaned forward to hear the answer.

"No. She was a member of the kitchen staff."

Northam milked it for the crowd. "Forgive me, Madame Devereux, but I must ask you to clarify . . . the prisoner in the dock, the Marchioness of Blackheath and my learned friend's wife . . . was your former *kitchen maid*?"

The Madame leveled her gaze at April. "Yes."

Laughter rippled through the courtroom. The judge pounded his gavel. April was mortified not for herself, but for Riley. He was expressionless.

Northam held up a book. "Madame Devereux, is this your diary?"

April held her breath. The Madame looked directly at her. "Yes."

"When was the last time you saw it?"

"October the eleventh, the day before the crime. I had asked April to crate it away, along with some other books in my study."

"And did she?"

"No. She absconded with it. She did not come down to work the following morning. Nor did Jenny Hare, one of my entertainers. They were very close. I thought something terrible had happened to them. But a few days later, a member of my clientele said that he saw them both at a country inn outside London. I did not suspect the diary was missing until April told me so last night."

Riley glanced at April. She bit her lip in consternation.

"She went to see you?" Northam asked.

"Indeed, she came to apologize. It was a very moving speech. She was most contrite. I wonder who was nobler—the peeress who came to beg forgiveness, or the abbess who gave it."

Riley stood up. "M'lord, I cannot see where this line of questioning is going. Does this witness have anything to contribute to the charge at hand?"

Northam responded. "I am getting to that, Lord Blackheath. Madame, do you know a man by the name of Jonah Hawthorne, the Duke of Westbrook?"

"I do."

"Is he a member of your 'gentlemen's club'?"

"No. We knew each other a long time ago. Twenty years ago, in fact."

"When you were a courtesan?"

"Yes."

"And you were keeping this particular diary then, is that correct?"

"Yes."

"Madame Devereux, it has been suggested by his honor the judge that this diary, having been written by a woman of loose moral character, might be a fabrication. Can you attest to the accuracy of the events described herein?"

"A woman of loose moral character?" She raised an imperious brow at the judge, making him squirm. "I assure his honor the judge that my profession has absolutely nothing whatever to do with my character. I was born into one of the oldest and noblest families in France, the school I attended was taught by nuns, and my reputation for piety was renowned and unimpeachable. The great irony of my life is that I was always taught that *prostituées* were lascivious and immoral women. I was not even allowed to look at them in the streets. Maybe if I had remained in France, I would be a 'decent' person today. But circumstances drove me to leave for England. It was *here* that I had to make certain . . . compromises."

Northam crossed his arms. "What compromises, Madame Devereux?"

"The kind that permit one to survive. My first night in London, I slept under a tree in Hyde Park. A beautiful, well-dressed woman, whom I later discovered was the famous Madame Davies, took me in. She gave me a place in her mansion, elegant clothes, everything I did not expect to ever see again. I soon discovered what the price of all this opulence would be. In return for her protection, I was to allow her to sell my personal services to gentlemen. Not as a streetwalker, but as a courtesan. We were to consider ourselves ladies, and must never act like anything less. I was surprised to learn that some of the other courtesans were as highborn as me. Her stable of women included an illegitimate Arab princess, a fallen Spanish noblewoman, and a famous Austrian actress. She confessed to me that my beauty and deportment caught her eye, and she knew that I would fetch many admirers. I never disappointed her in that respect.

"Her clientele was equally exclusive. Her criteria for accepting a man's patronage demanded that in addition to having the wealth to afford her ladies' favors, he must also have an outward appearance of respectability. I remained in her employ for many years, and so I developed a clientele of my own, all of whom are mentioned in that book you hold in your hand. But I was young and idealistic, and still entertained dreams of love and marriage. It was not long before I found a gentleman for whom I developed . . . tender feelings." Her voice trailed off.

"Was that gentleman the Duke of Westbrook?"

The Madame gazed at Jonah through eyes of regret. "Yes."

Murmurs sounded out around the courtroom. The judge had to pound the gavel several times to quiet the room.

"So you fell in love with Jonah Hawthorne. Did he reciprocate your affections?"

"I have no doubt that he did."

"Was your acquaintance an intimate one?"

The Madame regarded Jonah, who was leaning forward in his seat. "For a long time, no. But I loved him very much. What's more, I still do."

The courtroom erupted into a hive of gossip.

"You give an account in your diary, Madame, of when you became with child."

Riley jumped to his feet. "M'lord, I ask that you put a stop to this line of questioning. Does this woman's child have any bearing on the case before you?"

The judge peered over his spectacles. "Mr. Northam, *is* there any point to this?"

"Yes, sir. A little indulgence is all I ask."

"Get on with it, then."

"M'lord is most gracious. Madame, did you have a child by Jonah Hawthorne, the man you loved?"

"I had a child."

"And is that illegitimate child not in this very room, seated to the left of Jonah Hawthorne, in the person of Lord Jeremy Hawthorne, who is in fact engaged to be married the day after tomorrow to the Queen's own cousin, introducing his bastardy to the monarchy of this country?"

Tension charged the air. No one breathed.

The Madame stared at Jeremy. "A stunning boy. I see the resemblance. It could very well be said that he is mine."

Riley shut his eyes.

"But that would be wrong," the Madame continued. "I have never seen that boy in my life."

Beads of perspiration lined Northam's upper lip. "Madame Devereux, you are under oath! Is Jeremy Hawthorne your son?"

She smiled at Jeremy, and shook her head. "No."

Tears of happiness gathered in April's eyes.

"Madame, please reflect. Are you quite sure—"

Riley bolted up from his chair. "The witness has answered the question. Is the prosecution hard of hearing?"

Rattled, Northam turned to the judge. "M'lord, I declare that this witness has perjured herself before this court."

The judge's grizzled eyebrows flew upward. "You're

accusing *your own* witness of perjury? Do you have any evidence that refutes her testimony?"

Riley smirked at Northam. "If my learned friend wishes to have the jury discount his witness's entire testimony, the defense is not opposed."

Northam glowered in return. "I withdraw my request, m'lord. Madame Devereux, in your diary you claim that your baby was taken from your bosom. How can you be so sure that Jeremy Hawthorne is not the man your babe became?"

Her eyes were unemotional. "Because my babe died in my arms."

Riley hazarded a look at Jonah. The older man's eyes, so long covered by the scales of pride and arrogance, were now glistening with unshed tears. As he gazed at the Madame, his face shone with gratitude, regret, and tenderness.

Northam threw himself onto his seat. "I have no more questions for this witness, my lord."

"Lord Blackheath, your cross-examination?"

Riley rose and smiled at the Madame with unspoken appreciation. "I have no questions for Madame Devereux at this time, m'lord. The witness may step down."

Northam scowled at Madame Devereux as she passed in front of him. "M'lord, the prosecution rests."

The judge's quill scribbled furiously on the dossier. "In that case, Lord Blackheath, you may proceed with the case for the defense."

Riley stood and faced the jury. "Gentlemen of the jury, like any decent man, I want to live in a world that upholds justice. As a man of the law, I derive my professional satisfaction from seeking it out and enforcing it. Now, justice, as any reasonable person will tell you, means getting at the truth. Without truth, justice is merely revenge. But sometimes, the facts in a case point to one conclusion, and the truth points to another.

"My colleague has tried to confuse you with issues wholly irrelevant to this case. He has tried to blindfold you to the truth by offending your sensibilities with tawdry scandals and prurient gossip. Allow me to take the blindfold off. The truth of this case is this: first, the prisoner stole a diary from her employer, Madame Devereux, an act for which the elder lady admits to having forgiven her. Second, the prisoner approached a man who was named in the diary with a made-up story. The man admits he did not believe her, admits she did not pose a threat to him, and admits he gave her money of his own free will. Third, the prisoner approached my father with the same made-up story. He admits she did not coerce him into bequeathing her his property, and further admits she did not take a penny from him. In my fifteen years as a litigator and jurist, I can tell you that from all that I have told you, there is not one single crime. Not one. Lying? Yes. A bit of mischief, nothing more. But is lying a capital crime? This will be for you to decide. The only thing, gentlemen, that you do not know, is *why* she did it. This I would like you to hear from her own lips. The case for the defense has but one witness, and that is the prisoner herself, April Rose Hawthorne, Lady Blackheath."

Her hands shook as she looked around the room at all the faces who knew her now for a fraud and a liar. She felt a powerful urge to run, and she would have done so except that the only sanctuary she sought was in the arms of Riley.

She looked down on the face of her husband. Her answers would determine whether she would be released into his loving arms, or carted off to jail to await her execution. Worry was written in his eyes.

"Lady Blackheath, did you once serve as a scullery maid for Madame Devereux?"

She made a strangled answer, and had to clear her throat. "Yes."

"How long were you in her employ?"

"A little over a year."

"How did you come by this post?"

"My father had died shortly after my eighteenth birthday. I had been living alone with him since my mother died when I was a child. I had no other relations, so I set out to look for work. I can read and write, and have knowledge of books, so I tried to secure a position as a governess. But with the war in France, no one wanted to hire the daughter of a French chimney sweep, even though I am English by birth. I tried to hire myself out as a lady's maid, but there was no work to be had. Finally, I was evicted from our flat. I lived on the streets for about a week before I stumbled upon the Madame's business, which had a sign out front that said she was hiring. I inquired, but the Madame was looking for a... a... an entertainer. I told her that I couldn't do that, and begged her to hire me as a maid instead. She might very well have taken advantage of my desperation, but she took pity on me. She allowed me to work in service—for the time being."

"Why only temporarily?"

"She knew I was a maiden, and she wanted me to become accustomed to the profession, perhaps even be tempted to join it."

"And were you?"

"No. The idea of selling my body offends me. Mind you, I cannot judge those who are forced to engage in that profession. I know that if it were not for the Madame's good graces, I might have been one of their number. I do not feel anything but pity for a woman who must ply that trade. They do it only to survive. I know that nearly all of them, given the choice, would prefer another vocation if it were available. Despite my desperate circumstances, I was lucky enough to be able to hold on to my virtue."

"Did the Madame ever force you to prostitute yourself?"

"No, never. She was very considerate that way. But she frequently reminded me that a time would come when she would insist that I join the other girls."

"And did that time ever come?"

"Yes. The day before I took the diary. She said that I would have until the end of the week to decide or I would be discharged."

"Why did you not accept the discharge, or leave of your own volition?"

"I had no money. The Madame did not pay me for my work; she only provided room and board. I was terrified of having to return to living on the street. I had no family, no place to live, no money to buy food, no prospects for survival out on my own. It's bad enough having to find sustenance when everyone you meet is just as poor as you are. But it's the dangers . . . London at night is so full of people who mean to harm you. I know that if the Madame had discharged me, I faced almost certain death. Even so, I would have chosen to leave rather than be the prize in a virgin auction."

"A virgin auction?"

April shifted in her seat. "Yes, that's where a virgin is put up and men come to bid for her first night. A girl can make a lot of money selling her maidenhead. I have seen it done. By and large, it's a fool's enterprise. Some gullible men have been duped into bidding for what is in fact a 'professional' virgin."

The courtroom broke out into laughter.

"But," she continued, "on the rare occasion that a real virgin is procured, it can be a very lucrative night for her."

"You stated that you needed money very desperately. Why did you not take advantage of this opportunity?"

April shook her head. "A man can lose all his material possessions and still be a man, but if he sells his self-respect, he has nothing. Once one's honor is amputated, there isn't enough money in the world to bandage the wound. If I had branded myself a prostitute, I would have forfeited my dream for a better life. Dignity is not negotiable."

Riley smiled at her. "Thank you, Lady Blackheath. I have no more questions."

She watched him resume his seat. His expression was reassuring, and she was thrilled he was pleased with her responses.

It was now Northam's turn to question her. "Would you characterize your life as being 'better' now?"

"I'm sorry?"

"Well, you're dressed to the height of fashion, you took up residence in one of the grandest homes in all England, and a few days ago you married Society's most eligible bachelor. Few kitchen maids are ever quite so privileged."

His implications irritated her. "I'm sure you're right about that."

"Were these the lofty ambitions to which you aspired?"

"As I said, I just wanted a better life," she insisted.

"You mean you wanted a more lucrative life."

"Doesn't everyone?"

Northam crossed his arms. "Not at the expense of morality, madam. Whatever our plight in life, most English people observe the tenets of decency and the established order. We do not overleap the classes, obtaining lucre through flagitious acts of criminality."

"Objection, m'lord. Please restrain my learned colleague from being argumentative with the witness."

"Sustained. Mr. Northam, you may reserve your opinions for your summation."

"Yes, m'lord. *Mrs*. Hawthorne, is it your contention that you can buy respectability?"

April bit back a venomous reply at his insult. "Respectability is not what I was after. Before I stole the Madame's diary, I had done nothing to be ashamed about. No, I was respectable enough. I suppose what I really wanted was respect."

"And you thought you could obtain this respect by lying to members of the upper classes, posing as someone else? Presenting a false identity to all of Society, including Her Royal Majesty?"

April's brows connected in dismay. "Yes, I thought I could. But I was wrong."

"Explain yourself."

"Well, no one truly respects a maid. We are . . . inconsequential, dispensable. The only way I could obtain any measure of respect was to pretend to be someone I wasn't. It's a paradox really; by lying, I finally got everyone's respect, only it wasn't me they were respecting. But then I met Riley. He gave me love I did not earn, did not even deserve. He took me, just as I was, warts and all, and called me his 'lady.' Though to the world I was no one, to him, I was *the* one. That alone meant everything."

"You mean, that alone *bought* you everything. Riley Hawthorne is a very wealthy man."

"Mr. Northam, I would gladly forgo the home, the fashions, the titles—everything of monetary value I stand to gain. I have only one ambition in life now, one desire. The regard and happiness of my husband. I do . . . love him so."

Riley nodded stiffly at her, trying to keep his emotions in check.

Northam spat his words at her. "A touching sentiment, but wholly artificial, Mrs. Hawthorne. You cannot ingratiate yourself with the jury that way."

April wearily shook her head. "I don't expect anyone to believe me. I've told enough lies to cast doubt on every word I speak for the rest of my life. If the men of the jury are as skeptical about me as you are, then I will probably be condemned to death, and all I ask is an opportunity to say something to my husband now." She locked eyes with him. "Riley, I want you to know how much I love you. It is the only thing I know to be absolutely true. I want you to know that you were wrong to think I betrayed you. I went to see Northam that night because he was trying to blackmail me."

"I have no more questions for the prisoner," said Northam.

"He sent me a note telling me—"

Northam raised his voice. "The prosecution has finished its cross-examination."

"—that I was to bring him twenty thousand pounds or else he'd send the diary to the authorities."

"M'lord! Please instruct the prisoner to step down!" Northam boomed.

She opened her reticule and looked around for something. "I want you to know that I am telling the truth. Here is the note he sent me." She held the piece of paper aloft in her hand.

In mid-protest, Northam walked around the bar and approached the witness box with an arm outstretched to take the paper from April's hand.

Riley, however, had jumped over the bar in one lithe leap and seized the note from April's hand before Northam could reach it.

Officers rushed upon the floor to restrain the men who now wrestled each other for the piece of paper. The judge banged his gavel to silence the clamor that arose from the altercation. One officer had taken hold of Riley from behind, while another wrestled Northam to the ground. Taking advantage of their momentary separation, Riley read the note.

"Bailiff, bring that note to me," shouted the judge, and Riley surrendered it to one of them. "Gentlemen, please return to the bar, both of you!"

Both Riley and Northam began to talk heatedly to the judge, and he banged his gavel some more.

"I'll do the talking, if you don't mind." The flustered judge read the note aloud. " 'Naughty girl. Someone must pay for your crimes. Will it be you or your bridegroom? Bring twenty thousand pounds to the Hoof and Talon at midnight tonight, the eve of your wedding, or the rest of this diary goes to the constabulary. Tell no one, or you shall discover the true meaning of the word "scandal." ' " The judge turned to April. "Young woman, are you accusing Mr. Northam of blackmailing you?"

"Yes, m'lord. It's true. I paid him twenty thousand pounds, and he sent the diary to the constabulary anyway."

"How dare you!" Northam roared. "M'lord, I wish to officially declare that this woman has slandered my good name, and I intend to seek redress."

"But this note is unsigned. Lady Blackheath, what proof do you have that Mr. Northam was the one who wrote the note?"

Riley spoke up. "The proof is in your hands, m'lord. The language of the note implies that it was written on the eve of our wedding, four days ago. It is written on a page from the Madame's diary. The same diary that has been, by his own declaration, in Mr. Northam's keeping for *six weeks*."

"So he did," concurred the judge. The judge lifted a piece of paper and compared it with the note. "Mr. Northam, the handwriting on this note matches that of the report you submitted to this court. How do you explain this?"

Northam looked from the judge to April, and then to Riley. He chuckled, shaking his head.

The judge cocked his head. "Mr. Northam, do you have anything to say before I have the officers take you into custody for questioning?"

Northam looked over at Riley. Suddenly, he leapt upon the barristers' bench and ran across it toward Riley, his face a mask of rage. He knocked Riley over, sending him sprawling across the floor. Northam jumped on top of him and wrapped his hands around Riley's throat and squeezed, driving his thumbs into Riley's windpipe. With the only breath he had, Riley rammed his fist into Northam's rib cage, causing him to loosen his stranglehold and curl to the side. Riley took advantage of the opening and smashed his fist into Northam's chin. Northam flew backward, landing unconscious at the feet of the officers. The judge ordered the officers to haul him away and declared the trial in recess.

A FEW MINUTES LATER, THE JUDGE RETURNED to the bench. He removed his spectacles to address the stunned faces in the courtroom.

"The events that transpired at the close of the last session will kindly be disregarded by the jury. Everything since the presentation of the note by the prisoner has no bearing on the case at hand; however, it will be entered into evidence as part of a separate criminal trial. Although the prosecutor will not be participating in the remainder of this trial, the court recorder has noted that the prosecution did in fact finish his cross-examination of the defense's only witness. Lord Blackheath, if that is the end of the presentation of testimony, you may now give your closing remarks."

Riley stood and smoothed his hair, rumpled by his brawl with Northam. "Thank you, m'lord. Gentlemen of the jury, it is argued that sometimes it becomes necessary to violate the 'letter of the law' in order to act in harmony with the 'spirit of the law.' But truth always must triumph. My former colleague presented facts in this case that, by and large, the defense does not challenge. That on October eleventh, the prisoner stole a diary—for which she was forgiven—we do not dispute. That on October twelfth she lied to Sir Cedric Markham, and he gave her money of his own free will—we do not dispute. But why did she do these things? Because if she hadn't, she stood to have her body violated on October thirteenth.

"Gentlemen of the jury, you must determine for yourselves not whether a misdeed was committed, but to what extent it was justified. The prisoner was acting under the most extreme form of duress. Duress, gentlemen, is when a person performs a crime because of a threat of force by another. In this case, the threat came from Madame Devereux, who told her she was in imminent danger of losing her virtue to the highest bidder—a man to whom she was not married, whom she did not even know, who might very well have been cruel or even violent. Her alternative was a similar fate or even death on the streets all alone. The question I put to you, gentlemen, is this: what would you do? Consider if *you* were a destitute orphan female faced with only two, equally bleak, prospects: severe and demoralizing bodily violation and injury, or braving the dangers of the London streets alone, penniless and terrified. Which would you choose? Would you not, as decent human beings, try to create for yourself a separate destiny, one in which you could find the means you needed to survive, all within the boundaries of the law? That is what the prisoner did. She did the only thing she could do to try to escape death and a life of immorality. The prisoner you see here is not a delinquent; she is simply a human being trying to survive in a world that does not favor her kind . . . poor, unmarried, and female. Consider carefully, then, what justice there should be for one caught between Scylla and Charybdis.

"It is a dangerous thing when we become more concerned with people's station than their character. When we overlook integrity and kindness in favor of birthright and wealth, we become a civilization that will kill the spirit and nurture pride. I know that you have not been able to see into April's heart as I've been privileged to do. I pity you your loss. Because in my travels, as extensive as they have been, I have never met her equal in all the royal salons of Europe. I defy anyone to find a woman with as much courage, intelligence, and honor as the one that sits before you. When we were wed, she was accorded a title, that of Lady Blackheath. She became, by law, a noblewoman. But I tell you, gentlemen, that she was a noble woman long before we married. Holding fast to one's principles, even in the face of great adversity . . . that is what true nobility is all about. April Rose Jardine may not have been born a lady, but she has most definitely earned the title. I am proud to call this woman my wife."

Riley walked over to the dock and stretched out his hand. Tears streaming from her eyes, April put her hand in his. He pressed his lips firmly against the back of her hand. "I love her more than anything, and now more than ever. I hope that one day I will become worthy of her love for me." He turned back to the jury. "You have it in your power to give me the opportunity to become the man she deserves. Restore my wife to me. I pray you, proclaim her not guilty."

A silence fell on the courtroom, interrupted only by April's soft sobbing.

THE CHILL IN THE COURTROOM SEEMED to permeate April's bones. The place was overflowing with people, and even in their midst, she was all alone. In the distance, Big Ben struck three, and to April, it sounded like a death knell.

She looked for Riley, but could not find him. She wanted to tell him goodbye, to thank him. She wanted to show him, with one last kiss, how much she loved him.

How cruel life was. Now that she had found the man of her dreams, she was no longer free to have him. After all they'd been through, after all they struggled against, that it should come to this. Her only consolation, her only happiness, was that he would not be going to jail in her place.

A door opened and the jury filed in. She scanned their faces for a hint of encouragement, a sign of hope. But their faces were grave, forbidding, condemning. Her hands trembled violently. Riley walked in from a separate door, his dense black hair rumpled from the punishment of his nervous hands. He offered her a reassuring smile, but it was too late. She already knew the verdict. As the courtroom settled, she studied Riley's face, knowing it would be the last time she would see it, and burned into her mind all of his beautiful features. She loved him, more than she had ever loved anything or anyone in her life.

"The prisoner will stand," the court clerk ordered.

Her legs wobbled a bit as she obeyed. She glanced over at Riley, and they locked eyes. In that one look, they shared an eternity of love.

"Members of the jury, have you decided upon your verdict?"

A man stood, the one with the gravest face. "We have."

"Are you all agreed upon your verdict?"

"We are."

"Do you find the prisoner at the bar, April Rose Hawthorne, guilty or not guilty of larceny by trickery against Sir Cedric Markham?"

The man paused, and so did her heart. "Not guilty, m'lord."

Pandemonium erupted in the courtroom. Through the deafening uproar she called Riley's name. She looked for him in his chair, but he was gone. She scanned the floor for him, but he was nowhere.

A hand spun her around, and there he was, by her side.

She flew into Riley's arms, the only place she ever wanted to be.

Nineteen

THE CROWD THAT HAD FORMED OUTSIDE Riley's London town house swamped the street, slowing traffic to a crawl. His household servants were doing all they could to keep out the journalists, well-wishers, and curiosity-seekers from banging down the door.

News of the verdict had blazed across town. Their tempestuous three-day marriage was the most delectable bit of gossip around. It was a union that transcended the barriers of class, country, and crime, and everyone had an opinion about the two people whose marriage had become legendary—romantic for some, scandalous for others. Regardless, both their celebrity and notoriety made them impossible to ignore, and everyone wanted to meet the couple that had made the front pages sizzle. It was becoming patently clear that there would be no privacy or peace for Riley and April in London. Once they'd had a chance to bathe and have a decent meal, they set out for Blackheath Manor.

Ensconced in the carriage with Riley, April had never been so happy . . . and thankful that they were finally together. As Riley related his experiences at Newgate Prison, she shuddered at the thought of him in such a place for one night, let alone for years on end. As he recounted all he had seen and heard, she realized he had known precisely what he was getting himself into. The horror, the desolation, the despair—he had gone into the bowels of hell willingly. For her. He had sacrificed his honor, given up his comfort, and laid down his life. And when he was no longer permitted to do these things, he had fought to win her back, to spare her from the very punishment that he himself was willing to endure. No one deserved that kind of love, and yet, it had been given to April Rose Jardine. Given, not earned. Accepted, but not understood.

She hugged his arm even tighter, as if he would be taken from her again. Riley slipped his arm away and placed it around her shoulders.

"I came so close to losing you during the trial," he said, shaking his head. "I felt so helpless, so powerless. I don't know what I would have done if I had lost the case . . ."

She squeezed his hand. "I would have died a happy woman knowing you loved me as you did."

He kissed her temple. "I haven't yet begun to show you how much I love you."

As the carriage approached the hills of the manor, Riley did not slow the horses. She thought it a little strange, but when he missed the path altogether, she spoke up. "Where are we going?"

"Tonight, I want you all to myself. No visitors, no servants, no distractions. Just you and me." He led the horses along the path that overlooked the stream, and then she knew. They were going to the cave.

Night had fallen, but Riley's instinct was true, and they found the place that led to his secret dwelling. He helped her alight, and took the blankets from the carriage. The moon was full and the sky clear, offering them enough light to negotiate the rock face down to the cave.

The cave was quiet and still. Winter had made the

stream sluggish, and all nature had settled in for the night. Riley lit the lantern on the wall, its soft glow sheathing them in a yellow sphere of light. Sitting on the woolen blanket on the floor, April felt at once safe . . . and afraid. Not of being with Riley, but of disappointing him. Tonight had become their wedding night, and she wanted it to be perfect for him. She thought back to when Jenny had tried to give her some instruction; now April wished she had not interrupted her.

He sat down next to her. Now more than ever, she took stock of how large a man he was, his breadth dwarfing the size of the cave, and his long legs sprawling out beyond the edge of the blanket.

"Do you love me?" he asked.

She smiled. "Of course I do."

"No. Do you truly love me?"

April was hurt he would ask that again. "Riley, I truly love you. More than I've ever loved anyone else."

"That isn't enough. Do you love me enough to give me all of you for as long as you live? Do you trust me with everything you have and everything you are, and never hold anything back? Will you look for me when you are afraid, alone, or in need, and never try to face the world on your own again? Can you rely on my love for you, no matter what happens? Do you love me that much?"

His beautiful face became a blur as tears collected in her eyes. It was not an emotion he wanted, a feeling that would ebb and wane with the years and the trials of marriage. It was a decision he required, one that asked that she choose him and his love no matter what came their way. There would be many things in life that would conspire to break them apart, and he wanted to know that precisely at such times, they would decide to cling to each other more fiercely than ever. Now, this moment, he asked that she commit to him in times of confidence and uncertainty, in fortune and in poverty, in happiness and in tears. It was a monumental thing he asked of her . . . to love him as much as he loved her.

"Yes, Riley. I love you that much." She took his face in her hands, and gazed deeply into the blue-green eyes that, amazingly, became more tender and more confident at the same time. "And I promise that you will never want for anything as long as I live. You will never lose my love for you. You will never reach out for me and find me not there."

A smile spread across his face, and he kissed her. She encircled her arms around his neck, drawing him closer, and returned his kiss with the candor and sincerity overflowing in her heart. Gradually, the kisses deepened, growing more insistent, as if each were a profession of love that had to be proclaimed.

He took her hand in his, and peeled off her glove. She watched him as he brought his lips to her naked hand, fascinated that she no longer felt ashamed of her ugliest feature. As he did the same for her other hand, she entwined her fingers into the thick forest of his black hair, a sensation that made him moan. He knelt beside her and took off his coat, and rolled it up into a pillow for her. Resting her head on the navy blue fabric, she discovered that this, the scent of her husband, had become a powerful aphrodisiac.

At what point it happened, she did not know. But somehow, the ache in her heart had spread to her feminine places. The cry in her soul for Riley had become a hunger for him down there. Her mind, heart, and body—her entire being—all desired the same thing at once, and it was there, right before her. She wanted this man, and only this man.

As she watched him shrug out of his waistcoat and shirtsleeves, her breath began to quicken. She had seen many men in varying degrees of nudity. But none of them ever conveyed this masculine perfection, this healthy virility that made her pulse race. Massive arms. A square chest. Dense muscles bricking his abdomen. Sinew and vein lining his beefy forearms. The sight of his naked torso intoxicated her. Her maidenly reserve began to drown in the wellspring of her passion.

He lay down next to her, and she touched his hairy chest. So warm, so solid, so close . . . her body ached with the need of him. She watched in fascination as he deftly unbuttoned her bodice, and he nuzzled her neck as his large hand stroked the swell of her breasts. The contact of skin against skin made her yearn for more. As his soft lips whispered across the spot just below her earlobe, she rubbed her face against his cheek. His rougher skin felt glorious on her face, and it awakened an unquenchable desire to know him completely. She kissed his bare neck, heated with racing blood. Instinctively, her tongue leapt out and traced a line up to his jaw, and the hot saltiness increased her hunger for him. Her hands splayed across the curve of his back, relishing the feel of him. She had never before felt this longing for any man, and her need now flared with a vengeance. Her breathing grew labored as the yearning grew more intense, until she was ready to cry out with the pain of his absence from her body.

He must have sensed her mounting ache, because he shifted on top of her. The weight of his body over hers made her dizzy with bliss. Enclosed by his massive arms, she was imprisoned in a warm cage of flesh. The heat of his quickened breath on her neck descended to her breasts, which rose up to meet his kisses. He took her nipples in his mouth, coaxing and wooing them with his tongue, and her heated loins melted the honey inside her.

She felt him lift her skirt, and the sensation of the woolen blanket under her bare legs filled her with a wanton desire. The candle of her passion had blazed into a full-blown fire, and she was not about to burn alone.

A boldness seared her veins, and in breathless anticipation, she opened herself to him.

She felt him unbutton his breeches and position his hips between her open thighs. He placed a tender kiss on her lips, and slowly pushed himself inside her.

She cried out into his neck. He lay still, letting her body adapt to his girth, his kisses on her forehead softening her pained expression. The hurt soon suffused to a mild discomfort, diminished by the realization that they had finally become one flesh. The union of their two bodies felt so right, so perfect, she thought heaven could be no better.

His eyes smoldered as he moved gently inside her. The very tightness that had made her cringe was now inflicting upon him an excruciating ecstasy. She exulted in seeing him take his pleasure, knowing that it was she who was giving it to him, she from whom he wanted it.

Her body began to respond with a passion all its own. Her hands traveled freely over his body, delighting in the form and texture of him. Driven by her hungry ache, she gave free rein to all of her aroused passions. His whole body became a feast for her starving senses. He was outside of her, he was inside of her ... her fevered mind could no longer tell where one ended and the other began. The pleasure built up inside her, his thrusts coaxing the most beautiful sounds from her mouth. As his pace hastened, so did her moaning, her cries echoing in the yawning chasm of the cave. The double whimpers hastened his thrusting, and her desperate body could no longer hold back. A blinding flash of ecstasy flooded her body, and the waves of pleasure that followed made her womanhood contract around him, as if trying to pull him in further.

Riley watched her face flush becomingly, her lips forming a loose O. Her breathing became softer, deeper, and she started to relax.

"My God, you're beautiful."

As they lay intertwined, his manhood still throbbing within her, she knew the reason why. "You make me so."

His gaze kindled into a flame of passion, and he began to move inside her. She thought that she was past pleasuring, but she had been wrong. With every stroke, he reduced her to nothing but a complete longing for him. With every plundering thrust he banished her reserve, subjecting her to a position where she had no control—a position which she had always eluded, but which now she welcomed.

They reached their climax together, surging and ebbing in perfect unison, and they lay together, exhausted by the sheer pleasure of it.

Twenty

"ONE, TWO, THREE . . ." APRIL COUNTED, enumerating her trunks and suitcases arranged in the library of Riley's London town house. "Five, six, seven. That's everything, I think."

Riley stepped up behind her and threw his muscled arms around her. "You, madam, must have the largest trousseau in English history."

She turned in his arms. "Not all the cases are mine. Some of them are yours."

"Which one?"

"Very funny."

"I don't know why you're packing so many clothes. I don't intend for you to be dressed all that much." He began to fondle her bottom possessively.

"Riley," she protested halfheartedly. "People will see!"

Jeremy ambled in, clutching Emily's hand. "Too late. We've already seen. Quite shocking."

April pushed his reluctant hands away. Riley growled. "Jeremy, did I ever tell you how blasted inopportune your timing is?"

"Sorry, it's my fault," Emily offered. "Jeremy's taking

me home, but I left my parasol in here. So you two will be off on your honeymoon?"

"Yes," answered April. "We booked passage for Greece tomorrow. Right after your wedding reception."

"How long will you be away?" she asked.

Riley poured out four glasses of sherry. "Three months, maybe four."

"You'll miss the Easter term of the Assizes circuit. So you've definitely given up the bench?"

Riley nodded. "For the time being. I'm going to take up my old practice as a barrister. April's trial reminded me how much I really enjoyed arguing a case in court."

April looked at him askance. "Well, I'm glad one of us was having a good time."

Jeremy laughed. "Wait until you see his bill."

April held up her hands defensively. "Don't even think about it. I haven't any money, and I'm fresh out of diaries."

"What's holding up those sherries?" Jonah protested, poking his head into the library. "Ah, you're all here. Vivienne, step into the library for a moment, please."

Vivienne came in, wearing something April had never seen before: a genuine smile.

"And speaking of diaries," Riley said, "I have a present for you, Vivienne." He reached into his coat pocket and pulled out Vivienne's familiar red leather journal. "It's time it was returned to its rightful owner."

"Thank you," she said, turning the volume over. "The memories in here mean nothing to me now. I would see this in the fire. As for what concerns you, *mon petit ours*," she said, touching Jonah's whiskered cheek, "it is time we made new memories. There is only one thing in here that is absolutely irreplaceable." She opened up the journal and pulled out the folded patch of cream-colored silk.

She opened it up and showed the tiny blue handprint to Jeremy. "I made this when you were but ten months old.

I have treasured it all my days, thinking I would never see my child again." Her lips quivered as she placed her hands on Jeremy's face. "But as much as my heart broke with yearning to hold that child in my arms once more, I am happy that I gave him up to see you as the man you have become."

Overcome, Jeremy flung his arms around her.

"Come along, you two," Jonah admonished, wiping his eyes, "save some tears for the wedding."

Riley faced Vivienne. "I want to apologize again to you. I'm deeply ashamed of what I did so long ago, planting those rumors about you. I was very angry with Father, and I never truly forgave him. I simply couldn't understand the feelings that he had for you. At least, not until I fell in love with April. I cannot return to you the years you lost with Jeremy, but I can promise you that you will never lack anything more for as long as you live."

Vivienne nodded. "Thank you, Riley. It takes a noble man to admit his mistakes. But I do not reproach you. I would rather have one fleeting hour with my son than another age without him." She turned to April. "And as for you, I thank you for what you have taught me. You succeeded where I failed. You held on to the love you bore a Hawthorne man, and it saved you. Your passion reminded me—and Jonah— that it was only our hope that died, not our love."

Jonah squeezed her hand. "Well, Vivienne and I have a carriage waiting. Shall we?" He offered his arm, and Vivienne placed hers in it.

"We should be getting back, too," said Jeremy. "Lots to do."

Riley saw them out, and then returned to the library.

"Now that we are finally alone, madam wife, there is a legal matter I wish to discuss with you."

"A legal matter?" she said, her back leaning against a standing trunk.

"It concerns my conjugal rights."

"I see. What about them?" she asked innocently.

Placing one hand on the trunk beside her head, he brought his heavily muscled frame inches from hers. "I want what is rightfully mine."

"Hmm. I've been meaning to talk to you about that."

"Oh?"

"You see, my esteemed colleague, I've learned a thing or two about English law in the past few days, and I've come to understand that, as your wife, I have very few rights."

He nodded arrogantly. "Yes, I know."

"In fact, as a *feme covert*, I have no say over issues of money, or property, or even my own body."

He began to kiss the sensitive spot behind her ears. "Appalling state of affairs in this country, wouldn't you say?"

"Absolutely. And so, in order to recover my lost rights, I have decided that I must now become a *feme sole*. As my legal counsel, what do you think of that?"

His kisses trailed down to her neck, his mind absently answering her question. "There is only one way for you to become a *feme sole*, and that is for you to become—"

"Widowed, yes."

His lips halted, and he brought his gaze up to a level with hers. "So you're planning to end my life, is that it?"

Her voice danced innocently. "Only if you yourself won't oblige."

His eyes glinted as he considered the playful challenge in her face. "And just how do you intend to kill me?"

Her eyelids fell slowly. "With great pleasure."

His thick lashes narrowed on her. "Is that so? Well, let us see if that proves to be an efficacious weapon." He began to loosen the bow under her breasts that held her dress together.

"What do you mean?" she asked suspiciously.

"I have never heard of anyone dying from pleasure, but I'll be happy to become its first victim."

April glanced down at his expert fingers, loosening her gown. They brushed the flesh between her breasts, igniting sparks that burned a trail down to the V between her legs. His large hands curved down to her bottom, and began to gather her skirts slowly in his fists. She licked her dry lips, now swelling with passion. Somewhere in the back of her mind, there was a faint awareness that the library door was unlocked, but when Riley brought his hand around her waist and yanked her to him, all presence of mind evaporated.

He reached down and lifted her up against him. She gloried in the strength and closeness of him. He walked behind the wall of trunks to one that was lying flat on the ground. He set her down on it and knelt before her. His eyes smoldered at her as he ripped open the last constraints that kept her breasts from his hands, and she arched her back for him. His tongue danced on her breasts, making the points swell. She almost cried with the agony of her desire. She opened her eyes to see that he had taken off his jacket, but his breeches were as yet still fastened. She could kill him for making her wait.

She could take no more of this sweet torture. She gathered his hair in her fist and lifted his head off her swollen breasts.

He winced and gave her an amused look. "Are you trying to tell me something, my sweet?"

"Yes, damn it. Now!"

He cocked an eyebrow. "Such language from a lady! I see I shall have to teach you how to put that mouth to better use."

She groaned. "Riley, please . . ."

He gave her a devilish smile. "That's better."

He brought his hand to the opening between her legs, and his expert fingers began to dance upon her womanhood in the way that made her dissolve onto him.

She sank backward onto the trunk, and he leaned toward her. She glanced up through dreamy eyelids, and her eyes fell upon the monogram on one of the standing trunks: *AH*.

"Ahhh," she read, relishing the feeling of contentment it gave her to realize that it was her destiny to be thus. Her body grew hotter at his touch, as if the spirals of pleasure that carried her higher were drawing her nearer the sun, until she exploded into a million burning stars.

She smiled radiantly at him. "Riley?" she said, kissing his lips tenderly.

"Yes?"

"I love you."

"And I you," he said, kissing her neck.

"But I have a question."

He raised his head to look at her. "What is it, my sweet?"

"Do you think we'll ever make love on a real bed?"

A smile spread across his face, showing a row of perfect white teeth. "We have a lifetime together to find out."

Epilogue

25 April 1811

In honor of my birthday, the Marquess of Blackheath has given me this journal and a golden quill. He is very generous to me, and tonight I will give him something equally extraordinary.

It was not the only gift he gave me, however. Covering my eyes carefully with his large hands, he walked me into the Long Gallery. When he removed his hands, I looked up and beheld myself.

Where the large painting of him had hung before, there now was a painting of the two of us in Jeremy's vast garden of spring flowers. I sat in a chair, holding a profusion of roses in my lap, while he stood next to me, a gentle smile playing on his lips. It was magnificent.

Though I thought it an incredible likeness of us both, he held me close and told me that the artist had failed in his commission; namely, to capture my greatest beauty, the one that came from inside of me.

In word and deed, my husband never fails to pay me the greatest of compliments. That I am treasured.

I whirled around and thanked him for proving to me that I am beloved. As I did, I noticed that mine was not the only new painting in the gallery. Dozens of paintings had been replaced in it, paintings of the Hawthorne women throughout the ages.

Unable to contain my joy, I told him that there was a gift I had for him, as well. I pointed to our painting, and at the tiny white rosebud resting against my tummy. One day, I said, about seven months hence, that rosebud will flower into a beautiful child that would carry his honorable name into the future.

I was not prepared for his expression of happiness. He picked me up and whirled me around, and we kissed with the love of two people about to start a family. Our tears merged together, just as our love did in the creation of the child I now carry inside me.

I thank God that He led me to this man, and made all my dreams come true.
   —*April Rose Hawthorne, Lady Blackheath*

Acknowledgments

I couldn't let this book end without thanking a few people who had a great deal to do with getting it into your hands.

Above all, I'd like to thank God and Jesus, for showing me what true love is all about.

I'm also grateful to my parents, Lino and Juana Marcos, for forgoing their own aspirations and comforts throughout their lives so that their children's might be realized.

My four sisters and brother, and all my friends, have been great encouragers to me. And I cheerfully owe a special thanks to Mabel Marcos, one of my loving sisters, for introducing me to romance fiction and for serving as my sounding board on this novel every step of the way.

I have to gush about Rose Hilliard, my editor at St. Martin's Press. She was my very first fan, as excited about publishing this book as I was. I'm so grateful to her for believing in me.

And I was likewise blessed to have Cheryl Ferguson as my agent. I couldn't have wished for a more enthusiastic voice to champion my book.

Finally, thanks to Lisa Kleypas, one of my all-time favorite authors, who graciously agreed to read and endorse my book. What a sweetie!

A big kiss to all of you.

Read on for an excerpt from the next book by
MICHELLE MARCOS

Gentlemen Behaving Badly

Coming soon from St. Martin's Paperbacks

My dear Lord Prescott,

It has taken me a long time to find the courage to write this letter. I beg your forgiveness for corresponding with you without first having made your acquaintance, but this is a matter of greatest urgency. To put it plainly, I need you.

You see, as a lady of leisure in the employ of Madame Fynch, proprietress of the Pleasure Emporium, it is my duty to provide entertainment for the members of our exclusive club for gentlemen. The Madame has told me that I am idle and do not try hard enough. It is my belief that the ardor of my gentleman callers is evidence of my work, and I told her so. She was furious with my impertinent response and forced me to find a gentleman who would implement a course in humiliation under which I would learn to treat better those charges which she appoints me.

I know I've been very naughty in the past, but the Madame says this time she is prepared to discharge me for my insolence. She has given my performance here bottom marks, and she says that my only hope of reprieve is to have an impartial observer judge my innocence or guilt in the matter. I therefore come to you. If found guilty in your eyes, I am to submit to whatever brand and expression of discipline you see fit, even if it means you must give me "bottom marks" as well. Between us, sir, I will do anything—anything at all—to be able to remain here. Please come at once, and exercise your ruling. You have only to decree how grateful I should be.

Yours completely,
Lollie

Mina Halliday smirked wickedly as she folded the stiff blue paper. Whetting a man's appetite for sex was so very easy, especially when you knew precisely what form his appetites took. And at this incendiary invitation, this particular man would certainly come. She'd stake her entire collection of erotica on it.

With a practiced hand, she tilted her candle over the flap, and the red wax pooled into the shape of a heart. She glanced at the shelf above her writing desk, where a row of monogrammed seals sat like tiny soldiers awaiting orders. She ran her finger down the line until she found the right one, and then she pressed it firmly into the warm wax— *L.*

With customary neglect of the rules of propriety, Lollie flung open Mina's bedroom door. "Ye didn't come down for tea. So, nice as I am, I brought it up for you."

Mina smiled broadly. "I've got a good one for you, Lollie," she said, the gleam in her eye intensifying as she waved the letter at her. "And this one is very special indeed. To both of us."

Lollie pursed her generous lips as she snatched the letter from Mina's hands. "'Lord Roderick Prescott.' Who the 'ell is 'e?"

"It doesn't matter who he is." Mina shrugged. "He's a quill. The important thing is that he's got pots and pots of money. You want to take your time with this one. In fact, I wouldn't doubt it if he brought you a shiny bauble or two to relieve your discomfort."

"Relieve my—" Lollie's expression dissolved from puzzlement to dismay. "Oh, no . . . not another spanker!"

Mina held up her hands to calm her. "He's very rich, and—"

"No! I told you I don't want them kind o' quills. Give 'im to Serafina. She goes in for all that 'masterchism' or whatever you calls it."

"Please, Lollie. It's got to be you."

"Why?"

"Because . . . because . . ." Mina fumbled for a coherent order to express all her pent-up emotions. "Because I think this may be the man who had my father arrested."

"What?"

Mina pulled Lollie to her bed and sat her down. "First, you've got to swear to me you won't breathe a word of this to the Madame."

Lollie's graceful eyebrows drew together in concern. "Course I won't."

"Before I came to work here, my dad was a jeweler on Fulsom Street. A man came to my dad's jewelry shop and asked him to replace the fine jewels in a tiara with semi-precious stones." Afterward, Mina explained, the man claimed he had only brought the necklace in for cleaning, and it was returned to him with the jewels switched. Within four days, Mina's father was convicted of thievery and fraud—and shipped to Australia's penal colony.

"And you think this Prescott bloke turned yer dad in?" asked Lollie.

"That's what I want to find out. No one gets sentenced that quickly. No one! And to have a closed-door trial, where even I'm not allowed to testify on my father's behalf? Who can arrange that quick a conviction? It has to be someone high up in government."

"How do you know it was Prescott?"

"Well, I don't. Not for sure. But my dad had only a handful of clients with so much influence. In fact, only two men that I know of. The only thing that I know about him is his predilection for aggression because he had been bragging to my dad about a woman he had taught a lesson to the night before. So I have to find out for certain which of these two men is the one who ruined my father."

Lollie blinked her large blue eyes. "What are you going to do if it's 'im?"

The question hung in the air as Mina's anger filled the room. "Ruin him back."

Lollie's porcelain features twisted into a grimace. "Just how am I supposed to get him to admit to all of this?"

"Talk to him. All night if you have to."

She harrumphed. "I can see you've never been with a quill, 'specially not a spanker. Believe me, you don't want to entertain them all night. You'll be wanting them in and done with . . . right quick."

Mina shoved a lock of her straight brown hair behind one ear. "No. I mean, keep him in the salon. Sit at the bar, and I'll keep plying him with drinks. This way, I can listen in on your conversation."

"What am I supposed to do? Ask him if he had the owner of Halliday's Jewelry Shop arrested? He's not going to confess something like that to the likes of me."

"Of course he would!" Mina exclaimed, her brown eyes widening. "One of the most astonishing things I've seen since I started working here is how incredibly talkative these quills are with you girls. Men talk to courtesans as if you were the most discreet and sympathetic of confidantes. They share things with you they would never tell a father confessor, or even their own spouses. They brag about even the most depraved and wicked things they've done. And all because, as courtesans, you've no right to judge them." Mina gripped Lollie's arm tightly. "I'm sure you can get something out of Lord Prescott. All you need do is get him to talk about jewelry. Show him your necklace. Ask him what he thinks about it, or how much he thinks it may be worth. We'll see whether he brings up my father's name or his shop."

"I don't know, Mina. If this is so important to you, why don't you take this quill yourself?"

Mina backed away, her expression sobering with unspoken emotion. "You know that's impossible." Mina had long since accepted that she was no beauty. Of the dozen courtesans in the Madame's employ, none was less than flawless. With such a dazzling array of gorgeous women to satisfy the lust of a man's eyes, no one paid any attention to Mina. And although she served wine and port continuously throughout the salon, no one ever even looked at her face. She might as well be part of the furniture. "Please, Lollie. This is important to me. I'll give you one week's wages if you do this for me. A month's. Anything you ask. Please."

Lollie sighed noisily, her petulance only adding to her charm. "All right. But this better be the last perverted quill you get for me. The next one better be a good-looking prince eager to marry a Covent Garden tart."

Mina exhaled her relief. "I'll start making inquiries right away," she replied wryly.

But after Lollie left the room, doubts pressed heavily upon Mina. What if Lollie couldn't get Lord Prescott to open up? Worse still, what if neither of the men accepted her invitation to visit the bordello? How would she ever find out who had consigned her father to a hell on earth?

There was no room for failure. At all costs, she simply had to get Lord Prescott to come.

SALTER LAMBRICK LEANED OVER THE BODY of the dead man to get a look at his face. There was no mistaking it . . . Lord Prescott was no more.

Salter rubbed the thick black stubble on his face, a gesture that reminded him of the haste of the call. He stood up to get a better perspective on the murder scene, but was disappointed—not at what he saw, but at what he *didn't* see. Whoever had met Prescott here was careful not to leave any evidence of his presence.

Salter walked around the room slowly, allowing the alchemy of all his senses to paint a picture of what had happened last night. The victim and the murderer had met here in Lord Prescott's study. Prescott had been sitting at his desk, and at some point, the murderer had come around behind him and strangled him with a garrote. Prescott was wrestled to the floor, where he fell facedown. Once in the superior position, the murderer leveraged his weight to hold the victim down as he tightened the cord around the man's neck. From the boot scuffs on the marble floor, Salter could tell that Lord Prescott had thrashed a good deal. But with a man kneeling on his back, there was no way Prescott could have defended himself.

Salter crouched and turned the body over. Prescott's face was waxy and pallid, and his tongue spilled over his blue lips. It was a hideous death mask, but Salter had shed the horror of death long ago on the battlefield. He lifted the man's chin to get a closer look at the murder weapon. The crease between Salter's thick brows deepened as he realized it was not a garrote at all. He untwisted the cord embedded in the dead man's neck. It was a leather whip! Not a long one, like the kind used on carriage horses . . . nor even a bullwhip used on insubordinate soldiers. This was a peculiar instrument, with a sturdy handle and a thong about three feet long. Like the kind they used to chastise schoolboys.

Salter frowned. Why would a murderer bring an object like this to kill someone? If the murderer wanted to do Prescott in quietly, surely he would have brought a dagger or some poison, or even a better fashioned garrote than a whip.

Salter let the leather cord slither from his large hands. Perhaps the murderer wanted to sneak it in without detection. Or maybe the whip belonged to Prescott, and the murderer had obtained it here. The answer to that question would explain whether the murder was premeditated, or the tragic result of a vehement quarrel.

Salter fished around in Lord Prescott's pockets. He found the man's untouched billfold in his coat pocket. Evidently, robbery was not the motive. In his other breast pocket, Salter found two items: a folded piece of paper, and a leather tawse. Salter unfolded the piece of paper, and what he found astonished him.

My dear Lord Prescott,
It has taken me a long time to find the courage to write this letter.

As he read the rest of the missive, Salter had to smile. So that's where Prescott was headed with all these implements of torture . . . a bordello! Prescott seemed to have a peculiar affinity for dominating women, and he was being invited by a courtesan to indulge that inclination.

Salter shook his head at the writer's lewdness. He had never made use of a bordello, but had the letter been addressed to him, he just might have been tempted enough to try it.

Salter refolded the blue parchment, a frown casting a shadow over his hazel eyes. Come to think of it, there might be more to be read from this letter than a sexual proposition. What if Prescott's murderer was someone at this bordello? An irate Madame to whom he owed money? Another customer, jealous over his chosen courtesan? Or maybe even the very woman who wrote this letter . . .

"Alcott," he called out.

A young constable wearing a weathered brown coat came to the door. "Yes, sir?"

"Have you met with all the servants?"

"Yes, sir," he said, thumbing through his notepad. "Their statements ring true. None of them seemed to have any knowledge of the murder. After they retired for the night, no one 'eard a sound till this mornin' when the butler raised the alarm. Frankly," he said, lowering his voice, "I don't think any of them *could* do it. Cook's a frail woman, the maids are little things no bigger'n my sister, and the butler's older than the Lord Almighty."

Salter chuckled. "Fine. You can release them to their duties. Tell them that with their master gone, they should start looking for employment elsewhere."

"Right you are." Alcott jerked his head toward the body. "So what you reckon, Chief Constable?"

Salter put the letter in his coat pocket. "I think that this case isn't going to be easy. Lord Prescott was senior aide to the Lord Mayor of London. And the Lord Mayor is *not* going to like the scandal this will stir up. Besides, as the Chief Magistrate of London, his office will be placed under a great deal of scrutiny. I think we had better be prepared for the pressure to solve this case quickly and quietly."

"Any ideas who did it?"

"Not yet, but I've got a lead to track down. Ask that butler fellow to get me one of Prescott's coats. I think I'm going to do a bit of impersonating."

Alcott scratched his blond head with the end of his pencil. "Impersonatin', sir?"

Salter stood up straight. "Call me Lord Prescott."

He glanced down at the tawse in his hand, its supple leather strap split into two pain-inflicting tails.

Whoever wrote that letter had some explaining to do.